The Sexton Blake Library

Published 2021 by Rebellion Publishing Ltd,
Riverside House, Osney Mead, Oxford, OX2 0ES, UK

ISBN: 978-1-78108-802-9

10 9 8 7 6 5 4 3 2 1

A CIP catalogue record for this book is available
from the British Library.

Designed & typeset by Rebellion Publishing Ltd

Cover art by Crush Creative

Printed in Denmark

The Sexton Blake Library

ANTHOLOGY IV:

SEXTON BLAKE ON THE HOME FRONT

Selected, edited and discussed by Mark Hodder and Sexton Blake

BAKER STREET, LONDON

My FOURTH INTERVIEW with Sexton Blake was postponed. He telephoned from an untraceable number (believe me, I tried) to explain that "something had come up." Three days later, he called again, late in the evening, and invited me to have breakfast with him the following morning. "Be here by half seven."

Plainly, he was an early riser. I am not. Fortunately, Mrs Bardell had made a pot of very strong coffee. She'd also made kippers and poached eggs; toast smeared with salted lard; devilled kidneys; sliced ham; bacon; and buttered crumpets. It was an intimidating prospect for a cornflakes man such as myself, but once I started on it, a heavenly choir began to sing in my stomach.

We ate in the dining room on the ground floor of Blake's Baker Street residence, which, from the outside, didn't resemble a domestic residence at all. Between mouthfuls, we conversed, and I was by now sufficiently familiar with him to feel more relaxed in his presence. Even so, I was careful to avoid the subjects that had been proscribed prior to the first of our meetings, despite my burning curiosity. He took the lead, asking me questions about my background and current circumstances, enquiring as to my opinion in matters of politics and culture, technology and entertainment. I saw in him during that conversation a relentless curiosity, an insatiable need to comprehend how other people view the world around them.

For a man with such a powerful sense of justice, he seemed remarkably non-judgemental.

We finished, refilled our coffee cups, carried them up to his consulting room, and settled in the two armchairs by the fireplace. As I had done on the previous occasions, I took a binder from my briefcase and handed it to him.

"A change for this, the fourth anthology," I said. "Instead of three issues of the Union Jack story paper, we have two issues of The Sexton Blake Library."

"Longer tales," he noted.

I made a sound of affirmation. "The SBL, which had started in 1915, became your principal vehicle from 1940 onward, along with Knockout, which ran comic strips of a considerably more juvenile nature."

"Don't dismiss the Knockout," he said, reaching for his briar pipe.

I felt my eyebrows go up. "Don't dismiss it? Surely you're not suggesting that the strips were also inspired by real cases?"

"Mostly, yes, they were."

I blinked and sat back. "Phew! That casts rather a different light on matters!"

He opened a pouch of tobacco. "How so?"

"I was about to suggest that you did in the Second World War much as you had done in the First, which was to hunt spies and traitors at home with occasional forays to the front lines and into occupied territories."

Blake grunted and used a tool to pack the tobacco into the bowl of his pipe.

"Now, though," I said, "If the Knockout is to be believed, I have to take into consideration that you engaged with the enemy much more directly!"

"Yes, I did."

"In those bizarre machines, the Rolling Sphere and the Flying Disc!"

"That's correct."

"But they are impossible!" I exclaimed. "Or, at very least, it's impossible that they've remained a secret for all these years!"

"It only seems impossible," he said, "because you're unaware of how many secrets there are and of why those secrets are kept. That is the nature of secrets."

I took a deep breath and blew it out through my nose, slowly shaking my head. "How did you find the time to do it all?"

"It was a long war." He struck a match and lit up. "And you should take into account that, at the start of the decade, a great many of the stories in the SBL were reprinted accounts of earlier cases, so I wasn't as unrealistically active as it appears." He opened the binder and glanced at the covers of the two issues within. "Why these two?"

I answered, "Because I think they represent the two

principal themes of your 1940s experiences: one being your frequent routing of Nazi spies; the other, the more domestic mysteries, being cases involving fairly ordinary people caught up in murders, thefts, blackmail, and so forth."

Blake took a puff of his pipe then poked at the air with its stem. "You know, those readers who enjoyed the Union Jack in their youth identified the late forties and early fifties as my 'lean years.' They missed the extravagances of the old master crooks. Their enthusiasm waned."

"Perhaps they also felt that way," I ventured, "because the stories started to reflect a world with which they were very familiar—rather a grim one, too. By contrast, to later generations—my own, for example—those yarns are more enjoyable because they're brimming with a more distant social history."

He gave a thoughtful nod. "When I first gave my case notes to Amalgamated Press, it was with but a single intention, it being to influence the attitudes, beliefs and behaviours of my opponents. It never occurred to me that I would also cause to be recorded an ever-changing cultural climate."

"I find them extremely evocative," I said. "And it's incredible how, between the stories written at the start of the twentieth century and those from midway through, there's such an astonishing alteration in the attitudes and lifestyles portrayed."

"Fifty tumultuous years," he noted.

"And you with your finger on the pulse."

THE MAN FROM OCCUPIED FRANCE

BLAKE SUCKED AT his pipe and sent a blueish cloud rolling into the air. He removed the first of the two Sexton Blake Libraries from its plastic sleeve.

"Anthony Parsons," he murmured. "He was one of the mainstays of the period, an author to whom I entrusted many of my reports, often immediately after the affairs they described had occurred. Some of the pages in those reports were almost solid black, being so inked over with War Office redactions. Yet from what little hints remained, he was always able to construct a tale that actually bore a passing resemblance to the real events."

I indicated the issue in his hand. "A case in point?"

"Oh, definitely."

THE MAN FROM OCCUPIED FRANCE

by Anthony Parsons
THE SEXTON BLAKE LIBRARY 3rd series,
issue 8 (1941)

THE PROLOGUE

John Maynard's Vow.

"Ten years—"

The words seemed to rustle through the empty court like wind among dry leaves, yet the girl in the dock gave no sign that she had heard. She stood exactly as she had been standing throughout the whole of that incredible day, with her hands resting lightly on the dock rails and her grey eyes fixed on something that seemed above and beyond the judge. Not once, so far as he was aware, had she even looked at him. She had never once looked at the jury. So far as it was possible to judge from her attitude, she had at no time throughout her trial been aware either of them or him.

The dry voice continued to rustle through the dusty court. Assisting the King's enemies—a heinous offence— the lives of brave men endangered—the safety of the realm—his duty to pass sentence—

Ten years!

It was over at last. The thin voice tricked into

silence. In the hush that followed his lordship gathered up his papers and rose, but he did not at once withdraw. He paused for a moment, a vivid splash of colour against the sombre background of the court, his eyes seeking out the girl in the dock—that pathetically young, graceful girl, whose navy blue costume with the white ruff of lace at throat and cuffs was so soon to be exchanged for the grey garb of prison. He saw her delicately-cut face in sharp outline against the black oak panelling behind; felt again the calm serenity of her, the utter fearlessness of her. And once again he was reminded of that old picture of Joan of Arc at her trial. Then, as counsel bowed respectfully, he turned and disappeared through his private door at the back of the dais. Simultaneously, a wardress reached out and touched the prisoner's arm.

"That's all!" she whispered audibly. And with a jerk of her head towards the cells below: "Come on!"

The trial had been held in camera. No details had been given either of the charge or of Isobel Ensor herself. No details ever would be given. In tomorrow's papers there would be a brief paragraph announcing that Isobel Ensor, until recently employed as a secretary in a certain aircraft company, had been sentenced to ten years' imprisonment upon a charge of selling information to the enemy—but that was all the public would ever know.

The twelve good men and true filed noisily from their box, glad that the case was over. Upon the far side of the court, counsel for the Crown was gathering up his papers with an air of bored detachment odd in one who a few minutes ago had been all fire and indignation. But that had been mere play-acting, of course, part of the dramatics of the law. Robbed of its scarlet-robed judge and bewigged counsel, even the court itself took on the appearance of an empty stage.

Ten years!

In a close, stuffy little room down below, the convicted girl was taking leave of her fiancé. Behind the prisoner was a wardress, her eyes on the clock, as though one minute more or less could have any significance in the bottomless well of ten whole years! And behind John Maynard stood a police sergeant, keenly alert that nothing passed between the two that might in any way circumvent the ends of justice.

At last it was over. Dry-eyed, still smiling pathetically, Isobel was led away to commence her long sentence. John Maynard watched her all the way to the door and past it. When presently he turned to go, he found himself face to face with counsel for the defence, Gervase Crispin, K.C., the man he had himself briefed upon Isobel's behalf.

"I'm sorry I could do no more," the lawyer said, as their eyes met.

"You did your best. We must find Walter Paine now."

"Do you think that would be—of much use?"

"But of course it would. Paine is the one man who can clear her!"

The lawyer nodded his head slowly. It was plain that not even the verdict of the court meant anything to John Maynard. He simply would not accept it.

It was Maynard who had persuaded him to take up the case. He had come to his chambers with a faith it was impossible to ignore. In that dusty old room in the Middle

Temple John Maynard had seemed to the lawyer like a lighted lamp or a drawn sword—something you could neither put out nor break. His belief in the girl he loved was utterly and completely final. It was terrific. There had been no gainsaying it. Never for one moment had he doubted the outcome of the trial. Even as late as last night, when the K.C. had thought it necessary to sound a warning note, he had brushed it aside as impossible.

"But she is innocent!" he had said. And the force of his belief was such that even the lawyer himself had momentarily doubted.

Now, as the silence grew and lengthened between them, he drew a deep breath.

"It's too late, I'm afraid," he said, and his voice was harsher than he knew by reason of his own emotion. "Faith alone is not enough in a court of law, Maynard— we demand facts. Truth is, there is too much against her to make an alibi of much use. I'm sorry, but I conceive it my duty to make this quite clear to you. Having heard all the evidence, the court has sentenced Isobel Ensor to ten years' imprisonment; and nothing can alter that sentence short of a successful appeal. It is my duty to tell you that we have no possible grounds upon which to make such an appeal."

"But she is innocent, Mr. Crispin!"

"You think that she is innocent."

"But the alibi—"

"Walter Paine is most probably dead. He was reported 'Missing, believed killed' when the B.E.F.[1] evacuated from France; and since then nothing has been heard of him. In the opinion of the court, Walter Paine and the alibi were mere red herrings drawn across the trail by an astute defence. Frankly, they did not believe in Walter Paine. And, in any event, even if he were alive, I do not know what he could say. Nor do you. For that we have only Isobel Ensor's word, and that the court will not accept."

"Would they accept Walter Paine's own word?"

"I don't know." The lawyer avoided Maynard's eyes. It was like bludgeoning a helpless man, yet still he went on, convinced that it was kinder so. "The defence throughout the whole case has rested upon a flat denial of the charges—a denial unsupported by a scintilla of proof. We could not, for example, explain away the five thousand pounds that was paid into Miss Ensor's account upon the day after the plans were missed. Nor could we offer any convincing explanation of the tiny camera-watch found in her handbag. It is in evidence that she was a member of the Link,[2] and had pro-German sympathies before the war. It is also in evidence that she was accustomed to spending her holidays in Germany, where she has many friends and some relatives."

"Yes, but—"

"Wait!" the lawyer said flatly. "Against all that mass of circumstantial evidence our only answer was this alibi afforded by Walter Paine—by a dead man! Or, at any rate, a man who will shortly be presumed dead. Upon the night in question, Isobel Ensor says that she was with Walter Paine; but when the court calls upon us to produce this Walter Paine, all we can say is that unfortunately the gentleman did not come back from France, and therefore we cannot produce him! You see how weak it sounds? How much like a subterfuge designed for the sole purpose of creating doubt in the minds of the jury?"

"Yes, but it's true!" young Maynard cried. "That's what we have to remember—it's true! Isobel's innocent, I tell you. And Walter Paine can prove it."

"Not if he's killed."

"He may not have been killed. I have the feeling that he wasn't killed, Mr. Crispin. That report we had from his regiment—he was alive when they left him, wasn't he? And there was a nun with him, too. Help, that is. Maybe he survived. I'm going over there to find out."

"But you can't go to Occupied France, Maynard!"

"Can't I?"

"Of course, you can't! You can't get out of England, to begin with. There's a war on! And certainly you could never get through two million Germans."

"I'd get through two million hells if it meant freeing Isobel, Mr. Crispin!"

He threw back his head as he spoke. There was a sincerity, a compelling dignity about him that saved him from the taint of melodrama. Very slim he was, very straight—so that watching him, once again the lawyer caught himself thinking of a drawn sword flashing defiantly in the sunlight.

"I'll find Walter Paine!" he said simply. "If he is still alive, I'll find him and bring him back here so that he can speak for himself. He shall tell his story in court. They'll have to believe Isobel, then!"

The End of the Prologue

THE STORY

THE FIRST CHAPTER

Strict Orders.

"AND JUST A final word of warning, gentlemen!" said the C.O. with his grimmest smile. "Any fellow who leaves the escort to go looking for trouble on his own'll find that trouble—and not from a bat-eared Hun, either! He'll find it from me—good and plenty—within half a minute of his touching down here! Is that understood?"

The assembled pilots agreed that it was understood. They were most fervent about it. Too fervent, it seemed; for the C.O. repeated his warning, together with the information that he would accept no excuse from anyone who failed to return with the formation. Upon the last occasion when the squadron had done escort duty, two pilots had returned half an hour after the rest, with the excuse of engine trouble. Subsequent information had shown that the two pilots in question had dropped out of the formation half-way across the "ditch" and hared back to France to strafe an aerodrome they disliked. Then they sighted a Junkers 88 and stopped to have a crack at that; after which they had returned home full of beans and unblushingly announced "engine trouble."

The C.O. rose to his feet. The conference was at an end. But as he moved towards the door of the hut his eye alighted upon two sergeant-pilots who had been posted to his squadron only a few days previously.

"Oh, Wilkinson," he called to a flight-lieutenant.

"Sir?"

"Those two new men over there. This'll be their first operational flight, I think? Certainly their first escort job. See that they've fully understood their instructions."

"Very good, sir!" The flight-lieutenant saluted and fell back. The two men were in his flight, and although they had only just been posted to him, already he was aware of their quality. The taller of the two, Allen, had the makings of a crack Spitfire artist. The other, Green, was only an inch or two behind him. "Will you two fellows hang on for a moment?" he called to them across the room.

The other pilots were already streaming from the hut, their maps under their arms and their tongues going nineteen to the dozen. They did not like escort work, it was too dull. "Bus-conducting" they called it. "Going out with the crocodile." Trained to individual combat, they preferred to sally forth in twos and threes and beat up trouble in their own way. Most of them had a "sparring partner," and hunted in couples. The notion of going out "glued to a mob of bombers" was not attractive.

The flight-lieutenant explained this to Allen and Green, even while making it clear that duty was duty, and escort work was as much a part of their job as anything else. Then, for a time, the talk became highly technical as he went over the details of the forthcoming "sweep" over Northern France. At the end of if all he took out a packet of cigarettes.

"I expect you're feeling a bit hit-up—sort of?" he suggested, as he handed them round. "First time over, and all that—everybody has to go through it. The thing to avoid is getting over-anxious. If I were you, I'd have a drink in the mess and then buzz off to the first house of one of the shows in the town. What d'you think?"

"A good idea, sir!" Green admitted at once. "I've waited nine months for this moment, and now I'm all of a dither to be off. I wish it were to-night instead of to-morrow night!"

"And you, Sergeant Allen?"

"Oh, I'm all right, sir!"

The flight-lieutenant gave him a thoughtful glance. He was thinking of what one of the instructional staff from the Advanced Flying School had said a couple of days ago, when, having come over to the squadron on a day's leave, he had noticed Sergeant Allen standing on the tarmac.

"Hallo!" he had exclaimed. "So you've got 'Purposeful Percy,' have you? Sergeant Allen, I mean—Percy Allen," he explained, when the flight-lieutenant had stared his non-comprehension. "I had him in my class, and that was one of his nicknames. 'Purposeful Percy,' they called him. 'The gent who means to succeed.' I bet he will, too! I'll bet you he puts up the D.F.M.[3] within a month—"

Now, watching him, the flight-lieutenant nodded to himself thoughtfully. He agreed that Sergeant Allen probably would get his D.F.M. within the month—he had that look about him. Physically, although tall, he was very slight, suggesting the rapier rather than the broadsword. And although his features were small and his grey eyes curiously expressionless, you could not avoid an impression of tremendous inner strength.

"By the way, Allen, he asked suddenly, "were you ever at Repton?"

"I'm afraid not, sir."

"Any brother of yours there?"

"No, sir."

"I asked because your face strikes some chord in my memory—I thought it might be Repton. Sorry!" The flight-lieutenant nodded pleasantly to them and turned away.

"What's Repton?" Sergeant Green asked when he had gone.

"A rather famous public school," Allen answered him a bit dryly. "He was there himself."

"How do you know?"

"I don't. I merely guessed it from what he said just now."

Sergeant Green looked at him for a moment, then gathered up his maps. He had gone through the mill with Percy Allen—from elementary training to passing out, and now they had been posted to the same squadron and were going on their first flight across the "ditch" together—yet still he knew very little about him. He was thinking of that "mill" now as they moved towards the door. "Seems funny that we're here at last, doesn't it?" he said musingly. "I could never really see myself finishing. Could you?"

"You mean starting, don't you?"

"Well, starting, then, if you like it better. But you know what I mean: I could never see myself with a Spitfire of my own. I could never see myself finishing that course and being posted to a real squadron."

"Six months can be the deuce of a time!"

"I had nine months! I'd been at it three when you arrived, don't forget!"

His companion nodded. They were out on the tarmac now, and for a minute or two he stood gazing at the line of waspish fighters that were being groomed in readiness for the next morning's escort duty.

"Remember when old Backhouse said you'd got to go on bombers?" Green asked suddenly.

Percy Allen pulled a wry face. He had plumbed for fighters all along: it had been a bitter blow when he had been told to switch to bombers. Even now he could see the C.O.'s face when, having been called to the orderly-room at the end of that particular course, he had said: "I am recommending you for bombers, Sergeant Allen."

"Bombers?" he had gasped. "But I want fighters, sir. I mean—"

"What d'you mean?" rasped old Backhouse blankly. It is doubtful if anyone ever before had dared to question his decision in such a matter. "You're the type we want for bombers," he had snapped. "You've got the bomber temperament. You've got determination, and the cold, unhurrying purpose that is the very backbone of a good bomber pilot. I've watched you at your work here. I know what they call you; it's my business to know. You set yourself to come out on top here, and you've come out on top. Not because of any particular brilliance but from sheer dogged sticking at it. And that's what a bomber pilot needs more than anything else—dogged sticking at it."

"Yes, sir, but I—I was fighting to get on to Spitfires!"

"Spitfires—my foot! Spitfires aren't the only machines in the R.A.F."

"They are for me, sir!" Allen had told him simply.

He had got his way. There were those who maintained that in defying old Backhouse—a bomber man himself, and a power in the bomber circle—Sergeant Allen had thrown away his best chance of early promotion. But that was his own affair. Percy Allen did not want bombers, he wanted fighters—and a single-seater fighter, no less: "Purposeful Percy" they had called him after that. "The gent who means to succeed"—for single-seater fighter men were generally credited with having an eye to the records of Ball and McCudden[4] in the last show; and more particularly to their decorations!

"What about buzzing off to a show to-night?" Green asked as they moved towards their quarters.

"Not for me, Reg—I've got one or two things I want to do," Allen told him.

"Oh, nonsense, man—come on!"

"Not to-night, old chap. Sorry, but I'm busy."

Green clicked an impatient tongue.

"You're a queer fish!" he grumbled. "Don't you ever celebrate anything? I don't believe you've even wet your 'wings' yet—let alone celebrated your graduation. And to-morrow we're going over the 'ditch.' Come on! Let's go and shoot it up somewhere!"

"Not for me, Reg—thanks all the same."

"But why not, man?"

Allen shrugged.

"Perhaps because I want a clear head in the morning," he smiled in that slow, far-away fashion of his. "So-long, old boy!" he added more briskly. "See you later. A la bonne heure!"

"Aw! Don't sling your bloomin' French at me!" was all the other said irritably as he turned away.

That was another thing that had surprised the "boys"— the way in which Sergeant Allen swotted up French in every minute of his spare time. No matter what course he might be on, he always succeeded in rounding up some funny little "mousseer" to come and jabber with him in his quarters. You'd have thought he had notions of joining a Free French squadron the way he went on!

It was then five o'clock, and half an hour later saw Sergeant Green scrambling eagerly into the leave-tender en route for Dillborough six miles away. The evening was chilly, with a hint of worse to come, but he wore no overcoat—why should he? At twenty-one, in the uniform of the greatest air force on earth, with three stripes on your arms and a pair of brand-new wings on your chest—who wants an overcoat? Certainly not Sergeant

Reginald Green and his like. Later he would hang a few decorations under those wings, but for the moment they formed an elegant sufficiency of themselves. They kept him in a constant glow; and his only trouble was that he could not wear another pair on his right breast so that the pretty girls who passed him on that side should have equal chance with those who passed him on his left. For very pretty girls, it is true, he was in the habit of half-turning as though he had forgotten something—and why not, forsooth? A fellow who put up the wings of the R.AF. is no small beer! They are a decoration in themselves, and have always been counted as such—but a decoration that can never be given. The wings of the R.A.F.—like those of the R.F.C.—have to be earned. They have to be laboured for, in sweat, and often enough in blood. There are no "honorary" wings.

"Phwe-e-e!" observed Sergeant Green as the tender swung round a crossroads half-way to the town. "Oh boy, oh boy!" he gasped. "Stop the cab—it's me she's waiting for!" But his companions merely laughed. For after a quick glance into the tender as it sped past her, the young lady in question had continued her walk in the direction of the airfield.

"She didn't see me!" cried the sergeant in mock despair. "I've always said these tenders go too fast. She said she'd walk out to meet me—"

"Ger-cher!" they told him, their eyes fixed admiringly on the delectable bit of fluff that was now but a pinpoint in the distance. "She's waiting for somebody on foot—or on a bicycle! Somebody's fixed a date with her."

"Phwe-e-e!" whistled Sergeant Green again. Great stars above—was that why Purposeful Percy had refused to come in the tender? He had said that he was going into the town, but he would use his cycle. He always did use a cycle in preference to the leave tender. "Why, the bloomin' old sky-hawk!" grinned Sergeant Green, thinking that at last he had solved the secret of his friend's unsociability. He made a note to tax him with the intrigue when he got back to the airfeld, but when that time arrived, Purposeful Percy had not yet returned.

He was still absent at eleven o'clock that night.

When midnight struck, and still he had not returned, with a broad grin on his round, good-natured face, Sergeant Green walked across to the quarter-guard to warn the sergeant-in-charge that Purposeful Percy had blotted-his copy-book and would most likely come stealing home with the milk.

"He said something about wanting to keep his head clear for the morning," he sighed. "But if that was his headache tablet I saw along the road—oh boy, oh boy, why wasn't I born a chemist!"

THE SECOND CHAPTER

A Well Laid Trap.

ACTUALLY, TO DO him justice, no one could possibly have been more surprised than was Sergeant Percy Allen himself when the girl signalled him at the junction of the cross-roads.

He had seen her standing there as he came pedalling up the hill, and if he had thought anything at all it was that she was waiting for somebody from the airfield. It was, therefore, with a considerable amazement that he saw her wave her hand to him and call out—and even then he would not have stopped save for something about her which warned him that she was no mere camp-follower.

He braked his bicycle and got off.

"You want me?" he asked a bit doubtfully, his right hand automatically going to his cap.

"Please!" she said, as she hurried towards him through the growing dusk. "And do forgive me for stopping you?"

She had the voice of a lady: the bearing of one, too.

As he wheeled his bicycle to meet her, he caught an impression of expensive clothes and elegancy.

"It's my car," she said. "I've been here such a time. The wretched thing's come to a dead stop, and I can neither get her going again nor get help. I wondered if you would mind—"

She paused. She had come up with him now, and although she was rather older than at first he had taken her to be, she was also a great deal more beautiful, he saw. She had an air about her, too. She was dainty and very smart, from her red, high-heeled shoes to her red leather driving gloves, her red handbag, and the red turban affair she had wound round her platinum head. She was not particularly tall, yet she looked tall—mainly because of her slim figure and upright carriage. And when she smiled at him, her teeth were amazingly white and regular behind the scarlet of her lips.

"Where is your car?" Allen heard himself ask.

She told him that it was a hundred yards or so down the Ladcaster road—away from the direction in which he was going—and when mechanically he started back in that direction she fell into graceful step beside him.

"I dare say it's some silly little thing," she said, "but I'm such a fool where machinery is concerned. You're sure I'm not keeping you from—"

She did not say from what, but her manner suggested from some other appointment. Allen shook his head. He was going in to Dillborough Library but there was plenty of time.

"Oh, you're a pilot, I see!" she exclaimed suddenly.

"Yes."

"How wonderful!" Her voice dropped a note, became warm and caressing. Allen would scarcely have been a man had he failed to glow to the admiration he read in her eyes and glance. She was staring at him frankly, now, as though seeing him for the first time. Her eyes said plainly that she was conscious of looking at a superman—and she didn't care if he knew it. "You are the first Spitfire pilot to whom I have ever spoken!" she told him a moment later. "You don't know how we women think of you."

"Who told you I was a Spitfire pilot?" he laughed a bit awkwardly.

"I know you are; I've seen the Spitfires flying from your airfield."

"You live here, then?"

"Oh, yes! In Ladcaster. There's the car, look!" she added, as they passed the cross-roads and turned into the leafy tunnel that was the Ladcaster Road.

It was an M.G—a red M.G., hence her red gloves and shoes and bag and turban, he gathered. The bonnet was already open, and there was a variety of tools lying on the running board. He asked her what she had done.

"Well," she said, "I've taken the jet out—and that's O.K. I've tested the petrol—and that's O.K. I've taken the plugs out and tried to test those, but I hurt my wrist with the starting handle and—"

"Hurt it badly?" he cut in, noticing for the first time that she had a handkerchief tied round her right wrist just inside the red gauntlet.

"Sprained it a little, perhaps—nothing serious," she

assured him. "The wretched thing slipped out, just when I was pulling my hardest. I'll have it attended to as soon as I get home."

Allen leaned over the radiator and got busy. He could remember the day when a "Twenty-M.G." had seemed a big job to handle, but after a Spitfire engine it was almost like a sewing machine. The electrical installation was the trouble, he soon discovered; and after perhaps fifteen minutes of careful elimination, he arrived at the cause of it all. "Here you are," he announced, not without a certain satisfaction. "A broken carbon brush, you see?"

"Is that serious?" she smiled, after carefully investigating the fragment.

"It is unless you've got a spare."

They went round to the tool box to investigate. It was almost dark by now, but when the girl leaned down to pick up the inspection lamp she gave a sharp "Ouch!" of pain.

"I say!" Allen exclaimed on the instant. "You've hurt that wrist of yours. You'll never be able to drive home."

"Oh, I'll manage, Mr—er——"

"Allen is my name," he told her. "Sergeant Allen."

"I'm called Grantham. Wendy Grantham. I live with my father at the White House. You must come and see us, Mr. Allen. I know my father would like to thank you for helping me on my way."

"I'm thinking I'll have to take you on your way—by the look of that wrist."

"Oh, please! I couldn't dream of allowing you to waste still more of your time."

"I'm in no particular hurry, Miss Grantham. And you

certainly can't hold a bus like this with only one hand. But first things first!" he broke off when she would have protested again. "Unless we can find a spare brush, it won't be the car at all. It'll have to be the step of my bicycle!"

She laughed at that. Her laugh was low, and very pleasant to the ear. The notion of being carried pillion on a bicycle by a four-hundred-miles-an-hour Spitfire pilot tickled her sense of humour, it seemed.

He himself found the inspection lamp, and a few minutes later, in a small leather case of magneto spares, found a duplicate brush.

"Now we shan't be long!" he said, as he carried both lamp and spare brush round to the front of the car.

"Shall I hold the lamp for you?"

He handed it over and she took it in her left hand—holding it high above his head while he worked. For in spite of the fact that it still wanted a few minutes to official black-out time, under the thick archway of trees that spread across the Ladcaster Road it was quite dark.

Allen worked quickly, and was just about to replace the distributor when something—some sixth sense perhaps—caused him to look up into the girl's face. Why he looked up he could not have told you. It might have been the silence, or it might have been that—without knowing it—he had heard a strange rustle of leaves. Or, of course, it might have been that sixth sense of "Mind your tail" which every fighter pilot develops quite early in his fighting career—or goes under! In any event he did look up and it was what he saw in the girl's eyes that made him duck.

The light from the inspection lamp was full on her face, but her eyes—wide-stretched and frozen—were fixed in an expressionless stare at something just over his head. Her lips were parted. Her nostrils distended. Even as he looked up, her free hand went like a flash to her throat as though to stifle a scream.

It was then that Allen ducked. Had he been in his plane he would have dived. In the same split-second something whizzed past his head, carrying away his forage cap and literally lifting the hair from his skull by the speed of its passing. Even as he whirled round he heard the girl cry out as though in mortal fear.

"What was that?" he gasped, seeing nothing behind him. "What hit me? What were you looking at?" He snatched the inspection lamp from her hand, shining it this way and that along the road—but the road was empty.

"A snake!" she cried in a strangled voice.

"What—"

She pointed upwards into the trees. She tried to say something else, but the words would not come. Allen suddenly remembered that rustling he had half-heard and shone the light upwards.

"Hell," his lips formed soundlessly a split-second later, for there, just disappearing into the greenery immediately above his head was a thin black loop. It was twenty feet up, and it was gone even as he saw it—but he knew that he had seen it, and he knew that he had made no mistake. "A snake?" he whispered hoarsely. "In England?"

"Let's get away!" Suddenly she found her tongue. "Let's go! Now! I saw it above your head! At first I thought I

36

must be dreaming. Seeing things! Then it moved. It was a snake, I tell you! I saw its jaws!"

"But there are no snakes in England!"

"I'm frightened. Let's go!"

"Hop in, then!" Suddenly Sergeant Allen found that he, too, was sweating. He hated snakes, anyway. And after all, you could never be sure. Maybe a snake had escaped from somewhere—years ago—and made a nest in the Ladcaster woods. He had read of snakes that lay out along branches, in the jungle, waiting to strike down at anyone who might be unwary enough to pass immediately below them. Boa-constrictors he thought they were. Monstrous things. Foul things. Thirty feet long, and big round as a man's waist. They could crush an ox and swallow it whole.

He worked fast. Men do work fast in emergency, and faster still when in fear. And nothing turns a man's heart to water as quickly as fear of the Unknown—that blind, unreasoning fear, that has come down to us from the primeval slime. That fear which comes with the dark.

"Hurry! Hurry!" the girl shuddered.

It was not until they were clear of the woods and out between the open fields above Ladcaster village that sanity returned to either. Then, with a shamed laugh, Sergeant Allen stopped the car and fell to mopping his brow.

"We're a fine pair of lunatics!" he told her. "That was no snake—couldn't have been! It was a bat, or something!"

"It was a snake!" Her voice was hard and she was more shaken than he had realised. She was white as a sheet. "Where's your bicycle?"

"I'm holding it here on the running board."

"Will you drive me home?"

He thought for a moment.

"Well, I don't know," he said then. "I think I ought to go back there. I mean—well, dash it all!—I've left my cap behind, for one thing. And for another, if there really is a snake loose in the woods, it'll have to be rounded up."

"But not now—please? Please don't go back there! Please drive me home."

"Well, if you feel like that about it, of course."

"And would you pull the hood up, please?"

"The hood—"

"I'm cold!" She shivered.

"Oh, I see!" Releasing his bicycle for a moment, Allen did as he was bid. "Have we far to go?" he asked, as he screwed up the screen fastenings.

"Only just the other side of the village. I'll tell you when we get there."

He could scarcely see her now, but there was no gainsaying the urgency of her voice. She was scared stiff. She seemed to have gone all to pieces. For himself he was feeling supremely ridiculous. Try as he might, he could not think how he had come to make such an all-fired fool of himself! It was sheer bosh to talk about a boa-constrictor haunting the Ladcaster woods. It was crazy. What she had seen was a bat—one of those chaps that had streamers to their wings, he thought suddenly. That was the explanation! He hadn't thought of it before, but now he remembered seeing a picture of one in some nature notes he had read somewhere. It was a streamer-winged bat. Of course it was! Darkness and nerves had done the rest. Set him going, too! Well, thank heaven Reg Green hadn't been there and seen him sweating with terror! He'd never have heard the last of it.

Ladcaster village appeared to be a village of the dead as he drove slowly through the little High Street. The girl had leaned forward in her seat and with her hands on the dashboard was peering ahead through the screen.

"Mind your hands on the switches there!" he said suddenly. "You've put the tail lamp out."

"I've what?"

"You've put the tail lamp out!"

"Oh, I'm sorry!" In the darkness he could hear her fumbling around the board. "Never mind," she said then. "Here we are—the house on the left, look! Yes, straight in! The gate is open."

Obediently he swung the car through the dimly seen gateposts and continued up a drive half-hidden by rhododendron bushes. Presently the path broadened out, and there on his left, black and silent against the night sky, was the silhouette of a large country house.

"Home!" said the girl in a voice pregnant with relief. She sat for a moment as though collecting herself, then she opened the door and began to climb out. "You'll come in for a moment, won't you?" she asked.

"I really think I ought to be getting along now."

"Oh, no—please! You must come in for a moment. Look, I'll call my chauffeur!" she promised. "Then he can drive you wherever you want to go. It will be much quicker that way, I'm sure. Please come in!"

"Well, all right!" he smiled, letting go of his bicycle and stepping out upon that side. He might as well get a lift into Dillborough as pedal it, he supposed. And, after all, it had certainly been a rum night! Quite the rummiest he could remember, what with romantic encounters, snakes up trees, broken-down cars, and one thing and another. Suddenly he leaned towards her as they climbed the wide steps to the porticoed doorway. "I say!" he laughed a bit ruefully. "Don't you think it would be better if we said nothing about that snake business?"

He thought that she gestured agreement with the idea, though he could not be sure. Curiously enough, she seemed to have forgotten him now that she was safe home again. She was turned away from him, listening for something, he thought, and unconsciously he found himself listening, too. The house was extraordinarily still. Not a sound. Nothing. Not a thing was stirring anywhere. The thought flashed across Allen's mind—"It's too still!" And simultaneous with that thought came fear.

It was as though an alarm bell had been touched off deep down in his subconscious awareness. In a flash red flags were waving everywhere. Something was wrong; everything, right from that all-embracing flash he knew that everything was wrong: everything, right from the beginning! He became aware of a fierce and unreasoning desire to be gone; to get out of that place; to be away on the high road again. His hand dropped to his pocket where he carried a torch. He must have half-turned to go back down the steps when the girl spoke again.

"Ah!" she exclaimed. "Here's Mason at last. Poor old

chap, he is so dreadfully deaf. He never hears the bell until it has been ringing for half an hour, and even then he takes about a week to get to the door. Come on in, Mr. Allen."

It was like a douche of cold water. For the second time that night blind, unreasoning fear had to give way before barndoor common-sense. And although Allen was still aware of an immense disinclination to pass through that door, nevertheless, because he yet retained sufficient self-control to prevent him from again making a fool of himself, he allowed her to take his arm and pilot him into the Stygian blackness of the house.

"We'll have a light in a moment," she promised, as Mason closed the outer door softly behind them.

It was then that Sergeant Allen knew truth. It came to him in a flash—came with the sound of his shoes on bare boards and with the smell of damp and decay that assailed his nostrils.

"We'll have a light now!" he laughed harshly, thrusting the girl aside and snapping on his torch.

They were in an empty house—so much he saw at a glance. One wild sweep round showed him the girl cowering back against the wall where he had thrown her, and "Mason"—as black-browed a villain as any he had ever seen—caught neatly in the act of shooting the bolts on the door. In the same split second a door opened farther along the hall, and a man leapt out.

"Be careful!" shrieked the girl, as a yard of blue flame ripped from the gun he was carrying.

Allen ducked to the flash. Ping went a bullet past his

ear. Instinctively he turned to the door, only to catch his breath and leap back again when Mason, grinning evilly, whipped out another gun and took deliberate aim. Then he knew that they were out to murder him! He hadn't a chance. That girl had deliberately trapped him. Why, he did not know.

There was a staircase leading to the upper regions not a dozen feet from where he was standing—a wide staircase, which turned at right angles and crossed over the hall past what looked to be an imitation musician's gallery. In the split second before Mason fired, Allen switched off his torch and dived blindly for it; caught the balustrade, stumbled, recovered himself, and even as that second man switched on a torch and caught him plump in its beam, he was on his feet again and racing like a madman for the top.

Mason's bullet crashed into the rail barely an inch behind him. He raced on. Now he was at the bend and within sight of safety, but already someone was thundering up the stairs on his heels. A bullet scored his leg. Another nicked his hand. He was using his own torch now, and he took the first chance he saw. A door loomed up on his right—a bed-room door, he thought. A good solid one. In a single movement he caught the knob, turned it, leapt inside, banged it shut again behind him, and turned the key in the precise instant that his pursuer flung himself bodily against the other side.

Breathlessly the Spitfire pilot looked about him. The room itself was empty as the rest of the house; there was not even a blind-roller that he could use as a weapon. The window was his only chance. How high it was, or upon which side of the house it looked out, he had no idea. He would have to risk that.

Recklessly he drove his foot through the glass—frantically "winking" his torch the while on the off-chance that someone passing the house might notice the phenomenon and come to investigate. The glass seemed to be falling a very long way, but that couldn't be helped. He was just stamping off the broken bits of glass on the bottom of the frame when with a loud crash the panel of the door burst inwards and a hand clutching a revolver was thrust through the aperture.

Allen whirled at the first shot, caught his breath, then saw his chance. Snatching off one of his shoes he ran round the wall of the room until he came to within striking distance of that marauding hand.

Crack! There was a yell of agony as the heel of his shoe whanged down upon the exposed wrist. The hand went limp on the instant. The paralysed fingers loosed their hold of the gun. With a yelp of triumph Allen seized it before it fell to the ground, swung it round, and fired point-blank through the broken panels at its late owner.

The man lurched away. Allen could hear his feet sliding drunkenly along the corridor as he retired. Instinct warned him that whoever the man was, he'd got him all right!

He went out after him! Trained to accept odds as readily as lesser men accept equality, now that he was armed and able to defend himself, there was no need to take the hazard of that window. He would go out by the door, or know the reason why!

Slipping on his shoe again, with his torch in one hand and the gun in the other, he made his way cautiously to the stair-head. Mason was half-way up; he was evidently coming to the assistance of his confederate. But when his torch revealed Allen standing there he loosed a vicious curse and opened up on the instant.

Allen replied in kind. There was no other course open to him. A moment later Mason dropped his gun, clutched with both hands at his stomach, heeled over sideways, and somersaulted helplessly to the bottom of the stairs.

Simultaneously a sudden flurry of footsteps from the back of the house announced the arrival of reinforcements.

"Stick 'em up, you there!" somebody roared, but Allen was waiting for no more. A bullet spanged into the woodwork behind him as he switched off his torch, and then he was away to the room he had just left. It would have to be the window, after all, he saw.

He dropped on to soft earth and lay still for a moment, dazed. The shock had shaken his very teeth loose, he felt, as well as broken his spine. But when the stars had faded from before his eyes and the numbness passed from his jarred legs, he found that he could stand all right—and a minute or so later, even run! For not having found him inside the house, those murderers were starting to look outside!

He did not stop for his bicycle. In any event, he could not have got it, since the enemy were between him and the place where he had left it. Instead, he took to his heels across what appeared to be a lawn, and after crossing a ditch and a field or two, very suddenly he found himself back on the Ladcaster road.

Then, for the first time, Sergeant Percy Allen paused to think what he had done. Standing there beside a stile, with the vague white ribbon of road running away from him on either side, he passed a hand across his eyes and asked himself if he had not been dreaming? He must have been dreaming, surely? That girl? The broken-down car? The boa-constrictor among the trees? The way she had deliberately taken him into that house, knowing that men were waiting to murder him there? It didn't make sense! There was no reason why they should want to murder him—why anyone should want to murder him!

Unless it was because he was a Spitfire pilot, and every Spitfire man less was so much gain to the enemy?

But that was nonsense, he argued. What had happened was that they'd mistaken him for somebody else. It was not him they had sought to lure to his death, but some other pilot of the squadron. But who? And why? And if that were true, why hadn't the girl seen her mistake at once? And why hadn't the men? Surely they must have known the man they were seeking?

And suddenly, as he stood there pondering the amazing events of this most amazing night—suddenly he caught his breath. What put the thought into his mind he did not know, but in the strange way that such things do come to people, quite suddenly he understood what had happened in the trees over-head while he had been repairing that broken brush on the Ladcaster road.

He had been right in ridiculing the snake idea—it had not been a snake. Moreover, that girl had known it was not a snake. She had, indeed, of deliberate intent held the inspection lamp high above his head. And the intentness of her expression had been caused, not by fear for Percy Allen, but fear for the man who was lying out along that branch overhead. Fear that he might not drop his fatal noose cleanly about his victim's neck! Fear lest Percy Allen should hear something, or look up too soon and see the sudden death that was preparing to swish down upon his unsuspecting head.

That was why the car had been parked in that particular spot! That was why, when his sixth sense had caused him to look up and so escape by a hairsbreadth the practised swing of that garrotter's rope, she had urged him to take her away at once! To take her away before he had time to work things out and start investigations—investigations which could only have resulted in her accomplice's discovery and arrest. And, of course, having failed in their first attempt, she had straightway proceeded with the next. She had been determined, it seemed, upon his death. Nothing less would suffice.

It occurred to him, as he slipped from the stile and commenced a cautious journey back to the airfield, that if everything had gone right for that girl—and for her plans—at this present moment he would have been swinging uneasily from a tree in some quiet glade of Ladcaster Woods.

And failing to find any real reason for it, the coroner would have brought in a verdict of "suicide while of unsound mind."

"Blimey!" whispered the sergeant of the guard, when

just after two o'clock that morning, footsore and weary and more dishevelled than he knew, Sergeant Percy Allen reached the airfield. "Blimey! Do you know what time it is?"

Allen shook his head. His manner indicated that he neither knew nor cared. All he wanted was bed.

"H'm!" laughed the sergeant of the guard, as he passed him through. And with a slow droop of what he fondly hoped looked like an experienced eyelid: "Old Dad turn up unexpectedly, and took a dislike to you?" he asked sympathetically.

THE THIRD CHAPTER

In a Nasty Spot.

"WEATHER MISTING UP a bit over the 'ditch,' and cloud at three thousand, apparently!" the flight-lieutenant remarked, as he joined his little bunch of pilots on the tarmac the following evening. "Not so good, for us. Everybody O.K.?"

"O.K., sir!" they told him.

"Good!" He looked them over with an experienced eye. "Hallo!" he said then. "What have you been doing to your face, Allen?"

Sergeant Percy Allen gave a short laugh. In his helmet and goggles, his face telephone, "Mae West," and the rest of the stuff, he had hoped that his cut and bruised forehead might pass unnoticed—but he was out of luck. However, he had his answer ready, and he gave it with every assumption of ease.

"Fooling around with Green, sir," he said. "Playing polo on bicycles. We crashed!"

The flight-lieutenant snorted. At twenty-six he was already an old man by R.A.F. fighter standards, and a positive greybeard in the matter of experience. He glanced at his watch.

"Ten minutes to go," he announced. "Don't forget what I told you yesterday about keeping station when we get over there."

The six pilots of C Flight nodded their heads. They'd got it all in the bag, it seemed. Behind them, the engines of their Spitfires were ticking over smoothly, while they themselves—officers and sergeants all one together in the glorious brotherhood of the air—stood talking easily of this and that until the moment should arrive for them to take off. All, that is, with the exception of Sergeant Percy Allen—and he, the flight-lieutenant noticed, seemed strangely ill at ease and restless.

"Expecting anybody?" he asked, when for the fifth time in half as many minutes, Allen craned his neck in the direction of the aerodrome entrance.

Allen came round with a start.

"Who—me?" he almost stammered. He gave a nervous sort of laugh, and shook his head. "Heavens, no!" he said with exaggerated boisterousness. "I'm not expecting anybody, sir—why should I be?"

"I don't know." Wilkinson was watching him curiously. That clapping of hands; that hopping from one foot to the other? If he had not known the man better he would have said he was jumpy. He tried a word of advice. "Don't get over-anxious, Allen," he warned under his breath. "You won't let us down."

"Oh, it isn't that, sir!" the other came back at once. "It's just that I—well, I want to get away. I want to get away from here!" Even while he was speaking he had glanced again in the direction of the entrance. "It's the—the waiting," he repeated. "I want to get away."

"Anybody 'ud think—" The flight-lieutenant paused. "Say?" he asked suddenly. "You haven't been up to anything, have you?"

"What do you mean?"

"Anything you shouldn't? That face of yours—"

"Good heavens, no!"

The flight-lieutenant breathed again.

"Then what are you ditherin' about?" he grinned. "What's bitin' you, man?" He clapped him on the shoulder. "Tell your Uncle Richard all about her," he suggested. "Or if it's a long story, wait till we get back when I can lend you an ear untrammelled by telephones." He broke off short when someone called his name. It was the squadron adjutant. He was coming through the line of Spitfires, and with him was the "waiting" pilot —Sergeant Thompson—all dressed ready for the air. "Anything wrong, sir?" he asked.

"The commanding officer wants Sergeant Allen in his office, immediately," the adjutant said. "Sergeant Thompson will take his place in the formation."

The flight-lieutenant glanced swiftly at Allen. He had been right then—the fellow had been up to something he shouldn't. His face had gone chalk-white at the adjutant's order. He seemed dazed. Actually Sergeant Allen had been expecting that summons all day, but that it should come now, when there were only two or three minutes to go; when all he had worked for, all he had slaved for, was right under his hand—

"Stand by your machines!" bawled the station loudspeaker.

"You'll take Number 17 then—Sergeant Thompson!" the flight-lieutenant said quickly.

"He won't—by God!" Before anyone could stop him, Allen had spun round and was racing towards his machine with his equipment bouncing grotesquely about him. "Chocks away!" he shouted to his astonished mechanic. "Look lively, you fool!" Already he had his foot on the step and one hand on the rim of the cockpit when the adjutant's stentorian voice roared:

"Stop that man! Grab him. Don't let him get into that machine!"

The sudden roar of the engine drowned his words. Allen had got to the throttle, and regardless of the fact that he was only half inside the cockpit, he had opened it wide with the obvious intention of taking off. In another moment he would have been moving across the 'drome, but in that brief second of time the flight-sergeant—who happened to be standing by the next machine in the line—recovered from his amazement, and leapt. He caught Allen's hindmost foot, and in spite of the gale from the propeller, hung on.

Before Allen could kick himself free, he was overpowered and dragged out on to the ground by Wilkinson, the adjutant, and the pilot between them.

"You blasted young fool!" Wilkinson cursed him savagely.

"One minute to go!" warned the station loudspeaker.

"Hold him, sergeant!" The adjutant beckoned to two other N.C.O.'s as Thompson climbed into the Spitfire and eased back the throttle. "Get him out of the way of these machines!"

They pulled him behind the line; he did not resist them. All the fight had gone out of him, all the madness. He stood there breathing heavily, his eyes dazed, while the squadron taxied across the aerodrome, turned, and with a full-throated roar of superbly tuned engines, raced across the ground in perfect formation and took to the air. They hurtled over his head with a sound like tearing calico, swung on to their wing tips, and streaked back again—glistening like silver darts in the light from the setting sun.

"Another move like that, Sergeant Allen, and I'll have you put in handcuffs!" snarled the adjutant, as soon as he could make himself heard. "What's the matter with you, you crazy fool? Are you mad?"

He motioned the escort to take him along to the orderly room.

"And he's your prisoner, flight-sergeant!" he snapped. "Hold him outside until I call you."

"Very good, sir," the flight-sergeant saluted woodenly.

The adjutant went on ahead. Never in all his career could he remember anything even approaching the scene he had just witnessed. Another half-second and the madman would have been clean away in that Spitfire! It was incredible.

"Did you get him?" the C.O. asked when a few minutes later he stepped into the office.

"Yes—and he's under arrest, sir!" the adjutant reported. He glanced at the other man in the room—a man in civilian clothes—a man whom he now knew to be a detective-inspector of police from Dillborough. "He made a dash for a plane," he said. "And by gad—he almost succeeded in getting away in it, too!"

"What?" the C.O. gaped.

"Yes, sir!" He told them exactly what had happened. When he had finished, the policeman gave vent to a low whistle of astonishment.

"I think I'd better have a word with him right away, sir, if you've no objection," he said to the C.O. "He seems to be our man, right enough."

"Call him in, Simpson," the C.O. nodded.

The adjutant called "Sergeant Allen!"—and the prisoner was marched in, halted, and right turned before the C.O.'s table.

"Sergeant-Pilot Allen, sir!" he announced automatically.

"Let the escort wait outside, flight-sergeant."

"Very good, sir!" The escort was marched out again, but when the man from Dillborough rose swiftly to his feet:

"Just a moment!" the C.O. stopped him. No matter what Allen might have done, he was a sergeant of the Royal Air Force and amenable to Military Law. Furthermore, he was now under arrest upon a charge yet to be formulated, and no power on earth could take him out of Air Force custody save with the permission of the competent authority.

He explained that to the prisoner.

"Furthermore," he warned him, "you need not answer

any of the questions put to you unless you so desire. Right," he said to the Dillborough man, "go ahead!"

"Thank you, sir," the civilian smiled acidly. "You are Sergeant-Pilot Allen, I believe?" he began.

"I am," Allen said briefly.

"I am Detective-Inspector Scudamore, of the Dillborough Police, and I am inquiring into the death of a man which occurred in an empty house—known as the White House—near Ladcaster village last night, at approximately nine-thirty o'clock. I may say that a certain bicycle was found leaning against the shrubs in the drive; a bicycle which, upon investigation, proved to have been hired out to you by Messrs. Shaw and Co., Cycle Dealers, of Dillborough. Would you care to offer any explanation of how that bicycle got there?"

To the surprise of everyone, Allen gave a short laugh.

"Not at all," he said. "I rode it as far as the cross-roads, and from there it was carried on the running-board of a red M.G. belonging to Miss Wendy Grantham."

"Who is Miss Wendy Grantham?" the inspector flashed back.

"I haven't the remotest idea. I never met her in my life until last night. And then she tried to murder me."

"What do you mean?" The C.O. and the adjutant were frankly gaping, but if the inspector felt any surprise there was no sign of it on his face. He was watching Allen closely, warily even, but he was making no notes. "What do you mean?" he asked again.

"She told me that she lived at the White House with her father—"

"But the White House has been empty for years!"

"I know that myself—now. But at the time she told me, I didn't. I'd never even heard of the place."

"Would you care to tell me exactly what happened? The whole story, I mean?"

"I doubt if you'll believe me, inspector."

"I doubt if I shall!" the inspector's expression said plainly as though he had spoken aloud.

"Very well!" Seeing that no other course appeared open to him, Allen told the whole story. He told them everything, beginning with the girl stopping him at the cross-roads and continuing right up to that moment when, leaning exhausted against the stile, the real truth of that snake business had driven home to his understanding.

"I've been the victim of a plot," he wound up strongly. "It's quite obvious that those people mistook me for someone else. What I did, I did in self-defence. It was their lives or mine, inspector."

Nobody spoke. For once in a way even the inspector was speechless, while as for the R.A.F. officers—they were completely flabbergasted! Baron Munchausen had nothing on this young fellow.

It was the adjutant who finally broke the long silence.

"But if all this is true, Sergeant Allen," he asked, "why didn't you report it the moment you returned here?"

"Had I been a wiser man, that's what I should have done—but I didn't, sir. I felt I needed more time to think things over. I realised that mine was not a story many people would believe. I hadn't an atom of proof. The whole thing was too utterly fantastic, don't you see?"

The adjutant did see. The inspector saw, too. There were limits even to his credulity.

"You're not really expecting me to believe that you thought it was a snake up that tree?" he asked at last. "I mean—"

"I know what you mean, inspector." Allen took the words out of his mouth. "But you are forgetting the setting of it all, the atmosphere. The thing had knocked off my cap and missed my skull by the merest fraction of an inch—and there was the girl staring with her eyes wide and her mouth open and a look of frozen fear on her face. And when I looked up myself, by the light of that inspection lamp, a thin black loop was just disappearing among the leaves!" He snapped his fingers. "It was like that!" he added. "A flash! A lightning impression. And what with the girl urging me to get her out and so on— well, it wasn't until we got among the open fields that I sort of had a chance to think coherently. And even then I didn't think of an attempted garrotting. The explanation I gave it was a streamer-winged bat!"

"What was the number of this car you're speaking of?"

"I've no idea. It never occurred to me to notice it— any more than you would have noticed it in similar circumstances. Didn't you find the car in the drive?"

"No!" the inspector said a bit grimly.

"Then she must have got away in it. Taken her father with her, too, if he was her father—which I very much doubt. The other man she called Mason—for what it's worth."

The inspector was regarding him with growing scepticism.

"Why did you try to jump that plane just now?" he asked bluntly. "Wouldn't it be correct to say that you were trying to make your own escape?"

"It would be totally incorrect, inspector. I wanted to go on this flight."

"What—alone?"

"Anyhow, so long as I went!"

"But you couldn't have gone without your squadron."

"Who could have prevented my joining the squadron in the air, once I was clear of the ground? Who could have prevented me from taking my place in the formation?"

"But—er—" The C.O.'s voice trickled away into silence. That was a damned silly thing to say. "How in the world would that have helped you? You've admitted that you were expecting the police to come for you at any moment? Well, they'd have had you just the same when you came back."

"If he'd come back!" Inspector Scudamore said dryly.

"What d'you mean?"

The question came swift as a rapier thrust, and as violently. For a second the inspector could do nothing but stare. He was quite startled. Not once throughout the entire interview had the prisoner raised his voice beyond the level of ordinary conversation; indeed, whether he knew it or not, it was his matter-of-fact narration that had gone farther than anything else towards making even his fantastic story sound at any rate possible.

"What d'you mean?" he demanded again, his voice trembling with fury.

"What I say," the inspector drawled then. But although

his enunciation was slow, his brain was working at top speed. He had touched a raw spot there! That blind thrust of his had slipped under his adversary's guard and got home. The man had intended to fly off and land somewhere else!

"Where was the squadron going?" he jerked out a bit breathlessly.

"Northern France!" the adjutant said. "Occupied France, that is. We are escorting a bomber sweep."

The inspector's grin widened to triumphant proportions, but before he could say anything there was a tap at the door and an orderly came in. He handed the C.O. a card.

"Superintendent Venner. Criminal Investigation Department," it read. And in the left-hand corner: "New Scotland Yard, London, S.W.1."

"To see me?" the C.O. asked when he had read it.

"Yes, sir!"

The C.O. read it again, frowned, and pushed it across to Inspector Scudamore. "Is he with you?" he asked.

"Not so that you'd notice it!" gloomed the inspector after but the briefest glance. "The boot's on the other foot—unfortunately. I'm with him!"

"Then show the gentleman in!"

The orderly saluted and retired. One minute later the door opened again to admit that brightest of all Yard stars—Superintendent Venner! He sauntered in elegantly—grey suit, yellow gloves, malacca cane, pork-pie hat, and all the accessories complete. He bowed.

"Venner of the Yard!" he announced himself with terrifying simplicity. Then paused. His eye had alighted on Sergeant Allen standing there, had passed over him, shot back again, and now he was smiling in surprised recognition. "And they tell me there's no such thing as chance!" he said as he held out his hand. "I wondered where you'd disappeared to—and now you're a pilot, eh? Good for you, son! That's the stuff!" He passed on towards the C.O.'s table, but, becoming aware of a curious and extremely flat silence, he paused again. "Anything wrong?" he asked.

It was Inspector Scudamore who answered.

"Do I understand that you—that you're acquainted with Sergeant Allen?" he stammered.

"Sergeant Allen?" Venner echoed. "I don't know. I haven't seen him yet. Where is he?"

The inspector swallowed hard. "That's him!" he said. "You've just spoken to him. That's Sergeant Percy Allen!"

Venner turned slowly. To those watching him, his figure seemed to heighten by several inches, while his eyes— passing carefully over the prisoner from head to foot— seemed to be squeezed dry of all humanity. For perhaps two minutes he remained motionless, considering. Then he spoke.

"So that's the way of it, huh?" he said with great deliberation. He turned back to the C.O. "The last time I saw that young man was in the Old Bailey," he explained. "His name, at that time, was John Maynard. And his business at the Old Bailey was to say good-bye to his sweetheart—a girl named Isobel Ensor—who had just been sentenced ten years' imprisonment for selling aircraft secrets to the Germans!"

"A spy?" whispered the C.O.

"She got ten years for it!"

"And that man's masquerading here, under a false name—"

"And only just now tried to make good his escape in one of our latest Spitfires?" gasped the adjutant. "By heavens, he must be on the same game himself!"

Superintendent Venner smiled thinly.

"Rum thing is," he said, "the man lying dead in that place called the White House is also known to have been engaged in the espionage racket. In fact," he added as he peeled off his gloves, "that, gentlemen, is what brings Venner of the Yard to these parts!"

THE FOURTH CHAPTER

Delving Into Facts.

THERE CAN BE few houses in England receiving a greater variety of callers than the Baker Street home of that famous London criminologist, Sexton Blake. At one time or another men of almost every profession and trade under the sun have called there, and every nationality. Yet curiously enough, as the detective stood looking at this present slip of pasteboard Mrs. Bardell had handed him, he could not recall ever having had a K.C. client before.

"Gervase Crispin, K.C.," the card read. And Blake knew the name to be that of one of the best-known criminal lawyers of the day.

"I told 'im you wouldn't see 'im!" Mrs. Bardell said brightly, misconstruing his hesitation. "We don't eat 'em! I says, but you know—"

"Eat 'em?" Blake echoed.

"What he's sellin'—yes. Crispies. Little folded-up bit o'—"

Blake groaned aloud, though he had to laugh. Given the slightest chance to make a mistake, it was a safe bet that his landlady would make it.

"Crispin!" he said. "Not crispies. No, and he's nothing to do with the phenomenon of it raining for forty days, either—that was Saint Crispin. This is Gervase Crispin, the famous advocate. Show him into the consulting room, will you?"

The buxom dame retired chastened but in good order.

"Anyways, 'e lives in a pub!" she snorted as she went out. "It says so there on 'is card. 'Lincoln Inn,' it says, an' you can't get past that!"

Blake turned to his assistant.

"Crispin?" he asked when they were alone again. "Have we picked him up anywhere lately?"

"Not that I can remember," Tinker said. They were referring to their private index, a sort of cross-reference they maintained upon the more important events of the day. "He defended in that Mayo murder case, a month or so ago. I don't know if—"

Blake hunched his shoulders. There had been nothing of interest in that. He tapped out his pipe and laid it carefully on the mantelpiece.

"Let's see what he's got to say for himself," he suggested.

The detective rose as the K.C. entered. He was a tall man, of Blake's own height—but there the likeness ended, for while Blake was lean as a greyhound with a thin, almost ascetic-seeming face, Gervase Crispin was thick-set and corpulent, with baggy eyes, a big face, and a pronounced dewlap which began under his cleft chin and disappeared ignominiously into his "gates-ajar" collar.

"I've heard of you, of course," he said as they shook hands, "but I do not think that we have ever met. And frankly, Mr. Blake," he added, "you may take it as a testimony to your amazing reputation that I am here at all, even now." He had grasped the lapels of his coat with either hand, and was speaking precisely as though he were addressing a judge and jury. "My mission is no ordinary one, I would say. In fact, I find myself at some loss where and how to begin my story."

"The beginning is usually considered a convenient point, if I may suggest it!" Blake smiled dryly.

"Save that in this affair there is no beginning, my dear sir! That, in fact, is the trouble. I have come to you on behalf of a young client of mine. But if what he says is true, the cause of his trouble lies in something that happened six months ago, and for which a certain young woman is already serving a sentence of ten years' penal servitude."

"Her name?" Blake asked.

"Isobel Ensor."

"Ha—the spy case, you mean? The girl who was convicted of selling aircraft secrets to the Huns?"

"You have a remarkable memory, Mr. Blake."

"Part of my business, Mr. Crispin. You defended her, I believe?"

"That is so." The lawyer gave a twisted little smile. "You make things much easier for me," he confessed. "I did defend her, as you say, and I was in no way surprised by the verdict of the court. I want to make it quite clear to you that I agreed with that verdict. The girl was guilty

65

as hell, Mr. Blake. She hadn't a leg to stand on. In fact, when the brief was first offered me I refused it—for that very reason. But later I accepted it."

"Why?" Blake asked when he paused.

"Because of the belief of one man. Because the man to whom she was engaged to be married came to see me personally, and I could not refuse him. John Maynard believed in that girl with an intensity that—that—"

"Deceived even you?" Blake suggested when the lawyer appeared stuck for the word he wanted.

"That's the point!" The K.C. jumped to his feet and began a ponderous pacing of the room. "That's the very thing that has brought me here now!" he said. "At the time, the very intensity of his belief in the girl almost persuaded me of her innocence. Certainly it persuaded me into accepting her defence. But a couple of days ago I received an urgent appeal from the same man asking me to call upon him at Dillborough Aerodrome. I did call upon him—in the guard-room!"

"Guard-room?"

"He was under arrest, awaiting trial by court-martial upon a charge of attempting to steal a Spitfire fighter, and a second charge of fraudulent enlistment. He had enlisted in the R.A.F. under a false name. Instead of his real name—John Maynard—he taken the identity card and ration book of a close friend of his who had been killed in an air-raid, and using those as his own had voluntarily enlisted for flying duties in the R.A.F. under that man's name—Percy Allen. And it was as Sergeant-Pilot Percy Allen that I found him in his squadron's room—but that

66

isn't all. There is another and graver charge being preferred against him by the civil police—a charge to which, from all I can hear, he has already admitted himself guilty. The civil police are charging him with murder!"

"Murder of whom?" Blake asked after a moment's silence.

"A man by the name of Bernard Wise—or Weiss."

"Does he want you to defend him?"

"No. He hasn't got as far as that yet. What he wants me for, at the moment, is to clear him of the suspicion that he was stealing that Spitfire with the intention of flying it to Germany."

"I don't think I quite understand you there."

"The lawyer swung round from his pacings to face Blake squarely.

"Of course you don't!" he said. "That's the whole point at issue! Because I haven't got to that yet. That's the very reason that I'm here now. You see, right from the beginning of her trial, Isobel Ensor—that's Maynard's girl, you remember?—strongly maintained that a man named Walter Paine could completely clear her of the charge of trafficking with the Germans. Walter Paine had been a clerk in the same aircraft works, but had joined up in his age group and was actually in France at the time of the Dunkirk retreat. Now that man, she said, could afford her an unbreakable alibi for the night in question—but unfortunately, when we started to trace this Walter Paine, we found that he had never come back from France."

"You mean he'd been killed?"

"I don't know. Officially he is still 'missing, believed

killed'—and I have little doubt but that he is indeed dead. However, after the trial and conviction, Maynard told me that he was going to find Walter Paine—dead or alive, sort of thing—and bring him back to England. He was the only man who could clear Isobel Ensor, and Maynard was going to find him at all and any costs. I remember I told him that he couldn't do it. I told him that he would never be able to leave England, and certainly never be able to move about in Occupied France. He said that he could. And he said that he would. And his plan—so he says, now—was to join the R.A.F., get his 'wings' as a fighter pilot, fly over there to the village where Walter Paine was last seen lying by the side of the road with both legs blown off, land, destroy his machine, and then set about the task of tracing him. And that, he tells me, was why—when his C.O. sent for him at the request of the police over this murder business—he suddenly conceived the idea of jumping into his machine and flying over to France while he still had the chance!"

"Whereas the authorities see in it only a desperate effort to escape the consequences of his crime?" Blake asked.

"That is the police view, certainly," the lawyer agreed. "But now that they've discovered his connection with Isobel Ensor—a woman already convicted of selling aircraft secrets to the enemy—and discovered that in order to hide that connection he joined the R.A.F. under a false name, the Service authorities are strongly of the opinion that he and Isobel Ensor were working together, and that when she was caught, he decided to carry on alone. They contend that he joined the R.AF. and got his 'wings' for one purpose only—to keep the enemy informed of the latest developments in aircraft construction and, maybe, as and when the opportunity offered, to fly over an occasional machine for their inspection."

"I see." Blake was silent for a moment. "What were the circumstances of the actual murder?" he asked presently.

"I'll tell you." The K.C. sat down and leaned his elbows on Blake's desk. "And I think you'll agree with me that it is a most extraordinary story," he smiled. Thereupon he related everything that had happened that night between Percy Allen—or John Maynard, to give him his correct name—and the girl calling herself Wendy Grantham, and the men at the White House. "That such a girl was on the Ladcaster road that night is borne out by the evidence of other R.A.F. men who saw her there," he wound up. "But, of course, as the police maintain, that is no criterion that she played the part Maynard says she played—or even that she played any part at all. Maynard may merely have seen her on the road, as the other fellows did, and subsequently woven this little romance around her in order to explain his presence at the White House."

"He has no proof of his story, I gather?"

"Not a rag! Not a thing!"

"Any explanation of why these people should lie up for him?"

"Yes." The lawyer spoke slowly, rubbing his chin the while. "Yes," he said again. Rather abruptly he rose to his feet and resumed his pacing of the room. "And that's what brings me to see you, Mr. Blake," he admitted. "Maynard has an explanation. It's this: he says that those people were out to prevent him going to France! He says that by some means or other they must have got wind of his identity, learned how he had taken his 'wings,' followed him to his Operational Squadron, and pounced on him just when he was on the point of going.

"I understand that the police have long suspected the dead man—Bernard Weiss—of being concerned in the espionage ramp; and while that merely strengthens their conviction that Maynard was in with the same gang, on the other hand, knowing what I do know of Maynard's avowed intentions, it might be—might be, I say!—some slight corroboration of his theory that Weiss and the rest were out to stop him from trying to contact Walter Paine."

"Inferring that Walter Paine may still be alive?"

"Yes, it implies that—certainly."

"And something else, too!" Blake said, eyeing the other keenly.

"That's the point!" The great advocate spread his hands. "That's the whole thing in a nutshell," he agreed. "Now you appreciate my difficulty, Mr. Blake. If we accept that theory—with its inference that Walter Paine is still alive and that it is against somebody's interest for Maynard to have speech with him—where does Isobel Ensor stand?"

"Exactly."

"Mind you," the lawyer went on, "I never believed in Walter Paine myself—and the court, of course, pooh-poohed the suggestion from the start. After all, it's not much use trying to set up an alibi when the alibi himself is dead—or, at any rate, cannot be produced. But Isobel Ensor stuck to her story right through the piece, and unless young Maynard was in the game with her and was play-acting from first to last, then he, too, was convinced of Paine's ability to secure Miss Ensor's release.

"That is proved by his joining the R.A.F. and winning his 'wings' in record time. He was determined to make good his escape from this country!"

"Save that if he were himself a spy, it is scarcely likely that he would be attacked by other spies?"

"That's true—and a point in his favour. Unless, of course, they met in that empty house by arrangement, and fell out among themselves—perhaps over the girl."

"Do you believe his story?" Blake asked bluntly.

"I don't know. And up to a point I'm really not concerned. But the thing I can't entirely dismiss from my mind is the fact that if his story is true, then Isobel Ensor would appear to have been wrongfully convicted. That is the possibility that's kept me awake all night; that's been on my mind ever since I returned from Dillborough, yesterday. Because if someone is prepared to commit murder rather than run the risk of having Walter Paine produced in court, it can only mean that Paine holds information which—as my client maintained all through her trial—would not only secure her release but pin the blame upon the real culprit, the man who framed her.

"And who in that event is still at large, and still at his nefarious work in the factory," Blake said thoughtfully. "The man who—assuming Maynard's story to be true— would be the instigator of the attack on him at the White House. What exactly was the case against Miss Ensor, Mr. Crispin?"

The lawyer did not immediately reply. He appeared to be pondering the matter. For several minutes he continued pacing back and forth across the floor. Finally he came to a decision.

"Mr. Blake," he said. "I'd like you to see young Maynard. I'd like you to hear his story from his own lips, and at the same time to form your own estimate of his credibility. If you believe this fantastic story of his to be true, then manifestly I must reopen the case of Rex. v. Isobel Ensor with the Home Secretary—not only for her own sake, but for the sake of the country. Because if she isn't guilty of selling those plans to Germany, somebody else is. And in the interests of the country's security that person must be found and scotched before he has time to sell still more information. Will you do that for me?"

Blake thought for a moment.

"Yes," he said then. "I can go down to Dillborough this afternoon."

"I'm greatly obliged to you. You are taking a considerable load off my mind. If you believe his story, we will then review Isobel Ensor's case together, and decide what to do for the best. If, on the other hand, of your great experience you decide that John Maynard is just another renegade in the pay of Germany—no damage will have been done, and I, at least, shall be able to sleep peacefully again in my bed."

He held out his hand.

"If you would give me a ring as soon as you get back—"

"As soon as I get back, I will," he promised.

THE FIFTH CHAPTER

A Visit to Prison.

IF ISOBEL ENSOR experienced even the simple emotion of surprise upon hearing that she was wanted in the governor's office, the following afternoon, there was no sign of it on her face. She followed the wardress mechanically, her eyes fixed straight before her, her hands hanging listlessly at her sides—her whole bearing one of complete and utter resignation. For nearly seven months now she had lived within those grey walls, not a woman but a number. Even her once-vivid personality had become as grey as her clothes, as unobtrusive.

She did not even see her visitors until the governor himself called her attention to them.

"How do you do?" she said then, her voice a thin thread in the silence.

"You remember me, Miss Ensor?" Gervase Crispin asked anxiously.

"Yes."

"This is Mr. Sexton Blake, the famous detective, who is interesting himself in your case."

"How do you do?" she said in the same grey, expressionless voice.

Blake held out his hand. If he had been surprised by her appearance, he was still more surprised by the hopelessness and indifference of her manner. Save only in the matter of temperature, the hand she gave him might have been that of a dead woman. It was impossible to recognise in this grey-voiced, grey-garbed shadow, the vital personality John Maynard had described to him yesterday in the guard-room of Dillborough Aerodrome.

"I've come to talk to you upon a very important matter, Miss Ensor," he said. "I saw John Maynard yesterday."

"Oh, yes?"

"He's in the Air Force."

"Yes?"

"In trouble."

Automatically her lips formed that monotonous "Yes?" but no sound came. Blake pulled a fast one.

"He has been arrested on a charge of murder!" he said.

She caught her breath. She stood stock-still while the little colour that had been in her cheeks drained slowly downwards. She closed her eyes. Even her lips drained to that same ghastly grey.

"Sit down!" Blake's voice reached her from a very long way away.

She obeyed him mechanically. Gervase Crispin was watching her with anxious eyes, but when he whispered a suggestion that he should ring for assistance Blake shook his head. There was nothing wrong physically with the girl. Her trouble was mental. For seven months she had been living and moving in a state of mental stupor, a state of deliberate self-hypnosis—a prolongation of the condition of mind in which she had gone through her trial.

Blake knew the signs intimately. He had seen the same thing so often before in people of strong individuality and vivid imagination, to whom prison would have meant death had they not deliberately reduced themselves to the state of unthinking automatons. Such people dare not think. They would go mad if they did—or think they would go mad, which is the same thing.

Now, with only they two and Gervase Crispin in the well-appointed office—for the governor and the wardress had left them alone, upon instructions from the Home Office that the lawyer and Sexton Blake were to be allowed a private interview with the prisoner—Blake waited for the girl to recover herself. Already, he could see, her intelligence was beginning to reassert itself. It was like watching a rusty locomotive being forced into action by a powerful head of steam. Either the cylinders would burst or the machine would start to move. Blake knew that Isobel Ensor would either leap up and scream or rise to her feet and demand what he meant. What was he trying to tell her?

She reacted as he had hoped—in the latter fashion. After perhaps five minutes of breathless silence she sprang to her feet and faced him, frightened-eyed.

"What do you mean?" she whispered. "What has happened to him? Why have you come here?"

"Because I think you might be able to help him, Miss Ensor. Because I think that his trouble is rooted in yours."

"I don't understand."

"Isobel Ensor," began the K.C. pontifically—but stopped when she closed her eyes and for the first time—smiled. It was a funny, twisted, yet strangely ecstatic little smile. A secret smile, the meaning of which entirely evaded the practical man of law, but not Sexton Blake.

"Sounds good, that—eh?" he asked softly.

"Wonderful!" she said under her breath. "Isobel Ensor," she repeated. "Isobel!" She smiled again. "Funny, but I never cared much about the name 'Isobel'—until now." There was no need for her to touch the number she wore for Blake to know what she meant.

"Maybe be hearing more of it sooner than you think," he said with deliberate intent.

She looked at him, startled. It was plain that, though she was awakening rapidly, her apprehension was still a bit hazy. Or perhaps she was afraid to reach out for the meaning of what he was saying. She had put hope so far from her, that now even the distant thought of it scared her. She was like a starving man who refuses even to look at the food he knows he cannot get.

"You were saying?" she asked vaguely. "About John?"

Blake motioned the lawyer to tell her what Maynard had promised to do with regard to finding the missing soldier, Walter Paine. And although the K.C. spoke in his usual sonorous periods and rounded phrases—using twelve words where one would have been ample, for he loved the sound of his own voice—Blake thought that the girl understood.

"And now," he said when the other had finished, "that brings us to the affairs of to-day." Very briefly he related how John Maynard had enlisted in the R.A.F. under a false name—being afraid to apply for flying duties in his own name, owing to its close connection with her own—a convicted spy—and after six months' work had qualified for his "wings" and been posted to an Operational Fighter Squadron stationed at Dillborough Aerodrome.

"Yes, but I thought you said—"

"I'm coming to that now," he told her when she would have interrupted. "And I want you to listen very carefully, Miss Ensor. Won't you sit down?"

"I would prefer to stand!"

"Very well." Blake thereupon gave her a full and complete account of everything that, according to his own story, had happened to John Maynard upon the night in question—beginning with his meeting with Wendy Grantham and continuing right up to the moment when he was pulled out of his Spitfire. "The service case against him is that he was most probably engaged in subversive activities and, finding himself cornered, made a desperate effort to escape in that Spitfire to Occupied France," he summed up for her. "The police case is somewhat similar, save that they—perhaps understandably—maintain that he was trying to escape abroad from the consequences of his crime at the White House."

"But didn't he tell them that he was really going to find Walter Paine?" she asked when at last he had finished.

"He daren't!" Blake told her with a grim smile. "He has enough on his plate now without admitting that he joined the R.A.F. for no other reason than to get a plane in which he could fly to France and disappear! That—on top of the other fantastic story—even he felt would be just a bit too much!"

"But if he was doing it for me—"

"That is our whole point!" Blake nodded. "And the one point that brings Mr. Crispin and myself here to-day. I will say to you that I believe John Maynard. I have seen him and spoken with him, and I have also visited the house in question and I am convinced that no matter how far-fetched his story may sound, it is substantially true.

"I paid a visit to the spot where he says the M.G. was standing disabled, and along a branch of a tree immediately above that spot I certainly found marks such as might have been made by someone climbing into concealment there. I may add that those marks have been photographed and checked. They have also been pointed out to the police, and will be admitted as evidence at the appropriate moment—but it is not because of that alone that we are here now. It is the inference to be drawn from those marks that counts!"

"I don't understand you?"

"Yet it's very simple, Miss Ensor. If someone tried to kill Maynard rather than allow him to look for Walter Paine, then that 'someone' must obviously have a very vital reason for not wishing Paine to be found!"

"You mean—" She caught her breath. "You mean—you believe that there—is someone else? That it—it wasn't I who—sold those plans?"

Blake took a sharp turn across the room. It was a

difficult question.

"I can't answer that!" he said at last. "But this I can say: when we laid the facts before the Home Secretary, he at once gave us permission to interview you here."

"Yes; but—why?"

"Because if my theory is correct, Miss Ensor— the production of Walter Paine in Court would be extremely detrimental to that 'someone's' safety. At present, you are carrying the blame, and the case is closed. But if events should prove you to be innocent, the case will be thrown back into the melting-pot and the hunt will be on again. Do I make myself clear?"

She nodded her head. For a long minute she was silent, but when next she spoke it was impossible to hide—either in her voice or eyes—the new hope that was flooding her being.

"Ask me anything you like, and I will answer you!" she cried tensely. "But first, whether you believe me or not, let me say again what I haven't said since I came to this place—I am absolutely innocent!"

"Sit down, Miss Ensor!" was all Blake replied.

He asked her questions and she answered them frankly, without the least hesitation. She had been born at Streatham; lived there all her life. Her father was a bank manager until he had died, when Isobel was fifteen, and it was then that she had paid her first visit to Germany. Her mother's sister had married a German engineer. She had met him while he was studying at London University, and later had married him and gone to Germany with him, to Leipzig.

When Isobel's father had died, her mother had sent her to Aunt May for a time, for a holiday. She had stayed there for six months, and thereafter returned every year for periods varying between one and four months. She was very fond of Aunt May. Fond, too, of Uncle von Frielhausen. She liked them both, their friends, the people who came to the house. By now, of course, she spoke fluent German and was thoroughly at home there. When she was eighteen, there had even been a German boy—

It is difficult to live with people you like, and not see their good points. People who live very much as you live yourself, who play the same games, and laugh on the same note. She had never met the Prussian caste—the 'jackboot-brigade' as Uncle von Frielhausen laughingly called them. And perhaps because Aunt May was an Englishwoman, politics were seldom or never mentioned in the Von Frielhausen household. In any event, Uncle von Frielhausen wasn't interested in anything but his engineering works.

"What kind of engineering was he engaged upon?" Blake asked her.

"Aero engines," she told him steadily.

"Go on!"

She explained how the deterioration of friendship between the two countries had distressed her considerably. Over there, her friends would sometimes say 'Why is it that your countrymen won't like us? You like us, Isobel. Is it because you know us, and they don't?' She had done her little best to promote greater friendship between the countries. She was a member of the League of Nations Union; had spoken sometimes at the meetings of the Anglo-German Friendship League. She could not understand—being herself a post-war product—why English politicians insisted upon presenting German men and women as monsters, when all the Germans she knew were as simple and as homely as herself. It was absurd to think of Uncle von Frielhausen shouting frenzied "Heils" everywhere, and "Gott strafe England!" Why, nothing pleased him better, in the long winter nights, than to sit round the fire telling his children of the days in England when he had met their mother. The days when he had been carefree—a student![5] And his friends would often drop in to listen, and to ask questions. Everybody liked to hear of "Frau von Frielhausen's England."

"When did you first go to work at the Southern Aircraft Construction Company, Miss Ensor?"

"November, 1938," she told him.

"Did you answer an advertisement, or something?"

"No, I wrote and asked them if they had a vacancy."

"Why that firm, in particular?"

"I had a friend there."

"English?"

"No, she was German. Her people had been in England for a good many years; she was a member of the same Friendship League. That's how I met her."

"You see what the Defence had to contend with?" Gervase Crispin put in with a shrug. "You can imagine what capital the Prosecution made of all this detail?"

"Go on, Miss Ensor!" Blake nodded.

By now, she explained, her mother had died; and when she

was given a job as shorthand-typist in the Works Manager's office at the Southern Aircraft Company, she had gone to share a flat with her friend, Anne.

"That's the German girl you mentioned just now?"

"Yes. She called herself 'Anne Miller,' but her real name was 'Anna Muller.' As I said, she had lived in this country for many years, and her parents had long since taken to calling themselves 'Miller.' It was easier, you understand?"

"You knew that at the time?"

"Yes. She told me that in the beginning. I thought nothing of it. She was so entirely English in her outlook— and her people the same—that it was impossible to think of her being anything other than English. Besides, why shouldn't a German girl be as much at home in England as an English girl—myself, for example—had been at home in Germany? That was one of the planks in our Anglo-German Friendship League platform. And in any event, in the part of London where her people had lived for so long, everybody called them 'Miller'! The tradespeople and so on had changed the name for themselves, as they so frequently do."

"And then—"

Then the war clouds began to gather, she said. And with the heightening of the Polish crisis, the old spy-fever had raised its head in England. Authorities at the Southern Aircraft Company had begun to probe into the antecedents of the staff, and Anne Miller had seen the writing on the wall as plainly as the rest. "They'll sack me, Isobel!" she cried. "They'll turn me out!" She had been in despair. She did not want to go back to Germany; all her friends were in London. She was terrified lest they should find out at the works that her real name was Muller.

"You didn't tell them?" Blake asked.

"Of course not. A war between nations cannot break individual ties of friendship—or, at least, I thought not, then."

"But you've changed your mind, since?"

"Not wholly, no! Most have gone, of course—but I am certain that Anna is as much my friend now as she was then. Just as I feel the same about her."

"You actually lent her money to escape to Germany, I think?"

"Not to 'escape.' True, she would have been interned if she had stayed here, but she was not 'escaping.' She was merely going home. I had the money to spare; she hadn't. Also, I had a cousin in Switzerland to whom I could send her. She was my friend. I would have done anything in the world to save her from the miseries of internment. It was a pity ever to think of interning such people. Spies—yes! But not harmless girls such as my friend, Anna. Anna saw England through me; just as I saw Germany through Aunt Mary and Uncle von Frielhausen. War is made between strangers; never between friends."

"In any event you financed her departure, and then took over her job?"

"Yes, I was given her job by Mr. Ogilvie. He was furious when he learned that Anna was German; I think he was a bit frightened, too. She had been in charge of the Blue Print Department, and, of course, he thought the worst. He knew that I had sometimes helped her with the Department, and straightway he insisted upon going right through the files from A to Z and examining every single print with meticulous care. It took us a week, and I don't think he breathed freely until it was finished. Then he started on me."

Blake asked her what she meant, and she told him that Mr. Ogilvie had sent for her to his private office and told her that she must bring him her birth certificate, and at least two personal references from properly qualified people who had known her for five years or more. He did not intend to be caught napping again. She had given him the documents required, and he had put them before the general manager—and only then, when they had satisfied themselves of her pure British descent and unassailable integrity had Mr. Ogilvie put her in charge of the Blue Prints. That was immediately after the outbreak of war, and she had carried on in charge of the department right up to the moment of her arrest by the police.

"Tell me exactly what happened?"

She said that Mr. Ogilvie—the Works Manager—had sent for her to his office, one morning. He had kept here there for a very long time, talking about nothing in particular. Then two other men had entered the office, one of whom was carrying her handbag in his hand.

"Are you Isobel Ensor?" he asked.

She had told him yes.

"Is this your bag?"

Again she had told him yes.

"I'm looking for a watch that has been reported stolen. And I've found it in this bag. Have you any explanation to offer?"

She had been flabbergasted; utterly and completely bewildered. Was this why Mr. Ogilvie had kept her talking in there—so that these detectives might search her bag? She had drawn herself upright. She had been furious.

"I don't know what you're talking about!" she had flashed back at them. "The only watch in that bag is my own. It was given to me by a friend of mine, for a keepsake."

They had asked her friend's name, and she had told them. It was Anne Miller. She had no cause to be ashamed of her friend, just because she happened to be a German! Mr. Ogilvie, however, had gone white to the lips. "You—a friend of hers?" he stormed. "You never told me this before?"

There was no reason why she should have told him. What was it to do with Mr. Ogilvie how she spent her spare time or with whom she was friendly?

"But the girl was a German! An enemy!"

"German—yes. But not an enemy, Mr. Ogilvie. Anne Miller, as you knew her, was as loyal as I myself."

Possibly she had spoken more warmly than she knew, for one of the detectives gave a nasty laugh.

"Once a German, always a German!" he said shortly. Then, taking her arm, he had invited her along to the station to make a statement.

It was there, for the first time, that she learned something of the real seriousness of the situation. At first they had not told her anything; they had let her talk. But now she understood that certain plans of the new fighter which

Southern Aircraft had just put into production were already in German hands—and that she was suspected of having a part in the treachery! It was she who was in charge of the Master Plan—the main plan from which the details were taken for each individual operation in the factory. Each of those individual operations had its own blue print, but not even a dozen or two of those put together would give away the secret of the entire production. That could only be gained through sight of the Master Plan of which she herself was the sole custodian. It was one of the methods by which Southern Aircraft guarded their products while they were on the "Secret List" of the Air Ministry.

At first she had laughed at the ridiculous charge, but quite soon that laughter had changed to gravity—and then to fear. Within an hour of entering the police station she was terrified, for a net was being woven about her that, try as she might she could not break.

That was no casual call the police had made at the office! They had known all about her even before they entered the place—all about Aunt May and Uncle von Frielhausen, her visits to Germany, her friendship with Anna Muller, the fact that she had supplied Anna with money to escape the country—there was nothing with which they were not completely familiar, even down to her membership of the Anglo-German Friendship League, and her desire to see the two countries drawn closer together.

"But it's no crime to have German relations!" she had told them boldly. "To have German friends."

"Are you in receipt of an allowance from Germany?"

"Good heavens, no!"

"Your Uncle von Frielhausen doesn't send you money?"

"Of course not! He couldn't if he wanted to, poor man. The German Government do not allow private citizens to send money out of the country—even you should know that!"

"Carl von Frielhausen is a manufacturer of aero engines, is he not?"

"Yes."

"In Leipzig?"

"That is so."

"Are you in communication with him at all?"

"I can communicate with him—yes. Through a friend in Switzerland."

"When did you last hear from him?"

"I had word from Aunt May about two months ago."

"Nothing since?"

"No."

"Is that his writing?" From a drawer beside him the inspector questioning her produced an envelope which he slid across the table towards her. It bore a German stamp, and was addressed to Miss Isobel Ensor, care of an address in Berne, Switzerland. "Is that his writing?" he asked again.

She was staring at it in silence. Something—some inner prescience—warned her to have a care. The writing was Von Frielhausen's all right, but how had the police come into possession of it? What was it doing there? And since the envelope was open, what had been inside?

"Is that Carl von Frielhausen's handwriting?" the inspector snapped fiercely when she still hesitated.

"Yes. At least, it would appear so."

"Then perhaps you can explain the meaning of the letter it contained? I may add that it was intercepted by the Censor upon our instructions." From the same drawer he took out a typed sheet of paper. "That is a copy," he said as he handed it over.

She looked at it—at first with curiosity, then with a dreadful sinking at her heart. It contained these lines only.

"Dear Isobel,— Your photograph safely to hand. It does you great credit. £5,000 has to-day been placed to your credit at the Swiss Bank in Berne. I hope you will be very happy. Love from us both.
"CARL VON FRIELHAUSEN."

"Where did you have that photograph of yourself taken, Miss Ensor?" she heard the inspector ask softly.

She gave him the paper back. The whole thing was a trick. It was absurd. She had never had a photograph taken. As for Uncle von Frielhausen sending her five thousand pounds—it was too utterly absurd for words. For one thing, as she had already explained, he could not send her money from Germany. The Government had long since stopped all money from leaving the country.

"I expect he got special permission for this." The inspector smiled crookedly when she repeated that to him. "I think the Fuehrer would consider it money well spent. In any event, the money is there—for we have inquired about it! So it would seem that you are five thousand pounds richer than you thought, Miss Ensor!"

She had not known what to say. She was overwhelmed—and very frightened. She had the feeling a mouse must have when it realises it has stepped into a trap but is afraid to try to get out again lest it steps unwillingly on the trigger and finishes everything.

"You cannot tell me where you had that photograph taken?" he asked again.

"There was no photograph, I tell you! I don't understand this at all. It is a trick of some kind."

"I think there was a photograph, Miss Ensor."

"There was not a photograph! You can ask every photographer in England, if you like! I've never had a photograph taken for years—not even an amateur one."

"But this is one that you took yourself."

"What do you mean?"

He put Anna Muller's watch on the table, and she was aware of his light blue eyes boring into hers as she stared at it.

"You must not think that we are stupider than you, Miss Ensor," he purred. He touched a spring somewhere, and the back flew open. He touched another, and an inside case fell open. "You see?" he smiled, as she caught her breath. "A camera, huh? A very fine piece of work, a credit to its maker—to its German maker! The tiny lens is secreted in the hollow shaft of the pin carrying the hands. The postage-stamp size film is secreted at the back. You have had this watch for quite a long time, ever since Anna Muller thought it wiser to clear out of the country—ever since she made you her deputy and left you in charge of the plans at Southern Aircraft Construction Company. If I may venture an opinion, Miss Ensor, you appear to have proved yourself an exceedingly apt pupil!"

THE SIXTH CHAPTER

A Surprising Story.

WHILE ISOBEL ENSOR drank the water the lawyer had fetched for her, Sexton Blake stood staring thoughtfully through the window into the prison garden.

His task was not going to be easy. On the evidence offered at her trial—as the K.C. himself had already agreed—the girl was "guilty as hell." So far as defence was concerned she had never had a leg to stand on. From the hard facts of the case, the sentence meted out to her had been well and truly merited. And yet, if one was to believe John Maynard's story, there was more than a chance that she might yet be proved innocent!

While he waited for her to recover herself he ran over the salient features in his mind. The police case against her was clean-cut and exact, and had rested upon five main points:

1. Save for the heads of the firm, she was the only

person having access to the master plan.

2. The plan had been photographed on to postage-stamp size film, and in that shape smuggled into Germany. Isobel Ensor was actually found in possession of a secret camera—a "camera-watch"—capable of taking exactly such photographs.

3. The film was known to have been smuggled out of England and into Germany by a man known to the Special Branch as Larry Rue. Isobel Ensor was acquainted with Larry Rue, and upon the night of his disappearance from the country had actually dined with him at a questionable Soho dive known as the White Cat.

4. The sum of £5,000 had been paid into Isobel Ensor's account at the Swiss Bank in Berne for—"photograph safely to hand."

5. She was known to have relatives in Germany, and to have been strongly pro-German in her political outlook.

Such were the five basic points of the Prosecution's case, and against them the Defence had been able to produce nothing but a flat denial of the latter half of Point 3.

That was where Walter Paine and his alibi came in.

Of the remaining points, all were admitted. It was true, the Defence admitted, that Isobel Ensor certainly had had access to the master plan—but she had never photographed it.

It was true that the camera-watch had been found by the police in her handbag, but it had been given to her as a keepsake by Anna Muller, and she herself had had no idea even that it was a camera.

It was true that she had known Larry Rue, but only as a casual acquaintance. She had met him once or twice at the Anglo-German Friendship League meetings, and upon one or two occasions it was true that she had taken coffee with him and others at the White Cat—that being the league's more or less official club. But—and this was the Defence's one flat denial—Isobel Ensor had not dined with Larry Rue on the night in question, nor had she, upon that night, been anywhere near the White Cat.

For the rest—yes, it was admitted that she had friends and relatives in Germany, and—according to that letter—£5,000 certainly had been deposited to her credit in the Swiss Bank at Berne. But she knew nothing about it. That was as big a mystery to her as to the police—in fact, a bigger mystery—and taken in conjunction with the other items, could only point to a deliberate attempt on the part of the real culprits to frame her.

That was the submission put forward by the Defence. And it was backed by the statement that upon the night in question, contrary to dining with Larry Rue at the White Cat, Isobel Ensor had attended the Regal Cinema with a private soldier named Walter Paine. But it had to be revealed that Walter Paine, although on leave in England at the time, was now reported "missing, believed killed," and could not therefore, give evidence. Nor, unfortunately, had it been possible to find anyone at the cinema who could give sworn evidence on Miss Ensor's behalf.

On the facts of the case, and on the questions and answers as revealed in the official shorthand notes of the trial, no jury could have returned any verdict other than the one that had been returned—Guilty! No other verdict was possible. Indeed, as Gervase Crispin had already confessed, he had never expected any other.

And yet, if this story of John Maynard's were true, that verdict had been a wrong verdict—and Isobel Ensor was the victim of a miscarriage of justice as amazing as any in the history of British law.

That, then, was the problem confronting Sexton Blake as he waited for the girl to recover herself. Was that alibi true or false? Had she really gone to the Regal Cinema with Walter Paine that night, or was it just an attempt to red-herring the prosecution? Gervase Crispin thought it false—or at least he had thought it false at the time. Now he was not so sure. And it was this new-found doubt which had caused him to enlist the interest of Sexton Blake in the matter.

Suddenly, as though anxious not to strain their patience too severely, Isobel Ensor stood up.

"Thank you," she smiled wanly. "I can go on now, Mr. Blake."

"Good!" With a sigh of relief the detective turned back into the room and continued his examination. "The crucial factor of the whole thing," he said, "is that Larry Rue and the man John Maynard is accused of killing, are known to have been acquainted. Did you ever know a Bernard Wise—or Weiss, Miss Ensor?"

The girl thought for a moment. She shook her head.

"Not, that I can remember," she said.

Blake extracted a photograph from his pocket-book

and handed it over to her.

"Or that man?" he asked. "Have you ever met him, anywhere?"

"No," she said after a careful inspection. "I can't say that I have."

"He is Bernard Wise—or Weiss!"

"You mean?" She started violently.

"The man John Maynard is accused of shooting," Blake nodded. "The friend of Larry Rue. They were both in the same gang, it seems. Both of them were suspected of subversive activities although there was no real evidence upon which either could have been arrested and convicted. There are, of course, others. Some were members of the Anglo-German Friendship League while others are just small-time toughs hanging about the West End. The White Cat appears to have been their meeting-place; which is why the police have allowed it to remain open all this time. It is better to have such people where you can find them than to close their headquarters and have them disappear into the blue."

"You think that I made friends of such people?"

"I don't know. But I do think that your enthusiasms led you into quarters where you would otherwise never have gone—but that is neither here nor there. Enthusiasms frequently do lead perfectly respectable people into queer quarters. Elizabeth Fry, for example. The point is that whatever may have been your own intentions in joining the Anglo-German Friendship League, you cannot altogether disguise from yourself the fact that other people were less altruistic."

"Yet many of them had great names, Mr. Blake. Honoured names."

"I know—and that's the tragedy of it. People who ought to have known better. However, what's done is done, and it's no use crying over spilt milk. What we have to do now is to look to the future. It took you some little time to put forward the defence that you had been out with Walter Paine upon that particular night, I understand?"

"Yes, it did," she agreed. "But the whole thing had happened three months ago, you must remember, and that's a long time to bear in mind the happenings of one particular night. Especially when the happenings were of no significance."

"What eventually recalled the matter to your memory?"

"The fur collar I wore on my coat that night. I suddenly remembered that I had collected it from the cleaner's on my way home from the office—and that gave me the date and the day."

"Yes, that is perfectly correct," Mr. Crispin nodded in confirmation. "We checked up on that and proved from the dry-cleaner's books that the fur had indeed been collected upon that particular evening. But of course"— he shrugged his shoulders—"that didn't get us anywhere. It didn't, and couldn't, prove anything—one way or the other."

Blake asked what kind of a fur it was and she told him a big white fox fur.

"Actually, it had belonged to my mother," she said. "But I had a notion to try it in the new fashion."

"What fashion was that?"

"Oh, sort of standing up all round your head, like an Elizabethan ruff—only more so. But it didn't suit me. As a matter of fact, I dismantled it that same night when I got back from the pictures. I didn't like it at all."

"Why not?"

"It wasn't my type. It wouldn't have been so terribly noticeable had it been black, or even brown. But fierce snow white—"

"Noticeable?" Blake snapped.

"Well, I thought it was. I can't wear very noticeable trimmings, I'm not the type. It struck me as being loud, and vulgar, and cheap. Definitely not my style."

"I see." Blake was watching her thoughtfully. She was above the average in height, and he could quite imagine that in normal times, and in her own clothes, she would be as vivid a personality as young Maynard had described. While with a massive white fox fur framing her face—

He asked her how she had come to meet Walter Paine, and she told him. Before the war, Paine had been in the accountant's office which was next door to her own, and naturally they had met and talked. Then, later on, when he had gone to France after his training, she had sent him cigarettes and chocolates and so on. And sometimes she had written him letters.

"Then he came home on leave?"

"Yes," she said. "He walked into the office one afternoon—he was on ten days' leave, he said—gave us a terrific surprise. I think he had been home two or three days then, but he'd devoted himself to his mother and had not been out at all. He asked me what shows were

97

on, and what pictures were worth seeing, and I told him that I was going to see 'Honolulu Bound' that very night, at the Regal. He asked if he might go with me, and I said of course. We arranged to meet outside at half-past seven—"

"Outside the office?"

"No—outside the Regal. And it was on my way home that I thought of the white fox. 'I'll get it,' I thought, 'and wear it'!"

"How did you know that it would be ready?"

"Well, they'd had it for three weeks!"

She had meant to fetch it the week previous, she explained, but the shop was a bit out of her way and she had not bothered. In any event, it would not have mattered even if it had not been ready—it was of no importance. It was merely an idea that struck her with the notion of brightening things up a bit for a soldier on leave. As it happened, however, the fur was ready, and she had taken it home. In an hour she had transformed it into the new-type collar, and dead on time had met Walter Paine outside the Regal. They went into the three- and- sixpenny seats—"Let's dash it!" he had said—and had left at the end of the show, approximately at half-past ten.

"So that you were inside the Regal from roughly half-past seven until half-past ten?"

"Yes," she said.

"And then?"

"We came out, walked through the black-out to the stop, and caught the next bus to Edgware."

"What time was that?"

"As near as I can remember, about half-past eleven."

"And then?"

"Mr. Paine walked with me as far as the door of my flat, and said good-night."

"And the time then was?"

"Shortly before midnight, I imagine. I did not notice the time because I had no call to, but it takes about twenty minutes to walk from the terminus to where I live. Or, rather, where I used to live—then."

"Did nobody see you, or hear you enter?"

"Apparently not."

"What about Walter Paine? Where was he living?"

"With his widowed mother, some half-mile or so away."

"Wasn't she at home when he got in?"

"Yes, she was," the lawyer cut in dryly. "But she was in bed. I thought of that myself, and went to see her, but she told me that she was always in bed by ten o'clock and had no idea what time her son had got home that night nor when he had gone upstairs. I hoped, perhaps, that he might have mentioned something to her about going to the pictures with Miss Ensor, but he hadn't. Or if he had she'd forgotten it! At any rate, she would not give evidence for us."

"Could the bus conductor not recall seeing them?"

"No. Not a thing. The black-out defeated him, of course, and to make matters worse, it was a particularly dark night, anyhow."

Blake nodded, a bit ruefully. Everything appeared bunched together to defeat them. According to the evidence, Isobel Ensor had been with Larry Rue in the White Cat somewhere between nine and ten of that same night, and since she was quite well known there, and had been noticed by several people, it seemed impossible to believe that a mistake had been made. Yet according to her own story, it was impossible that she could have been in the place at all, either then or at any other time that night!

"Why did you carry that watch around in your handbag?" he asked her suddenly.

"I had no other means of carrying it, and I did not much care for the idea of leaving it in an empty flat all day; it was too valuable. It was a man's watch, you understand, a gold one. Anne told me that it had belonged to her father, but that she would like me to have it for a keepsake. It was all that she had to give."

"But did you never open it?"

"There was no reason why I should. It kept most excellent time, and, in any event, I know nothing about watches. Had it gone wrong I should have taken it to a watchmaker."

"It would have saved you much trouble if it had gone wrong!" Blake muttered under his breath. And aloud: "Why do you imagine Anna Muller gave you that watch?"

"I don't think she knew what it really was. I suppose her father had never told her."

"Your faith in human nature is greater than mine, I'm afraid, Miss Ensor. You are telling me the truth about Walter Paine?"

"Utterly!"

"And you did not meet Larry Rue in the White Cat that night?"

"I swear it, Mr. Blake!"

"Did you ever, at any time, use that watch of Anne Muller's for the purpose for which it was made?"

"Never. I was not even aware that it had a purpose other than that for which every watch is made."

"And the five thousand pounds paid into your account at the Swiss Bank of Berne?"

"I know nothing whatever about it, Mr. Blake. That is as great a mystery to me as it is to you. Yet the writing was Uncle von Frielhausen's, and the communication was sent to me through our secret address in Berne. I can only think that pressure was brought to bear on Uncle von Frielhausen to make him write the letter."

"By Anna Muller?"

"Oh, no! That's impossible! Anna is my friend!"

"I admire your loyalty more than your common sense," Blake told her dryly. "Anna Muller knew of your Uncle von Frielhausen, I take it?"

"Ye-s."

"And of your method of keeping in touch with him?"

"Ye-s," she admitted, more reluctantly still.

"Have you still got that white fox fur you spoke of?"

She was momentarily bewildered by the sudden turn of his questions.

"I think so," she said at last. "It should be in the box my landlady is keeping for me."

"Together with the other things you wore that night?"

"Yes, but—"

"If necessary, do you think you could reconstruct that collar?"

"What d'you mean?" she asked, suddenly breathless.

"I have an idea, Miss Ensor. It may work, or it may not. I can't tell. But if I can get permission to have the box you mention sent here, do you think you could reconstruct for me the entire suit of clothes—from hat to shoes—that you wore upon the night in question?"

She nodded her head. She was too breathless to speak. From the strange brightness of her eyes it was obvious that once again hope had taken possession of her.

"Could you?" Blake asked.

"Yes!" she whispered. "Yes, of—of course I could!"

"Then you may look to hear from me some time to-morrow, Miss Ensor. Good-afternoon!"

THE SEVENTH CHAPTER

On Blake's Tail.

BLAKE FOUND THE works of the Southern Aircraft Construction Company to be considerably larger than he had expected when he called there the morning with the idea of having a chat with Mr. Ogilvie. Since the outbreak of war, he learned, they had expanded to more than four times their original size, and extensive building. operations were still in progress.

"In fact, the sky's the limit—in more ways than one!" boasted the clerk who escorted him to the works manager's office. "Mr. Ogilvie," he said, as he opened the door.

The occupant of the room was seated behind a vast oak desk, but rose as the detective entered. He was a thick-set, heavily built man of fifty-two or three—a powerful-looking man of the "big-business" type, with a large head, large features, a somewhat thick-lipped, pursed-up mouth, and an uncompromising jowl. He stooped a little, so that his clothes "hung" on him rather than "sat" on him, thus giving the impression that they were a size too large for even his big frame.

"I hope nothing is wrong?" he said, glancing at the detective's card. His voice was very deep, but his hands, though large, were soft and podgy-looking; the hands of an office worker. Blake's immediate impression of the man was that he combined considerable force of character with a genius for organisation.

He took the chair offered him, and sat down. He had been commissioned by the Home Office to make an examination into the methods adopted for the safeguarding of key documents in Government offices, he explained mendaciously. And he would like an opportunity of examining the "clock system" which he understood was in use at the Southern Aircraft Construction Company for the safeguarding of important blue prints.

"There's an idea abroad that it's about the best system yet devised," he added tactfully.

"Thank you," said Ogilvie, smiling. And when Blake stared: "It's my patent!" he explained.

"Your patent? I had no idea of that!"

"The original idea was Chec. Came from the Skoda Works, I believe. But I improved upon it, and eventually applied the principle to locks. I'll show you!"

He rose as he spoke, and Blake got up with him. He had chosen this method of approaching the manager because he thought it more likely to produce reliable results. Ogilvie had been a good friend of Isobel Ensor, both before and during her trial. He had very definitely ranged himself upon her side. Indeed, at one point—so Gervase Crispin had told him—Ogilvie had come within an ace of being pulled up for perjury so ardently had he sought to defend her. It seemed to Blake, therefore—and particularly if Ogilvie should catch the impression that there was a chance of the case being re-opened—that the answers he would give to any direct question concerning Isobel Ensor might be more enthusiastic than strictly factual!

"There are two rooms in the Blue Print Department," Ogilvie told him now, as they walked down a long corridor. "An outer room where we keep the operational prints, and an inner where we store the master drawing. I'll show you how it works. Come in!"

He opened a door as he spoke, and Blake found himself in a large room, the walls of which were lined with steel filing drawers, each of which bore a number. Those drawers contained the blue prints of the thousand and one operational details which went to make up the component: parts of the finished product, explained. But the master drawings were kept in what appeared to be a strong-room built into the solid-concrete of the end wall.

"Now this is fireproof and blast-proof," Ogilvie informed him proudly, coming to a halt beside the huge green door. "And no one has a key to it except Mr. James over there—the keeper as we call him—the man who is in charge of the entire Blue Print Department. Oh, James!" he called.

"Sir!"

A man came over from a desk in one corner of the room. He was an elderly little man, with a puckered face, who peered out upon the world through a pair of extraordinarily thick lenses. Ogilvie explained to him that he was showing Mr. Blake how the "clock system" worked, and between them they proceeded to a practical demonstration.

James took a key from his pocket, unlocked the big green door, and slowly swung it back. Behind it lay a room of some twelve feet square, the walls of which were again lined with steel drawers.

"For convenience sake, each drawer bears the number of the plan it contains," Ogilvie pointed out. "'B.23' over there, for example, is the number we gave to one of our reconnaissance planes, and the master drawing of B.23 is kept in that drawer. But this is the crux of the system!"

He tapped what looked like a small cash register that was fixed to the back of the safe door.

"There's an electric clock in this box," he said, "and every time the door is opened a clock face showing the exact time is printed upon an internal roll of paper. You can see the paper through this slot here, and whoever comes for a drawing must sign his name in the slot together with the number of the drawing he takes out. When the drawing is returned, the procedure is the same. James opens the safe again, the plan is put back in its drawer, whoever has had it signs as returning it, and James signs his signature to make a second check. I'll show you a used roll so that you can see exactly how it works out."

He went into the strong room and came back with a roll of paper about three inches wide.

"I forgot to mention that at twelve midnight the clock automatically stamps the date of the next day, so that we know where we are." He opened the roll as he spoke. "June 21st, look, 1940," he said. "We'll take that day, shall we? Now let's see what happened on June 21st, 1940."

Blake looked where he was pointing. Down the narrow roll was a line of clock faces showing various times, and opposite each stamp was a man's signature, a figure, and then James' signature.

"Now these are the names of every man who had occasion to take out a master print upon June 21st, 1940," Ogilvie explained. "W. R. Nugent, for instance—that's one of our directors—he took out A.5 at twenty-two minutes past eleven and returned it to the safe again at three minutes to twelve—James countersigning both transactions. P. V. Harrison—he's our chief draughtsman—he took out B.16 at two-five and returned it at two-twenty-seven— you see the idea? Every time the safe door is opened the time is stamped on this roll, and unless there is a proper signature alongside every stamp—well, we know there's something wrong."

"I take it that not everyone would be allowed to handle the master plans?" Blake asked.

"No. That's where the check begins to operate. Only the directors, the chief draughtsman, myself, the designer of course, and the production manager, are allowed to handle these master plans. So that if anything goes wrong—if, for example, details of a new machine were to leak out—then manifestly the blame must rest with whichever of us has signed for that particular plan. And these rolls form a record for all time, don't you see?"

"Who is responsible for the plans outside this room?"

"They're never taken outside this room! Nor does James ever leave this room while a plan is out of the safe. Check and countercheck, you see? And another thing I forgot to mention, the safe itself can only be opened within certain specified hours. A time lock is fitted."

"You've certainly thought up a pretty water-tight arrangement, Mr. Ogilvie," Blake was forced to admit. "It would take a triple-gilt spy to get through your defences!"

"It would now we're awake," the other agreed with a short laugh. "But it didn't in the beginning, before we had time to realise what we were up against. Before James took over we had a girl on the job. Two, in fact. The first proved to be a German, above everything. While the second, an English girl, is now serving a ten years' sentence for selling our secrets to the enemy."

"You mean that she beat your 'clock system'?" Blake asked in well-simulated surprise.

"No, she didn't beat the system. She beat the men who ran the system, that was the trouble! She had a camera built into a watch, and the theory was that when one of us was examining that particular print she had leaned over his shoulder with her watch in her hand and taken a photograph of it."

"But wouldn't the man concerned know of that?"

"We didn't, anyway," Ogilvie shrugged. "We had a meeting on that very point—all of us whom the roll proved had handled that print. But none of us could remember a thing. I told them so in court at her trial."

"But they convicted her?"

"Yes. Of course, there was a lot more to it than that, you appreciate? It was revealed that she had German relatives and that she'd received German money for the photographs she had sent them. I dunno. I suppose she was guilty, all right."

"Was no one else ever suspected?"

"There was no one else they could suspect! It was proved from the roll that no one had ever touched the print save the managing director, myself, our chief draughtsman, and the designer—and none of us had got camera watches! She was the only other person who had ever seen the print, and, as I say, when they came to ferret out her back history and found that she was hand in glove with the Germans and was actually receiving money from them—" Ogilvie spread his hands. "She was a nice girl, too," he said thoughtfully. "The last girl in the world you'd ever have suspected of doing that kind of thing. Funny, wasn't it?"

"What did she say about it herself?"

"What could she say? She maintained that she knew nothing about it; that she was getting the blame for something she'd never done. That it was somebody else who had photographed them. Frankly, I more than half believed her—at the time. I mean, she'd been my shorthand typist for more than a year prior to that: I knew her well. Or thought I did. But I'm no detective, I suppose. I can only judge people as I find them, and once I've made up my mind about anyone it takes a lot of shifting."

"Heart versus head, huh?" Blake laughed easily.

"I suppose that's about the size of it."

Shortly afterwards they went back to the works manager's office, and later, Ogilvie suggested a trip round the factory. They finished up on the company's private aerodrome where for a time they stood watching the antics of what seemed to be an amazingly fast fighter with which the company's designers were experimenting both by day and by night.

"What do you call her?" Blake asked.

"Officially, A.1," Ogilvie told him. "Unofficially, it's known as Adolf's Surprise. Our chief test pilot has other names for it, some of them not quite so nice—particularly when after some slight alteration it has taken off and stood straight on its ear. Matter of fact, that's the third model you're watching now—and the best, so far. The first two he had to bale out of—one broke up in the air, and the other shed its tail while diving at a speed I can't mention. But it's hot."

"It is hot!" Blake said, following with a professional eye the streaking atom that was now dropping at incredible speed out of the sky. "I hope there are no spies watching the performance."

"Spies?" Ogilvie grinned. "They wouldn't get much out of watching that, Mr. Blake—save a crick in the neck and a big belly ache, perhaps. You've seen how we keep the only things spies would like to see; and once bitten, twice shy, as they say!"

They walked back to the office, and shortly afterwards Blake took his leave. He had much to think about. Unless there was some way of defeating that tell-tale clock behind the door of the strong room, it seemed impossible that anyone save Isobel Ensor herself could have photographed the plan. And in that event, the question of her alibi became of less importance. On the other hand—and in spite of all the evidence against her—if Maynard was correct in saying that he had been attacked by people who were determined to prevent him from contacting Walter Paine, then manifestly the alibi must be every bit as important as she said it was. It must be—or why should anyone be willing to risk hanging for the pleasure of preventing its establishment?

That seemed to Sexton Blake to be only common sense, and he was still debating the matter with himself when he reached Cricklewood. For some little time past, in a vague kind of way, he had been aware of the light van behind him—a van with canvas sides that were flapping wildly in the breeze. But it was not until he turned right into Kilburn High Street that it suddenly dawned upon him that he was being followed.

At first he refused to credit it. There was no earthly reason why anyone should follow him. To test the matter he turned into the first street that appeared on his left, but sure enough, a half-minute later, round sailed the van with the flying sides. He put on speed; so did the light van. He reduced speed; so did the light van.

Convinced now that he was being followed, Blake smiled to himself grimly. Two could play at that game.

Awaiting his opportunity he turned left again, braked hard immediately he was round the corner, and stopped against the kerb. When a half-minute later the light van came sailing round, the detective was already out on the pavement waiting for it.

But then a strange thing happened, for instead of going straight on, the van stopped dead. It pulled up as suddenly as Blake's own car had stopped, and its driver jumped out as quickly.

"I was afraid of that!" he grinned.

Blake clicked a disgusted tongue. One glance at that six-foot-three of smiling geniality was enough to tell him everything. The driver was none other than Detective-Inspector Belford of Scotland Yard, "handmaiden" and chief factotem to that brightest of all Yard constellations—Superintendent Venner.

"You shinned round there too fast, Mr. Blake," he chortled. "You bewildered the poor beast!"

"Eh?" Blake said inelegantly.

"The bird who was following you. C.O. 758. He picked you up outside the Southern Aircraft place, and he's been on your tail ever since. Black Ford 10, he was. He rolled up while you were inside; I saw him. Shouldn't have noticed him save that he didn't leave his car. Then, when you came out and drove off, he straightway started after you. So I started after him."

"Why?" Blake asked after a moment of dead silence.

Belford coughed.

"Well," he said. "I mean—"

"You mean, that you were tailing me, too, I suppose?"

112

Blake suggested acidly.

"Well, I wouldn't go as far as to say that, Mr. Blake. I mean—"

"What do you mean?" Blake snapped. "What's the great idea, Belford?"

The handmaiden drew a deep sigh. Life could be very difficult at times.

"It's no use blaming me," he said in a sudden burst of confidence. "You know what the sooper is, Mr. Blake. You've upset him, I tell you."

"Who? Me?"

"Yes, he phoned me yesterday about it. There he was, sitting pretty as a robin in Dillborough—roses round the door and pansies in his hair and that like—and suddenly you come barging in. Well, he wants to know what you're up to, and he details me to keep an eye on you. So far you've been to the Home Office, and had an interview with Isobel Ensor in jug, and now you've been to the Southern Aircraft works—I'm bewildered! And on top of that I see that you're being followed by a gent in a Ford Ten who's obviously been waiting for you—I mean, what am I going to tell the sooper?"

"So far as I'm concerned, you can tell him what you like, Belford," the detective grinned cheerfully. "But I'd like you to tell me something if you would?"

"Such as—what?"

"Are you speaking the truth about this fellow in the Ford Ten?"

"And me a detective-inspector of New Scotland Yard!" sighed the handmaiden. "However, overlook the

113

imputation and say that the answer's in the affirmative, Mr. Blake."

"When did he arrive there?"

"About a quarter of an hour before you came out."

"And he didn't leave his car?"

"No. He just sat there waiting."

"What sort of man was he?"

"I didn't see him. I shouldn't even have noticed him except from the manner in which he started off so promptly on your tail—and then I realised that he must have been waiting for you."

"And his number was C.O. 758, you say?"

"That's right. And he'd have been on your tail now if you hadn't snooped round that darned corner so fast. I take it from the easy way you shook him off that he's an amateur at the game."

"It would certainly seem so," Blake mused.

"I'll let you know who he is, if you like? I mean, I shall have to look him up, anyhow."

"I'd be glad if you would, Belford."

"Sure. One good turn deserves another. You're going to tell me what's afoot at the Southern Aircraft place and I'm going to tell you who owns the car C.O. 758," blandly proclaimed the handmaiden. "Or aren't you?" he added when Blake said nothing.

The private practitioner moved briskly towards his car. "Nothing's up," he said, "so it wouldn't be a fair bargain. I'm going home now by the way," he added pointedly.

"I'm going the same way," was all Belford said as he went to that dreadful van.

Blake pulled away, so did the van. When an hour later he drew up outside the Baker Street flat, so did the van.

"I like an hour and a half for my lunch," grinned the handmaiden cheerfully. "Is it a bargain?"

"I certainly shall not move out earlier than that," Blake agreed, as he ran up the steps.

Tinker met him in the hall. He had taken the box of clothes to the prison, he said, and Miss Ensor was already at work on the outfit. "How did you get on at the Southern Aircraft, guv'nor?" he asked eagerly.

Blake told him. At the end of it all he wrote down the letters and number of the Ford Ten and dispatched his assistant with instructions to locate the owner as soon as possible. "Get hold of Parkinson, at the Registration Department," he said, "and then canvass the insurance people. Understand?"

Tinker nodded, and set off on his task. He was gone for four hours. When he got back again he found Sexton Blake entertaining a young lady—a most extraordinary occurrence.

"Sorry!" Tinker said as he opened the door.

"It's quite all right, old son. Come in!" Blake called. He turned to the girl and smiled. "This is the young gentleman who will be your cavalier," he said. "Tinker, this is Miss Fisher—Miss Doris Fisher. You're taking her to dinner to-night at the White Cat."

"Am I?" Tinker asked blankly.

"How did you get on with that number?"

Tinker cleared his throat. Things appeared to be moving all ways at once.

"C.O. 758 belongs to a car owned by a man named Denham, living at Marlow," he said. "But he's dead. He was killed in the City during a raid, more than two months ago."

"What happened to his car?"

"Nobody knows. That's the rum part of it. He used it for going up and down to Town, and he had it with him the night he was killed. But it wasn't a Ford Ten, guv'nor."

"What was it, then?"

"A red M.G. Twenty."

Blake almost dropped his pipe in his surprise.

"A red M.G. Twenty?" he echoed.

"So they told me in the village."

There was a moment of silence. Then Blake knocked out his pipe and laid it with meticulous care along the front of the mantelpiece.

"The devil they did!" he said very thoughtfully.

THE EIGHTH CHAPTER

Blake Falls a Victim.

FROM OUTSIDE, AT any rate, there was nothing to differentiate the White Cat from any one of the dozen or so other small restaurants in Charlotte Street. The same curtained window fronted flat on to the pavement, and the discreet doorway exuded the same smell of garlic and Continental cooking. The ground floor and first-floor rooms were the restaurant, and above those were the store-rooms and the living accommodation of the proprietor and his family.

Eddy Paul kept the White Cat. Prior to the war he had been Eddino Paulioni, but since no one had ever called him anything but "Eddy" the change had little significance. He was a short, plump, round little man—a typical Italian, with pale skin, dark eyes, a "button" mouth, and a sad bald patch on the top of his head. Thirty years he had been in Charlotte Street, or within a stone's throw of it; and at one time or another had owned almost every restaurant on both sides of the road—or so at least he

117

would tell you.

He would tell you other things, too, for besides being an artist in food and drink, he was an expert in the noble art of suffering fools gladly. Particularly rich fools. He would speak to each new customer as though he alone mattered. As though it were for him alone that the chef had striven and the cooks laboured. He would descant learnedly and at length upon the merits of this or that wine until, having discovered that his customer didn't know a hock from a chianti anyway, he would fetch up a bottle of his worst rubbish—with a suitable flourish of napkin and ice-pail— and solemnly sell it for a guinea.

It was all part of his business, as was his execrable English. Experience had long since taught him that foreigners speaking fluent English were apt to be treated no better than the English themselves—whereas a foreigner with nothing but "comic" English could get away with anything, short of murder! All Soho knew him, and Eddy knew all Soho—that again was part of his business. And while no one knew where his political sympathies lay, they did know that his pocket was in Charlotte Street and that he was naturalised anyhow.

It was a few minutes past eight o'clock that night when Sexton Blake strolled into the place. For reasons of his own he had elected to disguise himself, and the effect was so startling—in war-time—that even the experienced Eddy was momentarily thrown out of his stride.

"The Last of the Bohemians!" he thought as his eyes took in the neat brown beard, black horn-rimmed glasses, the wide soft collar, floppy tie and velvet jacket of the fraternity. In the days of peace many such had been among his regular clientele, but since the war they had all disappeared. Certainly no such figure as this had been seen in the White Cat for ages.

"Signor!" he bowed mechanically.

"Padrone!" Blake nodded with a smile.

It was enough. The intonation, the accent, everything proclaimed that here was a true Bohemian—a citizen of the world. An artist. Eddy looked at him sharply, then bowed again.

"You honour my poor house, signor!" he said, turning with pride to lead this very special customer to the table reserved for those who mattered. He himself took the broad-brimmed hat, the stick, the gloves, the ulster, for in the little Italian's pantheon the Arts held a very honoured place.

Then he began to talk food.

He spoke in Italian, and Blake listened to him with the solemnity the occasion demanded, here and there throwing in a suggestion of his own which caused Eddy to beam with pleasure. For no matter what life had made him, Eddino Paulioni was a restaurateur born and bred, and nothing gave him greater pleasure than to design a meal for someone who could really appreciate the gastronomic art.

That, indeed, was why the detective had chosen to appear in this Bohemian guise; he wanted to get on the best terms possible with Eddy in the little time at his disposal.

Presently Eddy hurried away to give instructions to his kitchen staff, and Blake was at liberty to look about him.

The interior of the White Cat was entirely typical of its kind. The room was shaped to a rough "L," the longer leg of which formed the restaurant proper, and the shorter leg a kind of club-room for the habitues of the place. In the shorter leg, which was more or less private from the public restaurant, a few young people were lounging idly over the blue-and-white tablecloths, some talking, some playing cards, and some still eating. They were the "regulars." Young people who lived round about the district under heaven alone knew what circumstances, and who—when they had the money—took all their meals there. When they had no money, they either "went on the slate" or starved— according as Eddy assessed their credit.

They were artists for the most part, writers, pseudo-intellectuals, with a fair sprinkling of foreigners who might be—and probably were—anything. One or two of the black-haired, straight-fringed girls, might in better days have been artists' models, but now they were existing as best they could on whatever happened along—dance-hostesses, jobs in the various night clubs, work that was carrying them slowly yet irresistibly into the vortex of London's underworld. 'Poor little sheep who had lost their way," as Blake thought of them from his seat in the angle of the "L."

The longer leg of the room had small tables upon either side of the central gangway, but here the clientele was totally different. Here were the young fellows with their girls from the suburbs out for a night "up West"—bombs or no bombs! An elderly business man or two, a sprinkling of soldiers with their girls, shop-girls from round about—

all the various strata of life that go to make up work-a-day London.

In the long leg the sheep, Blake thought as Eddy ushered forward a waiter bearing two dry sherries "on the house." In the short leg—the goats!

"To your health, signor!" proclaimed Eddy, lifting his glass.

"Excellent," Blake complimented him after a first sip. It was plain that Eddy was giving of his very best; that he was really extending himself.

The waiter brought stuffed olives.

It was some half-hour later that Tinker entered the restaurant, with Doris Fisher. At the moment of their arrival Eddy was in deep and portentous discussion with Blake upon the topic of brandy, but even his voice tailed off for a second as the young woman sailed down the gangway towards the habitues' end of the restaurant.

"Lo, Eddy!" she smiled as she passed him.

"Signorina!" he bowed a bit blankly.

The hush in the restaurant was perceptible. Every woman in the place had paused to watch her along the gangway—even the waiters were staring. It was obvious that furs of the quality she was wearing were not common in the White Cat. And certainly not in the extravagant fashion in which she was wearing them. Indeed, as seen from Blake's table in the angle of the "L," her passage through the small restaurant had left behind a ripple of excitement comparable to that left behind by a speedboat passing through a quiet backwater.

"You are acquainted with the young lady?" he asked

softly as Eddy watched her take her seat at one of the blue-and-white check tables.

The plump little proprietor turned on the instant. He was full of apologies for neglecting the signor, but—yes, he knew the young lady although not quite— He spread his hands and shrugged.

"The signor will excuse for one moment?" he asked.

Blake inclined his head. In the normal course of events Eddy never greeted the habitues, but evidently in this case he intended making an exception. He went over there, beckoning a waiter to follow him. He bowed himself double. Some of the habitues knew her, apparently, for one or two had already waved to her while all were looking at her curiously.

Watching them, Blake remembered what Isobel Ensor had said with regard to that fur collar, and he was feign to agree. It definitely was not her style! It was too flamboyant. Too ultra-smart. It would have been noticeable even in a fashionable restaurant: it was a positive riot in the White Cat! The top of it was on a level with the top of its wearer's head, and from there it stood out on either side, in snowy magnificence, like an enormous Elizabethan ruff. It was as remarkable as a red suit would be on a man. It would be impossible to forget. In a year's time, if he were never to see her again, Eddy Paul would remember Doris Fisher by that enormous fur collar she was wearing—and therein lay the pith of Blake's experiment.

No one had ever mentioned that collar. Neither at the trial, nor at any of the identification parades, had anyone made a single reference to it. Eddy himself, and three of his waiters, had sworn to seeing Isobel Ensor in the company of Larry Rue on the night of the latter's disappearance. They had been able to swear to her because they were already acquainted with her—yet not one of them had mentioned the really startling fur collar she had been wearing upon an equally startling coat. They had been able to recall the girl but had forgotten the collar. Those same men who were now standing around staring at it as though fascinated.

Sitting back in his chair, with the smoke curling up lazily from his cigarette, Sexton Blake awaited the outcome of his subtle play. From the corner of his eye he could see Eddy engaged in what appeared to be vigorous protest against something the girl had said to him. He spread his hands. Alternatively, he raised them to high heaven to bear witness to the truth of what he was saying. His face became flushed with his exertions. His English went all to pieces. Finally, he appealed to the waiter, and that worthy seemed to support him—but then the girl laughed, and that upset Eddy's dignity. With a stiff little bow he turned and bounced away.

"A little trouble, padrone?" Blake asked lazily when he would have passed his table without speaking.

The Italian paused, then:

"No trouble—no!" he said. "It is just that I insulted haf been, signor!"

He spread one hand across his bosom. His funny round face wore an air of martyrdom. "I make-a da compliment to dat girl! I say what a magnifik fur! I tak-a dat liberty because I know dat girl—dat is understood! An' what she say to me? What dat girl say to me—I, who have-a da sense of dress? I—Eddino Paulioni! I—who nevaire forget-a da pretty woman or da smart dress! What dat girl say to me, you think?"

"I can't imagine," Blake said mendaciously.

"I tell you, signor! You—da great artist—you will unnerstan' my pain. I remain calm. Ozzer men may lose-a da temper, but not me. Not ze late Eddino Paulioni— now Eddy Paul. God save-a da King! She say to me: 'But, Eddy, you zis magnifik fur haf seen before'! An' I laugh myself, signor. What folly, I say. Pouf! As though I am a—a barbarian, signor! As though I the eyes not haf! The memory not possess-a! 'No!' I say—like-a that! 'Once seen, nevaire forgetted!' I say. An' then, what you tink?"

"I don't know," Blake admitted.

"She say to me that that same magnifik fur already come to this my restaurant! She say that it come here to eat. She say that it sit in dat very place and make-a da eats—an' I not know. I—da great Eddino Paulioni—late! I not see dat fur. I not know my eyes no good. My heart 'e stoppa da beat. Pah!"

He was trembling with indignation. He was completely outraged by such a suggestion, for like most Italian restaurateurs he prided himself upon never forgetting a face.

"You think I forgetta da face what sits inside dat magnifik fur?" he raved now. "You tink my waiters forget? You tink I one big dam fool? You tink I leave my country to come 'ere to be Englishman—Rule Britannia!—and leave-a da brain behind?"

"But from whom did she get the fur?" Blake asked when he could get a word in edgeways.

"From one of my habitues, she say! One of my habitues, mark you!—as though I do not know what my own peoples wear! She say it was six-seven months ago. I say six-seven years make-a no difference to me! I nevaire forget. My waiters nevaire forget! It is their job nevaire to forget. I train them nevaire to forget!"

"And do none of them remember that fur?"

"I show you!" Suddenly the excitable little man saw a way of proving his claim. "We ask them!" he said. "One by one. An' if even one remembers seeing that fur before, I make-a da present of da dinner to dat girl. There! I make-da bet!"

He called them up to him, one by one, and to each he put the same question. Had that fur ever been into the restaurant before? And one by one they shook their heads. Never, they said, or they would have remembered it. Who, indeed, could forget such a fur? It was unique. Never before had anything even approaching it come into the White Cat!

"You see?" Eddy asked proudly when the last of them had gone. "Could we all be mistaken, signor?"

Blake rose leisurely to his feet.

"It would be an amazing thing if you were," he agreed. "And doubly amazing in view of the fur's unusualness." He turned to put on his ulster, satisfied that he had driven the first wedge of doubt into the case against Isobel Ensor. But as he reached up for his broad-brimmed hat, he paused.

A girl was standing at the foot of the stairs leading to the upper regions. She was on her way out to the street, but in the second that Blake caught sight of her she came to an abrupt halt—to a startled halt, judging by the way in which one hand flew to her throat.

"Eddy!" she gasped.

The Italian heard her, and turned. She was only three or four steps from where they were standing, but she seemed not to have seen Sexton Blake. Her eyes were fixed upon something farther across the room, but in the brief moment of time before Eddy stepped across to her, and came between them, Blake had the curious feeling that he had seen her before somewhere. That he ought to know her. She was a tall girl, very pale, with red hair. A good-looking girl. He was certain he had seen her somewhere before, though where he could not remember.

Now Eddy himself had turned and was looking in the same direction. For a moment his face appeared as startled as her own had been, but almost at once he laughed.

"Nonsense!" Blake heard him whisper in Italian.

"You're sure?" the girl whispered back.

"Of course I'm sure!"

They were talking of Doris Fisher. A lightning glance behind him showed Blake that beyond the shadow of a doubt, for both the girl and Eddy had been looking in her direction. They were talking of Doris Fisher, who was wearing Isobel Ensor's clothes and—

Blake caught his breath. Whether it was the rapid association of ideas that jogged his memory, or whether it was due to some sudden move on the part of the girl, he could not have told you. It came to him like a flash of blinding light. For a moment he stood stock-still, literally dazed by the shock of it.

The girl standing at the foot of those stairs was Isobel Ensor's friend, Anne Miller!

Anna Muller—the German spy! The girl Isobel Ensor claimed to have sent back to Germany, via Switzerland; but who was still in England!

Anna Muller!

How he reached the door of the restaurant, Blake never really knew. His instinct was to run for it, to get out first, but to Tinker—who was watching him—his exit was so completely natural and leisurely that no one even looked up from his meal.

And his luck seemed to be in! A taxi was standing waiting by the edge of the kerb not a dozen yards away.

"Taxi!" he called.

"Sorry, sir. Engaged!" the driver's voice came back through the darkness.

Not so good! Blake clicked an impatient tongue, for there was nothing else in sight.

"Who's engaged you?" he asked, crossing to the driver's side. "My name is Sexton Blake!" he added when the fellow stared at him. "I'm on police business, you understand? There's a girl coming out of the White Cat whom I want to follow."

"A girl—" the driver asked after a moment of blank silence. "But I'm—I'm waitin' for a girl from the White Cat, guv'nor. It's a girl as rung for me."

"You've been here before?"

"Once or twice, guv'nor."

"A red-headed girl?"

"That's the one!"

"Driver—there's a fiver for you in this!" Blake whispered exultantly. "I've got to know where that girl lives. How can you carry me?"

The driver looked behind him. He seemed to be considering. But the door of the White Cat opened, and high heels began to click across the pavement towards where the cab was standing.

"Get down here by me!" he whispered hoarsely, pointing to the space beside his seat where the luggage is generally stowed. "Duck your head, guv'nor!" he urged as Blake jumped aboard and the high heels came up alongside.

"Taxi?" a girl's voice asked.

"Yes, miss—all ready!" the driver answered. He jumped down from his seat and, having put her inside, fumbled for his starting-handle—he was economising on petrol. He started his engine and climbed back into his seat. "Lower, guv'nor!" Blake heard him whisper. And, as though to impress the point, a rough hand reached out in the darkness and thrust him down.

Blake bent his head on to his knees. He could get no lower. Just when he was wondering why the fellow did not start away, something descended with crushing force on the back of his neck.

A jagged fork of blue light blinded him. His world dissolved into a million white-hot particles of pain.

When a minute or so later the taxi did move away, the body of London's most astute private investigator was acting as an unconscious footstool for the pretty feet of the girl with the red hair.

THE NINTH CHAPTER

At Pistol Point.

BLAKE CAME TO slowly, and to a sense of great discomfort. Even after full consciousness had returned, it was some little time before he succeeded in orientating himself sufficiently to realise, firstly, that he was gagged and trussed like a hog, and, secondly, that he was lying on the floor of what was almost certainly a coal-cellar.

It was very dark, and his head ached abominably. He felt sick. For a long time he lay motionless, trying to piece together the course of events which had led to this swift reversal of his fortunes; but although he recalled the girl with the red hair, and the taxi outside the White Cat, he could not for the life of him remember how he had come by that terrific blow on the back of his neck. He began to think that he must have fallen from his precarious perch, but in that case why was he not in hospital instead of lying gagged and bound in a coal-cellar? And the taximan would not have hit him, unless—

His thoughts stopped dead, then as suddenly raced on again. The taximan—of course! The oldest trick in the bag. He had gone to the White Cat to fetch Anna Muller, and, by the irony of Fate, Blake had walked straight up to him and said " Take me, too!"

The taxi had been stolen from somewhere—the driver was a fake. He was not a taximan at all, but a member of the gang. Like enough they used it for picking up innocent victims as well as their own members—particularly at night in the black-out. Had a private car picked up Anna Muller at the White Cat, someone might have noticed its make or its colour or its number. But who would remark a mere taxi? And what could be less suspicious?

Now Blake knew the truth, and lying there in the darkness he could have groaned aloud in his bitterness of spirit. Never could he remember a worse stroke of luck. Never could anyone have walked so plump into the lion's mouth. Never, he thought suddenly, could anyone have disappeared so completely or left so little trace of his passing! No wonder the fellow had seemed slow in the uptake! No wonder he had failed at first to grasp the amazing chance presented to him. "I am Sexton Blake," the detective had told him. "I'm on police business, you understand? There's a girl coming out of the White Cat whom I want to follow—a red-haired girl. I've got to know where she lives!"

It was incredible. It was too bad to be true. It didn't seem possible, and yet it had happened. By a chance in a million he had delivered himself to the enemy—trussed, browned to a turn, and on a charger!

He groaned again. Then he set to work on the bonds that held him; tentatively at first, but with increasing violence as they seemed to be working loose. He had no idea where he was, nor how long they had taken to bring him there; but back of his mind was a growing conviction that he was right in the centre of the web.

He was in the gang's headquarters; he was certain of it. Right from the beginning he had had the feeling that there yes more in this Isobel Ensor case than met the eye, and now he was sure of it. The reappearance of Anna Mulier in the country! The affair at Dillborough! The fact that he himself had been tailed from the Southern Aircraft Company's place only that very morning—why? Who could have known that he had gone there unless somebody at the factory had seen him and communicated with someone outside? Because no one had tailed him to the factory! The man in the Ford Ten had not arrived there until some fifteen minutes before he left the place—so that he could only have been called there by someone from inside.

It was from the Southern Aircraft Company, too, that the first lot of plans had leaked out—those alleged to have been photographed by Isobel Ensor on behalf of her German friend, Anna Muller. And now Anna Muller was back again in the country—and with his very own eyes Blake had only that morning witnessed the trials of the Southern Aircraft Company's latest and most secret production—the A.1 Fighter. Or "Adolf's Surprise," as the boys called it.

Was Anna Muller scheming to get hold of those plans, too? Was that why she had risked coming back here? If, indeed, she had ever left the country, as Isobel Ensor said she had?

As he worked silently at his bonds, Blake's thoughts went back to the White Cat and to the "late" Eddino Paulioni. Where did Eddy come in in the play? It was Eddy and three of his waiters who had sworn to seeing Isobel Ensor with Larry Rue upon the night of the latter's disappearance. It was, in fact, their evidence which had clinched the case against her. But had she been there with Larry Rue? If Eddy and his three waiters were sure enough to swear that she had been there on that particular night, then why had all four of them failed to recognise, or even to remember, that very striking fur?

Or was Isobel Ensor lying when she said that she had worn that fur on that particular night?

It was, at any rate, completely established that Eddy knew Anna Muller! And Blake had more than a suspicion that the girl was living at the White Cat, judging by the way in which she had walked down those stairs from the regions above.

She had certainly used Eddy's private phone to ring for her "taxi," since the public phone was in the restaurant—Blake had noticed that for himself. And it was equally certain that her sudden panic upon arrival at the foot of the stairs had been caused by sight of Doris Fisher wearing Isobel Ensor's clothes. The German girl had recognised them—had recognised the white fox fur. And for a moment she must have believed that Isobel Ensor herself was sitting there—hence her call to Eddy and the Italian's hasty disclaimer.

On the other hand, the fact that she had known fear over the incident, argued a point in Isobel Ensor's favour. Had the pair been in collaboration, as was suggested, surely she would have registered joy—not fear?

The cords about his wrists were giving perceptibly now. Given time, he believed he could get completely free, and his spirits rose accordingly. He strained his arms until the rope cut into his flesh. Relaxed and strained again until the sweat stood out in large drops on his brow.

Suddenly he stopped and lay still. Throughout all this time he had been alert for the least sound of movement— and now it came. Suddenly he was aware of voices. Then he heard the sound of approaching feet. One last frantic effort warned him that he could not free his hands before their arrival, so he composed himself and lay still. When a moment later a bolt was drawn and a torch was flashed into the cellar, he gave no sign of life.

There was a long moment of silence. Blake believed there were three of them, but only one was bending over him. Suddenly that one spoke.

"This isn't Sexton Blake, you fool!" he laughed harshly.

"Well, he said 'e was, baron!"

It was the "taximan" who spoke. Blake recognised his voice on the instant, but he could not recall ever having heard the voice of the man they addressed as "Baron." On the other hand, it seemed that the Baron was fairly familiar with his own appearance!

The next second he had proof of that, for with a sudden

and most painful tug his false beard was torn away!

"You're right, my friend—he is Sexton Blake!" the Baron said then, on a totally different note. "In disguise, at that; which can only mean one thing!"

"He's on to us, Baron—like I said?"

"We'll find out." The Baron's laugh sent a shiver of apprehension down Blake's spine. He would get no mercy from that quarter, he knew. "Watch him, both of you!" he snapped to his helpers. "I must think about this. Bring him up when I call. There's just a chance that he might be able to liquidate one of our dangers. If not, we shall have to liquidate him—that's all!"

He went out. Blake listened to his footsteps retreating along what appeared to be a stone corridor, then peeped between his closed lashes at the pair that were left on guard. As he had supposed, one of them was the taxi-driver who had bashed him. The other was a thin, dark, black-haired, Italianate-looking man in the late thirties—or, at least, appeared to be so in the light from the single torch.

It was the taxi-driver who spoke first.

"Funny 'e should 'ave come up to me, like that!" he mused. "It's like the Baron trippin' up to a cop and—"

"Shut up, you fool!" snarled the other. There was a shuffle of feet, and when a second later Blake was rolled unceremoniously on to his face, he guessed what had happened. The Italian had noticed his hands. Had seen the loosened cord in the beam from his torch. "Look at that!" he whispered.

"Aw! Would yer?" jeered the taximan, catching the

prone detective a vicious kick in his ribs. "Here! 'Old that light down, Antonio! The swine's gettin' loose!"

They re-tied him, and after that Blake lay still. He wondered who these people were? Wondered what the "Baron" had meant when he had spoken of "liquidating one of our dangers."

He was soon to know! Barely ten minutes had elapsed when a voice called them from up above somewhere, and in the same moment the taximan stooped down and cut the cords which held his ankles.

"Gerrup, Split!" he said roughly. "You'm wanted!"

Between them, they yanked him to his feet and hauled him from the cellar into a stone-flagged passage. It was agony walking, after he had been tied up for so long, but Blake offered no protest. For one thing he knew it would be useless. Only his wits could save him now; there could be no question of mercy from this lot.

They took him upstairs. Stone flags had given way to carpets, darkness to softly shaded lights. He appeared to be in a large country mansion somewhere, a well-kept, well-furnished place in which all the services were still functioning apparently. There was a telephone in the hall, he noticed—a white enamelled instrument set upon a lacquered stand. He would not have been surprised had a maid in cap and apron appeared and asked him for his card. The place gave you that impression.

"In 'ere!" the taxi-driver ordered, opening a certain door with his free hand and impelling Blake across the threshold in a staggering lurch.

"That will do!" snapped the Baron.

His captors released him, and very slowly Blake turned to face the man who appeared to be in charge. He was sitting behind a desk at the far end of the room, a man in black dinner clothes and immaculate linen. A thick-set, powerful looking man in the early forties, with strong features, a square head, eyes in which there was neither compassion nor any sign of human virtue, and a chin like a rock. His mouth was a straight line when Blake entered, but now, as they looked at each other, it gradually turned down at the corners in a mirthless smile.

"A bad mistake, Mr. Blake," he jibed.

"I agree," Blake told him pleasantly. "You wished to see me, I think?"

The Baron sat silent, thoughtfully nodding his head. Watching him closely, Blake was convinced that he had never seen the man before. So far as his appearance went he might have been anything, though the title seemed to suggest a Teutonic origin.

"Mr. Blake," he said suddenly. "From what I have heard of you, I take you to be a man of intelligence?"

"Even after my foolish mistake with regard to your private taxi?"

"Even after that," he said. "But this is no time for pleasantries, Mr. Blake. I will be perfectly frank and tell you that your life hangs by a thread. You are in my way. Your activities are hampering me in my work. My immediate decision upon hearing that you were in my hands was to order your elimination, but since then I have thought again. It occurs to me that you might be prepared to buy your life?"

"At what price?" Blake asked on exactly the same note.

"At the price of certain information which I am persuaded that you possess."

"Information touching—what?"

The Baron fixed him with an expressionless eye. There was a pregnant silence during which Blake instinctively braced himself. Then the Baron spoke again.

"Information concerning the whereabouts of the man, Walter Paine," he said slowly.

Blake did not speak. The silence grew and expanded until it became almost audible, yet still neither made any attempt to break it. What was in the Baron's mind, Blake had no means of knowing; but exulting through his own was the triumphant certainty; "I was right, after all! I was right, after all!"

"Well?" the Baron asked at last.

Blake hunched his shoulders. Instinct warned him that the man at that desk knew far more about Walter Paine than he knew himself, but as yet he was not aware of the fact! At the same time, experience warned him that the Baron would never have uncovered his hand to that extent if it was intended that Blake himself should leave that house alive.

"Walter Paine is reported 'missing, believed killed'," he said warily.

"I know that. I'm not asking you for 'reports' but for facts."

"And I'm asking for safeguards!" Blake retorted on the instant. "Just now, you credited me with possessing

137

intelligence. If I understand the situation aright, you are offering me my life in exchange for certain information as to Walter Paine's whereabouts. Is that correct?"

"It is correct!" the Baron said with more animation than he had yet shown. He leaned nearer across his desk. His eyes were suddenly eager. In a flash Blake knew that Walter Paine was not only alive and well, but that by some means or other he had managed to escape the Baron's net. The Baron had been after him as well, just as young Maynard had suggested. Almost it seemed that he had had him, too, but that he had got away again. It was exactly as Blake had figured might be the case; both sides were after the same man! One with the purpose of establishing an alibi, and the other with the avowed purpose of destroying that alibi utterly.

"Very well!" he said, with scarcely a a moment's pause. "Supposing I give you the information you seek—how then? How do I know you'll let me go?"

"You will have my word, Mr. Blake."

"But not my life!" Blake laughed in his face. "Do you think I'm crazy? I shall need much more than your bare word, Baron!"

"Baron?" whispered the other, half-rising in his chair.

"Well, that's what your men call you, isn't it?"

The other remained exactly as he was. His eyes switched to the taxi-driver who shuffled uneasily under that cold regard. Then they switched to the Italianate-looking man whose name was Antonio. Finally he sat down again, and joining the tips of his fingers stared thoughtfully at Sexton Blake.

"You want the information—I have it!" Blake boasted. "And it's no use glaring at me like that, Baron!" he laughed. "I don't care two straws for your glares. If you and I are to do business, it will be upon my terms and in my way—not yours! Of course, if you don't want my information, then shoot—and be damned to you!"

"It will be nothing so easy as shooting," the Baron said under his breath, but if he was hoping to break the nerve of Sexton Blake he had another thing coming to him, for by now Blake was very certain of his ground.

"Don't waste time being frightful, Baron," he jibed.

"You are right!" Suddenly the other stood up. He was smiling. Never once removing his eyes from those of his prisoner, he felt for the knob of a drawer on the right of his desk, found it, pulled the drawer open, and took out a heavy automatic. "Stand away, you two!" he commanded the taxi-man and Antonio.

They obeyed him with alacrity. They leapt for the door and stood cowering in an angle of the room furthest from the line of fire. Then, still with that snarling smile pinned to his mouth, the Baron advanced purposefully upon Sexton Blake.

And Blake smiled back at him! With his hands fastened behind him, he was quite helpless to resist; and although his legs were free, he knew that he could never open the door even if he could reach it before he was shot down.

A moment later, he felt the cold ring of the muzzle pressed hard against his temple.

"You crow too loudly, methinks!" purred the Baron.

"As cock o' the walk, why shouldn't I?" Blake flung

back at him pleasantly. "You surely can't be making the cardinal error of believing that you can frighten me with that thing? And not even I imagine you fool enough to shoot down your sole hope of information without at least trying something better than childish threats. Sit down, Baron! Be yourself!"

The Baron said nothing. His mouth was ugly, his eyes expressionless, his face set in hard, granite lines. In that moment Blake was as near death as ever he had been in all his adventurous career, but still he smiled, and still his eyes looked squarely into those of his murderer.

Finally the Baron spoke.

"Walter Paine was taken by a trick from the hospital where I had caused him to be held prisoner against my arrival there," he said, in a dead flat voice. "Who removed him?"

"You'd like to know, wouldn't you?" Sexton Blake laughed. "Well, I've told you my terms, Baron. No pay, no palaver, you know!"

"I'm not asking you the name of the person who removed him—merely the sex. Was it a man, or a woman?"

Blake looked at him, and his eyes narrowed. Now his life did indeed hang by a thread for already the Baron's forefinger was whitening about the trigger of his automatic. It was a test question, he realised. A question that he must answer—and answer correctly or have his brains spattered on the wall behind him.

He thought frantically. According to young Maynard, Walter Paine had been last seen by the men of his regiment lying beside the roadside with both his legs blown off. A

French nun had been leaning over him, and—

"Well—" he heard the Baron sneer.

Man or woman? Blake wondered frantically. A woman, surely—or why should he think to put the question at all? He tried to imagine the position—a hospital, a legless patient, a German guard. How would he himself have set about such a rescue? Obviously through one of the sisters. Perhaps an English sister, an English nun. A woman who had been working in the convent hospital before the war, and was still there. A woman who by some means or other had got wind of the Germans' intention towards her helpless countryman, and had planned to get him away before they could strike.

"Can it be that you were hoping to bluff me?" the Baron laughed menacingly. "That you know nothing at all?"

"Merely cautious, Baron!" Blake assured him. "We of the police have a rooted objection to saying more than we need. However, since you are so insistent, without giving away any of the vital information I hold, I don't mind telling you that you were beaten by a woman!"

He held his breath, but nothing happened. The revolver remained close to his temple, but no hot lead tore through his brains. After a dreadful moment of waiting he braced himself sufficiently to look into the Baron's face.

He breathed again!

He had been right. It was a woman.

"What sort of a woman?" the Baron asked harshly.

"A sister, since you ask the question. I won't say a beautiful one, because all sisters are beautiful. And that's all I'm telling you, Baron. The rest is a matter for

141

negotiation between us."

"You know where Walter Paine is now?"

"I know where Walter Paine is now!"

"Take him away!" The Baron lowered his automatic and returned to his desk. "Tie him up and watch him!" he snapped. "I must talk with the others. I call you later on!"

"Okay, Baron!" The taxi-driver and Antonio closed in on Blake and led him unresisting from the room. As they passed through the hall, Blake knew a wild desire to kick over that telephone, save that it would be useless. His time had not yet come, in spite of the respite his wits had gained him. He must be patient, he told himself. Must watch, and wait.

"Couldn't I have a wash?" he asked the taxi-driver as they descended the stairs to the basement.

"You don't want no wash!" was all the fellow said.

They took him back to the cellar and tied him up again. Gagged him, too. Then they propped him against one of the walls and left him; but a minute or two later the taxi-driver returned with a candle stuck in a saucer which he placed upon the floor outside the open cellar door.

Then he sat himself down on the doorstep to wait.

How long they sat there staring at each other, Blake could not be sure. It might have been ten minutes, or it might have been an hour. But whatever it was, and as though feeling the cold, the taxi-driver presently turned half away from him, turned up his jacket collar, propped his back against the lintel of the door, and fell to staring up the passage.

And now Blake started cautiously to work. By hook or by crook he had to get himself free before the Baron called to them; it was his only chance. He had bluffed the man once, but he could scarcely hope to bluff him again and, in any event, it was no part of the Baron's plan to allow him to escape with his life. He would not be such a fool. To do that would be to sign his own death warrant, and whatever else he might be, the man was certainly not crazy.

As he worked quietly at the cord which bound his wrists, Blake went over again in his mind everything that had happened to him since leaving "The White Cat." There could be no doubt but that he was at the heart of the organisation which was responsible not only for the framing of Isobel Ensor but also for the attack upon young Maynard in Ladcaster village. This man they called Baron appeared to be the head of it, and there could be little doubt but that Anna Muller was one of its leading members, and its object, so far as he could see at present, was the collection and dispatch of aircraft secrets to Germany.

He wondered who was working the racket inside the Southern Aircraft Company's place—because someone was! Isobel Ensor had been convicted of the last delinquency, but if she were innocent of the treachery, who was guilty? If she had not photographed those plans, who had? And who had deliberately framed her? Anna Muller had given her the secret camera, but it was not Anna Muller who had photographed the plans—couldn't have been, because they were not in existence when she bolted back to Germany. And even if—as Blake now thought likely—Anna Muller never had gone back to Germany, she still could not have photographed them since no one save the heads of the firm were allowed access to the plans. And Isobel Ensor herself, of course.

A sudden trickle of dust down the coal chute at the far end of the cellar broke the thread of Blake's cogitations and caused him to pause in his labours. Rats, he thought. So apparently did the taxi-driver, for after a suspicious glance in Blake's direction he turned back with a shrug to his contemplation of the passage and the guttering candle in front of him.

Cautiously Blake started to work again on his bonds, but he had scarcely got going when another rattle of dust down the chute caused the taxi-driver to turn for a second time. Upon that occasion he looked past Blake to the real seat of the noise, and watching him, Blake's heart gave a sudden and violent bound.

What gave him the idea he did not stop to think. But suddenly—so suddenly that it left him breathless and shaking—he thought of Tinker. No dust had come down the chute before. There had been no sound from anywhere. Now two lots had come down in quick succession. And even as he stared in that same direction, a third cataract came rattling down.

The taxi-driver rose to his feet. It was plain that he, too, thought the phenomenon demanded some investigation. Picking up the saucer containing the candle, he went over there, shielding the flame as he went.

Blake watched him with bated breath. He watched him

pick his way carefully over the piled coal. Saw him reach the end of the cellar and, holding the candle high above his head, peer up the angle of the chute.

What happened then Blake scarcely saw. He had an impression of something thrusting like lightning down the chute—something long and thick that locked like a pole. In the same split second the candle flew one way and the saucer the other as the taxi-driver clapped both hands to his middle and folded over like a shut knife. In the darkness that followed the extinguishing of the candle there was a terrific sliding noise in the chute itself, and then the sound of a crash. A moment later someone came staggering towards him over the coal.

Blake tried to cry out, but his gag prevented him. He banged his bound feet on the floor to indicate his whereabouts, for he knew it was Tinker now. But when a moment later the new-comer struck a match, he saw to his consternation that it was not Tinker, but a much older, heavier man. A man wearing the uniform of a well-known London dairy company.

"I've been waiting for that swab ever since they brought you down here!" he grinned, as he cut away Blake's gag and freed his hands and feet. "Did you observe the unerring marksmanship with which I drove the end of that line-prop wallop into the blighter's midriff? I'd have been crowned Queen of the May for a deed like that had I lived in ten-sixty-six."

Blake staggered to his feet. He was momentarily bewildered. The whole thing had happened so fast that he could scarcely grasp even now that he was free.

"I thought you were my assistant!" he gasped. "But you are not. Who are you? And how did you get here?"

"You saw how I got here," chuckled the newcomer. "Down the coal chute yonder. As to who I am—when I've washed my beautiful face, shaved, and cleaned my teeth, you'll recognise in me the Pride of the Secret Service— your old friend, Mister Beltom Brass, Esquire!"

THE TENTH CHAPTER

The House In Hampstead.

THERE WAS A long minute of silence.

Standing there in the dust and gloom of the cellar, Blake stared at the Secret Service ace as though even now he could not believe the evidence of his own ears.

Finally he drew a deep breath.

"Well, you're welcome, anyhow!" he said. "Never more so, in fact. But what brings you here; and why the uniform?"

"Oh, that's a long story, I'm afraid. Question now is: how are we going to get out of this place?"

"How about the chute?"

"No bon! That's a one-way entry. You can slide down it, but you can't slide up it, unfortunately. We shall have to find another way."

"Couldn't we make it between us?"

"Not without a rope. I've been hanging round here for ten days, and I know. You're not armed, of course?"

"No."

"Nor am I, unfortunately. And we're in a tough spot, Blake. I wouldn't have known you were here save that I saw a light shining up the chute and heard them talking. They don't mean you any good."

"Who's the bird they call the baron?"

"The owner of the place—Thomas Grey. He's a stockbroker in the City, and Julie's father."

"Whose father?" Blake asked sharply.

"Julie. The girl with the red hair. Only her name isn't Julie, and her hair isn't red."

"What d'you mean?"

"I saw her in Berlin the year before the war. She was in close confab with Von Strownitz, who at that time ran the German Secret Service. Ten days ago I ran across her in Piccadilly, and in spite of her changed colour and complexion I recognised her again. I wondered what the deuce she was up to in England, and I followed her. She came here. I put on a man to watch her; he didn't last twenty-four hours."

"You mean—they got him?"

"I don't know. He just disappeared. So I came along myself, having first of all arranged to muscle in on the milk delivery. I thought I might get chatty with the cook or the housemaid or something—but oysters are talkative bivalves compared with the domestic staff of this establishment. How did you get here?"

Blake ignored the question. Time enough for that later on.

"Where are we?" he asked instead.

"The Rowans, Church Avenue, Hampstead."

"Do you know how many people there are upstairs?"

Beltom Brass shook his head.

"But there must be a tidy few," he said. "Locally, Mr. Thomas Grey has the reputation of being a socialite. He entertains on a considerable scale, and he's entertaining to-night, judging by the number of cars that have rolled up while I've been lying in the shrubbery. I'd have had the numbers of 'em if it weren't so damnably dark."

Blake nodded. He was thinking of what the Baron had said about "talking with the others." He pushed the cellar door ajar, and glanced down the darkness of the passage.

"How about the kitchen door?" he asked.

"We couldn't make it, old man. There are two or three men in there now. I've heard them talking, and if I'm right in my theory about this place, they're killers."

"You may take it that you are right, Brass!" the detective told him grimly. "I don't know precisely what you're after, but I can tell you in advance that when you slid down that coal chute you slid into as pretty a nest of spies and traitors as any I've ever seen. How far are we from the local police station?"

"About a mile and a half. Maybe two. Why?"

"And you're working on your own, I suppose?"

"Naturally," shrugged the Secret Service man.

"Nobody knows you're here? Or that that girl is in England?"

"The Secret Service does not report methods. Only results!" Brass replied a bit stiffly.

"I thought as much. And as I've said before, Brass, you carry secrecy too far in your service. If we get scuppered

149

nobody will have the benefit of your work. The whole gang will go on completely unmolested."

"What about you? Doesn't Tinker know you're here?"

"Unfortunately, no. I didn't have a chance to tell him. Nor will anyone ever trace me here. I was fool enough to step into their private taxi, and they sloshed me right away. That's how I came here. Nor does anyone know about the girl. I didn't see her myself until to-night."

"You knew her, too?"

"Yes. I recognised her from a photograph. She is Anna Muller. Anne Miller, as she called herself."

The Secret Service man started.

"Anna Muller?" he exclaimed. "I seem to know that name."

"She worked at the Southern Aircraft Construction Company's place. It was she who gave the camera-watch—"

"The Isobel Ensor case!" Brass whispered. "By golly, I remember now. And she's that girl?"

"The same. I'm certain of it. Matter of fact, I'm working on that case, and it's my belief that Isobel Ensor is innocent. She was framed. And it's my guess that Anna Muller and this man they call the Baron are the two people who framed her. There may be others in the plot—Eddy Paul, of the White Cat restaurant in Charlotte Street, for example—but those two are the real culprits. I'm telling you this in case you should get through alive and I fail. The Baron offered me my life in return for the whereabouts of the man Isobel Ensor says could provide her with an alibi—"

"You mean Walter Paine?"

"That's the fellow. And I think he's not dead, as the prosecution maintained at her trial. He's alive and well, and it's my belief that he could not only supply Isobel Ensor with her alibi, but he could also tell us who was responsible for the theft of the plans. That, at least, is the impression I got from the Baron. And that, I think, explains his fear of the man."

"We're after Walter Paine ourselves," Beltom Brass said slowly.

"You?"

"We've been after him ever since he was mentioned at the trial. We thought it as well to make sure, because if Isobel Ensor was right in what she said it obviously meant that the real traitor was still at large and still able to function."

Blake clicked an impatient tongue.

"Pity you people have to be so secret with everything," he said. "If the defence had known that at the time it would have saved no end of trouble. Who is after him?"

"Mademoiselle."

"Good lor'!" Blake knew to whom he referred, of course—there was only one "mademoiselle." He meant the Mademoiselle Yvonne de Braselieu, star of the French Secret Service until France's collapse, and since then attached to De Gaulle and England. "Has she any news of him?"

"None, save that he was smuggled out of St. John's Convent Hospital at Amiens, and completely disappeared."

"Well, that's something, anyway!"

Blake was silent for a moment. "If you get out of this alive, you might say the Baron is moving heaven and earth to get him first. She ought to be put on her guard."

"She will be," Beltom Brass said flatly.

Blake glanced at him. He could trust Brass to do that, he knew, in view of the fact that the pair were half in love with each other.

"Right!" he said briskly. "Now we've two chances, Brass. One, the front door. And two, the telephone. If we can make the front door without raising the alarm, that's the way we'll go. If not, we'll try to dial 999 on the telephone and bawl for help. If the station is no farther away than a couple of miles, help might reach us before we get scuppered. If it doesn't—well, it can't be helped. Okay?"

"Lead on!" was all Mr. Brass said to that. "Or wait!" With the remaining light from the candle he searched the coals for two long, fairly narrow slivers that he could hold comfortably in each clenched fist. "Right!" he said then, the light of battle flaring strongly in his eyes. "An' heaven 'elp the blighter who gets this little lot!" he added fervently.

Blake opened the cellar door again and peeped out. The house was silent as a grave.

"The kitchen's at the end of this passage, on the left," Brass whispered. "The stairs must lead up on the right, I imagine."

"They do!" Blake had already been up there, and knew. "By the way," he said, his hand still on the door, "you said just now that that girl's name was not Julie, nor was her hair red. You were speaking of when you saw her in Berlin, I take it? What was her name then?"

"I don't know. I didn't hear. But obviously, since she's German, her name wouldn't be Julie Grey. And at that time she was a brunette."

"You didn't connect her with Anna Muller?"

"I didn't know Anna Muller. I've never met her in my life. She'd gone back to Germany long before the Isobel Ensor case happened. Anna Muller was never anything but a name to me until you yourself connected it just now with this girl upstairs."

Blake nodded his understanding. He had the feeling that, once out of this place, the solution to the mystery would not be long delayed.

"Come on!" he said softly.

Dousing the candle, they started off cautiously along the passage. As soon as their eyes became accustomed to the darkness they were able to make out the faint glow ahead caused by the lights in the hall shining down the basement stairs. There were two flights of those, Blake knew, and they constituted the worst danger points, since once embarked upon those there could be neither hiding nor retreat.

They reached the foot of them safely, and paused for a moment, listening. Behind them a shorter passage ended in a closed door—the kitchen door, as Brass supposed. And from beyond that came the murmur of several voices. Upstairs, however, all seemed silent and deserted: and remembering what he had seen up there, Blake thought it likely that the baron and his associates would be deep

153

in discussion in one or other of the rooms leading off the hall.

Testing the bottom step carefully for creaks, he commenced the ascent towards the light—Beltom Brass hard on his heels and both men stepping only on the extreme outer edges of the stairs. The farther they went, the stronger became the light; but they reached the first landing without anyone giving the alarm, and with high hopes set out on the second flight.

Their luck was in! Mounting steadily, they reached the top and stood for a moment listening, but still there was no sound. Either the hall was deserted, or whoever was on guard there was standing still. Or was he, too, listening?

Steadily Blake crept forward along the wall. The layout of the place was roughly in the form of a letter "T," of which they were now in the left "ear." Straight ahead of them the right "ear" led to the stairs giving access to the upper regions, while round the corner to their right lay the upright of the "T"—the main entrance-hall, a place of some thirty feet long by fifteen wide.

The telephone, so far as Blake could remember, was on their side of the hall and some yard or so round the corner.

The passage in which they were standing was some fifteen paces long and three wide, but there were no doors leading off it, and the left hand side was largely a balustrade overlooking the second flight of stairs down to the basement. It was thickly carpeted and their feet made no sound, which was all to the good. If only the main hall was empty, the rest would be easy.

A yard before the corner, Blake dropped to his knees and peeped. His heart sank. Contrary to the hall being empty there were two men there. They were seated on chairs upon either side of the door, and Blake knew instinctively that each was armed. The man on the right was staring at the wall ahead of him, but the one on the left was watching the door through which the taxi-driver had thrust Blake for his interview with the Baron. The front door they were guarding was closed, and probably locked. The distance between them and Blake was some thirty feet.

The detective saw at a glance that there was no hope that way. They would be shot down before they were half-way across the hall; and even should they succeed in reaching the door unharmed, they could never hope to get it open before the Baron and the rest of the gang rushed out to take them in the rear.

He drew back his head and indicated as much to Beltom Brass. Then he went forward again to look for the telephone.

For a full minute he knelt silent, considering. The lacquered stand bearing the instrument was some four feet round the corner, just where he had remembered it. And it looked to be about four feet six high. He estimated the main cord at five feet, which—assuming that he could lift the instrument without being seen—would enable him to bring it round the corner into the passage and there dial his number in comparative safety.

There was no time to waste. At any moment one of the doors in the passage opposite might open and reveal them crouching there to whoever came out. At any moment one of the guards on the main door might think to stretch his legs by a stroll to their end of the hall.

With a brief glance at his companion, Blake eased himself forward and slowly stretched up his hand towards the white-enamelled instrument on its lacquered stand. His fingers touched it. Encircled its base. He was just about to lift it when the guard on the left of the door looked directly his way.

Blake froze. He knew the man could not have heard anything, but he might have caught an impression of movement. Not daring to breathe, he waited—motionless, immobile; but the fellow's eyes were fixed at a man's height, he was not looking near the floor. And presently he looked away again, apparently satisfied that all was well.

Blake breathed again. Bracing himself, in a single movement he lifted the telephone from its stand and brought it—receiver and all—noiselessly round the corner to where he was crouching.

It just reached. Neither of the guards had seen him, and neither had observed the movement.

He dialled 999.

"Hallo?" came the answer so loudly that it seemed to ring through the house.

Beltom Brass crept nearer the corner. Blake had not reckoned on a bull-voice like that.

"Listen!" he whispered desperately. "The Rowans, Church Avenue, Hampstead. Sexton Blake. Send help immediately. Armed."

"What?" bawled the voice.

"Look out!" urged Beltom Brass under his breath. "They've heard us, Blake!"

"The Rowans, Church Avenue!" Blake repeated, sweat standing out on his brow. "Sexton Blake here. Break in! There are spies here: Murder! Come in force—"

"Look out!" urged Beltom Brass, leaping to his feet. The door across the way had opened, and there on the threshold was the Baron himself. Feet were thundering across the hall. Someone was shouting the alarm down below. Brass ducked as a bullet spanged into the wall behind him. "In here!" he shouted.

"Hurry!" Blake called into the phone. With a sudden wrench he snapped the instrument from its cord and hurled it full into the face of the nearest gunman. The Baron fired. Missed. Fired again. Brass had reached a door across the other side of the passage and directly facing the main hall. He'd got it open.

"In here!" he shouted.

Blake caught up the lacquered stand and sent it spinning through the air at the Baron. He ducked. A bullet from one of the gunmen nicked Blake's ear like a white-hot razor, but the next second that man staggered beneath the impact of a flung chair. Doors were opening everywhere. Men seemed to be coming from everywhere. Measuring his distance, Blake went through his own door in a flat dive, and a split second later Brass banged it shut and turned the key.

The detective was up again almost before he touched the ground.

"Stack up the furniture!" he gasped.

"Did you get through?"

"Yes!"

"Good man!" Brass laughed as a bullet ploughed through the panels of the door. "I wish I had a gun!"

They had taken refuge in what looked to be the dining-room of the mansion. There was a heavy sideboard alongside the door—an enormous thing of mahogany and glass. Hauling and shoving they got it across the door, and then piled up the heavy dining-table to back it.

"How about the window?"

"That bookcase will do!"

They wrenched the various sections from the wall and piled them one upon another against the window. If they could hold out for ten minutes or so help would arrive. Chairs went on top of the bookcase. Then a determined onslaught on the door smashed the lock and pushed the obstructing furniture a good foot into the room.

"Heave!" gasped Beltom Brass, as they pushed it back again.

The sudden smashing of glass at the window caused Blake to rush back there. He had grabbed a poker from the fireplace, and as an arm came through the frame, pushing away the bookcase, he lashed out violently. A wild yell of pain indicated that he had scored a bull. The arm disappeared. A moment later he was back again at the main barrier, adding his weight to that of Beltom Brass, who was straining mightily to keep out the attack from that direction.

The end came almost as suddenly as it had started. One moment the defenders were gasping to maintain their advantage, and the next—so suddenly that both of them slid over—the pressure on the door was released and the furniture shot forward with a crack against the wall.

"Eh?" panted Beltom Brass.

"They've given up!" Blake said.

"They're beating it!"

"You mean—the police are here?"

"Either that, or they've realised their danger in staying any longer!"

They stood for a moment, listening, but neither could hear anything beyond his own laboured breathing. Suddenly Blake sniffed.

"Petrol!" he whispered.

"You're right!" the Secret Service man confirmed. "I was just thinking the same thing. They're going to fire the place! Roast us out!"

"Or destroy us! And with us, the evidence!"

They listened for a moment longer, but when Brass would have pulled back the dining-table, Blake stopped him.

"Half a minute!" he whispered. "They're probably waiting on the far side for us—a trap! I can't smell fire yet."

"Nor can I, now you mention it!"

They were still undecided when the scream of brakes outside heralded the arrival of a car. It was followed by a second and a third. It did not need the ensuing onslaught on the front door and the almost immediate blast of a police whistle to assure them that help was at hand.

"Hi!" bawled Beltom Brass, seizing upon the table and dragging it back. "Here we are!"

Half a minute later an inspector and sergeant of the Metropolitan Police forced their way through the door and paused in amazement at sight of the two men whom they found confronting them.

Mr. Brass bowed.

"The Bearded Wonder and the Milkman King!" he said solemnly. "And very pleased to meet you, inspector!"

Blake took the bewildered man aside. He was not able to go into details, he explained, but he wanted the house searched and anyone in it taken into custody. "You'll find one man in the coal-cellar," he said. "And watch out for fire, inspector. I think they've put petrol down somewhere."

They went out into the hall, where the inspector issued the necessary orders to his men. Blake smiled as he looked round the ruin. The fight had been sharp and short, but effective. There was scarcely a thing that was not broken.

Suddenly he paused.

"What's that?" he said.

They listened. From somewhere close at hand was coming a curious knocking sound.

"By gad! There's somebody locked up somewhere!" Brass ejaculated. He looked behind him. "In one of these rooms, I think!"

"It isn't! It's down below somewhere!" Blake flashed back. "Let's look!"

He raced away down the stairs to the basement. The knocking was much louder now, and seemed to be coming from where Brass had placed the kitchen. It was the kitchen, Blake discovered a moment later—and empty. But from behind a door in one corner—

"Break it down!" he ordered sharply.

One of the constables had a tyre-lever in his hand—a useful weapon. In less than a couple of minutes he had prised back the lock and turned the handle.

The door came open with a bang.

"Hell!" gasped Beltom Brass, as a mummy-like figure fell out into the room from behind it.

It was Blake who caught the man. He was gagged and bound and helpless. Lowering him gently to the floor he untied the cloth that was bound across the man's face— and then almost dropped it in amazement.

For a second he was speechless. It took a lot to stagger Sexton Blake, but he was certainly staggered then.

"Who is he?" whispered Beltom Brass.

"It's Mr. Ogilvie!" Blake heard himself say. "Works manager to the Southern Aircraft Construction Company!"

THE ELEVENTH CHAPTER

Back to Baker Street.

OGILVIE'S FIRST WORDS were to ask for a telephone. No sooner had they cut him free and stood him on his feet when he clapped a hand to his head and demanded a phone.

"What's happened?" Blake asked him.

"I don't know!" he gasped. He was very pale. His hands were trembling visibly. "I must get through to the works! Now! At once!"

"I don't know if there's a phone left in the house!" Blake turned as he spoke. "Come upstairs!" he said. "We'll see." He went to the room where he had interviewed the Baron. "Ah!" he said, picking up a telephone on the desk. "Yes, and it's working!"

"Thank Heaven for that!" Ogilvie took the receiver and crumpled into the Baron's chair. He dialled a number. While he was waiting he mopped his brow, breathing heavily the while. He was plainly on the verge of collapse.

Suddenly he stiffened.

"Southern Aircraft?" he gasped. "Mr. Ogilvie speaking. Put me through to Mr. Barraclough—quickly!"

He waited again, his free hand constantly combing his hair. Beltom Brass had entered now, and was watching him curiously from the hearth.

Suddenly he spoke again.

"Is that you, Barraclough? Thank God for that! Ogilvie here. Listen, Barraclough!—something's happened! I want you to go to the Blue Print Department and make sure the safe's all right. What? I don't know, I tell you! I've been kidnapped. No, you fool—I'm not drunk! They're after the plans of the new fighter. Make sure the safe's all right, and then see that the key's on its hook in the office and that both the watchmen are there. Put an extra guard on, till I come! What? Yes, I'll wait here for you. But hurry, man! Hurry!"

He sat back in his chair, and for the first time his eyes lifted directly to Blake's.

"How did you come to find me?" he asked.

"We heard you knocking," Blake told him. Overhead, he could hear the police ransacking every room for signs of the late occupants. "But how did you get here, Ogilvie?"

"I don't know. They must have been waiting for me. I left my flat at seven, as I always do, and took a taxi to the club—"

"Where did you get the taxi?" Blake interrupted.

"From the rank. At least, it was coming towards me as I went out."

"Go on!"

164

"Well, I got in." Ogilvie paused, and frowned, and again he passed his hand over his head in that curious fashion. "I don't know what happened then—not exactly," he complained. "I suppose there must have been somebody else sitting in the taxi, although I didn't see anyone in the dark. Anyway, something hit me in the face, and then a cloth was over my mouth. I think it was chloroform. At any rate, the next thing I knew I was lying on a couch in a strange room with three men watching me. I tried to sit up, and one of them gave me a drink. I felt a bit better after that. I asked them what had happened, and they laughed. Then one of them began to ask me about the plans of Southern Aircraft's new fighter."

"What time was it then?"

"I've no idea. I don't even know where I am!"

"No matter. Go on!"

"Well, as they went on talking, mad as it seemed I began to realise that I'd been kidnapped by spies. I began to realise that they were pumping me. And as time went on, I realised something worse than that—I saw that they intended to kill me unless I told them what they wanted to know!"

"Did you tell 'em?" Beltom Brass cut in from the hearth.

"Did I—hell!" said Ogilvie with more spirit than he had hitherto shown. "I told them to go to blazes. I told them I didn't know the secret, anyhow. I told them no one but the designer knew that—and he wasn't sure of it, yet! Then they started threatening me with all manner of things, and finally they said give me time to think it over. The swine tied me up like a mummy and put me away

165

in that cupboard. Then I heard what I thought sounded like shots, and I thought it might mean rescue. So I began banging my tied hands against the door. Then you people came!"

He turned back to the phone again.

"Come on! Come on!" he urged under his breath.

"Is that true about only the designer knowing the actual secret of the new fighter?" Blake asked after a minute or two of silence.

Ogilvie looked up from the telephone.

"In a way—yes," he said. "The general plan is there, of course; but the real secret of its performance—the real secret of its amazing speed—that is still on paper. It's still being experimented with—just a moment!" He addressed himself to the phone. "Yes?" he said. "Yes?" He listened, eagerly, and presently his face broke into smile. "You're sure, Barraclough?" he asked. "Good! That's fine! I'll be with you as soon as I can get there. My God, what a night!"

He replaced the receiver and stood up. Relief was written all over him; he was a different man.

"The plans are safe, anyhow!" he told them. "How can I get a car? I must go out there immediately. I'm scared. I'm going to arrange for a military guard, or something. It's too big a responsibility with people like these still at large. You won't want me again here, I take it?"

Blake shook his head.

"We can probably send you in a police car," he said.

"I'd be grateful if you could. You know where to find me should anything turn up?"

166

Blake nodded and went outside to see the inspector. He found him talking with his sergeant in the hall.

"I was just coming to find you, Mr. Blake," the inspector said when he saw him. "There isn't a soul in the place. Not even in the coal cellar!"

"You're sure?"

"I've been down there myself. They've cleared off and taken their casualties with them, apparently—manservants, maidservants, and all!" His eyes switched to Ogilvie's who had come into the hall with Beltom Brass. "That gentleman's the only one they've left behind," he said.

"And he hasn't got what they want," grinned the Secret Service man. "Evidently, they don't believe in carrying excess baggage, inspector! How about a car?"

That was arranged, and a few minutes later Mr. Ogilvie left in the care of a stalwart constable. Before he went, he thanked Blake profusely for all that he had done, and promised to help in any way open to him should his unknown assailants be captured. From the description he gave, the chief of those assailants was evidently the Baron himself, but the other two Blake failed to recognise either as the taxi-driver or the man he had heard addressed as Antonio.

"Well," said the local inspector when the car had gone. "If anyone had told me, even an hour ago, that Mr. Thomas Grey was a German spy—I'd have arrested him as a raving lunatic!"

"That's why he is a German spy!" shrugged the Secret Service ace. "How long have you known him?"

167

"Ten years or more. And in all that time I've never heard a word against him. He's one of our best-known men. The wealthy stockbroker par excellence!"

"Of course he is! They all are!" grinned Beltom Brass. "That's how they get away with it. Some of 'em have been in this country since the last war, digging 'emselves in and entrenching themselves behind a facade of respectability so as to be ready to jump off with both feet when this war started. Trouble all along this country has been that people expect German spies to sneak round in wide-brimmed hats and black cloaks, carrying a smoking bomb in one hand and a tommy-gun in the other. They don't! The German spy of to-day is the very ordinary bloke next door—old Tomkins, who's worked at the factory for ten or fifteen years and goes every Saturday to the dogs—isn't that so, Blake?"

The private practitioner looked up at the sound of his name. It was plain that he had not been listening.

"Sorry!" he apologised. And then: "I was thinking about Ogilvie," he admitted. "Wondering why they'd stopped to collect everybody else but left him behind. There doesn't seem any sense in that move—that I can see."

"Unless they thought we shouldn't find him! And that they could come back for him later on."

"But if it's the plans they're after, Ogilvie is their king piece, surely?"

"Perhaps they hadn't time to collect him?" the inspector suggested, but Blake shook his head. "They had time to collect the taxi-driver from the cellar," he pointed out, "And Ogilvie was worth fifty taxi-drivers, remember!"

"But he didn't know the secret they were after, Blake!"

"Didn't he?" Blake hunched his shoulders. "He knew a good deal about it, anyway," he said. "Must have done. But apart from that, by leaving Ogilvie behind to tell his story, they've let us know that it's the plans they're after. They've played right into our hands, don't you see? Given us both time and opportunity to take precautions against them. You heard what Ogilvie said just now about arranging for a military guard to—"

He stopped. For a second he stood rigid, staring.

"Damn!" he ripped out then, snapping his fingers as he turned and leapt for the basement stairs—but he was too late. He was too late by half a minute. Even as he reached the first landing, a constable came racing up from below bawling: "Fire! Fire!"

"Look out, sir!" he shouted when Blake thrust him aside and tore on down the remaining stairs.

The corridor was filled with swirling black clouds of greasy smoke—petrol! Holding his nose, Blake reached the kitchen in time to see the whole of one corner burst into flames. He tried to get in but the heat drove him back. He had no option but to retire. Beltom Brass, who had followed him down, grabbed the back of his jacket and literally hauled him out to the stairs.

"There's your answer!" he gasped as they fought their way back to the hall. "The swine never intended him to tell anybody anything! They never intended him to live! They banked on him being roasted alive before anyone could rescue him—that's the petrol we smelt, you remember? They must have soaked that cupboard in the stuff, and then put a slow match to it!"

"Why a slow match?"

"To give themselves a chance to get away, of course! They didn't want to have the house in flames before they themselves were well clear of it—and clear of the immediate vicinity, too! Grey was known, remember! He might have been stopped and recognised by the police. Looks like they hoped to roast us; as well! Nobody knew that any of us were here so that our remains—if any— would have been taken to be theirs, while they got clean away to start up somewhere else!"

They reached the hall in time to see the inspector running from the room Ogilvie had just used. He had phoned for the brigade, he told them.

"We'd better get out of this, quick!" he advised. "It'll go like dry tinder!"

"Wait!" Blake dashed into the room and literally tore open the drawers in his desk. They were empty. There was not a thing there. Either he had cleared them out himself, or he had been too astute ever to use them.

"Come on!" Beltom Brass shouted as a vicious red tongue of flame shot up past the window.

They ran outside. Already the lower part of the house was sheathed in fire, in a few minutes' time it would be a beacon visible for miles away. There must have been petrol stowed away in that basement, judging by the thick black smoke.

Suddenly the flames turned to green; then to blue.

"What the devil's that?" bawled the inspector above the din.

"Chemicals!" laughed Beltom Brass. "Signal fires! If there's a Hun plane within sight, he'll like enough read from that display that their chief spy is in trouble. That'll put 'em on their guard when his next reports come in— are they genuine, or not? Catch the idea? The Hun never leaves anything to chance, inspector!"

His voice was drowned in the clatter of the first engine to arrive. By now the flames were bursting from the third floor windows and it was plain that the whole building was doomed. If anything had been left behind—any papers or anything—they would never be found now. Nothing would ever be found! As Brass had rightly observed, the Huns left nothing to chance.

Another engine arrived, and yet a third. Seeing that he could do nothing else at the moment, Blake suggested to the Secret Service man that they return to the flat.

"I've got something I'd like to show you," he said.

"Something in a bottle?" grinned Mr. Brass.

"That, too, if you like!"

They borrowed a police car for the journey. When some half-hour later they arrived in Baker Street, Blake let himself in with his key and straightaway made for the bath-room.

"We'd better tidy up a bit," he said. "We don't want Mrs Bardell in hysterics!"

That done, and feeling all the better for it, the two retired to the sitting-room where Blake rang for his landlady.

"No," she said, in response to his inquiry for Tinker. "He hasn't come home yet, but he's telephoned four times to ask if you've come home. Very h'agitated I thought 'e seemed," she added gratuitously.

"Did he leave no message?"

"No, not a word, sir."

Blake thought for a moment. "All right!" he said then, as soon as Mrs. Bardell had left the room he crossed to the concealed wall-safe, opened it, and came back with a photograph showing two girls walking along Hastings front.

"Recognise either of those?" he asked.

Brass took the photograph, glanced at it, and whistled.

"Where did you get this?' he demanded.

"D'you recognise them?"

"Of course! One is Isobel Ensor, and the other's the red-haired girl—the one you say is Anna Muller."

"Correct! But what I'm trying to get at is this: is the girl I call Anna Muller—the one in that photograph there—the same girl that you saw talking to Von Strownitz in Berlin the year before the war?"

"Yes," Brass said without the hesitation. "She's the same girl."

"You're quite sure?"

"I'm positive. In fact, it's easier to recognise her from this photograph than it was when I saw her in the flesh in Piccadilly. You were darned lucky to strike this, you know!"

"I appreciate that myself. In a photograph red hair comes out like brown hair, or any other colour hair. Matter of fact, I had no idea what colour Anna Muller's hair was, so that I experienced no shock when I saw that it was red. All I remembered was the face; and when I saw that girl standing at the foot of the stairs in the White Cat restaurant, I knew her in a moment for the girl of that photograph. For Anna Muller!"

"But from where did you get the photograph, Blake—that's what intrigues me. You may not know it, but while the Isobel Ensor case was proceeding, we of the Secret Service searched high and low for a photograph of this much-discussed Anna Muller. We wanted to check up on her, and try to locate her, you understand? Up till then, none of us had even heard of such a girl, much less seen her—there was no reason why we should. She had been just an unknown clerk in the employ of Southern Aircraft, and she'd been left for five or six months before anything happened. Had I seen that photograph at the time of the trial, Isobel Ensor would have stood even less chance than she did, for at once I'd have recognised her friend as the girl I had seen talking with Von Strownitz in Berlin. In short, for the spy she undoubtedly was—and is!"

"Which is why you never found the photograph," Blake laughed softly. "Actually, I got it from the woman who owns the flat they lived in. It was taken in July, before the war, while both the girls were on holiday at Hastings, but it didn't arrive at the flat until Anna Muller had bolted—which explains why it's there at all. It is, I should imagine, the only photograph extant of her; and that wouldn't have been there had she known of it. She'd have destroyed it for a certainty, before leaving. But she didn't know of it! And when it came by post, Isobel Ensor kept it—naturally."

"But why didn't the Service find it?"

"Because when Isobel Ensor was arrested for her friendship with Anna Muller, her landlady—who appears to be genuinely fond of the girl—saw that photograph in the flat and realised its capacity for harm. So she took it away, and hid it in her own flat, determined to keep it dark. Yesterday, however, when I went round there to collect some clothes of Miss Ensor's, we had a chat. And when she found that I was working to secure Miss Ensor's pardon, and that—at any rate in my opinion—it was Anna Muller who was responsible for all the trouble, she showed me that photograph."

"My gosh! And then you have the nerve to tell me you don't believe in luck!" snorted Mr. Brass. "You get that photograph one day, and the very next, for no reason at all, you walk into the White Cat and see the blessed girl in question standing slap-bang-wallop in front of you!"

"Scarcely that!" Blake protested. "In the first place I had a very good reason for going to the White Cat. And in the second, I have the feeling that Anna Muller has been frequenting the White Cat for months past. I have the feeling that I might have seen her there a dozen times had I had any reason for going to the place. She was perfectly safe there, because nobody knew her. All the old lot had gone!"

"Have it your own way." The Secret Service man pitched his cigarette-end into the fire and rose. "It's the dickens of a mess-up, whichever way you look at it," he said. "What's your next move, Blake?"

"I'm going up to Dillborough."

"To where?"

"Dillborough," Blake said again. "I've a hunch I can pin something on Anna Muller that might yet pull down the whole gang of 'em!"

"How do you mean?"

Very briefly he related the story of all that had happened

to John Maynard—or Sergeant-Pilot Percy Allen, as the R.A.F. still insisted upon calling him. He explained why young Maynard had joined the Air Force, and precisely why he had tried to jump his Spitfire rather than be baulked at the last moment by the consequences of the shooting affray at the White House in Ladcaster village.

"Now the girl who stopped Maynard that night was a very smart platinum blonde," he said. "She was tall and slim, and she wore—"

"Anna Muller?" gasped the Secret Service man.

"I think so," Blake smiled. "I believe that platinum blondes can be turned out in a few hours, and that a platinum blonde can revert to a redhead—or a brunette—in a similar period of time. Certainly Anna Muller appears to be addicted to that type of disguise; and beyond any doubt whatever the problem of finding Walter Paine is the prime concern of the gang. It is that necessity that is motivating all their efforts. It is that necessity which forced the Baron to reveal himself to me to-night. And if it's that which motivated the attack on John Maynard at Ladcaster, then it's a thousand pounds to a penny that the girl who stopped Maynard was Anna Muller!"

"But d'you think he'd recognise her again, Blake?"

"Why not?" Blake tapped the photograph and smiled. "As I remarked before, there's nothing here to show whether her hair is red, green, blue, blonde, or any other colour. All it shows here is her face. And I think he'll remember that all right!"

"When are you going?"

"To-night! Now!"

"Is there anything you'd like me to do?"

"Two things, if you will. In the first place, can you get into touch with mademoiselle in France?"

"Yes."

"Then do. Find out where she is and what she's doing, and let me know as soon as you can."

"Right! And the second?"

"Have your men keep an eye on Eddy at the White Cat. I've got a notion that he's the go-between for the various members of the gang, a sort of poste restante for them. And, incidentally, if our theory is correct, when he swore in Court to seeing Isobel Ensor with Larry Rue that night, he was swearing to the blackest lie of his life—and that's where we're going to get him. He's the weakest link of the chain, and he'll snap first, if I'm any judge of a man!"

"Right you are!" They shook hands. But just as Mr. Brass was moving towards the door, the phone rang.

"That'll be Tinker, I expect!" Blake went over to answer it. "Yes?" he said. "Speaking, old son. What's the trouble?" He was silent for a moment, listening. "What?" he gasped so suddenly that Beltom Brass spun round to stare. "You're sure?" There was a short pause, then: "Very well," he said. "Yes, come right along. I'll wait for you."

He replaced the receiver and stood for a moment thinking. Finally he shrugged.

"That was Tinker," he said. "Eddy was found dead on the floor of his office at the White Cat, just after eleven to-night."

"Murdered?"

"Stabbed in the back!"

THE TWELFTH
CHAPTER

Bigwigs Confer.

TWO DAYS LATER Sexton Blake was called to appear before
a board as strange as any that even Whitehall could
remember.

In addition to the Home Secretary and the Minister of
Aircraft Production, there were two members of the War
Cabinet, the Commissioner of the C.I.D., the Chief of the
Secret Service, the Chief of Staff of the R.A.F., Beltom
Brass, and Gervase Crispin, K.C.

Gervase Crispin had already opened the ball by giving a
brief explanation of the John Maynard case and the reasons
which had led him to call in the assistance of Sexton Blake.

"The truth is," he said, "we are faced with a situation for
which I can find no parallel in legal history. If Mr. Blake
is right in his reconstruction of the affair, not only have
we sentenced an innocent girl to ten years' imprisonment,
but, unless we can find and bring to the court the person
of the man, Walter Paine, she will have to stay there while

the guilty go free. Nor is that all! Unless we can find Walter Paine and bring him home, the secrets of our best and latest fighter will almost certainly pass into German hands, exactly as did the secrets of its predecessor!"

He sat down, and everyone round the table looked at Sexton Blake. They already knew the gist of what had happened, since Blake had previously had a long conference with the Home Secretary, and the latter had told them when convening the meeting.

"It's those plans we're afraid of!" the Home Secretary said now. "I don't think we can hold ourselves to blame over the conviction of Isobel Ensor, though that, of course, will have to be straightened out and put right. But the immediate danger—the really desperate danger—is to our latest fighter. If the plans of that find their way into German hands, bang goes the result of nearly two years' work, and bang goes our best chance of winning the war!"

"I'd rather burn both the plane and the plans than risk that!" snapped the Minister of Aircraft Production. "But we want that plane in service, and to get it into service I'm willing to commit murder or anything else. But murder won't help us, it seems!"

"We don't know who to murder!" the Home Secretary retorted. "That's the rub. We've got ten men—any one of whom might be the responsible party. On the other hand, those ten are known to most of us here as among the best brains in the industry and the most loyal of men. And in the end it may be somebody of whom we've never even thought! There's a traitor somewhere, of course! But the question is—where? And who is he?"

"And how can we prove anything against him?" Blake put in quietly. "That's the whole point at issue, sir. I've spent two days in that factory, and it employs ten thousand men. It might be any one of them. That Isobel Ensor was well and truly framed, I think we can frankly admit. I think we can say that we know who framed her. I think beyond the shadow of a doubt it was Anna Muller and the man known as Thomas Grey, until recently a well-known and respected stockbroker in the City—"

"You haven't found, either of those people yet?" interrupted one of the members of the War Cabinet.

"Unfortunately, no. Mind you, I've no doubt but that we shall find them—but my dread is that it might be too late. It's impossible to be sure that part, at any rate, of the plans is not even now in their hands—but I'm positive that the real secret of the plane is still unknown to them. That's why they're still here. That's what they're waiting for."

"We've got a heavy guard on the place, you know!"

"I don't think it matters, sir. These people have brains beyond the ordinary and daring beyond the extraordinary! They'll stick at nothing. They've got a channel of information of which we know nothing, and a channel that can function perfectly well, no matter what guard we put on. Between the man they call the Baron—that's Thomas Grey—and the inner brains of Southern Aircraft, there's a link that can hold fast in spite of all the guards on earth!"

"Well, at any rate, we can cut the works manager out, I suppose—seeing that it's only by the mercy of heaven that those devils didn't roast him alive?"

"Not even him, sir!"

"But dammit, man—"

"Blake thinks all that may have been a blind," Beltom Brass put in wickedly. "He has the notion that Ogilvie might have tried to set himself on fire."

"And kidnapped himself? And tied himself up? And locked himself in that cupboard and thrown away the key from the outside?" snorted the chief of the C.I.D. incredulously. He gave a short laugh. "My dear Mister Blake!" he said. "Where would be the sense in that? What purpose could he possibly have in doing that? Why, dammit—it was he who first put you wise to the fact that they were after the plans at all!

"If he hadn't told you that, you'd never have got anywhere. You'd never have known a thing. And, in any event, since you had never suspected him of anything, why in the world should he risk the success of his scheme, not to mention his life, by forcing upon your attention the fact that he was in that house at all? Why didn't he go away with the others and keep his mouth shut? Why try to put thoughts into your head that were not there?"

"You're not forgetting that Brass has a head, too?"

"I don't follow you."

"Well, what about the others at the top?" the Home Secretary cut in, anxious to pour oil upon what looked like becoming troubled waters between the Yard chief and the private detective. "Have you considered those?"

"Yes, I have."

"Do they pass?"

Blake shrugged.

"Three of them could be arrested to-morrow," he said.

"Probably a fourth. But—"

"What?" gasped several voices at once.

"But that doesn't make them guilty of treachery," Blake went on coolly, glancing with some amusement round the circle of startled faces. "In fact, I mention the detail only to show you how next to impossible it is to comb through these people in the time at our disposal. We've got to take a short cut, gentlemen, that's the crux of the matter—if we're to save that new fighter for England. In other words, we've got to find Walter Paine!"

"Why?" asked one of the members of the War Cabinet.

"Because Walter Paine is not only in a position to clear Miss Ensor of the charge of meeting Larry Rue in the White Cat that night, he can say who did meet Larry Rue!"

"Who told you that?" rapped out the Chief of the C.I.D., who himself had given considerable thought to the matter.

"I deduce it, Sir Edward. And I deduce it from otherwise unexplainable facts. Right from the beginning, both Mr. Crispin and I realised that if the attack on John Maynard was delivered with the object of preventing him from flying to France to locate Walter Paine, then whoever attacked him must himself be interested in having Paine remain lost! That, I think, is self-evident?"

"Quite!" several voices agreed.

"Very well. Our first notion, then, was that someone was afraid of Walter Paine because it was realised that he could provide Isobel Ensor with the alibi she so badly needed. His evidence would go far to cutting the first strands of the web of circumstantial evidence which, over the years, this gang of spies had so carefully woven about her. But also it was realised that if he did that, and Miss Ensor was acquitted, quite obviously the case would be re-opened and the police would pursue their investigations along those new lines. And this time, they thought, they might themselves be suspected. For that reason alone, I think, it became essential to their safety that Paine should be located and scotched, and at all costs kept where he was in Occupied France."

"You think they knew, even then, that Paine was alive?" the Home Secretary asked.

"I'm sure they did," Blake told him. "In fact, the Baron admitted as much. He told me with his own lips—at a time when he never dreamt that I should live to repeat it—that Walter Paine had been taken by a trick from the hospital where he himself had ordered him to be detained. He also confirmed that it was a woman who had got him out, and that that woman was a nursing sister!"

"But what could Paine have known?" protested the Chief of the C.I.D.

"Well, as to that, I have my own ideas, Sir Edward. But, quite apart from theory, it's plain as a pikestaff that the Baron would not have risked trying to murder John Maynard unless the object of Maynard's search would prove fatal to him. In fact, it's my belief that the Baron thought Maynard was flying to France for no other purpose than to fetch Walter Paine home!"

There was a moment of surprised silence. Then the Chief of the C.I.D. shook a doubtful head. He smiled.

"I'm bound to say for you, Blake, that you're never afraid to take long leaps in the dark," he said on a faintly jibing note. "What makes you so sure that it was the Baron who actually arranged the attack on John Maynard?"

"Because the Baron is the head of the whole complicated system over here, with Anna Muller either his daughter or his chief lieutenant, I'm not sure which. In his character as Thomas Grey he had a daughter living with him—except for long periods when she was away 'at school' or 'staying with relatives in the country.' That girl was undoubtedly the girl we know as Anna Muller. The moment I showed John Maynard a photograph of Anna Muller, he said: 'By heavens, that's her! That's Wendy Grantham, Mr. Blake—the girl who stopped me that night with the red M.G.' And if it was Anna Muller who decoyed Maynard to that empty house in Ladcaster, Sir Edward, you may be perfectly certain that it was the Baron and his gang who were waiting for him there!"

Suddenly Blake jumped to his feet.

"But all this is wasting time!" he cried. "What I really want to make clear to you is the fact that, unless we can lay our hands on Walter Paine in the next day or two, we may as well say good-bye to that new fighter forever. It'll be useless to us. It would be foolish to under-estimate either the cunning or the resource of this man we call the Baron. I want you to realise that the circumstances which convicted Isobel Ensor, while allowing him and his gang to go not only free but completely unsuspected—those circumstances are not unique. They have been carefully duplicated in a dozen other directions.

"At this present moment I've no doubt but that there are dozens of other people in key positions who have been similarly tied up. People who, unknown to themselves, have been surrounded with a web of circumstantial evidence which at any moment can be pulled tight—just as it was pulled tight about Isobel Ensor. And with the same disastrous results! Each of these people will in turn be used as a scapegoat for some activity of the Baron—and always the Baron will go free to wreak further trouble for us!"

"But, Mr. Blake—"

"Just a moment, sir? Please allow me to finish. It is truth I am telling you, gentlemen. I say again that all the detail of Isobel Ensor's frame-up was complete before ever Anna Muller left her. It was complete, and ready to be used at a moment's notice. The fact that it was not used for a considerable time only goes to prove the efficacy of the gang's methods. They had no need of a scapegoat! Their activities were passing unnoticed. Their spying was not detected. But suddenly it failed. Something went wrong over the photographs of that first fighter. Somebody tripped. The police got wind of it, and the entire system of collecting information from this country and dispatching it to Germany was in dire peril. So what happens?"

He paused for a moment.

"I'll tell you!" he said. "Like an expert chess player, the Baron calmly plays his check. From the back of the board, where he has held her for just this emergency, he brings out Isobel Ensor, plays her like a master, and so saves both himself and the game!"

He paused again.

"But that isn't all!" he went on when no one spoke. "I am perfectly certain that there are other scapegoats standing

184

by at this very moment, each of them framed tightly in advance to take the rap whenever it should become necessary. At the Southern Aircraft Works, for example, the damnable traitor who photographed that first set of plans was covered by Isobel Ensor. Now that he's ready to communicate the contents of another set, he will be covered by someone else—should a cover become necessary. Who his next victim will be I do not know—but he knows. And Eddy Paul at the White Cat knows—or did know! That's why he was killed. They didn't trust him not to break down under pressure. The moment the Baron realised that we were connecting Anna Muller with the White Cat Restaurant, he knew that Eddy would be questioned—and would likely enough break down. So Eddy was promptly murdered before he had the chance to speak at all!"

"Well, what do you suggest?" the Home Secretary asked, after a long silence.

"We've got to find Walter Paine, sir—that's the first job. In a few days' time that new fighter will be finished, and unless we do something about it the plans will flow down the prepared channel to Germany without let or hindrance from us. Nothing is more certain than that. They're waiting for them now. And don't let the fact that we've roasted the Baron out of Hampstead worry you any—because it's not worrying him! He has other addresses and other identities besides that of 'Thomas Grey.'

"In fact, I've no doubt whatever but at this present moment he's lounging elegantly in the garden of some country house which he has owned for years, and where he is quite well known. Our sole chance of defeating the

Baron lies in holding up the final touches on the fighter until we've located Walter Paine, and by hook or by crook brought him back to this country. Paine can establish Miss Ensor's alibi, and Paine alone can tell us who did meet Larry Rue and hand over those photographs that night. We must have Walter Paine, sir!"

"But we don't know where he is!" cut in the Chief of the C.I.D.

"We know near enough for Mr. Brass and myself to start work!" said Sexton Blake on the instant. He turned to the Chief of the Secret Service. "Would you mind informing these gentlemen what mademoiselle has to say about Walter Paine?"

The Secret Service Chief rose slowly to his feet. It was gall and wormwood to him to have to speak at all about his department's activities, but when in addition he had to admit defeat—

"I do not intend to go into needless detail," he said cautiously, "or to explain the reasons which induced me to take the course; but I may say that an agent of mine has been on the trail of this Walter Paine ever since the trial in question. At Mr. Blake's request we contacted the lady, and I heard this morning that she has traced Walter Paine to Rouen, but has lost him again. He arrived there two months ago, she says, in the care of the nun who rescued him from the hospital at Amiens, but they're both lying low and she is unable to find them."

"So what?" snapped the Chief of the C.I.D., irritably.

"Mr. Brass and I suggest that we cross to Rouen to assist her," smiled the private practitioner. "Three heads are better than one, and we could easily be dropped over there by parachute if we are given the necessary permission. We are ready to go to-night."

For a moment nobody spoke. They were rather staggered by the boldness of the proposition. It was left to the C.I.D. man to throw the first cold water.

"You're crazy!" he said. "Even if you succeeded in finding him, what could you do with him—a man with no legs? How d'you think you could get him away?"

"We have a scheme for that, too." Blake told him equably. "Rouen is not a great distance from the coast, and—always assuming that we found him—neither Brass nor I have any doubt on the score of our ability to get him to the sea. Somehow!" he added.

"And then swim it, I suppose?"

Blake glanced covertly at the two members of the War Cabinet, both of whom were leaning forward attentively in their chairs. "From there we should need a ship!" he said boldly.

"A ship would never get over! Certainly, it would never get back!"

"Yet the British Navy very successfully landed upon the Lofoten Islands, and equally successfully brought off a party of Norwegian patriots," Blake said quietly.

"My God!—are you suggesting a raid on the French Coast?" gasped one of the members of the War Cabinet.

"Desperate diseases demand desperate remedies," Blake said. "As a matter of fact, there's a secluded little village on that coast, sir, with a still more secluded little harbour. If a British destroyer should happen to poke her nose in there, quite soon—say one week from to-night—and if her crew should happen to feel like creating a merry diversion ashore while Brass and I got our man through the defences and down to the ship, I think we could guarantee Walter Paine's presence in London, and, incidentally, guarantee that the plans of that magnificent fighter should never get into German hands until we've got an even better one to take her place in the air. Of course," he added, "if in your opinion the fighter is not worth the risk—"

"Risk?" bawled the Minister of Aircraft Production. "That new fighter?" For a moment he was positively speechless. He could not find words in which to express himself. The fastest thing in the skies? The slickest, slimmest, most deadly weapon of war that the mind of man had so far achieved? Risk?

Suddenly he thumped both hands on the table before him and leapt to his feet.

"Risk?" he cried in a choking voice. "You talk to me of risk?"

Blake glanced at Beltom Brass and the two grinned at each other. There was no need for them to worry any more.

Thirty hours later, under a coal-black sky, the two adventurers shook hands with the second-pilot of a black Blenheim, and one after the other jumped out into the night. They went down in sprawling somersaults for four thousand feet; then they pulled their rip cords.

Two black silk parachutes fluttered above them wildly for a moment, then filled and steadied. Rouen was dimly visible below and to their left.

They sailed down slowly, invisibly, purposefully.

THE THIRTEENTH
CHAPTER

In Enemy Territory.

THEY LANDED IN a field—or, rather, in adjacent fields, for Beltom Brass misjudged his landing and was dragged head-first through a hedge before he could spill the wind from his parachute and stop himself.

When eventually Blake found him, he was sitting knee deep in a tangle of silk and cordage, ruefully rubbing the back of his head.

"You all right?" Blake whispered.

"Oh, I'm fine!" groaned the Secret Service ace. "In fact I feel like that bird who tried to get a job in the theatre at diving from the balcony and landing on his head in the middle of the stage. 'Well, that's all right,' the manager said when he'd shown him what he could do. 'But couldn't you make it higher?' 'Sure!' said the bloke, determined to please. So he went to the top of the gallery, dived off that, turned a somersault in mid-air, and landed plonk on his head in the middle of the stage. Then he got up, bowed stiffly, put a hand to the side of his face and swayed off the stage. 'Hey!' bawled the manager, up in arms in a moment. 'That's all right, but can the Cissy stuff!' 'Cissy stuff, be damned!' shouted the bird. 'I've broke my blinkin' neck!' Do you know where we are, exactly?"

"About five miles north-west of the town," Blake told him. "We'd better get rid of these parachutes as soon as you're ready."

They carried them to a corner of the field and buried them deeply as they could in the soft earth. Then, having smoothed down the ground again, they washed their hands in a nearby ditch and presently set off in search of the road.

There was no hurry. It still wanted an hour or more to dawn. And although both of them were wearing the clothes of French farm-workers, and both spoke the language fluently, they had no wish to fall in with a German patrol before it was daylight. Short of a direct challenge they had little to fear, but there was no point in taking any unnecessary risks.

They found the road and sat down to wait. To their left lay Rouen in the darkness, but in every other direction there seemed little but miles and miles of green billowing country with an occasional wood here and there. At that hour of the morning everything seemed so peaceful that it was almost impossible to realise that war had so recently swept over it; but in the full light of day, no doubt, the scene would be very different.

It was! As the light strengthened and objects near at

hand became more clearly visible, Brass touched the detective's arm and pointed along the road. Not fifty yards away, lying grotesquely on its side on the grass verge, was the wreckage of a French heavy tank. While in the field beyond, standing up starkly against the dawn, was the bullet-riddled tail of a shattered Morane fighter plane.

"Heil, Laval!"[6] said Mr. Brass—and spat pleasantly.

The French are early risers, and in spite of the fact that there is now little to rise for, the habits of a lifetime cannot easily be changed. Soon odd figures began to appear in the fields, and presently farm carts began to make their appearance on the road. When at last full daylight was come, the two Englishmen rose stiffly to their feet and started out on the long walk into Rouen.

Now the signs of German occupation became more marked. A squadron of Heinkels flew overhead, and twice a convoy of armoured cars roared past, driving everything else relentlessly into the ditch.

"What you need in this country is a travelling cuspidor!" observed Mr. Brass as he spat religiously after the departing Huns.

Half-way into the town they overtook an old man with whom they kept company for a time. He came from a village some way back, and had been walking half the night since the Germans had taken his horse and cart. He was going to see his daughter, he told them, who lived in the Rue Marie-Therese.

"We're strangers round here, monsieur," Blake said. "Are we likely to have difficulty in getting about Rouen?"

"Not unless you make difficulty yourself, monsieur," the old man told him. "It is, of course, wiser to keep from the main streets, but in the smaller streets—no, there the German does not go. Maybe he does not like our small streets, Maybe our small streets are not enough for him. I am an old man, monsieur. I do not know these things, In the last war things were different. Then France was great. I who speak, I know—for was I not a soldier of France under the great Marechal? But to-day we have M. Laval—"

He paused, eyeing them sideways.

"Forward the cuspidors!" beamed Mr. Brass on the instant.

They spat together, all three of them solemnly and with considerable fervour, pausing in the middle of the road to do it. And when that little ceremony was over:

"If one wished to enter Rouen and avoid all chance of being grunted at by pigs," the old man observed softly, "one would naturally take the second turning on the right of this road which brings one in by the poorer section of the town instead of over the bridge. Also one would not let it be known that one was a workless stranger, otherwise one might be taken against one's will to do work in the farmyard across the Rhine."

"One is grateful for the information, monsieur," Blake thanked him in the same impersonal fashion. But as they quickened their pace and drew away: "Vive la France, monsieur!" grinned Beltom Brass. "And watch out for the R.A.F.!" he added under his breath.

They took the second turning on the right and after a

long detour found themselves on the southern outskirts of the city. Here the signs of war were more apparent, but as the old man had predicted, they met no Germans and encountered no trouble.

"Our Teutonic friends evidently prefer the bright lights and the big squares!" Brass observed as they stumbled over the cobbled roads. "Or else they don't trust the French peasant! Do you see where we are, yet?"

"Not yet," Blake said.

They walked steadily forward for perhaps an hour longer—for there were neither tramcars nor buses running. Indeed, it was largely due to the empty streets that they had such difficulty in finding their way. But then Brass got his bearings, and finally, towards eleven o'clock, he turned into a narrow alley and came to a halt before the dirtiest, most villainous looking estaminet it had ever been Blake's bad fortune to encounter.

"Home!" he grinned, bowing to his companion to enter.

Blake ducked his head under the low doorway, crinkling his nose as he did so; for bad as was the outside, the inside was even worse. Cold cabbage water, dirt, damp, stale beer—each strove for the mastery. But if Brass noticed anything wrong with the atmosphere he gave no sign. He threw himself into a broken old chair as easily as though it had been a padded seat at the Ritz, and banging loudly on the zinc-covered table, called for monsieur the proprietor.

Monsieur the proprietor entered from the rear of the place. An ancient, moth-eaten bear, would have been neat by comparison. He was an enormous man, with shaggy beard and shaggy hair; with a great fat paunch, tiny pig's eyes, a toothless mouth, and an expression such as no doubt the wolf wore when he saw Red Riding Hood enter his bed-room.

"Bon jour, monsieur!" Brass greeted him boisterously. "Amer Picon, I think. Two!"

"Two?" snarled monsieur the proprietor.

"Three, then—I'm sorry!"

Glasses and a bottle were produced, and the drinks poured out.

"Tell me, monsieur,"' Brass asked. "If a man were looking for his grandmother in Rouen, where should he start?"

Monsieur the proprietor drained his glass, set it down again, refilled it, and frowned.

"That depends upon the age of the grandmother," he said at last.

"The age of the grandmother is one hundred and two, monsieur."

The pig-like eyes narrowed. Monsieur the proprietor rubbed his hand on his hip and then held it out palm upwards to the Secret Service man. When a moment later he closed it again, he closed it upon a one hundred franc note.

"Number 10, Rue de la Poste," he said in a hoarse whisper. "Knock three times, monsieur, and ask for Madame Lobel."

Brass thanked the man, and soon afterwards rose to go. From what he remembered of the Rue de la Poste it was no health resort, and when some half hour later he arrived there with his companion he perceived that his memory was not at fault. It was in the older part of the town—a narrow, winding street, lined with old-fashioned stone houses which, though picturesque enough at one time, were now dilapidated and incredibly sordid. After a brief search they located Number 10 and knocked three times on its sun-blistered door.

A slatternly woman, hand on hip, answered them.

"Well?" she demanded brusquely.

"We wish to see Madame Lobel, madame?"

"Huh?" She looked them over from head to heel, but softened somewhat when Brass produced a five franc note. "All right!" she gave in grudgingly, opening the door for them to enter. "Number 16, on the third landing—that's where you'll find her."

They went up the uncarpeted stairs. The place was like a rabbit warren. Arrived on the third landing they knocked upon the door marked "16" and with rapidly beating hearts stood back to wait.

The next moment they got the shock of their lives for the door was opened by an old woman who peered at them myopically. She was eighty if she was a day, bent, shrivelled, and grey as a badger. She was in rags, and she was dirty.

"I beg your pardon, madame—" Brass was beginning, but before he could get any further she literally threw herself on his bosom.

"Why, it's my little cabbages!" she shrilled in a cracked, high-pitched voice that was tremulous with age and woe. "My two little cabbages, come at last to see their poor old mother!" Doors opened all along the landing and from every door popped a tousled head to witness the touching scene. "Come in!" she cried. "Come in, my little cabbages!"

The little cabbages entered—it was journey's end for them. For incredible as it seemed that ancient hag was none other than Yvonne de Braselieu—crack agent of the French Secret Service and now working for de Gaulle and England.

Yvonne de Braselieu—one of the most elegant women in Europe!

"AND NOW, MESSIEURS, to work!" she laughed softly when, greetings over, both men had congratulated her upon the excellence of her disguise. "Four weeks have I spent in this place and yet I am no nearer my object than when I started. But first—what has happened in England to make them risk sending you over here?" she demanded, waving them to the only seats in the room—the dilapidated bed. "Why has this Walter Paine became suddenly of such importance?"

"Tell her, Blake!" sighed Mr. Brass, his eyes on that ravaged face. "And to think that I once kissed her just—"

"Monsieur!"

"By mistake, of course!" he assured her quickly. "You were asleep at the time and I mistook you for my poor old mother. Too bad!"

Blake told him to shut up. Then, as briefly as possible he explained to mademoiselle all that had happened in England over the last few days.

"So you see," he said when at last he had made an end of it, "by hook or by crook we've got to find Walter Paine and take him back to London. Only he can save an innocent woman from serving the remainder of a ten years' sentence, and only he can give us the information we want that will enable us to round up the worst and most dangerous gang of spies that has ever afflicted England in war-time. Why are you so sure that he's still in Rouen, mademoiselle?"

"Well, that's a long story, I'm afraid." She crossed over to the door and listened for a while intently. Then, having satisfied herself that the keyhole was properly filled with paper, she came back to the one and only chair the room boasted.

"In the beginning," she said as she sat down again, "my mission was largely routine. I was sent over here to make sure that Walter Paine was indeed dead—or, if he was not dead, then I must get into touch with him and find out if that girl's alibi was true. That was necessary, you appreciate, as a check-up for the Service. Since if by some extraordinary chance her alibi was true—then she had not met Larry Rue in the White Cat that night— then the entire case against her became a frame-up and somebody else was guilty. What was more, that unknown 'someone else' would still be at large and capable of further treacheries. In which case, it was our business to scotch him. You understand?"

"Go on!" said Blake.

"Well, I soon found out that Walter Paine had not, as we had supposed, died immediately of his injuries. He had been taken to a St. John's Home in a village outside Amiens—but when I reached there I found the place the centre of a most violent storm. It appeared that for some reason or, other the Germans had suddenly become interested in this same man, and a guard had been put on the home. Precisely why a German guard was necessary over a man with no feet, no one seemed to know. But a guard was posted—and evaded!"

"By a woman?" Blake asked quickly.

"By a woman," nodded mademoiselle. "Though how you know that is a matter I do not understand. But you are perfectly correct, just the same. Walter Paine was removed from that home, and he was removed by a woman known as Sister Agnes. The two disappeared one night—how, nobody knows. Or if anyone does know, she will not say. At any rate, the German guard was successfully hoodwinked and eluded, and both Sister Agnes and her charge completely disappeared."

"Was Sister Agnes looking after Walter Paine?"

"Yes; she was his nurse. It was she who found him by the roadside during the retreat, and she who caused him to be carried to the home where she served. She was an Englishwoman."

"I thought as much!" Blake snapped. "Yes, go on, mademoiselle?"

"An Englishwoman who had lived over twenty years in France," smiled mademoiselle. "A nun, you understand. In what is called a 'nursing order.'"

"Just a moment," Brass interrupted. "You say that Sister Agnes took Paine away just before you got there?

How long had she had charge of him before that?"

"From the day of his injuries, of course! She had taken care of him from the beginning. He had been a patient there for—well, two or three months, I suppose."

"The Germans hadn't clamped down on him before then?"

"No. So far as I could gather they knew he was there but took little notice of him. I suppose he was too hors de combat for them to be concerned. They showed no particular interest in Walter Paine until a few days before I arrived there myself—"

"In other words, until his name was mentioned at the trial of Isobel Ensor?" Blake put in.

"Exactly, monsieur. And then they put a guard on both him and the home and showed the keenest interest in his welfare. But even so, as I have told you, Sister Agnes managed to save him from their clutches, and get him safely away to some secret place."

"How did she manage it?"

"I don't know how she managed the actual disappearance, but that was only the beginning. Instantly—as you can easily imagine—the Germans gave orders for all roads to be guarded and all hospitals searched. On the face of it, and knowing something of German thoroughness, you would say it was impossible for an elderly woman to get a footless man from Amiens to Rouen without being apprehended—but impossible or not, that is exactly what Sister Agnes achieved with Walter Paine. It took her months to do it, but she did do it. And about a month ago she reached Rouen."

"How do you know that?" Blake asked.

"She arrived here as a refugee, with all her worldly belongings wrapped in a sheet and piled high on a blue perambulator. Hundreds of other women arrived in like case. For days on end they filled the roads—women from Holland and Belgium who had walked hundreds of miles, sleeping in the fields, eating what they could get, all intent upon placing as much distance as possible themselves and their ruined homes, all intent upon reaching Unoccupied France. And the Germans were letting them through. In those days, they didn't care. And somewhere in that crowd was Sister Agnes with Walter Paine."

"You mean she'd got him in the perambulator?"

"Yes. She'd got a baby there, too. It was a big perambulator—a Dutch perambulator. I expect its owner had died, or been killed, and Sister Agnes had taken it over from her, the baby as well. You see, the Germans were looking for a nun with a wounded and footless man. They were not looking for a bedraggled Dutchwoman pushing a battered perambulator containing a baby and all her foolish bits and pieces. But under those pieces was Walter Paine, and on the top of Walter Paine was the baby. And high above all was that big roll of sheeted possessions!"

"She had courage, if nothing else," Blake said softly after a thoughtful silence. "She was wearing the Dutch woman's clothes, too, I take it?"

"Yes. She was when she arrived here. How long she had been wearing them I do not know, because before that time she must have been carrying him in some other way. She had to await her chance, you understand. A few miles, perhaps, and then a long wait until something else presented itself. Quite obviously she was hoping to get right through France and possibly into Spain—I don't know. I should think that was her idea."

"Where did she hide in between the bursts of travelling?"

"Ha! That I do not know. The Germans do not know, either, nor can they find out. I should have said that being a nun she would have made straight for the village priest, but she is not doing that here. The Germans have already searched the house of every priest in Rouen—the churches, too. But still they have not found her. Yet she is still here!"

"What makes you so sure of that, mademoiselle?"

"Because the Germans have not removed their guards from the main roads running out of the town. Because they have issued orders that whoever is found harbouring a crippled Englishman will be shot."

"There was no guard on the road we used, this morning!"

"There was further out. They do not guard the small roads, only the big main roads along which she must travel if she is to leave Rouen for any other place. You know the French road system."

"But what makes them think that she is here at all?"

"Someone gave her away, monsieur. Some Quisling among the refugees. Perhaps someone saw something, I not know. All I do know is that the blue perambulator was found abandoned in the middle of the town, but that neither Waiter Paine nor the baby was in it. Evidently,

Sister Agnes got word in time, and abandoned the perambulator before its discovery could give her away. She has the brains—that one!"

"She sure has!" Beltom Brass frowned. He was silent for a moment, thinking. Suddenly he turned to Sexton Blake. "You know, there's something just the least shade fantastic about this affair," he said. "Something I haven't got hold of yet. Even allowing that Walter Paine could confirm the Ensor alibi, I still can't see that it would be worth all this trouble to Germany. I mean, would the hard-boiled Hun waste time searching and guarding half France for the sake of a single wounded tommy? It doesn't make sense to me. And why should Sister Agnes risk her life for him? He'd be quite safe as a prisoner of war. I mean, if the man were a blessed army corps they couldn't be making more fuss about him!"

"But perhaps that's just what he is, Brass!"

"Eh?" the Secret Service man asked after a moment of blank silence.

Blake smiled.

"If my notion of Walter Paine is the correct one," he said, "I should imagine that's just about what he does represent to Adolf Hitler, alive—or dead! That's why it's so important that we get him first. Question is: how best to set about doing it!"

THE FOURTEENTH CHAPTER

At Last!

THE NEXT FEW days were destined to be among the most desperate Blake could remember. He had known from the start that it was no easy job he was tackling, but never in his most pessimistic moments had he imagined anything even one half as baffling as this task of one ex-nun among the thousands of people that formed the population of Rouen.

Time and again the three met to discuss the situation. Mademoiselle, efficient as she was, had already admitted herself at the end of her resources before Blake and his companion arrived. And although the private practitioner had brought out a few bright ideas of his own, one and all of them proved useless.

It was Beltom Brass who thought of the medical supplies. It suddenly struck him that with a case such as Walter Paine on her hands, Sister Agnes would perforce have to purchase considerable supplies of bandages and ointments and lint. She could not have brought much with her—certainly not a month's supply for a case so severe as Paine's must be—and therefore she would have to procure more locally.

"She's got two possible sources of supply," he argued. "The hospitals and the chemists. But I doubt if she would risk the hospitals because they'd want to know too much. That leaves her with only the chemists; and I suggest we call on every chemist in Rouen to try to find out if a tall, pale-faced, elderly woman, most likely wearing a close-fitting hat, has been noticed making extensive purchases of medicaments lately."

The "close-fitting hat" detail was mademoiselle's contribution. One of the greatest difficulties of the search was the fact that they had no photograph of Sister Agnes, and very little actual description of her. None of them had ever seen her, and all mademoiselle had been able to gather from the sisters at the St. John's Home was the somewhat negative information that Sister Agnes was a little taller than most women, of middle age perhaps, and rather pale as to colouring. Her eyes—having no time for such vanities—they had never noticed. Nor had anyone ever seen her bare head. But being a nun, it followed automatically that her head would be shorn—and although her hair would doubtless have grown in the months since she had given up her nun's coif, it would, mademoiselle argued, still be on the short side and would demand a close-fitting hat to hide it. Thus, a close-fitting hat had become part and parcel of the imaginary Sister Agnes' description.

On the third day of the search they adopted Brass' suggestion and toured the chemists—again with no success. If any such woman had made such purchases she had certainly not been remarked. As a last resource they risked inquiries of the hospitals, but there again drew blank. In any event, the hospitals did not sell medicaments to private persons—and that, in turn, caused Blake to think of doctors.

Had Sister Agnes called in a doctor to see Walter Paine? The next day they tested that idea, only to discover that the Germans had already tried it—and failed. If any doctor had been called in, he was not admitting it—either to them or to the Germans themselves. The priests of the town were, if anything, more hopeless still. Their lips, of course—even had they known anything—would have been sealed by the confessional.

In other circumstances it would have been possible to use the "Agony" columns of the local press, but the Germans had long since forbidden such advertisements and none could now be printed anywhere in France—so that that was barred. And, of course, no help could be obtained from what was left of the local police—since for their own safety they were compelled to avoid the police as carefully as they avoided the Germans. In Occupied France it is impossible to tell friend from foe. And as a rule, one makes only one mistake!

By the end of the fourth day, even Blake himself was beginning to lose confidence. At this time they were lodging in a house in the Rue des Heures, mademoiselle having thought it wiser to give up her room at Number 10,

Rue de la Poste, now that her "sons" had at last returned home! She was still an old woman—indeed, she had no option in that respect since the powerful astringent with which she had "wrinkled" her face took a considerable time to wear away—but now she was more the "dear old lady" type, while her sons were respectable middle-class citizens. Their rise in the social scale had been dictated entirely by the exigencies of their task, since a good middle-class citizen can appear freely in many places where a peasant would merely invite comment from the watchful Hun.

"Well, what's the next step?" Brass asked now as they sat around the table discussing the day's failure.

Blake thrust back his chair and rose. The situation was beginning to appear hopeless. The latter part of the afternoon and evening he had spent fruitlessly patrolling the "Bloomsbury" district of the town, hoping against hope that he might hit upon the woman by sheer chance while the others were maintaining a similar patrol in other likely districts. But as was only to be expected, none of them had had even a bite.

"And yet, if she knew we were here, Sister Agnes would be even more anxious to find us than we are to find here—if such a thing were possible!" he said as he took a worried turn across the little room. "That's the cruel part of it all! She's here, and we're here, and yet it seems beyond our powers to think up a way of finding her. It's crazy, really!"

"But after all, we are in Occupied France!" Mr. Brass pointed out. "It isn't as though we were in London, with a hundred aids ready to our hand. Matter of fact, I'm wondering if Walter Paine mightn't have died on her, and—"

"He couldn't have died on her, or the Germans would know of it!" mademoiselle interrupted with decision. "No one can be buried here without permission—the Huns have been alive to that chance right from the beginning. Also to the possibility that she might dose him with morphia or something and get him out of the town in the guise of a corpse in its coffin on the way to be buried in some other town! They're wary—these Bosches!"

"You're tellin' me, sweetheart!"

"Monsieur!"

"So to speak, of course! So to speak, mademoiselle!" the Secret Service ace corrected himself cheerfully. "Though after all, if a son can't call his mother—"

"Shut up, you two!" growled Blake from the window. "Give your tongues a rest, and use your heads for a bit. Let's consider the matter again; there must be some point we could get her on if we could think of it. After all, she's not an ordinary woman—she's a nun! That's the one thing that stands out a mile in my own mind. She's a nun—and has been a nun all her life. Therefore at all times and in all circumstances she will act like a nun, because there's nothing so absolutely routine-making as life in a religious order."

"So what?" Mr. Brass asked stolidly.

Blake spread his hands.

"So what?" he echoed. Always the argument came back to that same place. Time and again he had propounded the same thesis but always the answer was the same—"So what?" He did not know. They had already exhausted the points of distinction between a nun and an ordinary woman, and still they were no better off. Not one of them offered a handle with which they might dig her out. They had thought of them all. Her short hair, the fact that she would go to Mass more regularly—mademoiselle had haunted the three churches in Rouen until she knew them off by heart, but yet had seen no such woman as the one for whom she was searching. The Germans were watching the churches, too. They'd tumbled to that possibility.

Yet still the belief persisted in Blake's mind that it was through the nun side of her that they stood their best chance.

"A nun is a nun!" he would say. "She must give herself away—some time!"

She did!

It was on the sixth morning of their stay in Rouen. For the last three days Blake himself had attended every Mass at the Church of the Sacre Coeur in the Rue Jeanne d'Arc—beginning at six o'clock and continuing at intervals until nine. The other two were being watched by mademoiselle and Beltom Brass, but always it had been Blake's belief that the Rue Jeanne d'Arc church was in the most likely district for Sister Agnes to be in hiding.

Now, as he sat on his cane chair at back of the fine old church, he watched the people coming towards him from the nave. Mass was over. Already the priest had retired to his sacristy. Being the first Mass of the day, the worshippers were mostly of the labouring class, or those whose work began early, and Blake noticed that the hands which dipped into the font were for the most part the hands of working people.

He watched them closely as they followed one another towards the door. Each dipped his fingers into the font, crossed himself, and went out with bowed head and eyes on the floor. Each had been taught as a child to do that, and each, as an adult, still went through exactly the same motions. Old men, young men, women, girls—one after another they passed Blake's chair—but of a middle-aged, tall, pale-faced woman, wearing a tight-fitting hat, there was still no sign.

A stoutish woman was crossing herself now; he watched her mechanically. She slipped her hands along her forearms and with bowed head followed the others towards the door.

Suddenly Blake's heart gave a violent bound. For one single instant of time he sat there motionless, mouth agape. For a split second he was too utterly taken aback to do more than stare; then, with a catch of his breath that whistled audibly in the silence, he leapt to his feet and followed her outside.

She was standing in the vestibule. She was looking through the window to where four German soldiers were standing on the far side of the street watching the people leave. Without a second's hesitation Blake brushed past her, turned, and came straight back so that the two met face to face.

"Sister Agnes!" he said under his breath.

She did not speak. She remained still as a statue. Not a flicker of recognition passed across her face; not a muscle moved. Only her hands slid quietly along her forearms in the one movement that had given her away. That peculiar movement, common to nuns all the world over, of hiding their hands in their capacious sleeves!

"Sister Agnes!" he whispered triumphantly, certain now that he had made no mistake. "I've been searching all Rouen for you. Have no fear. I am English, too! I and my companions have come from England especially to take you and Walter Paine back home. My name is Sexton Blake—though I do not suppose that you have ever heard of me."

Still the woman he had addressed as Sister Agnes remained silent—but not even she could control her quickened breath. Her lips tightened. A tiny pulse woke to sudden and violent life in her throat.

"In another moment the church will have emptied!" he urged. "Already we are among the last to leave, and there are Germans watching us. Where can we go, Sister? Quick!"

She swallowed her fears. Her grey eyes searched his desperately. But, before she could say anything, the door behind them opened again and the priest himself came out into the vestibule.

"Monsieur le Cure!" she called swiftly.

The priest turned. He was on old man, with a grey beard and long grey bushy eyebrows. The glance he shot at Blake warned the detective intuitively that he, too, was in Sister Agnes' secret.

"Daughter?" he answered her softly.

Sister Agnes hesitated. It was plain that she had spoken on the spur of the moment, and now was at a loss how best to proceed. Plainly she could not risk involving Monsieur le Cure in what, after all, might be only a trap. Suddenly she swung back to Blake himself.

"How do I know I can—trust you?" she breathed.

Blake glanced again at the priest. Time was pressing; somehow or other he had to prove himself. He noted the old man's penetrating gaze, his firm mouth—the benignity of his countenance. He was a man totally devoid of fear. Just the type of man upon whom other men could lean— and never be let down.

"Monsieur le Cure," he said with sudden confidence, "I am an English detective. Together with my friend, an agent of the British Secret Service, I was dropped by parachute from a British bomber, six nights ago. My mission was to find Sister Agnes and Walter Paine, and take both of them back to England. Sister Agnes I have already found. Walter Paine I must find. If you doubt my credentials, call over those German soldiers outside and tell them what I have just told you. But if you do that, not only shall I suffer death, but an innocent girl in England will continue to serve a long term of imprisonment for a treachery she never committed. Walter Paine can clear that girl. That is why I want him."

"Her name?" gasped Sister Agnes.

"Isobel Ensor."

"Why didn't you say so before?" The absurdity of the question was no greater than the relief which flooded the

Sister's whole being. Even the priest relaxed something of his strained attitude. "Mon Dieu, mon Dieu!" he breathed. "At last! A little longer, my son, and you might have been too late."

"He is ill, you mean?"

"In mind and in body, my son."

"When may I see him?"

"After dark to-night. After vespers. Meet me here, monsieur. You, too, my daughter."

"I may bring my friends, monsieur? There will be several arrangements to be made; plans to be settled. We shall be leaving for England to-morrow."

"To-morrow!" echoed the priest. "But how can you— No, don't tell me!" he interrupted himself quickly. "It is better that I do not know." He glanced through the window at the waiting Germans. "Go now!" he said abruptly. "And return after vespers to-night."

When an hour later Blake let himself into the house in the Rue des Heures, he was figuratively walking on air. For a long time the other two simply could not believe his story. They could not even now believe that their task was finished. Then doubts began to show their heads. Had Blake allowed himself to be fooled? Had he been wrong in allowing the woman to go without tailing her and making sure where she was living? Never had a day seemed so long. Never had night seemed so slow in coming.

When at long last they did set out for the church, Brass—for one—was literally sweating with impatience.

Sister Agnes was awaiting them in the darkened

vestibule, but she did not speak. Instead, touching her lips to indicate silence, she glided noiselessly as a shadow into the church.

"I was right about the close-fitting hat, you see!" mademoiselle whispered when she had gone. "But they told me at the Home that she was thin."

"I expect she's padded!" Blake whispered back.

The last of the congregation had already gone, yet the sacristans were still straightening up and the organ still throbbed through the vaulted aisles. But presently the men went and the last of the music died away. One by one the candles on the altar were snuffed out—and silence reigned.

"This way!" a voice whispered suddenly through the darkness. "Take my hand, please."

Blake reached out and found the hand offered—the hand of Monsieur le Cure. His other hand he gave to Brass, who in turn linked up with mademoiselle.

"It would be unwise to risk a lamp!"

"We can manage!" Blake whispered back.

They crossed the church by the main aisle. After that, Blake thought they went behind the High Altar, and soon, after descending a winding flight of stone steps, he knew that they were in the crypt. For what seemed a considerable distance they continued down a narrow corridor—a stone corridor, judging by the walls. Then, so suddenly that they all bumped into one another, Monsieur le Curé stopped before an ancient, iron-bound door.

He switched on an electric torch.

"In days gone by," he said, as he fumbled in his cassock

for a key, "this was the treasure chamber of the church. I should perhaps explain that as soon as it became clear what France must expect from her conquerors, churchmen all over the country immediately took steps to safeguard those same treasures from this newest of vandals—this newest of Huns. In church, misdoubting the security of the medieval treasure chamber, we designed a new one. And thus, when Sister Agnes came to me in her trouble, I was able to offer her a sanctuary the existence of which is known to none save myself and the twenty lay-brothers who built it. Please to enter!"

He opened the old door as he spoke and led the way in. When they were all inside, he turned and locked it again. The light from his torch revealed a low-roofed stone chamber, the walls of which were set out like shelves in a larder, but all of them were empty.

"This is the medieval treasure chamber," he explained. "And here"—he touched something in the wall which caused a narrow panel to slide open under the urge of some hidden mechanism—"here is the new!"

But neither Blake not his companions were interested in treasure chambers—as such. Their eyes had shot straight through the aperture to where, propped high on a camp bed and with Sister Agnes standing beside him, lay the man they had come so far to find.

"Mon Dieu!" whispered the old priest, as he, too, looked in, "Hurry, monsieur! Hurry!"

Blake stepped swiftly to the bedside. One glance was enough to show him that he was only just in time. In the light from the lamp the man's face was ghastly. It was sheet white—grey—and already damp with the dew of death.

"Are you Walter Paine?" he whispered.

"Yes."

The answer was so faint as to be scarcely audible. It was a mere thread of sound in the heavy silence of that subterranean room. But though, the voice was faint, the spirit behind it was unmistakable. It was written large in the glittering eyes, in the breathless eagerness with which he was trying to raise himself in bed.

"Drink this, my son!"

From somewhere at the back of the room the old priest had produced a beaker containing some brownish fluid which he held to the dying man's lips. Paine drank eagerly.

"Who are you?" he gasped when he had finished, his eyes seeking out the detective again.

"I am Sexton Blake—here on behalf of Scotland Yard. My companions are Mademoiselle Yvonne de Braselieu, of the French Secret Service, and Mr. Beltom Brass of the British Secret Service."

"Enough. I was—Mahomet—trying to get to—the mountain," he said twistedly. "I—never thought that—the mountain might—come to Mahomet!"

"We had to come, Paine. There were questions to which we must have an answer. You remember Isobel Ensor?"

"Yes."

"She was arrested for trafficking with the Germans. She was framed from A to Z—and all the way between. She was accused of photographing the plans of a British fighter plane and selling them to Germany through a man named Larry Rue, whom she was supposed to have met in a Charlotte Street restaurant known as the White Cat, and she had no defence save you. Upon the night in question, contrary to being with Larry Rue in the White Cat, she claims to have been with you in the Regal Cinema. That was her alibi against the whole infamous charge, but it broke down because at the time of her trial you, unfortunately, had been reported 'missing, believed killed,' and could not be produced in court. The judge took the view that it was a red herring alibi, and in the event sentenced Isobel Ensor to ten years' imprisonment—of which so far she has completed six months."

He paused while Sister Agnes wiped the dying man's lips with a moistened handkerchief.

"Courage, Walter, my friend! Courage!" he heard her whisper.

"Walter Paine,' Blake said when she had finished, "do you confirm that Isobel Ensor was with you that night in the Regal Cinema?"

"Yes, I do! She was with me that night in the Regal Cinema!"

"But—" Beltom Brass paused; there was a puzzled expression on his face. "But you don't know which night we're—"

"Just a moment, Brass!" Blake checked him quietly. "If my notion's right about this man, I think you'll find that he knows a good deal more than you think." He leaned closer over the dying man, and in spite of himself his eyes were very hard.

"Upon the night that you took Isobel Ensor to the Regal,"

he said, "somebody did hand over the photographs of those plans in the White Cat—but it wasn't to Larry Rue, I think?"

"No," the other's lips formed soundlessly.

"In fact, it's in my mind that it was Larry Rue who handed them to someone else. To someone whose job it was to get them over to France! Who was that someone else, Paine?"

The dying man raised himself a fraction of an inch on his pillows. He tried to speak, but the words would not come. Twice he tried. Then Blake could stand it no longer.

"Was it you?" he challenged him bleakly.

"'Yes—it was me!'"

"What?" Brass whispered, stark incredulity glazing his eyes.

"He knows!" croaked the dying man, stabbing a trembling finger towards Sexton Blake. "That's why I took her to the pictures, so that we'd know where she'd been in case we had to fix her. But you'll find it all in the paper I've written for you. It's all there, I tell you! Everything! Sign it! Sign it now, while I can see you! I want to get straight. I can't—can't meet the—the boys I saw killed till I'm straight. Sign it now! All of you!"

Sister Agnes thrust forward several sheets of closely written foolscap.

"It's a full confession,' she whispered. "He wants you to sign it. He has signed it, look!"

Blake picked up a pen from the table beside the bed. In his bold handwriting he sighed "Sexton Blake," and the date. Then he handed the pen to Beltom Brass, who

217

also signed, followed by mademoiselle, and the old priest. Sister Agnes had already signed her name.

"Me!"

It was Walter Paine's last word. With the pen Sister Agnes put his trembling fingers, very carefully he inscribed his own name again—right across the foot of the last page. For a moment he sat looking at it, satisfied. He even smiled.

Then the pen slipped from his nerveless fingers.

When they lifted him up, he was dead.

THE FIFTEENTH CHAPTER

Confession.

WHEN BLAKE HAD finished reading through the eight pages which comprised the full confession of the dead man, Walter Paine, he folded it into his breast pocket and waited for Sister Agnes and the old priest to finish their last offices.

"Sister," he asked, when at last she rose from her knees, "how did all this extraordinary business come about?"

She told him. She explained how, after the battle, she had found a young soldier lying badly injured beside the road, and, having given him first aid, she eventually collected assistance and had him carried to the St. John's Home, of which she was a nursing sister.

There they operated. A double amputation. No other course was open to them. But the man was young and strong and would have undoubtedly made a complete recovery, save that his nerve went. He could not, he moaned, face life as a cripple. He would not face life as a cripple! He began to threaten suicide. He would kill himself rather than hobble through life without feet!

"I talked to him," Sister Agnes explained. "I tried to make him understand that, just as we cannot live by bread alone, so no man need lose heart because, in a just cause, he happens to lose his feet. I told him that I was English, too. I besought him to take heart, to be a man, to face up to his troubles and beat them."

A wan little smile passed over her face as she described how bit by bit her teachings seem to take root. The unrest passed. He became reconciled to his fate. But then something else happened. Quite suddenly he became moody and depressed. She had thought it a passing fit, but as time went on, instead of getting better, he became worse. He would cry out in his sleep. He became frightened. Time and again he would ask her what he had said the night before? He became afraid to sleep at all.

"I know now, of course, that it was his conscience," she said. "It was waking up. It was stabbing him. As he lay there flat on his back in that little room, he was thinking of the girl in England whom he and his like had condemned to a similar fate—but without her deserving it. I think he pictured her in prison. I suppose he remembered the various little kindnesses she had shown him—and in return he had done that. It preyed on his mind. Already low in health and resistance, he began to brood on it. He thought, too, of the boys of his regiment whom he had seen blown to pieces by enemy dive-bombers; those infernal machines from which the fighter he had stolen was designed to save them all.

"But at the time I did not know that, of course. At the time, you understand, I knew nothing whatever. If there was any particular thought in my mind it was that he was brooding over what he called 'being finished.' He was depressed because he could do no more for England."

They had talked a lot about England, in those days, she went on to explain. Perhaps her own love for her country had peeped out a bit too strongly. Her admiration for its soldiers and sailors, past and present, and the brave men who were ranging the skies by night and by day— no doubt her conversation had trickled like acid over the raw wounds of his conscience.

"And one day he told me everything," she said quietly. "It was the culminating point of a bad week—a week of physical pain and mental torture. At any rate, he told me the whole story from beginning to end.

"I was horrified! I was so distressed that for a time I could scarcely bring myself to touch him. He asked me what he should do, and I told him that he must at once write out a full confession, and that I would try to get it sent over to England."

But before that could happen, before he could bring himself to that pitch, one day a German officer appeared at the hospital and announced that the Englishman, Walter Paine, would from then onwards be in the care of the German Army and must consider himself under their protection. He was not to be moved without permission, and would be guarded by day and by night. The officer talked with him privately for a time, and after he had gone, Paine told her that they intended to kill him.

"They think I've split!" he said. "Something must have happened, and they suspect me." And then he had said: "Supposing they put me out of the way before I can put England wise to her peril?"

In the days immediately following, that had been his one dread. By now he had worked himself into a state bordering upon emotional hysteria. He must, at all costs, undo the harm he had done to England. He must get straight with the boys. Unless he could get back to England, other plans would be stolen. The organisation of which he had been a member lay like a octopus over the land—stealing, stealing, stealing. Undermining our best efforts. Wrecking our most deadly surprises.

"And I myself," she admitted, "I was dreadfully afraid of the same thing, could not bear that England should go down because of a treacherous crowd of Germans. I began to see it as my special duty to save my country. To get this man away to some place where he could talk, or write, or in some way let England know of her peril. He had the information, but he could not move. I could move, but I had not the information. The obvious solution was that we must help each other. We must take our courage in both hands and try to work our way through France into Spain, and then to Lisbon."

And so they had started off. By a neat trick they outwitted the German guard on the hospital, and then had begun that long epic of courage and endurance by which an elderly Englishwoman had hidden and transported a helpless cripple across more than one hundred miles of Occupied France—with every German soldier on the watch for her.

Yet in describing the journey it was not of herself that she spoke, but of Walter Paine. His courage, it seemed, had been magnificent. Traitor he may have been—spy, false friend! But in the end he had washed himself clean in the waters of sacrifice, and done everything he could to atone. His physical sufferings had induced in him such mental exaltation that never once had he doubted his ability to endure to the end—but it was not to be!

At Rouen she had had to seek the assistance of her friend, the old priest—and he, a qualified doctor, had forbidden her to proceed. The Englishman must be rested, he said, and to that end he had agreed to hide him in the church's secret treasure chamber until such time as it was safe to go on again. But Walter Paine had shot his bolt. He had no more strength. It was plain that he had not much longer to live—and knowing it, he had spent his last days in writing out a full account of his treachery so that it might be forwarded to England at the first opportunity.

"Did he know we were here?" Blake asked Sister Agnes when at last she had come to the end of her story. "Before he actually saw us enter this room, I mean?"

It was the old priest who answered.

"Yes," he said. "I told him this morning, after I left you, and when at last I had convinced him of the truth of it, he said: 'Then I needn't struggle any longer, father?' It was his warrant of release, I think. He knew, then, that his task was to be taken safely out of his hands. His incentive to endure was removed. His will to live, relaxed. As you saw for he gave up the struggle with relief. De mortuis nil nisi bonum," he quoted softly, drawing the sheet over the dead man's face. "Requiescat in pace. Amen."

There was a long silence in the room.

Staring at that sheeted figure, Blake could not help but reflect upon the odd chance that had sent Walter Paine, a renegade Englishman, to rest side by side with the dust of generations of Bishops of Rouen—because that's where he would have to lie. They dare not take him outside because of the German edict; he would have to be buried in the church's crypt.

"How long have you known the truth about Walter Paine, Blake?" Beltom Brass asked suddenly.

The detective shrugged.

"If you mean actually known it—no longer than yourself," he said, "But if you mean guessed it, I'd say from the moment when the Baron told me that he had ordered his arrest."

"I don't get you!"

"Yet it's simple enough. If all the Baron had to fear was that Walter Paine might be able to provide an alibi for Isobel Ensor—what would he do? He'd eliminate him, wouldn't he? Instead of ordering his arrest, he'd have ordered him to be shot. He would have taken no risks. Therefore, I argued, since he did not have him shot, there must be something he wanted from him. And that was amplified and made completely obvious by the way he was being searched for over here. As you said yourself, he might have been an army corps, and he was worth an army corps to Germany because of what he knew!"

"And is that how you worked round to the Larry Rue business?"

"Partly, yes. But my real hunch there came from the fact that if the gang had intended to frame Isobel Ensor upon that particular night, surely they would have taken the elementary precaution of making sure that she could not prove an alibi. You would yourself, wouldn't you? It would be your first thought. If you were going to frame a woman with being in a certain place at a certain time, you'd take jolly good care that she couldn't get up and say 'But I was at a party at that time, and I've fifty people to prove it!'"

"Yes. It's on top that I seem to need it," Mr. Brass conceded gracefully.

"And so I looked at her alibi from the other side. Since she was obviously the framed party, supposing that it was her partner who was seeking the alibi? Supposing it was Walter Paine who might want to say: 'But I was at the Regal that night, with Isobel Ensor, and what's more I can prove it!' How then? It was an odd thing that he should be going back to France just when those photographs had to be taken over! And it was odd, too, that his mother was unable to say what time he had arrived home that night, or what time he had gone upstairs. Maybe she hadn't wanted to know! Maybe, instead of going home after leaving Miss Ensor, he had doubled back to the White Cat, received the photographs from Larry Rue, and dashed back again. It was an odd coincidence, too, that he should have happened along to the Southern Aircraft place on that particular afternoon, and made a point of seeing Miss Ensor and talking about pictures. It all fitted just a shade too happily, don't you see?"

"Now you mention it, quite! And of course, it was easy as kiss-my-hand for Paine to carry the photographs as far as France. Who would ever dream of examining the kit of a tommy returning from leave?"

"Nobody! That's the devilish cunning of it. And according to what he says in his confession, he handed them over later on to Larry Rue, in France, after the latter had reached the country via Switzerland. It was Larry's business to complete the trip to Berlin, but he was a bit too well known here to risk giving him the photos to take across the Channel!"

"It was my seeing Larry Rue near the German border that started the ball rolling," put in mademoiselle, speaking for the first time. "I reported it, and our Berlin Agent picked him up again on the other side. That's how it all began."

"And that's why Isobel Ensor is in prison now," Blake said a bit grimly. "If Larry had got through unobserved, nothing more would have been heard of it all until the Germans suddenly came back at us with 'planes as good as our own—and then it would have been too late. But he tripped up somewhere, and to cover himself the Baron had to move forward the prepared scapegoat—in this case, Isobel Ensor. But we bore you with our shop, Monsieur le Cure," he broke off sharply.

"On the contrary, I find your 'shop' intensely interesting," the old priest denied. "In the good old days it was we of the church who were credited with the cunning of serpents. Now, I fear, we could scarcely enter the field with you of the police."

"Well, not all the police, monsieur," grinned Beltom Brass. "Sexton Blake is by way of being rather an outsize in boa-constrictors compared with the ordinary run of wormy police. I'm no small fry myself, of course, if it comes to that," he added modestly. 'Only it's not my day out, to-day. And talking of days out, Blake—what about to-morrow? The loss of Walter Paine's going to simplify matters considerably, isn't it?"

Blake nodded. For the transport of Paine to the village where they were hoping to be taken off to-morrow night, he had arranged a daring and remarkable scheme, but now there would be no need for it. Mademoiselle could make her own way there, and so could he and Brass. None of them had anything whatever to worry about. The only possible snags were the written confession and Sister Agnes, and those, when presently he mentioned the matter, Monsieur le Cure himself volunteered to take care of.

"My son," he said, "I have but two compensations in the France of to-day. One, I am free to go where I like, when I like, and how I like. And two, it is my privilege to marry those of my flock who may wish to be married, and afterwards to bless their new home. At what hour have you to be there?"

"One-hour after midnight, at the Coq d'Or, monsieur, on the east side of the harbour."

"We shall be there to meet you, never fear. And since nuns are married, not given in marriage, it would be strange indeed if any Hun guard should think to look twice at the spouse of the man I shall choose for Sister

Agnes! We shall arrive in the bridal cart, during the late afternoon. You shall see!"

Shortly afterwards, they left the old man with Sister Agnes and the dead. Nor did they see him again until, late the following afternoon, hearing a considerable commotion in the village street, they went to the window in time to see a decorated farm cart turn in beneath the archway of the Coq d'Or. In the front seat, gay in their bridal attire, sat a man whom they had never seen before, and his bride—Sister Agnes! While in the back of the cart, beaming upon all and sundry, sat Monsieur le Cure of Rouen, whom everybody—even the Germans lounging in the street outside—knew very well indeed.

"Pouf!" the old man said when presently he came up to the room where the two 'little cabbages' were sitting with their 'old mother.' "It was easy."

He went to the window and looked out across the harbour. "You had no trouble?" he asked softly, handing over Walter Paine's confession.

"Not a bit," Blake thanked him. "The Huns are looking only for a cripple."

"What our friends the Americanos would call the one track mind, I think?"

Beltom Brass ordered four Amer Picons, and they drank in silence to the success of their journey. Then they composed themselves to patience, their eyes on the sea, their thoughts on the lean grey shapes that were even then creeping cautiously down the Channel.

Six hundred years have gone to the making of the British Navy. Tradition counts. From the moment when, sharp on the tick of time, Blake observed a tiny pin-point of light far out at sea, everything went like clockwork. The first intimation that anything was in any way amiss came with a sudden swirl of water in the harbour.

The next moment, or so at least it seemed to those hiding in the archway of the Coq d'Or, there was a flurry of feet on the cobbled road. Bare steel gleamed wickedly in the darkness.

"Who's for England?" roared a stentorian voice, as the landing party swept on up the street.

"We are!" Blake shouted back.

A petty officer loomed enormous in the gloom. "All correct, sir?" he asked on a lower note.

"All correct!" Blake told him.

"First on the right, sir, and straight down. Fast as you like!" the man laughed gaily, as he raced away to catch up with his men. "Who's for England?" they could hear him calling in the distance.

They found the ship and were helped up the gangway by willing hands. Up on the heights overlooking the town, great guns were roaring. They were answered by flashes from far out at sea, where the escort waited.

Three short hoots on the siren brought the landing-party back at the double. No time was wasted. Almost before the last of them was off the gangway, the destroyer was backing towards the sea.

"Any luck?" the commander asked the officer in charge of the landing-party.

"Laid a dozen or more out, sir, and fired the barracks—look!"

"Not so bad. We'll make Pompey by dawn, with a bit of ginger!"

At ten o'clock of that same morning Sexton Blake and his party reached London. At eleven, having deposited Sister Agnes and mademoiselle at a convenient hotel, Blake and Beltom Brass were closeted with various important personages at the Home Office. Before twelve, eighteen powerful cars had left Scotland Yard for destinations in the country and suburbs.

It was exactly ten minutes to one when Sexton Blake walked into the offices of the Southern Aircraft Construction Company and sent in his card to the works manager—Mr. Ogilvie.

THE SIXTEENTH CHAPTER

Finale.

OGLIVIE RECEIVED HIM in his private office. If he was surprised by the detective's call, there was no sign of it, on his face.

"I've been wondering once or twice what had happened to you, my dear Blake," he said in that smooth voice of his. "I was hoping that you would have news for me before this."

"I have news, Mr. Ogilvie." Sexton Blake sat down in the same chair that he had occupied upon the previous occasion when he had visited the works. "News from France," he said.

"From France—"

"From Walter Paine."

The big man did not immediately reply. Only his mouth pursed to a smaller compass, while his jowl hardened perceptibly.

"That is interesting," he said. "Do you mean that Walter Paine is still—alive?"

"No, he is dead."

"Ah, you mean news of him! Not from him?"

"Both, I'm glad to say. And I have evidence now in my possession that will, I think, completely clear your recent employee—I refer to Miss Isobel Ensor—of all complicity in the treacherous plot which had for its object the destruction of British aerial supremacy."

It was a ponderous, pontifical speech, exactly as Blake had intended it to be—but it had its effect. From the sheer complacency with which he had listened to the opening words, Ogilvie's vast face registered the whole descending gamut of emotion until, by the time Blake had made an end of it, he was reflecting downright fear.

"I do not—quite understand you," he said at last.

"We have unmasked the whole astounding plot, Mr. Ogilvie."

"What d'you mean?"

"Walter Paine has confessed."

For a full moment there was silence in the room. But when the works manager would have risen from his chair, Blake waved him back again. "Just a moment, Mr. Ogilvie," he said. "There is someone outside who would like a word with you."

"What do you—mean?"

"Mr. Beltom Brass, of the British Secret Service. Late milkman, as you may recall, at the house of a friend of yours, Mr. Thomas Grey. Better known perhaps as the Baron."

"God! Are you—crazy, man?"

"Not noticeably so, I trust."

"But that was where they—tried to murder me!"

"No, my friend!" Blake crossed swiftly to the door to admit the Secret Service ace. "No, my friend!" he said again as Beltom Brass stepped into the room. "You over-reached yourself there. Had you gone off with the rest I should never have suspected you, but you were just a shade too clever—you and the Baron between you."

"You appreciate that I shall call you to answer for this infamous calumny, Mr. Blake!"

"I admire your nerve, Ogilvie—but it's no use. You've shot your bolt. You're finished," Blake laughed softly. "You are just one more traitor removed from the list. I'll tell you precisely why we were allowed to find you trussed and tied up like a mummy in that cupboard at the Rowans. The Baron had seen Mr. Brass here, standing beside me in the corridor. He had seen two men, where before there was only myself. He saw that the other was in the uniform of the company that supplied his milk, and straightway his nimble wits flashed to the thought 'Spy!'"

"I think you're quite mad!" Ogilvie repeated with an almost pathetic attempt at dignity. "I haven't the least idea what you're talking about."

"Instantly the Baron asked himself how much that milkman had seen," Blake went on as though the other had not spoken. "Had he, for example, seen you descend from the taxi which later on was destined to bring Anna Muller and myself to the house? Had he seen you rush out of the room into the hall when the first shots were fired? He did not know. He could not be sure. And since you were the king-pin of the whole elaborate organisation,

233

he dare not take any risk. If the milkman had seen you, and you were to disappear with the rest, immediately we should know that you were one of the gang. But if they tied you up and left you to die—if they made it appear that they had kidnapped you in order to force you to reveal the secrets of the new plane—"

Blake paused, but the works manager did not speak. His big face was ghastly. It was green.

"The only thing against the notion was that it would put us wise to the fact that the gang was after those plans—but was that of any real consequence?" he asked. "Provided that you yourself remained unsuspected, did it matter? As you yourself so nobly promised you would apply for a military guard to be put on the plans! It was too risky not having a guard, you said. But even had the entire British Army been put there on guard—the secrets of the new plane would inevitably have become known to you, and you, when the time came, would have passed them on to the Germans."

He paused again, but still the big man remained silent. So damning was the tale of Blake's reconstruction of the affair that he could think of nothing to say.

"The petrol, and the switch to the slow match in that cupboard, were a standing device to ensure the immediate destruction of the house should it ever become necessary," Blake shrugged. "But in this case, in order to heighten the impression that you were on the opposite side from the gang, they left you to throw the switch when you were 'rescued'—hoping to make it appear that they had fired the house and callously left you to be roasted alive in the cupboard. Very effective, Mr. Ogilvie!"

"But not effective enough!" grinned Beltom Brass. "And the same applies to the happenings in the taxi, Mr Ogilvie. That was a good story, as you told it, and it fitted in very neatly with what had actually happened to my friend Blake—in the same taxi! But it was all boloney. That taxi belonged to the gang, and it was used to convey members to and from the Hampstead headquarters. Taxis are so common in London. And so inconspicuous! Much better than red M.G.'s, for example—"

"You appreciate, of course, that I haven't the remotest idea of what you're talking about?" Ogilvie snarled.

Blake studied him for a moment, thoughtfully.

"So far as the red M.G. goes, I'm inclined to believe you," he said quietly. "But that's all. The red M.G. was no doubt picked up by the Baron, and used by Anna Muller—largely because she liked it and because its owner was dead and in no case to argue the point. But for the rest—no! You have been the Baron's right-hand man all the way through the piece, and when the time comes, I shall prove it. It was you who photographed the first set of prints, and it was you who passed on the negative to Walter Paine when he called here, that afternoon, ostensibly to see his old colleagues and to chat with Isobel Ensor. In fact, Ogilvie, the person who beat your 'clock-lock' was none other than yourself."

"That is sheer nonsense!"

"On the contrary, it is strictest fact. You had a camera-watch exactly similar to the one that Anna Muller gave Isobel Ensor, but whereas Miss Ensor was entirely ignorant of the real purpose of hers, you had yours for that one purpose alone. You and Anna Muller were working hand in glove together, and it was you two, between you, who gradually built up the web of evidence that later on was destined to trap her—"

"Then why do you imagine that I defended her so vigorously at her trial?" Ogilvie interrupted sneeringly. "I was her only friend. The only man who believed in her. I was actually choked off by the judge for pretty well perjuring myself on her behalf!"

"You'll soon be believing that yourself!" Blake jibed back at him. "And I admit that it was a clever move on your part. But it won't do, Ogilvie. All that was sheer play-acting. Stuff designed to throw the police off the real scent. The more stoutly you defended that girl, the deeper you damned her and the more you threw suspicion from yourself. It deceived the police. It deceived Miss Ensor herself. It even deceived me, at first—but as soon as I suspected Walter Paine of being a member of the gang, in that moment I also suspected you, Ogilvie! It was you who caused me to be followed from these works when I first came to see you. By some means or other you communicated with the gang, so that by the time I left here a man of yours was waiting to follow me to see where I went. You must have suspected my purpose in coming here. Doubtless, having a guilty conscience, you perceived the drift of my questions. That is why you kept me here, showed me round the works and all the rest of it—you were angling for time until your man could arrive outside ready to tail me when I left."

Ogilvie tried to smile. He was recovering himself now. "You certainly have a vivid imagination, Mr. Blake!" he jeered. "Why in the world should I want to tail you?"

"Because you were nervous! Because you were not quite sure of my real purpose in coming here. And above all else, because the whole gang had been put on its guard by your failure to silence John Maynard at Ladcaster."

"It would be quite useless saying that never in my life have I even been to Ladcaster?"

"On the contrary—I neither know nor care!" Blake assured him. "All that concerns me is that you were second-in-command of the gang that tried to kill Maynard up there. You knew that his purpose in joining the R.A.F. was to fly to France in order to find Walter Paine. You knew it, and the Baron knew it—and both of you realised your peril. So you determined to put it out of his power to fly anywhere!"

"I have never even met this John Maynard."

"Maybe not. I had never met Walter Paine until yesterday, but that did not prevent me from knowing the part he had played in stealing those plans. You, Ogilvie, have for years been setting the stage ready for this war! Ably assisted by Anna Muller, you chose Isobel Ensor as your scapegoat with the very greatest care. Anna Muller found her through the Anglo-German League, and straightway you marked her down for your victim. It was through Anna Muller that she was persuaded to apply for a job here, and when she did, you made her your private typist. Then Anna Muller worked her into the Blue Print Department, so that when the time came for she herself to 'bolt,' Miss Ensor could—without arousing any suspicion—be quietly tucked into the same job and so be all set for the gigantic frame-up."

"You forget that Miss Ensor was given that job with the expressed approval of the directors—"

"No, I don't!" Blake cut him short. "I know she was—but the directors knew nothing about her. That again was sheer bluff on your part. You vouched for her, and the directors took your word that she was okay."

"You won't find it easy to prove that, my dear Blake!"

"Don't delude yourself! By now, I imagine, the whole gang is safely in our hands. Including the Baron and Anna Muller herself. Scotland Yard acted an hour ago, Ogilvie. As I said in the beginning, your hour has struck. The game's played out. You've lost!"

Ogilvie paled a shade, but he still maintained his phlegm.

"You can't prove a thing!" he said again. "Not a thing, I tell you!"

"Aren't you forgetting that Walter Paine has confessed?"

"Walter Paine didn't know anything to confess!"

"He knows that your mother was a German."

Ogilvie started as to a blow. It was plain that he had not expected that. For a moment he sat rigid, staring, then he shrugged.

"I deny it!" he said.

"You may do—but it's true!" Blake went on remorselessly, "Also that you hold considerable industrial interests in Germany that you're trying to save for yourself by spying on your own works over here and passing on the secrets of your plane construction to your German masters! They got at you years ago, Ogilvie! They got at you the moment you assumed the position of manager in this company. In return for your work here they increased your holdings in Krupps and one or two other companies—in fact, they made you a rich man, in Germany, in consideration of your selling British plane secrets to them in case of war!"

It was too much. With a lightning movement, Ogilvie snatched open the top drawer of his desk and made a frantic grab for something inside.

Crack! Like a striking snake, Mr. Brass' fist flashed across the intervening space to whang home mightily on the big man's jaw. The works manager remained quite still for a moment where he sat. Then his jaw dropped, his eyes glazed, and like a pricked balloon he sagged forward over his desk.

"Just a lee-tle too high!" proclaimed Mr. Brass regretfully, always a stickler for perfection in such matters.

Blake looked into the open drawer. There was a .45 automatic lying there fully loaded and with one up the spout. The phone bell rang.

"Hallo?" Blake asked. "Sexton Blake speaking."

"Hallo, old boy!" bawled the voice at the other end. "Venner here—you asked me to ring you. I've got the Baron! Caught him like a bird at the address you gave me! We've got the others as well—the whole bang shootin' match. But I got the Baron. He pulled on me, as well. Fired twice at point-blank range, the swine—he'd have nailed me if I hadn't been so quick on my pins. But you know me, Blake, old boy! Lightning's slow compared with Venner of the Yard. He got me through the front of my hat—the Press chaps are taking a picture of that, now! You know what they are. You can't stop 'em when they're hot on a story. Half an inch lower, an' it have spattered my brains—"

"It wouldn't!" Blake said icily, as he clapped down the receiver.

AMONG THOSE PRESENT at the nuptials of Miss Isobel Ensor and Sergeant Pilot John Maynard, several weeks later, were Sexton Blake and Tinker, Gervase Crispin, K.C., Mademoiselle Yvonne de Braselieu and Sister Agnes, and last but not least, that Flower of the Secret Service as he persisted in referring to himself, Mister Beltom Brass, Esquire.

Gervase Crispin made the speech of his life. His theme was the Mills of God—and if Beltom Brass had not forcibly pulled him down he might still have been speaking now.

It was left to Blake to outline the course of events which had led to Miss Ensor's release and the squashing of the charge against Sergeant-Pilot John Maynard—as he was now known officially in the Service. Miss Ensor, of course, had been handsomely recompensed by the State for her sufferings and wrongful imprisonment; and with a fine gesture had handed over the money to the R.A.F. Benevolent Fund.

"The thing that defeats me," young Maynard said when Blake had finished his reconstruction of the affair, "is why they let me go on until the very last moment before attempting to scotch me? I mean, why didn't they have a cut at me before?"

"Well, for one thing, there was no need," Blake told him. "Walter Paine was their own man, and even had you found him, he would only have lied to you. At that time they had nothing to fear from Paine. He would have repudiated Miss Ensor's story as readily as Eddy Paul at the White Cat repudiated it. They were all in the game together, don't you see? But when Paine disappeared with Sister Agnes—when, in short, he appeared to be ready to rat on them—then they did have something to worry about! They became afraid of what he might do; of what he might say. And when they realised that you intended going over there—for all they knew with the consent of the Government and maybe even with precise information as to his whereabouts—then they took alarm. They feared that you might be intending to bring him back with you."

"But how do you imagine they tumbled to the fact that I was going to look for Paine?"

"I guess they watched you. Maybe they heard of the French lessons you were taking, and certainly they knew that you had enlisted under a false name. It wouldn't take them long to put two and two together and make four of them, you know. They weren't fools. And it was easier to get you on this side than the other. Had they had any clue to Paine's hiding-place—no, I don't think they would have tried for you over here. But when they didn't know where he was, and therefore could have no idea as to where you were going to land, obviously they had to strike while the iron was hot, so to speak."

"Even now I cannot think of Walter Paine as a traitor," Miss Ensor put in, with a shudder. "Why did he join them, Mr. Blake?"

"Money!" the detective shrugged. "They paid him well. According to what he wrote in his confession, Ogilvie got hold of him first, some years ago. It seemed that he used to do odd jobs for the man—work late at the office, and all that kind of thing. Ogilvie realised that he liked money, and would do almost anything to get it. From work in the office he put him on to his own private work, paying him more and more as time went on. Bit by bit he let him into the secret of his German investments—all the time testing him, testing him, to see how far he'd be prepared to go provided only that the money was big enough. I imagine that's how the gang got together. That's how the taxi-driver and the Italian, Antonio, were roped in. There are men who'll do anything for money—even murder!"

"You don't think Ogilvie was among those who attacked me at Ladcaster?" Maynard asked.

Blake shook his head.

"No," he said. "They wouldn't risk that. Ogilvie was too precious to risk in a brawl. Ogilvie, you must appreciate, was the technical head of the gang. It was he who collected the information and passed it on to the Baron for transmission to Germany. And not only information from his own works, remember! Ogilvie was well in with the heads of the Aircraft Supply Ministry, and he knew the secrets of the entire industry. That, indeed, is what kept suspicion away from him since it was not only the secrets of Southern Aircraft that were leaking across to Germany, but the secrets of half a dozen other firms! Odds and ends of all kinds were continually leaking out—"

"Even after my arrest and—and conviction?" Miss Ensor asked swiftly.

It was Beltom Brass who answered that question.

"Yes," he said. "In fact, my dear young lady, it was largely owing to the fact that information was still leaking out that we thought to follow up that suggested alibi of yours. That is why mademoiselle went over to France in the first place. It occurred to us that if, by any chance, you were speaking the truth about Walter Paine—mad as it sounded—then you yourself would have been wrongfully convicted and the real traitor be still at large and still on the job! And in that case, the sooner we got after him and snapped him up, the sooner we should stop the leak!"

"Did Paine always take information across the Channel?" Maynard asked, after a short silence.

"I don't know," Blake admitted. "But I think that Ogilvie always envisaged the possibility of conscription being enforced in the country should war ever come, and in view of the thoroughness of the rest of his preparations I can't help thinking that Walter Paine's call-up was very carefully considered and allowed for. He had not, at any rate, taken over any other photographs, although he admits to having carried verbal messages. He's had a lot of leave that you people never heard of, it seems. Special leaves—upon excuses engineered by Ogilvie and the Baron. Whenever they wanted him they could get him, he said. And there can be little doubt but that they've used him upon each and every occasion."

"They took some risks, didn't they?"

"How do you mean?"

"Well, I was thinking of the Ladcaster affair. After all, Anna Muller couldn't have been certain that I had not seen that photograph of her with Isobel—the one you showed me, you remember? Suppose I had seen it and recognised her—"

Blake interrupted him, with a smile. "But Anna Muller did not know that that photograph was in existence. That's the explanation of that! She had never seen it—and, as we know now, was completely unaware that the fellow had taken it! That was Miss Ensor's secret. She had seen the fellow taking the picture, and had surreptitiously slipped him the shilling required and told him to forward the prints to her address in London. She had intended the photograph to be a surprise for Anna Muller, because the German girl had always, right from the beginning, studiously avoided having her photograph taken—for obvious reasons! But by the time the prints arrived Anna Muller had gone!"

"Maybe if she had known about that picture, she would never have continued her work over here," Beltom Brass put in. "Upon such tiny hairs do fates hang, you see? Otherwise, with this continual dyeing of her hair and altering her complexion, she was safe as a house. But she's tough—our Anna!"

"You're telling me, she's tough!" young Maynard agreed, his thoughts back on that fatal night. He was remembering her face as he had seen it when she stood waiting for her accomplice up the tree to drop that noose about his neck. When she had stood there actually shining a light upon his head so that there should be no mistake! "All the nerve on earth!" he said softly. "And then some!"

"Yet I lived with her for a year and never saw anything wrong with her," Isobel put in. "I must have been blind."

"There was no reason why you should see anything wrong with her," Blake smiled. "In fact, at that time there wasn't anything wrong with her. She was in the same category as 'Thomas Grey.' She was merely waiting for what she knew must one day happen. That's where the German espionage service is so cunning. They employ people for years on the off-chance of one day having need of them. Under the name of 'Thomas Grey' the Baron had been working as a stockbroker in the City for fifteen years or more—and making money there, too! Anna never spoke of him, I suppose?"

"Not that I remember. Although she used to visit a relative out at Hampstead. Do you think he really is her father?"

"I shouldn't be surprised. I haven't proved it yet, but I've a strong suspicion that the life she told you about where the tradespeople took to calling them 'Miller' instead of 'Muller' actually happened. Like enough, it was just another identity which, if pressed, the Baron could have reassured as a hide-out."

"Where was he when you arrested him?"

"Out at Highbury. He had a fine house there; was living

as a retired solicitor. Sidesman of the local church. An expert on miniatures—travelled the country looking for them. You get the cunning of it? Actually, he couldn't have spent one quarter of his time there, yet he worked things so cleverly—he and his German servants between them—that people were quite surprised to learn that he had not spent all his time there! It was the same at Hampstead. His organisation was worthy of a better cause."

"Still, he was a German! I mean, he was working for his own country. He wasn't a dirty traitor, like Ogilvie!" young Maynard said.

"No. He had at least that in his favour."

"Though Ogilvie would never have got away with another major betrayal, would he? I mean, he'd never have got away with the plans of this second fighter? Somebody, surely, would have suspected him?"

Blake nodded, "Yes," he said. "I think you're right there. And I think Ogilvie knew it, too. But I don't think he intended to face another trial. Mind you, he had somebody framed ready to take the blame, but I don't think he would have relied on that this time. It's in my mind that he intended to make a bolt for it. I think he would have collected the plans, and disappeared. After all, it's extremely unlikely that we shall produce another plane as revolutionary in design as this latest one, and I think both he and the Germans would consider that he had earned his pay in stealing the plans of it. That, I believe, is why he was so ready to accept the risk of being found bound and gagged on the Hampstead premises— he knew he hadn't much further to go. If he could only stave off suspicion for another day or two, until the plane was finished; nothing else mattered. He'd be gone before his crime was discovered. He might even have planned to fly his plane over there complete. I dare say he did!"

"You don't know who that other scapegoat was to be?"

"No. And I don't suppose we ever shall, for the simple reason that he—or she—would not know himself. Whoever they framed would know no more about it than Miss Ensor knew—or Mrs. Maynard, I should say, of course!"

Young Maynard looked at his wife. They smiled at each other. It would soon be time for them to leave.

"What'll happen to the Baron eventually?"

"He'll be going upstairs, with the rest of his gang!" Mr. Brass said grimly. "Including the fair Anna, if I'm any judge of a case. But don't let's talk about bad smells at a wedding, friends! Let's be gay and 'earty, as the prophet says. Where's that war-time fizz that was here just now? Hey, Crispin—"

His voice was drowned in a mighty roar from overhead. Running to the window, they saw twelve silver darts turning in a perfect loop. They rolled and they span. They shot straight up to heaven, and dived straight down again—and never with more than a yard or so from wing-tip to wing-tip. Finally they swept down in graceful salute, their engines screaming in concert so that it sounded like a giant tearing a giant length of calico.

"My squadron!" whispered Sergeant-Pilot John Maynard when at last they were gone. "The new fighters, Blake! 'Adolf's Surprise' they call them at the works."

"Well, there's one thing about it," said Beltom Brass. "I'll bet little Adolf will be surprised—when he don't get the plans of it, as he expected!"

THE END

Notes

1. The British Expeditionary Force. The name of the British Army in Western Europe during the Second World War in the period 2nd September 1939 to 31st May 1940.

2. The Link. A politically independent organisation established in July 1937 to promote Anglo-German friendship.

3. Distinguished Flying Medal.

4. Albert Ball and James McCudden were celebrated flying aces during WW1.

5. The word "carefree" replaces "gay"—used in the original publication—in order to avoid any misunderstanding. In 1941, "gay" was not widely employed as a reference to homosexuality.

6. Pierre Laval, a French politician and Nazi sympathiser. He was executed for high treason in 1945.

THE HOUSE ON
THE HILL

"EVEN IN THE midst of war," I said, "you were also taking on cases that involved ordinary crimes being committed against ordinary people."

"I had always done so," Blake remarked.

"True, but previously, that sort of tale tended to get lost amid the glamour of the master crooks and their ambitious schemes. You claimed, in one of our previous interviews, that such villains owed their existence to a phenomenon you call the Credibility Gap, but by the forties, they were noticeably absent. The stories started to feel more realistic in the sense that the criminals, crimes and victims were, by comparison, bordering on the mundane. Had the Credibility Gap closed?"

He made a sound of confirmation. "The second conflict slammed it shut. There was no cognitive dissonance, as there had been when the Great War erupted. Instead, there was a weary sense of familiarity; a horrible feeling of 'here we go again.'" He brushed a strand of tobacco from his trouser leg. "It led to a post-war period of what might be termed 'cosy crimes.'"

I consulted my notepad. "With titles such as The Case of the Night Lorry Driver, The Holiday Camp Mystery, The Case of the Doped Heavyweight, The Income-Tax Conspiracy, The Riddle of the Night Garage, The Mystery of the Missing Angler, and so forth. Didn't you start to feel bored?"

Blake put aside his pipe and sighed. "I didn't choose to become a detective because I wanted to be entertained. My motive has always been a straightforward one: to help people in distress and to right wrongs. It matters not one jot to me whether a crime is against a lord or a labourer, whether it is committed by a Zenith or a zero. So, no, I didn't get bored." He gave a rueful smile. "I'm not sure the same can be said of the readers."

I made a sound of agreement. "By the early fifties, sales of The Sexton Blake Library had dropped considerably," I noted. "The next story, though, dates from 1945. It was written by John Drummond."

"His real name was John Newton Chance," Blake said. "He was a good one for mysteries."

"A bit of an Agatha Christie."

"Yes." He smiled. "Are you aware that, back in 1926, Mrs Christie went missing for ten days?"

"I recall reading something about it, yes."

"It remains one of my favourite cases."

"You were involved?"

"It was I who found her."

"What? That's ... but why was the story never

published? It'd be a sensation!"

"She made me take a vow of secrecy."

"Why? What happened?"

"Can't tell you." He raised his eyebrows. "The vow!"

THE HOUSE ON THE HILL

by John Drummond (John Newton Chance)
THE SEXTON BLAKE LIBRARY 3rd series,
issue 91 (1945)

THE FIRST CHAPTER

The Makings of Murder.

THE NIGHT WAS dark and still, with such a heaviness in the air that it seemed to hang like a stifling blanket. A belt of trees which stood around the small house on the edge of the park were stiff and silent. No leaf moved.

At an open window of the house a girl sat, sewing by the faint light of an oil lantern. The warmth from that tiny flame seemed to add to the stifling heat of the night.

Several times the girl drew back her head from the pale of the light, as if to escape the heat of it for a second. And when she did this, she peered out into the gathering shadows of the night, as if expecting to see or hear someone coming.

But there was no sound anywhere. The sudden brushing flutter of a blind bat dashing against the window pane made her start violently. The leathery flapping was eerie, like the sudden rapping of a dead hand, fleshless and cold, against the glass.

She shuddered and glanced round at the shadowy face

of a clock in the corner. Its tick was faint, so that it seemed almost a part of the silence.

"Mother should be back by now," Jane said, half aloud, as if to give herself courage against the smothering loneliness of the dark. "But then she does forget the time so, once she starts gossiping."

Outside another bat went by with a faint wittering sound, and then in the distance she heard the sound of footsteps approaching the house.

She stopped sewing and stared out through the dark gap of the open window.

The steps grew louder, and then in the dusky gloom outside the grey figure of a man appeared, like a phantom materialising out of a screen of black smoke.

Once more the girl looked towards the shadowy clock, and frowned this time.

"Jim's been working late at the mill again," she thought. "But I didn't expect him yet."

She laid her sewing on the table and rose. The footsteps were loud now, crunching on the gravel, then halted altogether.

There came a knock at the door.

This time the girl started. So the man in the garden was not Jim Drake at all. Jim had been lodging at this house for three years. He had his key. He would never knock.

The outer door of the cottage was only just across the room from where the girl stood, her face softly lit by the lamp on the table below her.

"Can I come in?" said a voice through the panels of the door.

Before there was time to answer, the handle rattled and the door came open. The visitor lounged into the room, a grin on his face.

He stuffed his hands into the pockets of his grey suit and halted, legs wide apart, by the door which fell slowly to behind him.

"What—all alone?" said the visitor with cheerful insolence, and the grin became broader on his face.

"Mr. Ansell!" said the girl, astonished.

"You have a very sharp eye, my dear," said Ansell, with a soft laugh. "Yes, it is I. No more, no less."

The girl seemed flustered. The suddenness of the surprise had caused her some confusion.

"Won't you sit down?" she said at last.

"No, I won't," said Ansell cheerfully, and strolled across to the mantelpiece to gaze at a photograph, dim in the shade of the lamplight. He stared at it for a moment, bending very close, then turned back to her.

"I know that face," he said, with a sly grin.

"That's—that's Mr. Drake," she stammered, flushing deeply.

"Drake? Drake?" said Ansell, and gazed at the shadowy ceiling. "Isn't he one of my engineers at the mill?"

"Yes, that's right," said Jane Wray huskily.

"I must get to know my employees better," grinned Ansell, leaning with one shoulder against the mantelpiece. "Except that it's going to take some time—with a couple of thousand of them!"

He laughed suddenly.

"Still, my old man's been dead only three weeks," he

went on, wandering nervously across the room again. "You can't expect me to learn everything in three weeks."

He gazed around the room quizzically, then grinned again.

"I suppose this cottage belongs to me, too, doesn't it?" he said. "It seems to be on my estate."

"Yes, Mr, Ansell; it does," said the girl uneasily.

There was something queer about the visitor's familiarity. It deepened the sense of uncertainty and dread which she had felt, sitting there alone in the stillness by the hot lamp.

"And why have you got Drake's picture on the mantelpiece?" said Ansell, nodding lightly towards the fireplace again.

"We—we're engaged to be married," said the girl, flushing again.

"H'm!" said Ansell, staring out of the window. "Bit of a dull life being married to a chap like that, eh? Same old grind, day after day. Doing the washing, darning his socks, cooking his dinners—"

His voice faded, and he looked into her astonished face with a broader grin than ever.

"I—I'm afraid I don't understand you, Mr. Ansell!" said Jane hotly.

"Very few people do," said the young man, shrugging. "In fact, some call me vague. But I'll try and explain myself a little better."

He brought out a cigarette case and offered it to the girl. She shook her head without taking her wondering eyes off his face.

"I'm pretty rich now," he said, puffing out a cloud of smoke that whirled thickly in the lamplight. "True, the old man's demise was recent, but what he had is all mine—the mill, the Grange, the estate, a fortune—"

He looked towards the window again and sighed, as if it were a sad thing to have become the owner of so much.

"Of course," he went on, "it's only three weeks since I first saw you, up at the mill, but that's enough. It shouldn't make people talk too much."

"Talk too much?" The girl felt her forehead, as if this strange riddle was beyond her understanding.

"Yes; I mean, it's quite a reasonable thing," said Ansell, sitting down on the table and looking up at her. "You're good-looking, nice figure, pleasant manners—you'd do all right in the part."

"Mr. Ansell,' said the girl, angry at last, "I can't understand one word of what you're saying!"

"All right. If I've got to be blunt about it—" Ansell shrugged and made a grimace. "I mean that you'd do quite well as my wife."

There was a silence that seemed to hang for seconds. Even the faint ticking of the clock seemed dulled by it.

Jane Wray looked at him as she would have looked at a madman.

"Mr. Ansell!" she said at last. "You must be mad!"

"No, not mad," said Ansell lightly, but there was a curious dark gleam in his eyes now which belied his casual attitude. "Not joking, either. I mean what I say. I want you to marry me, and as soon as possible."

She laughed breathlessly.

"Really, Mr. Ansell!" she said. "There is only one answer to that. No! Surely you didn't expect me to say yes, did you?"

"Not at first," said Ansell. "But later on."

Again the girl searched his eyes, but there was no longer the mocking glint of humour in them. There was a flat menace of a mind made up; the stare of a man past joking, and ready to enforce his will if need be.

"It's impossible,' she said with a slight tremor. "I have never heard of anything like this before."

"I don't care what you've heard of before," he said sharply. "I've made up my mind about this thing, and there's the end of it. Believe me, you'll say yes sooner than you think."

There was a dull flaring glow in his dark eyes now that made her shiver suddenly.

"You're mistaken, Mr. Ansell," she said, trying to sort out some kind of sense from the confusion in her brain. "Of course, you must be joking."

"I tell you I'm not!" he shouted with a sudden violence, and started up from the table. For a moment he stood rigid, half-crouching, then relaxed, but no smile or trace of humour came into his face.

Again the idea came into her head that he must be mad. There seemed no other explanation to it, this sudden extraordinary demand.

"When I get the idea that I want something, I go out and get it," he said, with a bitter inflection in his voice. "That's my way of doing things. And that's the way I'm doing it now. You understand that?"

She did not answer.

"Make up your mind by to-morrow," he said with sudden impatience. "Or, if you like, I'll try and make it up for you now. It isn't such a bad offer, is it? You'll have plenty of money, a big house, servants—"

"I don't want any of those things," she interrupted. "I couldn't be happy like that!"

"Well, you certainly won't be happy if you turn it down!" he said, his voice quietening. "You realise that I have the power to turn you out of here, sack you from the mill, and make it hell for you to try and get another living anywhere? And the same goes for Drake, too. You realise that?"

The girl stopped with her mouth half open, watching him as if she could no longer believe what she was hearing.

"You would—do that?" she whispered, horrified at the insane egotism of the man.

"I'd do anything to get my own way," he said, and the faint shadow of a smile twisted a corner of his mouth. But it was a hard, vicious smile.

"Now I'm sure you're mad!" she said desperately. "Or if this is your idea of a hoax, it's a cruel and wretched thing to do."

"How many more times do I have to tell you?" he snarled, stepping closer to her. "I am not joking. If you don't believe me, you'll damned soon find out!"

He calmed down a little, and half smiled in a cunning sort of way.

"Well, are you going to risk waiting to see if I mean what I say?" he said. "Or are you going to be sensible?"

Again a silence fell. The girl closed her eyes momentarily as if to find some temporary relief from this madness. Almost as if she hoped that when she opened her eyes again he would be gone, like a wraith in a nightmare.

But he was still there, watching her with the wild light of excitement in his eyes.

"Well? Yes or no?" he shouted suddenly.

In a flash the girl realised that she would have to go warily. She could not understand what was in the man's mind, and she must have time to talk this over sanely with somebody else.

"I can't tell you now," she said huskily. "It's—it's such a shock. Too much of a surprise. I—I must have time."

"You'll have time," he said, stepping back from her. "You can have till to-morrow morning. If I don't hear from you by then, you'll hear from me."

"What—what do you mean?" she whispered.

He had turned towards the door to go, but now he turned back, his black eyes gleaming.

"Didn't I make it clear just now?" he shouted. "Drake goes, your job goes, and I'll be back to-morrow evening to find out how you like that! Get it now?"

"I see." Her voice was hardly audible.

He hesitated a moment longer, then went out of the cottage and slammed the door. She heard his hurried footsteps crunching away down the drive, gradually fading into the same stifling silence from which he had come.

THE SECOND CHAPTER

A Man Means Murder.

THE OPPRESSIVE SILENCE in the house seemed heavier than before, and to the girl it felt that the loneliness had increased. As if a solid, stifling blanket of warm darkness had cut her off from the outer world.

She stood by the fireplace, staring at the photograph of Jim, just as Clive Ansell had done only a few minutes ago.

She jerked her head away from it and looked round at the clock again. The dim face gleamed faintly in the shadows of the corner, and mixed with the soft, muffled ticking, she heard again the sound of footsteps on the path outside.

She turned nervously towards the door, and seemed to relax with a little sigh of relief as she recognised the quick, heavy tread.

The door came open, and Jim Drake came in, a battered old felt on the back of his curly head and a shabby raincoat slung over his shoulder.

He snatched off his hat and threw both it and the raincoat down on a chair. His blue eyes seemed to laugh as he looked at her, then grew more serious as he saw her pale face and anxious, frightened look.

"Darling! What's happened?" he said, halting before her. "You look as if there's bad news." He looked quickly round the room. "Mother all right?"

She nodded, hesitated a brief second, and then began to speak with a rush.

"She's out," Jane said. "She went to see Auntie, but she'll be back very soon now. Jim, there's something I've got to tell you before she comes back—something that she mustn't know about."

His eyes searched her face anxiously, and he fumbled automatically in his pocket for an old pipe. He had the quick, direct mind of an engineer, and he did not waste time in asking questions.

He could see quite clearly that she was more upset than he had ever seen her, and that was enough for him.

"Let's hear it, Janey," he said quietly.

"I—I hardly know how to start," she said, then paused and bit her lip. "The whole thing's so crazy, and yet— somehow I can't believe he was playing some wicked hoax. He—he meant it."

Jim nodded, as if he understood what she was talking about, and this seemed to calm her. She got her thoughts into order and told him quickly and directly what had happened between her and Clive Ansell.

At first he chewed his pipe, frowning, then he took the battered old relic from his mouth, and the cheerful, humorous lines of his face changed and hardened into an expression so angry that even the girl stopped in sudden alarm.

"Go on, dear," he said impatiently, but without moving his mouth much. "Don't stop now."

The usual laughing light, in his eyes had died into a sullen gleam of fury, and the girl went on, more slowly now, watching him as if frightened of the storm which she had roused in him.

"He's mad, Jim," she ended. "He must be crazy. If he isn't, then what reason could he have had for such a thing?"

There was a brief silence. Jim looked at the little oil lamp as if to hide the expression in his eyes from her.

"He's not crazy," he said in a quiet voice that trembled slightly. "I know him well enough for that. He means what he says. He'll do what he says. He'll do what he threatens to do. That's his kind. There's nothing of the snake in Clive Ansell. He's in the open—outright damn cruel, like a spoilt kid. That's the type he is. He's been spoilt all his life—too much money, too much power— and now he's come into the fortune, he's going enjoy himself."

"But, Jim! Why—why me?" she said blankly.

Jim looked at her and his face softened. He gave a short grin.

"I can think of a reason for that," he said. "You're not exactly an ugly duckling, sweetheart." The faint light of puzzlement came into his face now. "But why marriage? Why the hell marriage? That isn't the game for the Ansell type."

"That's what makes the whole thing so mad," Jane said, frowning. "Honestly, Jim, I couldn't believe it. It was fantastic."

Jim slowly put the pipe back into his mouth and began to draw at it, though it was out.

"Of course," he said slowly, "he knows you. He's obviously had his eye on you for some time. You see, it's possible that he never thought you'd refuse. Some girls would have jumped at it. Perhaps he thought you would, too."

"Well, if he wanted that type of girl there must be plenty about," she said angrily. "He didn't have to come here in that mad way."

Jim dropped into a chair, as if to think it over.

"And he threatens to do all he says if he doesn't get his way," he said, almost to himself. "That doesn't leave us much time, does it?"

He looked up and gave a queer laugh.

"What are we going to do?" she said urgently. "We've got to do something, Jim, otherwise—"

"I think," Jim interrupted quietly, "that you'd better leave me to handle this. I know him fairly well, darling. I might be able to find out just what his game is. On the face of it, it seems mad, unbelievable. There doesn't appear to be any reason for it, yet there must be. Just how did he behave when he was here? Strangely?"

"At first he just behaved like a bad-mannered boy who thought he owned the place—" She broke off and laughed a little at herself for making this comparison. "He does own it, of course, but it would have been the same if he

266

hadn't. Then I thought he seemed surprised when I said no. After that he just got angry in a nasty, threatening way—as if he meant to have his own way, no matter what happened."

"Was he excited at all?" Jim queried.

"Well, no—not until towards the end," she said, staring. "Then he did seem to be furious. But that may have been his vanity."

Jim nodded.

"It's a queer set-up," he said softly, but the hard, bright light in his eyes belied the semi-humorous words. "As a matter of fact, I've never heard of anything queerer. I've heard of wealthy men trying to buy up girls as if they were so much merchandise, but never of trying to force marriage on them."

He laughed, but there was no humour in his voice.

Jane jerked round towards the window. Outside she could hear the light, quick footsteps of her mother approaching.

"Mother mustn't know!" Jane reminded him urgently.

Jim stood up suddenly, caught her arm gently and squeezed it.

"She won't darling," he said softly. "Now, you've got to leave this to me. However crazy it seems, it's a man's job to deal with it. Don't worry. Leave it to me."

He kissed her ear lightly and drew away just as the door opened and a little old lady came in, breathless and agitated.

"Good gracious, dear!" she gasped, putting a basket down on top of Jim's coat on the chair by the door. "I hurried as fast as I could. I'm sure there's a storm coming.

Certain. I can feel it in the air. We must cover all the mirrors and hide the knives—"

"Not before we've had supper, mother dear," said Jane, kissing the little old lady's bird-like nose. "It's ready. I'll go and get it now."

She went through a door into the little kitchen, and Jim helped Mrs. Wray off with her coat.

"It's hot as hot, you've no idea!" cried Mrs. Wray. "And dark, too. My word, you can cut it with a knife, it's so dark. It's the sort of night when terrible things happen. I'm no child, goodness knows, but it's the sort of night I sleep with my head under the bedclothes, I don't mind admitting."

"I don't think it's as bad as that, mother," Jim said cheerfully, and began to set to and lay the table for supper. "We might get a storm, as you say, but it'll clear the air."

"I hate storms," said Mrs. Wray, speaking in the same high-pitched, breathless voice. "I said to Jessie to-night, I said, 'My word, Jessie, though you are my sister and we was brought up together; I don't know how you can lie in your bed like that and not worry about storms,' I said."

Jane came into the room, carrying a tray with the supper on it. The old lady chattered about storms, and her sister Jessie lying in her bed, throughout the meal, until suddenly something caught her notice.

"My gracious me, Jim! What's the matter with your appetite, boy? You're pecking at that food. Pecking at it, and you need a lot, a big man like you."

"I'm not hungry, mother," said Jim, pushing his plate away. "It's the heat, I reckon."

"Yes, it certainly does take the edge off one's appetite,

I must admit," said Mrs. Wray, shovelling another large helping out of the basin on to her plate. "As I said to Jessie this evening—"

She broke off suddenly, and her sharp little eyes darted round the room as a faint growl of thunder sounded in the distance.

"Oh, my!" she said, dropping her knife and fork. "There it is, now! We must cover up the mirrors, Jim. And don't forget, there may be some old ones down in that awful cellar. Oh, how I hate that cellar!"

She darted about the room, snatching up knives, draping Jim's coat over the mirror above the fireplace, talking at a great rate all the time.

The others humoured her, for this old lady was a lion for courage in every other danger in life, but she just could not stand thunderstorms.

Jim took a torch from his pocket and went outside the house. The cottage had been built more than a hundred years before, but it had been built over the ruins of another, much older, with the result that there was an old cellar beneath the cottage.

It was large, and the only entrance to it was through an opening in the outside wall at the back of the house, and this opening was now mostly overgrown with bushes and weeds.

In the cellar itself there was a mass of forgotten things which did not belong to the Wrays at all. They had been there before, unclaimed and forgotten. Old broken heaps of furniture, crates, wooden beams and rubbish strewn about on the earth floor.

Jim did not intend to cover any old pieces of broken mirror which he might find down there. He did not even go down there. He stood at the entrance, lit a cigarette, waited in the electric stillness for a little while, then went back into the cottage.

By the time he arrived back all knives had been hidden and all Mrs. Wray's precautions taken. She was busy closing the windows.

He took his raincoat from the mirror and replaced it with a tablecloth. Then he took his hat and went to the door.

Mrs. Wray started and looked round at him.

"My goodness, boy!" she gasped. "You're surely not going out?"

"I'm sorry, mother," he said with a grin. "I have to."

His sparkling eyes turned to where Jane was standing near the kitchen door, and in his glance she understood the meaning of his going.

He was going in order to be alone to think of some way out of their difficulty.

"There's a new machine I have in mind, mother," he said uncomfortably. "I want to take a walk and think it over."

"Work, work, work!" said Mrs. Wray. "My word, you don't take much time off, child. Always working or thinking about work."

"That's the way to get on, mother," he said, and opened the door. There was no further sound of thunder. "I think the storm's passing the other way. Don't be frightened while I'm gone."

He went out into the brooding silence and closed the door behind him.

THE THIRD CHAPTER

The Mirage of Murder.

THE CALM BEFORE that storm remained for several hours. Mrs. Wray and her daughter went to bed and slept, in spite of the heat.

Jane had carried the little oil-lamp upstairs and stood it on a chair by the stair-head for Jim when he came back. It was beginning to smoke a little when the first approaching mutter of thunder sounded in the distance.

Outside, the dim flare of lightning flickered in the faraway sky and died again. A few seconds passed before the thunder of it growled in the air round the cottage. The next flare was brighter, and the thunder more rapid and louder.

A few heavy drops of rain pattered sullenly on the trees around the cottage. The rain seemed uncertain at first, then quickened up as the thunder grew louder, and settled into a steady, drenching hiss that seemed to become more and more vicious as the minute passed.

Lightning flared brightly round the cottage, and the thunder became loud and very sharp.

Jane awoke suddenly, startled from sleep by a splitting crash from the giant's skittle-alley in the heavens above. She looked towards the window, which suddenly flared up in a brilliant blue square with the fire of the lightning, and against the jagged fork she could see the streaming rain, like blue glass rods beating down outside the open window.

It was like a wild scene in a nightmare.

The echo of the thunder died, and above the hiss of the rain she could hear spattering drops hitting the oil-cloth on the floor inside the window.

She got out of bed to shut the window. The lightning blazed, and she instinctively halted in the middle of the little room and put her hands to her ears to muffle the crashing barrage which followed the flash.

She went on again to the window, but the storm was overhead now, and as she gripped the streaming woodwork to pull the sash down, the lightning blazed again.

The whole garden and the still trees were silhouetted in the blue-green glare, shining through the sheen of the rain like a scene built of sequins.

And suddenly she stopped, the rain beating in her face, staring down at the garden while the unearthly light glared down upon the weird scene.

There was the figure of a man, lying sprawled on the ground, and another, bending over him, arm raised to strike. Both figures glistened with rain, and in the eerie light looked transparent, like moulded figures of green glass.

The lightning died, and by contrast her eyes seemed to see red and yellow flashes in the sudden darkness that followed. The thunder roared in her ears with a violence that seemed to make the cottage shiver on its foundations.

She stood there stiff and still, as if the lightning had struck her motionless where she stood, her eyes still turned on the spot where she had seen the two figures in the garden.

Again the lightning flared, this time with a jagged fork that seemed to stab down at the earth behind the belt of trees. Its glow lit up the garden once more, but the eerie scene of the two men was not there now.

There was just a shapeless heap of rubble by the flower-beds, gleaming and shining with wet in the blue light, and that was all.

Her heart began to beat again, heavily, raggedly. She slammed the window shut and turned back, putting a hand to her wet forehead.

"It—it looked just like two men," she whispered. "Just like. I—I could have sworn—"

She turned towards the door of her room, and then suddenly noticed the light under the door. It was only a thin strip of yellow light, but it was startlingly clear in the darkness of the room.

She went to the door and opened it. On the chair by the stair-head the oil lamp still burned, a little rippling pillar of oily smoke rising upwards from its blackened shade.

The sight of the lamp burning low like this gave her

another shock. She crossed to it, thinking that Jim had forgotten to put it out.

She bent over it, then stopped again. She caught sight of Jim's bed-room door, which yawned wide open. The lamplight spread into the room in a yellow beam which lit up the empty, untouched bed.

Jim was not back yet.

"Then I could have only been asleep a little while,' she muttered. "It seemed like hours! Jim must have got caught in the storm somewhere."

From downstairs there came a sudden soft chime from the old clock in the parlour. Slowly and carefully it tolled three times, and then fell silent again.

The solemn tell-tale chime seemed to unnerve her. After the tension of the storm and the events of that evening, she became suddenly frightened.

Jim had been out for hours.

Until that moment she had been heavy, half-asleep. Now quite suddenly she realised that she had not believed the thing she had seen in the garden. She thought that her eyes and the sudden glare of the lightning had thrown shadows which had formed the grotesque shapes by the flower beds.

But now she began to wonder. The heap of rubbish might have looked like two men in the sudden glare; and the whole thing might have been no more than a trick of her sleepy sight, as she had thought at first.

But had it been?

Jim had never been out as late as this before, and she knew that he had gone to try and see Ansell.

Suppose that the two had met, and that—something dreadful had happened?

As her frightened thoughts raced in her brain the images she had seen in the garden seemed to grow clearer. More and more she began to believe that she had seen two men there, and that one had lain helpless on the ground while the other battered the brains out of him!

Above her the thunder cracked again, but she did not seem to hear it now. She snatched up the little lamp and proceeded downstairs and into the parlour.

As she came into the little room the outer door opened. Outside the lightning flared again, and in the opening the wild, bedraggled figure of Jim was suddenly silhouetted against the blue glare.

He seemed to start violently as he saw the girl with the lamp, then slammed the door to behind him.

"Janey! What are you doing down here at this time of night?"

In the dim light from the little lamp she could see that he was soaking wet, with mud and rain dripping off him on to the floor. He had no hat, and his curly hair was streaky and plastered to his face with the rain.

Great patches of dark, wet stuff stained the faded raincoat and streamed down in broad streaks, like running blood, as he stood there.

"I—I thought I saw somebody in the garden," she faltered, her eyes wide in horror.

"You did?" he said, and began to struggle out of his streaming coat. "That's funny. So did I. In the garden at the back?"

She nodded, but did not speak. Her eyes were fixed steadily on him, and the fear that burnt in them was clear to see.

But he seemed too excited to notice.

"Wasn't anybody, though," he went on. "A trick of the lightning."

"Jim," she said suddenly, "where have you been?"

He looked at her and his mouth hardened.

"Trying to get hold of Ansell," he said. "But I didn't succeed."

He looked round for somewhere to put his coat.

"Did you—did you fall in the stream?" she said, nodding mechanically at the coat.

He shrugged irritably and tossed the coat away into a corner.

"It was a ditch this morning, but it's a stream now." he said. "Liquid mud. Gosh, there's some rain dropping down—"

There was a pause. Both seemed to listen to the furious hissing of the rain outside.

"Are you sure there was nobody in the garden?" Jane said, with a slight shudder.

He jerked his head round to her and looked curiously into her strained face.

"Of course I am," he said angrily. "I went to make sure. It was a trick of the lightning."

"It's funny we should have both seen it—from different places," she said. There was a dull, frightened tone in her voice now.

"Rubbish!" he said. "Sudden glare like that could make

276

tree shadows look like a herd of elephants. You can't trust your eyesight, my dear. Not on nights like this."

"It—it seemed so real!" she whispered, her eyes still steadily fixed on him.

"Oh, don't bother about it any more!" he said curtly. "There was no one there."

"Perhaps—there was someone there and he ran away before you really saw him," said Jane, in the same frightened tone.

"He couldn't have done!" snapped Jim. "I came in by the back gate myself. We'd have run into each other if he'd been trying to get away. Now, don't worry any more about it, dear," he added in a softer tone. "You're worried. It's made you imagine things."

"Yes," she said, her eyes dully fixed on the stained heap of the coat in the corner. "Yes, perhaps I am. I must go back to bed."

She turned and went out and up the stairs, leaving him alone in the darkness of the parlour. At the top of the stairs she realised what she had done and looked back. He had not come out of the parlour, so she put the lamp back where it had been before, then went into her own room and shut the door.

She went to the window, where the rain slashed savagely against the panes. A glare of lightning, farther away this time, shed long black shadows through the streaming garden.

The mound of rubbish appeared—very like the huddled figure of a man lying on the ground.

But it did not look like two men—one on the ground,

and another bending over him, striking at his head. No, it did not look like that.

The electric glare died and she was left in darkness again.

Her heart beat fast, and there was a chill of terror running through her when she thought of Jim.

There had been something strange about him that night. As if the visit of Clive Ansell had changed his whole character.

Jim had always been determined and strong willed, but his strength had always been tempered by humour and kindness. To-night there had been no humour at all. He had seemed hard and grim.

As she stood there thinking of him, she listened through the clatter of the storm for the sound of him mounting the stairs, but it did not come.

The thin line of light still shone under the door, growing fainter as the oil in the lamp burnt lower.

Frequently the flare of distant lightning sprayed into the garden, gleaming on the tiny racing river of rain which covered the path to the back gate.

Each time the flashes came she watched the heap of rubble trying to make herself see it as she had seen it that first time, so that it appeared like the figures of two men.

But no matter how she looked at it, she could not see that eerie scene again.

She began to realise that, at the back of her mind, she had doubted the sudden evidence of her eyes all along until Jim had come back.

And then his strange behaviour had convinced her that the scene had been real, and not a mirage.

She put her hands to her temples. Her head throbbed and ached terribly, and she still did not seem to be able to think clearly. In her mind the whole series of events, beginning with Ansell's visit, had the unreal quality of a nightmare.

She seemed unable to reason the thing out. She was frightened, yet did not know why. She thought she had seen something like murder in the garden, yet in the queer confusion of her brain, she could not be sure of it.

But now that the headache was becoming more painful, so her thoughts seemed to clear, as if recovering from the effects of a drug.

She began to realise other things—things which she had seen at the time of their happening, yet which her fogged mind had taken no notice of.

She saw again the queer, bright look in Jim's eyes when he had come back to the house. It was a look which had seemed unnatural for him; an expression so unlike his normal one.

And the second thing struck her even more forcibly than the first.

Her mother, nervous and frightened to an alarming degree of storms, had slept throughout the tearing din of the thunder.

Through the window the first grey light of dawn came creeping over the drenched land. The rain had gone, but in the garden pools spread over the grass, and in the pathway water ran like a miniature stream.

Had there been anyone in the garden that night, the water would have washed away all trace of his footprints.

She turned suddenly and went out of the room. On the landing the wick of the lamp still smouldered redly. She turned it out and looked curiously round to the door of Jim's bedroom. The door was still open, but in the dawnlight, she saw Jim's figure, fully dressed, sprawled face down across the bed. The sound of his heavy breathing was loud and clear.

She hurried downstairs into the kitchen and crossed to the sink. She halted there, staring at the supper things which she had washed the night before and neatly stacked.

There had been nothing left from the meal—no food over at all. She remembered that her mother had finished up the last little bit.

She was trembling nervously, as if with cold, but in spite of her headache, her brain was working fast.

She went upstairs again to her mother's room. The little old lady was in bed, fast asleep. The girl touched her shoulder and shook her.

For a minute or more Mrs. Wray went on sleeping. Jane shook harder.

"Mother! Wake up!"

The old lady's eyes flickered open, but did not focus on the girl at all. She stared dazedly at the ceiling.

"Mother! Are you all right?"

Mrs. Wray blinked, then gave a groan.

"My! I've a splitting headache," she moaned. "Is the storm over? Let me alone, Jane. I've a bad headache."

The words faded away, and in another second the old lady dropped back into a heavy sleep again.

Jane went to the window and opened it. The cold fresh

air of the dawn made her feel better, but the clearer her mind became the greater grew her fear and sense of dread.

"It was a drug," she whispered to herself. "We were drugged. If I'd eaten more, I should have slept and seen nothing."

She shuddered violently.

Outside the rain dripped from the drenched trees, with a faint dismal rhythm.

One storm was over, but she knew now that in the clamour of the heavens another storm had broken—a storm between men, as violent as the thunder which had covered it.

That was the meaning of these weird happenings.

THE FOURTH CHAPTER

The Missing Man.

THE GRANGE WAS a big old house, set in amongst a cluster of great elm trees on the top of a hill. Little of the house itself could be seen peering through the trees around it.

Inside the building the trees which shadowed the windows made the place seem dark, and soon there was an air of emptiness about it, as if nobody really lived there.

The evening after the storm a big, loose built man, with a slight stoop, came silently along the broad main corridor of the house and turned into the housekeeper's room.

The man wore the dress of a butler, and had a heavy pasty face that might have been modelled from grey clay. There was an insolent half-humorous twist to the droop of his heavy eyelids.

As he came into the little room, a tall, thin woman looked up from a table by the window, where she was writing a letter. She was dressed in black, and with a back so straight she might have been a guardsman.

"I've told you before, Vernon—knock before you come in here!" she said.

At first it seemed as if her tone was one of anger, but there was also a note of excitement or fear in it, as if her nerves were out of order.

Vernon leant his back against the door and yawned heavily.

"My dear Mrs. Marion," he said with lazy cheerfulness, "surely we servants are not supposed to knock at each other? Don't be such a stickler for etiquette. After all, the dear young master is away, and we have the place to ourselves, eh?" He chuckled softly. "What about you and me having supper in the dining-room?" he went on, shutting one eye. "Just like the family! The other servants would wait on us, and—"

"Don't be such a fool, Vernon!" snapped the woman irritably. "Mr. Ansell will be back."

"When?" queried Vernon, with a queer look at the ceiling.

"I don't know," she said quickly.

"No more do I," said Vernon, "He didn't come back, last night, you know. Do you think he's gone off on a rip and forgot to tell us?"

The woman shrugged and jerked her head round to the window. She stared for a moment at the dark shadows of the trees.

"I suppose it's all right?" she said, turning slowly back to the lounging butler.

"I suppose so," said Vernon, more keenly. "After all, he's a wild young rake, as far as I've heard, and he hasn't got used to having his old man's money yet. He's probably gone off on a bender."

The woman stared at the fireplace.

"Wild," she repeated, half to herself. "Yes, he was always wild. I remember him as a boy. Quick-tempered and spiteful when he couldn't get his own way. Violent, too. I don't suppose he's changed much. He's probably just learned to hide it better."

"I don't think he's troubled to hide it much," said Vernon dryly. "Did I tell you about the other night? About the radio?"

The woman stared, her black eyes shining like coals, puzzled.

"What about it?" she said, tight-lipped.

"Nothing," said Vernon, shrugging. "He asked me to get the news for him, and I told him it was too late. Then he lost his temper and threw the decanter of whisky at me. It smashed against the wall. Missed me, luckily."

"So that's where the stain on the wall came from," she said. "I noticed it yesterday."

"Yes, that's where it came from," said Vernon sarcastically. "The little gentleman did it."

A silence fell in the room. Outside, the trees rustled faintly, and from the servants' hall at the back of the house there was a faint sound of a wireless playing.

Vernon listened for a moment, then leant away from the door.

"Well, my dear housekeeper," he said, with an ironic

tone in his voice, "what is to be done? Shall I lay supper for him, in case he comes back? Or shall we just wait until we hear from him? Or do you think we should tell the police?"

Mrs. Marion started violently, and her pen dropped with a tiny clatter to the floor.

"Tell the police?" she stammered. "What for?"

"Sorry. I didn't mean to alarm you," said Vernon gravely. "I only thought it was a little strange that he should have gone off without a word like this. It might be a case of loss of memory, perhaps. He might be wandering about the country, not knowing who he is, eh?"

Mrs. Marion shrugged impatiently.

She stood up suddenly and smoothed down her dress with her hands. The tall, rigid woman was nervous and upset. The heavy-lidded eyes of the butler could see this very clearly.

"Nonsense!" she snapped, with a trace of breathlessness. "Of course, he's gone off on some jaunt. That's all!"

"I forgot to mention," said the butler casually, "that—"

He broke off, his shadowed eyes on her as if deliberately tantalising her.

"You forgot to mention what?" she echoed.

"That he didn't take any clothes with him," said Vernon. "Not even a coat, and it rained like hell last night."

"I've told you before to be more careful with your language!" she flared angrily.

"Well, if that wasn't raining hell, I must be a goat," he answered slyly. "Anyhow, what are we going to do about him?"

"Wait, of course!" she said fiercely. "He won't like it if you ask the police to start hunting for him. He probably has a good reason for going off like this."

"Maybe somebody else had a good reason for him going off like this," said Vernon, in a very soft voice.

The woman stared at him, startled and afraid.

"What do you mean?" she said, her voice a whisper.

He shrugged and gave a heavy sigh.

"It was just an idea that struck me," he said. "You see, Mr. Ansell told me to lay out the whisky and cigars for him last evening." Vernon interrupted himself with a yawn. "Which is a sure sign that he meant to come back."

"But he never did come back. He's not back now."

"You make it sound very sinister," she said. "But don't forget, he's got a lot of queer ways. This may be one of them."

"Queer ways," said Vernon, nodding slowly. "Yes, they're queer all right. He didn't seem to bother much when his old man was taken ill, did he? Didn't seem to care at all."

"Don't say such horrible things!" she said angrily.

"Perhaps they are horrible things to say," he rejoined in the same slow voice, "but they're the truth. You can't get away from that, Mrs. Marion, can you now?"

She gave a sudden uncontrollable shudder and turned away from him to collect up her writing things. He watched her quizzically.

"Well, we haven't yet decided what we ought to do," he said in an idle sort of way. "Do we prepare supper, or what?"

"I'll deal with it," she said sharply. "I'll see that something cold is ready if he comes back."

"Yes—if he comes' back," said Vernon, nodding.

She swung round to him in a fury.

"Why do you keep on saying it like that?" she cried. "Do you think he's had an accident?"

Vernon watched her without replying. She waited for several seconds, then the shudder came again, and she walked quickly out of the room.

"And some," said Vernon, to the empty room, "refuse to look facts in the face."

He looked carefully round the room, then went silently out and along the corridor to the library. He switched on the lights, drew the curtains, and set out the whisky on a table by the armchair which Ansell always used.

Silently he moved about, putting everything just where Ansell would want it—if he ever came back. When Vernon had finished he looked round again, shook his head almost sadly, and went out again, closing the door behind him without any sound.

THE FIFTH CHAPTER

The Course of Rumour.

THE DAYS PASSED, and nothing was seen of Clive Ansell. At the Grange the servants talked; Vernon talked; Mrs. Marion talked, but that did not bring back the missing man.

Vernon argued with the housekeeper, but Mrs. Marion opposed the butler's desire to bring in the police.

"He was always a wild boy," she said. "He was always likely to do things like this. He'll be back."

Vernon did not agree, but he shrugged and went silently on with his work, laying out the whisky decanter and cigars night after night in the library—and clearing them away the next morning.

Mrs. Marion became more abrupt and taciturn as the days passed. She said hardly anything to the other servants in the huge old house, except to forbid them to talk about the young master.

Vernon watched her with interest during this time; as

if he could not quite understand why she should feel so unworried about Ansell's disappearance. In his own room at the top of the house he made an entry in his large diary each day.

The diary had been a habit of his for many years, and he had a good many volumes of books filled with his daily doings of the past years. And one day he said to Mrs. Marion:

"It should come in useful if the police want to look up anything."

"The police!" she cried. "Why do you keep bringing them into this?"

"My dear Mrs. Marion!" he protested, with the half-humorous droop of his heavy eyelids. "I haven't brought them in at all—yet."

With that he walked silently away, leaving her to stare fearfully after him.

In the town and at the mill there was a good deal of whispering and conjecture as to the disappearance of Ansell. He had not been seen by anyone in that district since the night of the storm.

Even then it did not create as much interest as it might have done had Ansell been better known. As it was, he had avoided Westhall as much as he could all his life.

He had not lived there at all while his father had been alive, and his brief visits to the Grange were mainly concerned with borrowing more money.

The whole district knew him as a rake, and an undisciplined spendthrift, which is why nothing much was done about his disappearance for so long.

Many people merely dismissed it, thinking that the spoilt boy had just gone away with some light of love for a week or two. Others assumed he had gone away on some wild adventure, leaving the estate to rot.

During those days Jane heard a lot of the girls at the mill talking about him, giggling and whispering together as they imagined some lurid explanation for the disappearance.

But as the days passed the cramping cold in her heart increased to a dull dread. Many times, when her mother and Jim were out in the evening, she went into the garden near the spot where she had seemed to see the murder scene in the storm, and tried to find some mark which would tell her that what she had seen had been real.

But the savage rains of the night had washed the garden clean of any trace that there might have been. If any strange footprints had been there they had dissolved into liquid mud and were lost for ever.

To her frightened mind the queerest thing about the disappearance was that Jim would not talk about it. He had become moody and depressed, and the bare mention of Ansell was enough to make him irritable and short-tempered.

She said nothing about the suspicions she had had of the supper on the night of the storm. For some reason she had become frightened to mention that, too.

In her own mind she was sure that somehow the food had been tampered with, and that on that night both she and her mother had suffered the effects of some drug.

Nothing else could explain the mother's heavy sleeping

through the storm. Jane, too, would have slept through it all had she not had her appetite upset by Ansell's visit.

It was that which had kept her awake and uneasy, and which had brought her to the window at the very moment when the strange scene in the garden had been enacted.

More than a week later her mother, Jim, and herself were at supper. The little old lady had just returned from another visit to her sister Jessie, and was as bright and chatty as a twittering little bird.

"Everyone seems to be talking about young Mr. Ansell," she said rapidly. "It really is very queer how he went away like that, isn't it? What do you think, Jim?"

Jim chewed slowly and stared at her, almost as if he were annoyed by the question. Jane watched him with a frightened light in her eyes.

"I don't know," he said at last. "He was always a queer type. Might do anything."

"But surely," protested Mrs. Wray—"surely he would settle down when his father died and he came into all that money? He wouldn't want to roam about goodness knows where, do you think? It doesn't seem natural to me."

Fortunately, Mrs. Wray could never keep to one subject for long, and she immediately switched off on to something else which had nothing to do with the missing Ansell.

For the rest of the meal Jim said nothing. He was dull and preoccupied. He had something on his mind.

The meal ended, and he helped Jane to clear it away. The old lady picked up some sewing and sat herself down at the table.

It was then that the dog began to howl.

The eerie wail sounded distant, as if coming from somewhere in the trees outside the house.

Mrs. Wray dropped her sewing and shuddered.

"Oh dear! Oh dear! That awful noise!" she cried. "It always means somebody is going to die!"

Jim was wiping plates by the sink. He became still, his eyes staring blankly at the curtained window. Jane looked quickly at him and went pale.

There was something eerie and dreadful about the howling dog, like the cry of a ghost in outer darkness. It echoed amongst the trees and then died away.

"I hate that sound!" said Jane in a voice hardly above a whisper. She went on washing-up.

Suddenly the howling started again, much louder now, as if the stray dog had got into the garden outside the window.

"Damn!" said Jim. "It's got in through the gate."

He threw down the drying cloth and went out into the garden through the back door. The thin slice of a new moon shone through the trees, shedding a yellow silver light in the garden.

Jim stopped as he saw the shape of a dog slinking away towards the open garden gate. The animal's tail was between his legs, and his ears were pricked back as if mortally scared.

It reached the gate, and then suddenly streaked out like a greyhound released from the trap. The racing form vanished into the moonlit shadows and was gone.

Jim looked quickly round the garden, but could see

nothing unusual about it. He turned slowly and went back into the house. Mother and daughter were silent, watching him as he came in.

The sight of their still, half-frightened stares seemed to irritate him more than ever.

"What's the matter?" he snapped suddenly. "Haven't you seen me before?"

Jane flushed and looked away quickly. Mrs. Wray swallowed and went on with her sewing at a terrific pace, so fast it seemed she might sew her fingers to the work before she would have time to stop herself.

"They make me nervous, dogs howling," she confessed, without looking up. "As children we were always taught they meant somebody was going to die."

"An old wives' tale," said Jim sourly and lit a cigarette. "There must be thousands of silly stories like that still going about."

He sat down in a chair away from them and puffed quickly at his cigarette.

"Was the dog in the garden?" said Jane softly.

He started and looked round at her.

"Yes, it was. The back gate was open," he said.

"It sounded right underneath the kitchen window—the last time," Jane went on, bending to watch her mother's sewing.

"It was," he said dryly.

He frowned suddenly and looked away to the dim shadows in one corner of the room, as if trying to remember something. From the wood came the faint, distant sound of the howling dog.

Jim got up suddenly.

"I'm going for a walk," he said, throwing his cigarette down into the fireplace.

He took his hat and went out of the house. They listened to the sound of his footsteps dying away on the gravel.

"I think that boy's sickening for something," said Mrs. Wray firmly. "He hasn't been himself at all just lately. Going about like a man in a dream. I think he ought to see a doctor. It's all very well, but these strong fellows are the first to go if anything goes wrong. I remember my Uncle Arthur, going out one night without a coat—"

She stopped suddenly and looked up with a curious little frown.

"Yes, and talking about coats—has Jim lost his raincoat?" she said.

There was a dead silence. Jane started visibly, and looked round the room.

"His—his raincoat?" she said huskily.

"Yes, you know—his old yellow raincoat," said Mrs. Wray impatiently. "It had a tear in the pocket, I noticed, and I meant to sew it up for him. But the other day I was looking for it, and I couldn't find it anywhere. Has he lost it?"

Jane turned away from the light so that her mother could not see the sudden paleness in her face.

"I don't know," she said. "I hadn't noticed it had gone."

"Perhaps he left it at the office," said Mrs. Wray more cheerfully. "But it's funny, all the same, because he used to carry it everywhere, slung over his shoulder like an old sack."

"Yes, I expect he's left it at the office," said Jane.

She remembered the sight of that coat on the night of the storm, streaming wet, and shining darkly with something that looked like blood. And he had thrown it carelessly down.

And since then she had forgotten it. But now she came to think of it, she had never seen it since.

Of course, the stains on it might have been mud, as Jim had said, but somehow . . .

She shook herself impatiently as if to try and throw aside these strange and dreadful thoughts which had been growing so terribly in her mind during the last few days.

For since the strange visit of Ansell her life had changed absolutely. It was as if he had been an evil sprite who had come and left his dark spell over the house, so that the whole place had become shadowed with dread.

There was some ironing which had to be done, and she set about it with some relief, as if the work would take her mind off the dark thoughts which were becoming a part of her life.

Yet as she worked she found herself thinking of the same things. She wondered where Jim had been that night, and why he had behaved so strangely ever since. He had not been himself. He had become morose and secretive and no longer shared his thoughts with her.

That alone had upset her, for she could think of no reason for it unless he was brooding over some secret which he could share with no one.

Her mother went to bed, and Jane kept on with her work for a long time after that. The shadowy clock in the corner ticked on quietly, and when at last she had finished the pile of ironing she looked up and saw that it was a quarter to twelve.

She put the things away and quickly got together the things for breakfast. The clock struck twelve when she finally came back into the parlour.

Jim was not back yet. She hesitated over the lamp, wondering whether to put it out or leave it on for him, and finally decided to put it out.

She needed no light to go upstairs by, and found her way to her bedroom without any difficulty. The new moon shone faintly through the open doorway of Jim's room and cast its faint pale light down the stairs.

She came into her room and went to the window. The moon shone like a silver rind in the clear sky, and the garden was sharply lit in its light. Once again she stared at the silent, shadowed heap of refuse in the garden, and into her frightened mind there came once more the memory of the tableau she had seen there on the night of the storm.

She shuddered slightly, and was about to turn away when suddenly she saw something moving in the garden. It was a flitting shadow, as quick and fleeting as the passing of a bat, but it was enough to catch her eye. She bent closer to the glass and peered down to a spot almost beneath her own window.

The queer, elongated shadow of a man lay across the grass at an angle. Almost as soon as she saw it, it seemed to step into the wall beneath her and vanish.

The garden lay quiet and motionless under the moon.

But there was a man down there, and from what she had seen it seemed as if he had been clambering through the lower window.

She turned towards the door and went out silently on to the landing. There she hesitated, her eyes on the door of her mother's room, but there was no sound from the old lady, and the girl went on down the stairs, making no sound as she went.

She came down into the kitchen and halted by the garden door.

There was no sound from outside, and the only thing she could hear was the ticking of the clock from the next room. That faint, regular beat seemed only to make the silence deeper.

She turned the key in the door. The faint click of the wards made her heart jump, and for a moment she stood rigid, wondering if the marauder outside had heard.

Still no sound came.

Slowly she pulled the door open. The moonlight seemed stronger and the heavily etched details of the garden stood out black and clear to her, like a drawing shaded with Indian ink.

She went out on to the step. There was a faint rustling sound close by her feet, and she stiffened involuntarily, jerking her head to one side to see what it was.

There was nothing there, save the thick bush which hid the unsightly entrance to the old cellar. It was still, but upon its branches there was a white gash which seemed to move in the faint night breeze.

She bent forward to see it more closely, and then she

made out the long, torn shape of a white handkerchief which had been caught on the branches.

And as she stared the brambles moved slightly in the breeze, and a faint yellow gleam of light from the cellar appeared between them.

The branches closed again almost at once, and there was only darkness in the heart of the bush.

But there was somebody down the cellar.

For several seconds she stood there, her heart beating like a hammer, trying to make her mind up what was best to be done. If there was a burglar in the cellar, there would be very little that she could do against a powerful and perhaps desperate man.

Yet there was no one to whom she could call for help. Jim had not come home.

She crept forward to the bush, bent and parted the branches.

From the gloomy interior of the cellar below the ground a solitary yellow candle-light shone. Its wavering light sprayed on to the heaps of forgotten rubbish piled in the vault, throwing eerie and distorted shadows along the blotched walls.

And by the candle, close to the far wall, was a man with his back to her. He was leaning back on a spade, staring down at a long hole which he had dug at his feet.

Jane caught her breath, and for a moment her brain whirled round, as if she was about to faint. But she managed to keep a grip on herself and choke back the horror which rose in her.

For in the hole sprawled the twisted, shattered body of

Ansell, spattered with mud and clay and dried blood.

And the man who stood over the corpse, staring down at it, was Jim Drake.

She drew back and clung to the rough brick wall of the house for support. For several seconds she could not think clearly, and then she turned and went back into the house, going as quietly as she had come.

Silent as a ghost, she went upstairs to her room and locked the door. She sat down on the edge of the bed and stared at the window, stunned, not knowing what to do.

The thing she had feared through these last days was true.

Ansell and Jim had quarrelled, and murder had been done.

The dark shadow of dread which had preyed on her mind had become a reality. There was no escape from it now; the greatest tragedy of all had happened during the storm that night.

She sat there until the moon sank and the first light of dawn streamed through the window, but she did not hear the sound of Jim coming into the house again.

THE SIXTH CHAPTER

The Black Visitors.

INSPECTOR GRIMES, OF the Westhall police, was a sour and disbelieving man. He was a born sceptic, and challenged everybody on principle. But if he once found out that anyone was speaking the truth, there was no keener listener than Inspector Grimes.

That morning he was short-tempered, and eyed his two visitors with no very great enthusiasm.

In fact, the visitors, dressed in the black uniform of their service and moving with the silence that went with it, were enough to depress anybody.

Mrs. Marion was stiff and tight-lipped, as if she had finally persuaded herself to come here against her own will. Vernon, the butler, looked as if he had come out of pure, but polite, curiosity. His heavy-lidded eyes looked sleepy as he viewed the inspector.

"We came because we thought it time the police looked into the disappearance of Mr. Ansell," said Mrs. Marion sharply. "I was all against it myself, but he's been gone too long now for my comfort, and he's got no family to start up a fuss, so we thought it was our duty to do it."

Suddenly the inspector's interest flamed up within him. He had heard much about Ansell's disappearance during the last week, and had himself been wondering if it were all above board; but he had been powerless to act on his own.

He had to have some authority on which to work, and it looked very much as if this would be it.

"Just give me the details, will you, ha?" he said quickly.

He seemed always to stick on "ha" at the end of a sentence, but nobody knew why.

Sharply and shortly the stiff, black-dressed woman gave him the details far as she knew them. Vernon smothered a yawn, but otherwise contributed nothing to the tale.

The inspector made a lot of rapid notes, then looked up again.

"Do you know where he went when he left the house that night, ha?"

Marion shook her head abruptly, and the inspector's eyes flicked round to Vernon. The butler seemed to be staring out of the window, idle and bored, but he started violently when the power of the inspector's gaze penetrated his blankness.

"Me, sir?" he said, drawing himself up.

"Yes, you, Mr. Vernon."

"I'm afraid, sir," said the butler urbanely, "that I did not hear the question."

A momentary frown darkened the inspector's keen face, but he repeated the query carefully.

"Oh—ah!—I see, sir," said Vernon, straightening his black tie and clearing his throat. "Well, yes, sir. I have an idea where he went, as you might say. That is, he said he was going to a certain place, sir, but whether he actually went there or not is another matter."

"Well?"

"I might add, sir, that it would be a most unlikely place for Mr. Ansell to go, sir," said the butler, determined not to be hustled.

"We are not really concerned with what you may consider to be likely or unlikely," said the inspector, with pleasing sarcasm. "Where was the place he said he would go to?"

"Laburn Cottage, sir," said the butler, and coughed, as if he really apologised for mentioning such a hovel to a gentleman like the inspector.

"Laburn Cottage?" said the inspector, squinting at the ceiling. "That's on the south side of the estate, isn't it, ha?"

"Exactly so, sir," said Vernon. "It used to be a labourer's cottage, sir, but now I understand it is let to a Mrs. Wray."

"I see," said Grimes, making a note. "Then that cottage would be Mr. Ansell's property, ha?"

"Quite so, sir."

"Then why is it unlikely that he should go and visit a piece of his own property?" demanded the inspector, in some surprise.

"At that time of night, sir," countered the butler, raising his eyebrows. "You will mark, sir, that the time he left the Grange was half-past eight, sir. Surely no time to call upon one's tenants?"

"Hum, ha," grunted the inspector, as if he reluctantly agreed. "Anyhow, it's the only guide we have as to where he may have gone."

Vernon shrugged very faintly, as if to indicate that if the inspector insisted on grubbing around dirty little hovels, he, Vernon, washed his hands of the whole affair.

The black garbed visitors had nothing more by which they could help the inspector, and they left, taking with them his assurance that if he required them again, he would call at the Grange.

"And I hope," remarked Vernon under his breath, "that he calls at the tradesmen's door."

The inspector did not hear this remark, and, therefore, was in a good humour when he rang the bell for Sergeant Sale. The sergeant was a huge man with a red face, and ears that stuck out from his head-like jug handles. But he had shrewd blue eyes and a tread as light as a cat's.

He listened carefully while the inspector told him what had happened during the visit of the Grange servants.

"I see, sir," he said slowly. "As a matter of fact, you probably know, sir, there's been a good deal of talk in the town just lately about Ansell. One half says he's out on some gigantic spree, and the other half say there's been dirty work. It's past time something was done to clear it up."

The inspector agreed, and in a few minutes he and Sale were on their way in a police car to Laburn Cottage. Once there they found little Mrs. Wray in the middle of her housework, and the old lady was put into a bother by the appearance of her unexpected visitors.

"I'm afraid you've caught me in my old working

clothes," she apologised with a nervous laugh. "But sit down, do, and I'll get you a cup of tea."

"I'm afraid we haven't time for that, madam," said the inspector kindly. "We called to find out if you have seen Mr. Ansell recently, ha?"

"Mr. Ansell?" she said, rather flustered. "Oh, you mean young Mr. Ansell, of course, because his father died, A few weeks ago, I remember. Very sad. But young Mr. Ansell—" She frowned at the inspector and shook her head. "As far as I can remember, I've never seen the boy in my life."

The inspector and Sale exchanged glances.

"Were you in on the evening of September the thirteenth?" said the inspector patiently.

"Oh dear—oh dear! I'm sure I never can remember dates!" fluttered the little old lady. "Let me see now. The thirteenth would have been—Friday, Thursday, Wednesday—" She counted the days backwards on her fingers, then brightened up a lot.

"Oh yes! Last Thursday week. Yesterday week, you mean!" she cried. "Yes, I remember that, because I always go and see my sister Jessie on Thursdays."

"Then you weren't in on that evening—the evening of Thursday the thirteenth?" persisted Grimes.

"No, no. That is, not until ten o'clock, I think it was," she said. "It was very late, I remember, and I ran all the way home because of the storm."

The inspector looked pleased about this. The evidence about the storm made it certain that the old lady did remember what she was talking about. In spite of her nervousness, she was a very good witness.

"We understand that Mr. Ansell may have called-here that night, while you were out," said Grimes gently. "Was there anyone in at that time?"

"Oh yes!" said Mrs. Wray eagerly. "My daughter was in, but I'm sure that she would have told me if Mr. Ansell had called. After all, it would be quite an important occasion, wouldn't it?" She laughed breathlessly. "I'll ask her. She's kept to her bed to-day because of a bad headache. But I sent a message to the mill where she works, to tell them, so that everything's all right."

She went out of the room, wiping her hands on her apron as she went.

"Nice little old dame," said Sale comfortably. "I bet she can cook the way mother used to."

"You have a tendency to think of your stomach before everything," said Grimes dryly. "And it's not surprising considering your stomach stands well before the rest of you."

The sergeant made a straining effort to pull his corporation in, but found the strain too much and let it go again with a satisfied grin.

"Better than being dyspeptic," he said. "My brother now, can't keep anything down without patent drugs. Bad thing that. Always taking things for his stomach, he is. Never seems happy. Drugs always send me bang off to sleep, and give me a headache afterwards."

"Drugs never act the same way on two different people," said Grimes, staring round the room. "You should know that by now."

Mrs. Wray came back, her face wrinkled with worry.

"I'm sorry, gentlemen," she said. "I can't think what's come over my daughter. She's locked herself in her room there, and won't answer properly. But she says she's never seen Mr. Ansell."

"That settles it, then," said the inspector, turning towards the door. "Well, thank you very much, Mrs. Wray. We're sorry to have troubled you."

"It's been a pleasure, of course," said Mrs. Wray happily. "Are you sure you won't have a cup of tea before you go?"

"Certain, thanks," said the inspector, stepping out into the garden. He looked from the road along the side of the house to the back garden gate.

"Is that a short cut up to the Grange?" he asked.

"Well, yes, it is," said Mrs. Wray. "Though it's not very short—it's the shortest, if you know what I mean. The path goes out by the gate and through the wood. You can't miss your way."

"I think we'll try it," said Grimes, looking up at the bright sunny sky. "Tell the driver to go round by the road and meet us up at the Grange, Sale. A walk will do us good, and we shall have to search the wood and sooner or later—perhaps."

He added the last sentence in a low voice so that the old lady did not hear it. Sale went and gave the order to the driver, and then returned to the inspector.

Together they began to stroll through the little garden. By the kitchen door Grimes halted and brought out a small notebook in which he made a jotting.

Sale looked round the neat garden with a critical eye,

for he was a keen amateur gardener himself.

"Can't understand why that ugly great gorse bush is plunked up against the wall there," he said, nodding at the bush. "Seems out of place, somehow. Great untidy straggling bits of gorse like that."

The inspector glanced round at it and grinned.

"You're too keen on neatness, Sale," he said. "It looks all right to me."

His eyes flicked upwards to the window high above the bush, and then down again to the garden.

"Don't look now, but there's a girl staring down from the window up there," he whispered. "That must be the locked-in daughter. She looks as pale as a ghost, too. Wonder what she's up to?"

Both men turned as the kitchen door came open and beaming Mrs. Wray appeared with a plate and some jam tarts on it.

"At least," she said, "you can eat a tart before you go. I made them only just now, and I'm sure you must get very hungry, asking people all these questions."

"No, thank you," said the inspector.

"Afraid not, ma," said the sergeant, shaking his head regretfully. "I was just asking the inspector," he went on, pointing at the bush, "why you have that there? Being a bit of a gardener myself I wondered a bit."

"That? Oh, that hides the cellar entrance," said Mrs. Wray.

"The cellar entrance?" echoed the inspector, looking round suddenly. "That's a funny idea, isn't it? Why not a door?"

"Well, you see, it's not exactly part of this house," said the old lady. "It's part of the one that was here before, and they sort of left it underneath. Nobody ever goes down there. It's too damp to be any good, you see."

"Ha, quite a curio," said the inspector. "Well, we mustn't hang about any more." He put his notebook away. "We must get along up to the Grange."

"Well now, that's funny," said Mrs. Wray, staring at the bush. "There's one of Jim's handkerchiefs hanging on the bush. I wonder how it got there?"

She pattered across to the bush and picked the white, torn rag from the brambles. In the moonlight it had looked white, but now in the bright sun of day it was dirty and stained, and there were brown smudges on it.

"Well, now, that is funny," she said, staring at it. "This is the handkerchief with the initial on it, and I haven't had that to wash this week. I thought he'd lost it."

"Handkerchiefs get lost by dozen the every day," smiled the inspector. "Well, good-bye, Mrs. Wray, and thank you—"

He broke off, his keen eyes fixed on the corner of the handkerchief and the initial "A" which showed faintly there. The old lady was peering shortsightedly at it, and it was clear to the inspector that she was too shortsighted to read actually what the initial was.

"This belongs to a friend of yours?" he queried.

"Why, yes, I think so," said Mrs. Wray, turning the corner of the stained rag this way and that in an effort to read the small letter. "And yet—that's funny—it looks more like an 'H' to me."

"It's an 'A'," said the inspector, watching the old lady start.

"Is it?" she said. "Good gracious! Then it must belong to somebody else. It can't be his at all! I wonder, now—"

She turned and peered at the bush again as if that spiky mass could tell her to whom the rag belonged.

"It looks to me," said the inspector slowly, "as if somebody has been down your cellar recently. Is there anything down there that anyone might want to steal?"

"Why, no! Only some old rubbish," said Mrs. Wray, with a startled look at the inspector. "Now I wonder whose this is? If it was a 'D' it would be Jim's, but—"

"Who is Jim?" asked the sergeant.

"Jim Drake. He lodges with us," she answered. "Such a nice boy, and engaged to my daughter. A nice couple they'll make, too. So devoted. He's an engineer at the mill, you know, and is often on night work. Works all hours, he's so anxious to get on."

"Has he been on night work recently, then?" said the inspector, rather curious to know why this information should suddenly have popped into the old woman's head.

"Well, I think he must have been on last night after all," she said, frowning. "He hasn't been here this morning yet, so I suppose he hasn't finished. But, of course, he often works at odd hours on his inventions."

"You mean that he has been away all night and hasn't been back this morning?" said the inspector.

"I suppose so," she said, nodding quickly.

Now the inspector was not a slow-witted man. He had seen a very pretty girl at the window above, and he knew

310

more than a little about Ansell's reputation in the matter of pretty girls.

He also knew something of jealous lovers, for he had been dealing with such unlucky fellows during a great part of his career, and the vague shape of a suspicion took place in his mind.

The only thing which brought it into his mind was that the girl above was well enough to watch them from a window, but was not well enough to answer any questions in a satisfactory manner.

"Mrs. Wray," said the inspector, turning away from the bush, "I'm afraid I must insist on seeing your daughter. I think she may be of great help to us."

A sudden hush fell upon the garden, and the sergeant looked surprised.

THE SEVENTH CHAPTER

And Graves Give Up Their Dead.

MRS. WRAY HURRIED upstairs for the second time and rapped quickly on the door. From inside came the tired, strained voice of the girl, hardly audible.

"I'm coming, mother. I heard through the window."

The old lady was startled. She bent and whispered through the keyhole.

"Janey darling! Whatever's the matter? Let me in!"

The key turned in the lock and the door opened. Mrs. Wray ran in and clasped her daughter to her.

"What is the matter with you, darling? You look so upset and ill! Shall I send for the doctor?"

"No, mother. It's all right. Listen to me," she said, in an urgent, husky voice. "Listen, I want you to go to Aunt Jessie and stay there for to-day."

"But my dear child!" protested Mrs. Wray. "I was there yesterday!"

"I know," Jane said. "But you must go again. Will you,

313

mother? It's—it's dreadfully important!"

"But I don't understand, dear! Why do you want me to—"

"Mother! Never mind that. Will you go? Will you go to—to please me?"

Mrs. Wray looked at her daughter's drawn white face, and suddenly became surprisingly calm and determined.

"No, dear," she said. "If you're in trouble, and I believe you must be, I stay with you. That's a mother's job, you know, dear. I'll stay with you."

"But, mother darling—"

"No!" Mrs. Wray shook her head. "I'll stay with you, dear. That's final. Don't talk about it any more." She turned towards the door. "Now let's go downstairs. These policemen are waiting. But don't be frightened, my dear. There's never anything wrong that can't be put right."

"Sometimes—there is," said the girl, half choking.

"Never, my dear," said Mrs. Wray firmly, "There, now! Trust an old woman's experience of these things. Nothing ever goes wrong that can't be put right, dear. Keep that in mind, and you won't be frightened."

Jane watched the tiny old lady for several seconds, but there was no sign of wavering in the lined little face. Mrs. Wray had made up her mind to stand by her daughter whatever happened, and that was all there was to it.

"Listen, mother," said Jane, keeping her voice low. "I'm going to tell you something that you must know before I talk to the police." She shuddered suddenly and looked away. "It's—it's horrible, but I know you'll be brave enough—"

"Of course I will, dear," said Mrs. Wray, and patted her daughter's hand reassuringly.

"Ansell did come here that night," Jane said in a whisper. "He came and tried to force me to marry him."

There was a silence. From downstairs came the impatient, soft sound of the inspector, pacing up and down the parlour.

"Go on, dear," said Mrs. Wray, her little face hardening.

"I—I told Jim, and he went out that night to try and see Ansell. He—he said he hadn't seen him, but he came back very late, and there was a lot of blood on his raincoat."

"So that's why it disappeared," said Mrs. Wray, half to herself.

"Yes, that's why," said Jane, shuddering again. "But last night I—I saw somebody in the garden. I went down and there—"

She broke off, and it was several seconds before she could force herself to tell her mother the horror of the scene in the cellar last night.

Mrs. Wray gripped her daughter's wrist hard, as if the grip helped her not to cry out in horror. The little old face went white and looked like wrinkled parchment, but the determined light in her birdlike eyes burnt steadily.

After a minute her grip relaxed somewhat.

"My poor dear," she said softly, "you should have told me before. You've made yourself ill trying to keep his terrible secret."

Jane suddenly lost control and burst into tears. It was a relief to cry on her mother's shoulder. In a short while she felt better, and almost ready to face the inquisitors below.

The impatient men downstairs were rewarded at last, and both turned to see the white-faced girl as she entered the room.

The recent upset, the faint marks of tragedy and horror seemed, if anything, to have made her beauty more startling. The sergeant looked aside to his superior as if in approval, but Grimes was staring at the girl.

Jane sat down at the table. The inspector began to make himself as pleasant as possible, in order to put her at ease.

"Miss Wray, do you live here with your mother?"

Jane nodded.

"All day? Are you in the house all day?

She looked up, slightly puzzled.

"No. I work at the mill in the town," she said.

Instinctively the inspector's eyes dropped to her hands.

"What do you do there?"

"I am in the accounting department," she said. "Keeping the books for the firm."

"You must have seen Mr. Ansell many times, then?"

"Which one? I knew old Mr. Ansell very well. Sometimes I used to do personal work for him at his house—when he was ill. I can type as well, you see."

"You were a frequent visitor to the Grange?" said the inspector, with quickening interest.

"I went whenever Mr. Ansell called for me," she said. "It was not often. Only when he felt ill and had some letters or figures which he wanted to get done. Then I used to go there."

"Did you ever see young Mr. Ansell there?"

"I only saw him once at the Grange,' she said, a slight

frown of puzzlement lining her face. She could not see the purpose of this questioning.

"When was that?"

"On the day old Mr. Ansell died," she answered.

"But you saw young Mr. Ansell a good deal at the mill, perhaps?" said the inspector persuasively.

She nodded, but said nothing.

"You mean that Mr. Ansell would know you very well by sight?" said the inspector.

Of the three people in that room with the inspector, only Sale could see the slow cunning trend of these questions. Grimes knew well that to put the main question first was to shock the witness and put her on her guard.

But he was putting the secondary questions first. In fact, clearing up the loose ends before he cut his cloth.

"He did know me quite well, I believe," she said in a small voice.

"Do you remember the night of Thursday, September the thirteenth?" said the inspector softly.

"Yes. It was the night of the storm," she said.

Sale noticed the old lady was locking and unlocking her fingers together in an extremely agitated manner.

"Do you remember anything else about that night?" said Grimes.

The girl caught her breath, and her eyes flicked wildly towards her mother, as if searching for advice. The old lady nodded quickly, like a bird pecking.

"Yes," said Jane, in a dry, husky voice. "It was the night that young Mr. Ansell called here."

"Ah," said Grimes very softly. "You saw him that night,

then, ha?"

"Yes."

"But you have not seen him since?"

It seemed suddenly as if the girl could pretend no longer. The massed feelings within her suddenly burst out, as if she had no longer control over them.

She jumped to her feet, her face white as clay.

"Yes, I have seen him since. In the cellar under this house. Go and find him! Go and find him!"

She collapsed into the chair, hid her face in her hands and cried bitterly. Mrs. Wray darted forward to comfort her.

Grimes, startled out of his calm, jerked his head as a sign to the sergeant, and both men went quietly out of the room.

They said nothing as they rounded the house and came to the bush against the wall. The inspector brought a torch from his pocket, looked briefly at Sale, then ducked down and plunged into the damp-smelling gloom of the cellar.

He stood up inside the vault, and Sale came blundering after him. The torch-light sprayed round the walls, shining on the heaps of rubbish and the curious, smooth face of the mud floor.

The surface of the floor was like a sand beach when the tide has gone out, but across the smooth surface were several mixed tracks of feet, leading from the cellar entrance to a place near the far wall.

The policemen went slowly across to where the tracks broke out into a confused mess of trampling on the mud, a mess which took up an area seven feet long by three wide.

"Somebody's been digging here," said Grimes hoarsely. "And stamped it down again afterwards."

"It's about the size—" said Sale, and swallowed. "About the size of a grave." He looked round. "I wonder if there's a spade about here?"

They made a rapid search of the place, but found no spade. Sale went up into the garden again and looked round him there, but could not find one.

He called at the house again, and Mrs. Wray told him there was a spade in the gardening shed at the bottom of the garden, because she had seen it there herself yesterday, leaning against the hut, and she had put it inside the hut to stop it getting rusty.

Sergeant Sale went to the hut, looked all round it inside and outside, but found no spade at all.

Disappointed, he returned to the cellar, where he found Grimes had dug some of the softened mud away with a broken piece of board.

The inspector was standing back, looking down at the hole he had made in the mud. The torch, lying on the ground, cut a brilliant path of light along the ruffled surface of the trampled mud.

In that light the shape of a human foot, encased in a muddy shoe, showed clearly in the hole.

"Get to the nearest phone-box," said Grimes, without looking round at the sergeant. "You know who to ask for."

Sale nodded, looked at the grotesque foot poking out of the ground, then swallowed again and went out of the cellar.

Grimes looked carefully around him, then picked up his torch and went out of the cellar after Sale. He entered the house again.

Jane and her mother were still in the front parlour, white-faced but determined. Their eyes turned to the inspector as he came in.

Grimes stopped in the doorway.

"I've sent for some help," he said quietly. "I'm afraid this is a dreadful thing for you both. I'm sorry."

Both women ignored his well-meant apology.

"But there is one thing I must know," he went on, after a while. "Where is Mr. Drake?"

THE EIGHTH CHAPTER

The Net.

SERGEANT SALE WAS no slow thinker. Years of working with the inspector had led both men to think along similar lines, and when he reached a telephone-box the sergeant gave the following message to the police station in the town.

"We've found Ansell, it looks like. Anyhow, there's a dead 'un buried in an old cellar at Laburn Cottage. Send out the necessary. And one other thing. Send out an alarm for a James Drake, who works as an engineer at the mill. We want him, and we want him bad."

The wheels of the law were set in motion by that call. Three cars left the station, two headed for the cottage, and the third went to the mill.

Detective-Sergeant Butters was in the third car, and he wasted no time at the mill. He got his information quickly and left again.

James Drake had not been to the office that day. During

the last week Mr. Drake had been acting strangely—in a distant and moody sort of way, which wasn't like him at all.

The staff at the mill had noticed a change in him as from the morning of Friday, the fourteenth of September. They remembered it was Friday, because Friday was pay-day, and Drake had forgotten to collect his pay envelope on the fourteenth.

Drake had never forgotten to collect his pay before. He was a cheerful, rather wild type of young man, brilliant in a way, hot-tempered, and with an inventive mind. But he was not forgetful.

Drake was six feet tall, broad, with untidy yellow hair, grey eyes, and wrinkles under them as if he laughed a lot. There was nothing unusual about him save for the little finger of his right hand, which bent inwards. That was all.

That was the information which Butters collected, and it was enough for him to go on with. He returned to the Station to await orders.

As soon as he had orders from the inspector, that description would be circulated throughout the country. But he must have the go-ahead from Grimes first.

Two hours later he got it. The inspector came back to the station to eat a quick sandwich lunch and carry on a short conference with his men at the same time.

"It's a clear case of murder against Drake," he said. "Everything's there—motive, opportunity, physical strength, and finally clearing out once he knew the girl had found him out. There's no doubt about this case. All we want to finish it is Drake."

The description was broadcast at once. Grimes continued to bite at sandwiches and make observations, which a shorthand writer took down.

"The girl gives a confused story about seeing two men in the garden during the storm," Grimes went on. "Says she saw it in a lightning flash. Two men fighting near the rubbish heap.

"But at the same time she says that she and her mother were drugged by something which must have been put into the supper salad. The old lady agrees that she might have been drugged, but can't be sure."

"Can it be proved, one way or the other?" asked Butters.

"No trace was left. The girl washed everything up before she realised there may have been something in the food," said Sale, pulling one of his huge ears.

"One thing disproves it," said Grimes. "If anyone drugged the supper it must have been Drake. It would have been a reasonable precaution for him to take in order to make sure neither the girl nor her mother should see what he was up to.

"But the snag is, both girl and mother swear he ate some of the stuff himself. And he certainly wouldn't have done that if he'd drugged the stuff, would he, ha?"

"There couldn't have been any drug then," said Butters, shrugging. "Girl's imagination. Maybe the storm upset her tummy. Storms upset lots of people, and make them feel ill. My wife gets right queer during a thunderstorm."

"Yes, it's a pretty common thing," agreed Grimes. "Anyhow, I think we can write off the drug story, ha! Put it down to imagination and effects of the storm."

"And of course," said Sergeant Sale, "the girl was upset in any case, due to Ansell's blackmail visit."

"She was in a pretty good state to imagine anything, by the time she'd been awake all night as well," said Grimes, nodding. "What's more, there's another thing she thinks she saw that night—Drake's raincoat.

"She swears he came in wearing the raincoat, and she thinks there was blood on it. But she must have been wrong. He could not have been wearing the coat at all."

"Why not?" Butters asked.

"Sorry. I didn't tell you about that," said Grimes, taking a huge bite of sandwich. "Drake's raincoat was wrapped round the body of Ansell."

Butters whistled.

"Hell! That was a damnfool thing to do!" he said.

"Perhaps," said Grimes. "But then Drake hoped that the body would never be found. If he hadn't gone back and dug it up last night, we shouldn't have found it ever, I should think. You see, all trace of the digging when the corpse was buried was washed clean out by floodwater rushing through the cellar during the storm.

"It left the whole of that mud floor like a new washed beach, with no marks there at all. If Drake hadn't lost his nerve, Ansell wouldn't have been found now. As it was, something made him go back there last night—no doubt with the idea of shifting the body to a place he thought would be safer.

"But the girl saw him, and he knew it. So he left it where it was and bunked. That's about the size of this case."

There seemed to be a general agreement amongst the

inspector's assistants.

"There is another thing," said Butters. "This story about Ansell forcing the girl to marry him sounds phoney. He wasn't the type to think about marriage."

"I think she just said marriage, just to make it sound nicer, ha," said Grimes. "We all know what she means, anyway. We know what Ansell meant, too."

"And as far as the motive goes, it's just the same thing," said Sergeant Sale complacently.

But it was not the same thing at all. Ignoring such details as that was like leaving "not" out of the sentence, "He did not do it."

Yet at that time it was almost impossible to see the importance of the smaller clues which did not seem to fit in with the obvious theory of a crime of passion.

THE NINTH CHAPTER

Shadow of the Noose.

JIM DRAKE TURNED from where he stood and plunged away, through the thickness of the wood. He had seen enough to know what was afoot.

Standing on the fringe of the wood around the cottage, he had seen the inspector and the sergeant go down the cellar. He had seen them come up again, grim and silent, and he had known too well that the secret of the cellar had been discovered.

There was no sense in hanging about the district any longer. His plan had failed, but he had not lost the game yet.

There was hope for him still. But he must have time. He needed a long time, perhaps weeks, to find the answer to this terrible riddle.

And he would not find it by sitting in a cell, waiting for his trial on a charge of a murder he could not deny.

That was why he turned and went away through the

wood, heading south over the moors. He wished he could have left some message for Jane, but he dared not.

Not only would such a thing ruin his chances of freedom, but more than that—it would implicate her in the terrible affair. It would put her in the position of being an accomplice, an accessory after the fact.

It was better that she should suffer in ignorance than that she should get drawn into the meshes of the police net, with all its sordid implications.

The sun shone brightly over the land then, growing hotter as he trudged along, but he saw no brightness in the scene at all. To him it seemed that a great shadow hung over everything, like the deep clouds of a storm, holding the air still and breathless.

As he crossed the country roads he sometimes saw people walking towards him. The very sight of them seemed to make his heart race, and he darted through the hedges and out of sight before they could get near enough to recognise him.

He was wise to take the precaution, for he knew perfectly well that the police would waste no time in setting their traps for him.

The moors and country lanes were lonely places, but he could not keep to them for ever. Some time that day he would have to go into a town, and get to a railway station for the journey south.

It was there that his greatest danger would lie. At the railway station; for the police would be watching at the barriers.

Late in the afternoon he was high on the desolate moor,

looking down upon the sprawling, smoky mass of a city in the valley. Already the yellow winking eyes of lights were shining in the tiny, sooty blocks of the buildings.

Overhead the evening was drawing across the sky, and he guessed that by the time he had reached the town below, it would be dark, and darkness is a friend to the hunted.

The shadows grew deeper as he went on down the rough, winding track, and when he reached the road that wound through the trough of the valley, it was quite dark. He kept along the side of the road. Trucks and lorries went by occasionally, driving into the city, and he kept out of the range of their headlights.

Often, when lights appeared on the road, he crouched back into the hedge and waited until the bright, staring eyes had passed before he went on again.

Street lamps appeared ahead of him, and for a moment he halted, staring at them, as if they, too, were watching and waiting for him. He cursed himself for a fool for letting his nerves run away with him like this, and pressed on again.

He knew what the trouble was. He was hungry. He had eaten nothing for over twenty-four hours, and if he went on like this his strength would quickly go.

For if he was going to succeed in this trip, he had got to be fit.

He came into the quiet, lamplit streets at the outskirts of the town, and kept on until he came to the shape of a public house on a corner. It was a small place, and looked quiet enough.

"I've got to get something somewhere," he muttered, staring at the little inn. "Might as well be here."

He pushed open the swing door, and came into a small parlour, with a tiny semi-circular counter in one corner. Behind this counter a little man was sitting, clad in shirtsleeves and a bowler hat. He was squinting through gold rimmed glasses at the evening paper.

Jim asked for a pint of beer and some bread and cheese. The little man seemed pleased to have a customer to talk to, and when he had served the young man, he settled down for a chat while Jim ate.

"Nasty business this murder, eh?" said the landlord, taking off his bowler hat and putting it on again.

"Murder?" said Jim, as if he had not heard of such a thing before.

"Yes. This here playboy feller," said the landlord, licking his lips. "Knocked on the head and buried down a cellar, eh? I spect that's what happens to most of 'em, sooner or later. Too much money, that's what's the matter with 'em. Too much wonga. Gets you into trouble in the end. Sure to."

"I suppose so," said Jim, looking idly at the paper which now lay on the counter.

The murder was on the front page, and there was a description of James Drake set in a black box in the page centre—but there was no photograph.

He felt relieved about that. Very few people would recognise a man from his description alone, but they would find it easy to compare a man with his photograph.

"Yerss, nasty business," said the landlord; shaking his

head. "Of course, you must have murders, I suppose. Primitive passions and all that, eh? Proper messy though, all the same."

Jim agreed with the little man, paid for what he had had and went out into the streets again. The encounter had given him more confidence, and the food and drink had refreshed him.

Now he had to find his way to the railway station, and he would have to find it himself. It would be foolish to ask the way of anyone he might meet in the street. To do that would be to confess himself a stranger, and to be a stranger is always to attract notice.

There were a few people about in the streets, but all seemed to be hurrying homewards, and none took any notice of him at all.

He came upon the station suddenly. It lay at the end of a street leading off to his right, its open, empty doorway gaping into the roadway. Inside the warmly lit booking hall he could see two or three people standing about waiting, with suitcases standing on the floor by them.

But close to the doorway stood a policeman, thumbs in his belt, legs wide apart, staring out into the dark road.

Automatically Jim Drake halted as he saw that figure, and for a second or two he watched the uniformed man, wondering what was best to do.

Policemen often hung about stations, just making a break in their beats. But this one might be there for a special purpose.

He might be waiting there in the hope that Jim Drake would come along.

Drake pushed his hat back on his head, and continued to stand at the street corner, staring down towards the station.

He wanted to go into that station and catch a train going south. That was an essential part of his scheme now, and the only one in which he could see any hope for himself.

There was no way of finding out whether that policeman was merely idling there or looking for Jim Drake other than by putting the thing to the test.

Drake buttoned his jacket and strode down the street towards the station. His heart faltered as he stepped out into the road and made his way across to the lighted mouth of the station.

He could almost feel the policeman's eyes on him, but he kept on. He came to the doorway and mounted the steps. The policeman watched him.

"Warm, still," said Jim, nodding.

"Too true, sir," said the policeman. "Stormy, like."

Jim did not whistle aloud with relief, but he felt a little weak as he crossed to the booking-office and bought himself a ticket for London.

While he was waiting for his change he glanced quickly round to the policeman. He jerked his head back quickly, for the officer had half turned and was staring across at the booking-office.

The skin at the back of his neck seemed to grow tight as he took his change and went towards the platform gates. Although he had his back to the constable, he could almost see the man staring at him, watching every move he made and comparing it mentally with the description of the wanted murderer.

Jim passed through the gates, but the policeman did not follow.

He walked down to a dimly-lit part of the platform, near the luggage lift at the end, and took out a cigarette. There was some little time to wait for the train, and that wait, he knew, was going to be an unpleasant one.

He sat down on a seat to watch the distant coloured lights of a signal gantry. Beyond it the orange glow from a shunting engine shone a beam into the sky, but there was no sign of the London train.

He looked back at the platform gate. His heart quickened again, for the policeman was chatting with the ticket collector, close by the gates.

He watched them for a minute or two and then the policeman went away into the booking-hall again.

The minutes passed with agonising slowness. The fugitive watched the signal gantry and the platform gates by turns. But the policeman did not come back, and at last one of the signals on the gantry dropped and in the far distance sounded the faint shriek of a locomotive whistle.

Drake got up and began to pace slowly towards the platform gate. The collector was there, leaning against the gate and eating a bit of a sandwich. He watched Jim carelessly, finished his sandwich and dusted his hands with a red handkerchief.

Jim could see into the booking-hall, but he could no longer see the policeman.

The few passengers who were waiting for the train

came out of the waiting-rooms. Drake kept his face turned down to the line towards the train and away from the passengers.

But behind him the ticket collector was staring steadfastly at the back of his head and frowning. It was clear that for a moment or two the collector could not make up his mind, and then, as the train came into the platform, the collector made a signal to someone in the booking-hall.

Drake saw nothing of this. He was in amongst the other passengers, and as the train drew to a halt the doors of the compartments opened and people poured out of it.

The comparatively deserted platform became suddenly alive with people and their luggage. Boxes and crates were piled out of the luggage vans, and porters hurried up and down the platform, dexterously pushing their loaded trolleys in amongst the mass of people.

And in this temporary confusion Drake entered the train and found an empty compartment. He sat down in one corner and stared out at the busy station. He peered carefully in amongst the moving, bustling mass of people, but could see nothing to alarm him.

The crowd cut him off from the platform gates.

Gradually the crowd thinned and poured out through the gates like sand through the neck of an hour glass. The platform cleared a lot, and along the train doors slammed.

The shrill whine of the whistle came from along the platform, and Drake gave a sigh of relief. They were going at last.

The engine gave a short blast, and then the train began to move slowly forward.

But as it went, two men appeared at the platform gate, and behind them came the policeman. These two men appeared to be in a hurry.

Drake saw them shout something to the collector, and that official pointed to the train and nodded.

The two men rushed forward, with the policeman behind them. The train was gathering speed, and threatened to leave the running men behind on the platform.

Drake got to his feet and peered out through the window. His heart stopped altogether as he watched.

He saw one of the men jump into an open door at the end of the train, and then turn to drag his colleague in. The second man only just made it.

For a moment it looked as if he would be dragged forcibly along the length of the platform, but the strength of his companion got him safely in through the door.

Of the trio only the policeman was left behind on the platform.

He came to a standstill, panting and staring after the end of the train.

But the danger was on board. Drake knew that those two men were plain clothes detectives. There could be no doubt of that whatever.

The ticket collector had recognised the fugitive, and he had not been slow to put the information in the right place.

The train gathered speed, rocking and swaying over the network of switches outside the station. It was heading south for London, but it was very unlikely now that Drake would ever reach that city.

For a minute he stood still in the compartment, not

knowing what to do. He knew perfectly well that the detectives were even then working their way through the length of the train, searching for him. He had no disguise—nothing that could cheat them at all.

It seemed to be just a matter of waiting until they reached his compartment, and then to give himself up.

The lights of the outskirts of the town were flashing by now, for the train was heading fast into the darkness of the south.

He started suddenly as someone appeared in the doorway of the compartment. He looked round into the small face of a man in the short white jacket of a dining car attendant.

"Would you like to book for dinner, sir?" said the man.

Drake's brain worked very fast now. He had not known there was a dining car on the train, but suddenly he saw a means of temporary escape.

"Where's the dining car?" he countered.

"Next coach," said the waiter, pointing to the front of the train. "Shall I book you a seat, sir?"

"No, thanks. I've just eaten," said Drake.

The attendant nodded and went on down the corridor. As soon as he had gone, Drake darted out into the rocking corridor. He looked along it, both ways, but it was completely empty.

He turned towards the head of the train and went along to the next coach. The hot smell of cooking left no doubt as to what coach it was.

He halted. Immediately ahead of him was the short passage which led alongside the galley, and beyond that to the dining compartment.

But beside the galley was a small recess, in which were stacked crates of empty bottles. And hanging on a hook above them there were two short white jackets.

Drake gave a sudden grin, snatched one of the jackets down and slipped it on over his own. He fastened the front of it, then darted back into the corridor of his own coach.

As he came into the corridor, he saw the door at the far end open, and the first of the detectives appear. His companion was close behind him. They were staring into the compartments as they came along.

Drake marched towards them, and stopped in front of them.

"Dinner, sir?" he said. "It's just being served. I could fix you up with two seats right away."

"No, thanks," said the leading detective, and pushed by without another glance.

His companion followed him. Drake went down to the end of the coach and round the angle of the corridor. There he stopped and peered back.

He saw the detectives complete their search of the compartments and move on into the dining coach.

Drake slipped off the coat, opened the lavatory door, which was close beside him, and hung the jacket on a hook inside. He shut the door again and mopped his brow.

"That gives me another mile or two before they rumble what's happened," he thought.

Quite suddenly he grinned. For the first time he realised that it was not all hell being hunted. There was the spice of adventure in it from time to time.

He lit a cigarette and leant against the open window

close by him. Outside the dark, countryside roared by, lit by the racing orange glow from the engine.

He grinned again, but it was a short-lived grin.

He had dodged the detectives for the time being, but they were still on the train, and soon they would be coming back again.

One thing was certain. He had better not be seen by those two men again—not without the white coat!

For a long time he stood there, staring out at the dark country, watching the opposite track racing by in the light thrown down from the racing train windows.

Then from the corner of his eye he saw someone move along the corridor. He turned his head quickly, and at the end of the long narrow passage he saw the two detectives returning.

The leading one caught sight of him, halted, and turned his head to say something to his companion behind. What he said could not be heard in the roaring racket of the swaying train, but Jim Drake could see what he meant.

They had recognised him—without the white coat.

They came forward quickly down the corridor.

Jim looked round him. There was no way of escape inside the train. The place was a trap that not even a rat could get out of now.

Then he grasped the handle of the door by which he stood, and jumped out into the dark racing air that whined past like an acrid smelling hurricane.

As he went he saw the detectives start forward to try and save him from that death plunge. The door swung wildly, driven wide open by the fury of the slipstream. As

Drake went, his fingers gripped the edge of the window and held on with all the strength he had.

As the door swung round, he went round with it, and when the door crashed wide open, he was still hanging to it, though winded and dazed by the crash.

From the corridor it looked as if the fugitive had thrown himself clean out on to the tracks.

The chief detective reached up and pulled the alarm cord. All along the train the sharp hiss of brakes broke out, and the coaches shuddered and rocked under the violence of the slowing down.

Half frozen with the smoky wind, Jim Drake hung on to the open door with one hand and fumbled round the end of the coach with the other. He got a grip on a sooty rail put there to allow cleaners to climb up on to the coach roof, and let go the door.

He got his foot on the buffers and pressed himself back in the gap between the two coaches. At his back the corridor concertina groaned and rattled as the train drew to a stand-still.

He could hear the detectives shouting something from the open doorway, but he could not make out what it was.

With a last grinding shriek the train jerked to a stop, and at once the chief detective leapt down on to the tracks. The drop was further than he thought, and he tripped and rolled over on the sleepers.

Jim Drake watched him pick himself up, cursing aloud, then begin to run back down the train. The second detective let himself down more gingerly, reached the tracks, and began to run back after his boss.

The pair met the guard approaching them along the lines, and shouted something to him. The words were lost against the impatient droning hiss of the locomotive in the darkness ahead.

Jim clambered down from the buffer and waited in the shadows between the coaches until the detectives and the guard were far enough away, then he darted under the train and out on the other side.

He ran down an embankment, climbed over the wire fence at the bottom and vanished into the darkness of a wood beside the line.

On the tracks the detectives went back, searching every inch of the lines for nearly a quarter of a mile, and found nothing.

The chief pushed his hat back and frowned at his colleague in the darkness.

"Is it possible that this fellow's tricked us for the second time in half an hour?" he said.

"Either that, or he's made of rubber and just bounced away," said his assistant.

"We can't hold the train any longer," said the guard irritably.

From his attitude it was clear he thought these detectives were drunk. After all, what man could jump out of a train doing sixty and not be spread all over the northbound track?

"Nobody but a gremlin or a pink elephant," thought the guard, with a sour expression.

THE TENTH CHAPTER

The Trap on the Road.

THE ROAD WAS broad and quiet. Drake kept on walking fast, still heading south, until the yellow glare of headlights sprayed the road behind him and grew brighter.

He turned. The dim shape of a truck could just be seen behind the glaring headlights. He jerked his thumb for the driver to see, and the hiss of brakes answered him. The truck pulled up beside him, and the driver peered down from his cabin.

"London," said the driver. "'Ighgit."

"That'll do fine," said Jim, and opened the door and clambered into the cab.

The truck started off again.

"Should be there by six in the morning," said the driver, changing into top. "If I don't get no more interruptions."

"Had a breakdown?" Jim queried.

"No, not that," said the driver. "Ruddy police. Been stopped twice already. I said to 'em, I said, 'Strike a light!

You don't think I'd give a killer a lift, do yer?' I says. 'Why I'd run a ruddy mile, I would!"

"Cigarette?" said Jim, bringing out a packet.

The driver shook his head, and kept his eyes glued on the road.

"Goin' south for a job?" he asked.

"That's roughly the idea," said Jim. "I've got the job, but not the money for the fare."

"It's always like that," said the driver, nodding sagely.

He was driving fast now, as if he wanted to get the journey over as quickly as possible. The road streamed by in the headlight glare. Sometimes another lorry came up and passed, going the other way, but the roads were almost deserted that night.

Jim was tired, and the effect of the racing road passing under the truck made him sleepy. He had been through enough that day, and although he did not realise it, he was close to exhaustion.

His eyes closed once, and he jerked them open again. The driver was talking, but Drake could no longer be bothered to hear what was said.

The voice droned on, mixing with the roar of the truck, and sounds gradually grew farther and farther away. His eyes closed again, but this time he did not reopen them.

He was asleep.

The driver noticed that his listener had dozed off and fell to whistling. After a while he stopped that, too.

Jim slumped sideways until he was almost lying along the seat.

"I envy you, mate," said the driver. "I could do with a

drop of that myself."

For another half hour they raced on, and then, at the entrance to a town, the silver buttons and badge of a policeman's uniform gleamed in the headlights.

The constable was in the middle of the road, signalling with a flashlight, and holding his other hand up.

"Another of 'em," grunted the driver, and braked to a standstill.

The policeman came round to the driver's seat.

"Anybody with you?" said the constable.

"A mate—he's asleep," said the driver. "Wish I was, too, I don't mind admittin'."

"Seen anybody on the road?"

The driver yawned, and then shrugged.

"Few lorries—nothing else."

The policeman stared.

"You'd better watch it in case you drop off," he said sternly. "You look tired."

"Ah, hell!" said the driver, "I'm always tired."

"You'd better pull in and have some coffee first stall you come to," said the constable. "O.K!"

He signalled the driver on, and the truck moved forward again into the night.

In the seat beside the driver the man slept on.

The driver began to whistle again, as if accompanying his idle thoughts with a tune. But the whistling got slower and quieter and then died away altogether.

The driver slowly turned his head and frowned down at the sleeping man on the seat. He stared for a moment, then switched his eyes back to the road.

But he scratched his head.

"I wonder?" he muttered. "Couldn't be, could it? Naow! 'Corse not! And yet—"

The germ of an idea had entered his slow-moving mind, and he could not get rid of it. Several times he looked at the sleeping man again.

"Yellow 'air, and tall—'bout six foot—" He scratched his jaw. "Might be—might be. Cor! Suppose it is— I am a ruddy fool!"

Suddenly he reached out, grabbed Drake's shoulder and shook him. Jim was awake on the instant, like a cat.

"Ere!" said the driver roughly. "Who are you, eh? Who are you?"

"Why?" said Jim, sitting up. "What's happened?"

"Nothink's happened—yet," said the driver. "Only it just struck me as curious like, that just the night when the cops are looking for a chap lookin' like you, you turn up for a lift. Dint strike me before, it dint."

Drake laughed.

"You fool!" he said. "Do I look like a murderer?"

The driver scratched his jaw again.

"No, you don't," he admitted. "You look like a gent in some ways. That's why I dint think of it before. But I just wondered—"

Drake could see that the man was suspicious now.

"What suddenly put this idea in your head?" he said, pulling out his cigarettes.

"We was stopped a few miles back," said the driver. "The cops again."

"Oh, you were stopped, were you?" said Drake, half-

344

closing his eyes. "What happened? What did you do?"

The driver told him.

"Well, listen, my friend,' said Jim quietly. "You could have told that policeman then. You didn't, did you? Supposing I am the man they want—do you know what you'll be? You'll be an accomplice! You'll be helping a murderer to escape!"

"God!" The driver hissed in the sudden shock of the realisation. "You're damned right, you are! What a fool I am—a ruddy fool! I must have been half asleep—"

"You were," said Jim, settling back in the seat. "But listen, Joe, or whatever your name is—"

"Bert," said the driver automatically.

"Well, listen, Bert," said Drake—"as far as I know, I'm not a murderer."

"Not! Phew!" Bert whistled with relief and mopped his brow. "Thank the lord for that."

"But I am the man the police want."

"What?" Bert fairly shouted, looked round at his passenger and almost swerved off the road.

"I've been framed," said Drake quickly. "I tell you, Bert, I'm not trying to escape from the police. What I'm trying to do is get to London to get help. Do you understand that?"

"Framed, eh?" said Bert breathlessly. "Gaw! Why did this have to happen to me?"

"Never mind that," said Drake sharply. 'Well, I've put my cards on the table. If you're scared, I'll get out now. But you might as well go on with it now that you've gone so far. What do you think?"

Bert stared ahead, closed one eye, stroked his jaw, and coughed.

"Dunno," he said hoarsely. "Dunno what's best, s'truth I don't!"

"At least I'll get a few miles nearer while you're trying to make up your mind," said Drake.

"You're a cool customer, you are," said Bert, shaking his head. "I reckon you deserve to get there! All right! I'll take you, but if there's any more hold-ups you'll have to get out and run fer it. I ain't going to get into trouble on your account, mate. I'll pretend I never knew who you were, then they won't be able to fix me as an accomplice, eh?"

"All right," said Drake, relieved.

The truck roared on. Bert had got over his sleepiness. He was ill at ease and jerky in his movements. He was frightened of the man beside him and frightened in case another police trap should suddenly appear round the next bend.

In short, Bert was scared all ways, and was taking the easiest way out of his difficulties. As he went he cursed himself for having been so slow before.

If only he'd tumbled to it when the last copper had stopped him! He wouldn't have any troubles at all now. This chap would have been in the clink, and everybody would have been happy.

Except, of course, the chap in the clink.

Suddenly the headlight glare seemed to brighten, and Bert drew closer in to the side of the road, realising that there was a car overtaking him from behind.

Then above the roar of the truck there sounded the shrill peal of a police car gong.

"Gawd!" gasped Bert, hardly knowing what to do. "It's the cops!"

"Don't mind me," said Jim, opening the cab door. "I'm off! Pretend you've been alone all the way."

He went out through the door and slammed it. Bert braked heavily as the police car came alongside and drew ahead.

With his heart beating fast, Bert came to a standstill behind the police car. Two policemen came out of the car and came back to the truck.

"What's up?" demanded Bert, sticking his head out of the cabin window. His heart beat so heavily now that it seemed to be thudding in his throat, nearly choking him.

"Your rear light's out, mate," said the leading policeman. "You'd better fix it right away."

"Eh?" said Bert. His heart stopped altogether. He felt as if he was in the middle of some curious dream where everybody was making a fool of him.

"Got a spare bulb?" asked the policeman. "If you have, fix that rear light and we'll say no more about it."

"Thanks, thanks!" stammered Bert, and began to search for his spare bulbs.

He found them and clambered out on to the road. The policeman watched while he replaced the broken bulb in the rear light, and then moved away.

"Right, mate," said the police driver. "Good-night!"

Like a man in a daze, Bert watched the police car drive away, and then he climbed back into his cab. He started as he sat down, for in the seat beside him was Jim Drake.

"I thought you'd gone!" he said hoarsely.

"Not yet, Bert," said Jim. "I want to cover a few more miles yet."

Bert started off again. The sweat was sticky on his face.

"This is the wust night I ever had," he said, almost to himself—"the wust!" He wiped his brow with his sleeve. "But how did you get back in here?"

"I climbed out of the door and up on to your load," said Jim. "I just got under the tarpaulin and waited there till the cops went."

"You're pretty smart," said Bert, swallowing hard—"pretty smart!"

Jim looked at his watch.

"How much further to go?" he asked.

"Not far now," the man's voice grated. "Fifteen mile, about. We're ahead of time."

Jim nodded. Through a break in the trees lining the road he could see the eastern sky turning grey with the coming of a new day.

Ahead the first houses of the outskirts of the city showed in the growing, misty light.

"This'll do, Bert," said Jim, opening the door. "I'll drop off here."

"Thank Gawd!" said Bert, with a noisy grunt of relief.

"You'll get your reward for this," grinned Jim. "Somebody'll do you a good turn one day."

"Uhuh!" groaned Bert. "Go away quick, for Gawd's sake! I've had enough."

Jim turned off from the road and went in amongst the

348

trees of a common. The truck moved away at a fast speed, as if anxious to leave the fugitive as far behind as possible.

Jim Drake came out of the common about a mile away and entered the broad quiet roads of a suburb. An early bus went by, and a few people were coming out of the houses and hurrying away to work.

He walked on for twenty minutes and then, ahead of him, he saw the entrance to a tube station. His pace quickened as he saw it.

Streams of early workers were going into the station, and he was pretty sure of being lost amongst them.

And apart from that, he believed that the police did not think he had got as far south as this, otherwise the men in the police car two hours ago would have asked Bert about him.

He went into the station and bought a ticket at an automatic machine. He went in amongst the crowd down to the platform and a train came in almost at once.

A few of the passengers had newspapers. He noticed them suddenly and with a sense of shock as great as he would have felt if he had felt a tap on his shoulder.

His picture would be in those papers. And once they were aboard the train these men would begin to look through the papers.

It was too late to change his mind. The doors of the train yawned open. He found himself borne forward on the crowd going into the train.

For the second time in a few hours he felt that a train was going to prove his undoing. Once inside the coach he would be trapped.

"But I'm likely to be trapped anywhere else," he thought. "On the streets, in a bus—anywhere. And I've got to get there—I've got to get there!"

He went into the train. The coach was full with people standing along its whole length. He took up a place near the door and stared out through the door into the darkness of the tunnel while the train clattered on towards the city.

Furtively he watched the faces of his fellow-passengers as they peered into the columns of the morning papers. At any moment he expected to see someone turn to him, stare and give a shout of recognition.

But nobody did.

The train came to the station he wanted, and he almost ran up the escalator to reach the street. He was so near to his objective now that he took no further notice of whether anybody was watching him or not.

The street was strange to him, but he hurried along it, reading the numbers of the houses almost aloud in his excitement, and then he found the one he wanted.

He rang, and the door was answered by a stout little woman. He told her what he wanted, and she looked doubtful for a moment, then shrugged.

"I've just taken up the breakfast," she said. "But I 'spect, it will be all right."

She showed him upstairs and into a room where a tall man in a dressing-gown was reading the morning papers and eating his breakfast off a tray.

The woman closed the door behind him, and the breakfaster looked up with a cold, grey eye that seemed to penetrate.

"You're wanted by the police, Mr. Drake," said Sexton Blake, laying his paper down.

"I know," said Drake breathlessly. "That's why I've come to see you. I hate reminding you. It seems rather mean on my part, but you remember I had the pleasure of helping Tinker out of a nasty spot in Manchester two years ago. You made me promise—"

Blake eyed the young man again, then turned from his breakfast-tray and reached out for a pipe and tobacco pouch which were lying on the table.

"I remember quite well. But surely it's a little too late for a visit to me?" said Blake, raising his eyebrows.

"I know," said Drake. "But—but I must have your help! I've been travelling all night, trying to get down here. I didn't think I was going to do it, but here I am, and—and I want you to help me!"

Blake filled his pipe.

"Sit down," he said calmly. "Help yourself to a cup of coffee."

Drake did as he was told. He was so glad at being in the presence of this master of mystery at last that he obeyed Blake like a child.

THE ELEVENTH CHAPTER

The Story of a Crime.

BLAKE LIT HIS pipe and puffed out a cloud of strong tobacco smoke. He watched the young man drink his coffee almost in a series of gulps.

"There's some toast," said the detective, pushing the plate towards Drake. "You eat, first. We can talk afterwards."

Drake was more grateful than ever. The events of the past night had left him ravenous, and he cleared up the toast in no time.

And while he ate the detective appeared to be reading the newspaper again. When Drake had finished eating, Blake put down the paper and looked up.

"Right, now!" said the detective. "I want you to be frank with me, Mr. Drake. If you're a genuine man, I'll do all I can to help. But I don't help guilty men to escape— you understand?"

"Yes, yes. I understand that," said Jim, swallowing.

"Did you do this murder?" said Blake, in a level voice.

Drake swallowed again, and tapped on the table edge with his finger. After a second or so he looked up.

"I was afraid you'd ask that," he said hoarsely.

"Well, what did you expect me to ask?" demanded Blake. "Did you do it?"

"That's the very point, Mr. Blake," was the answer. "That is why I want your help. I want you to find out if I did, or not."

Blake took his pipe out of his mouth, and for a moment there was a dead silence. In the distance the traffic roared, but so far away and muffled that it seemed part of another world.

"I believe," said Blake, after a while, "that that is the most extraordinary thing that has ever been said in this room."

Jim tapped on the table again, nervously. "That's the point, Mr. Blake," he said, in a voice that had become a husky whisper. "If I am a murderer, I'll give myself up. If I'm being framed, I want you to find the killer, and help me out of this mess."

"I see," said the detective.

He got up and went to his favourite position by the fire. He relit his pipe which had gone out, then reached out and rang a bell beside the fireplace.

"Have you any objection to my assistant Tinker listening to your story?" he asked.

Drake shook his head.

"Of course not," he said.

Almost as soon as Drake answered, Tinker came into the room.

"Ah, Tinker," said the detective, "this is Mr. Drake! He is wanted for murder, but at present there is a doubt about his guilt, and I would like you to listen to his story, and make any notes which occur to you."

"O-K., guv'nor!" said Tinker, with a curious glance at Jim Drake.

"Now, if you'll carry on, we'll see what we can do," said the detective, puffing slowly at his pipe. "But there is just one thing. Put in every small detail that you can remember, even if it seems to have nothing to do with the case."

Jim Drake told Blake of his own job, where he lived, his relationship with Jane and Mrs. Wray, and of Clive Ansell. He told this quickly, while Tinker made a brief note or two, and then he came to the night of September the thirteenth.

"It was a heavy night," he said, "with a storm that had been threatening all day. Everybody seemed to be on edge—you know how they do get when the air is sort of oppressive and electric."

"Do you normally feel any sensations like that?" said Blake.

"I usually feel a bit sickish and thick in the head," Jim confessed. "I believe quite a lot of people do."

"And did you feel like that on the thirteenth?"

"Yes, I did."

"Carry on," said Blake.

"I came home late. I'd been working in the drawing office on an invention of my own, and when I got back Jane told me that Ansell had just called, and tried to blackmail her into marrying him."

"Marrying is exactly the word you want, is it?" queried Blake sharply. "He doesn't seem to be the marrying type."

"Marrying is the word," said Drake firmly, and told of the threats which Ansell had made. "But before we could discuss it properly, Mrs. Wray came in. We had supper, and then I went out."

"You went out with the intention of seeing Ansell, did you?"

"Yes, I did," said Jim.

"No doubt you were in a furious temper about the whole thing?" said the detective.

"I was in a towering rage," said Jim, flushing. "I was determined to see him and have the whole thing out with him."

The detective knocked out his pipe on the mantelshelf.

"How did you mean to do that?" he asked shrewdly.

"I meant to make him see reason," said Jim. "And if he wouldn't—I meant to thrash him, and put him off the idea that way."

"I see," said Blake softly. "And so you went out to the Grange?"

"I started towards the Grange," said Jim. "And then I began to feel dizzy. I thought I was going to faint. I remember getting hold of a tree-trunk to steady myself, and that's all."

"You fainted?"

"Something like it," said Jim. "I went out, anyway."

"What is the next thing you remember?"

"Waking up on my bed next morning," said Jim. "I was

356

lying face down across it, fully dressed. My shoes and socks were soaked and plastered with mud. My trousers, too, were in a devil of a mess. There was blood on my suit, and I'd cut my left hand quite deeply, but when I woke the blood had dried on it, and the cut was almost healed."

"Healed in an hour or two?" said Blake. "Is that usual with you?"

"Normally I heal pretty quickly," said Jim. "I'm pretty fit. But I was surprised at this cut, because it was a deep one, even if it was only small."

"Have you any idea what you might have done during the time when you were—unconscious?" Tinker put in. "Is there anything you might have found afterwards which could give you a clue?"

"My raincoat," said Drake. "You'll see from the newspaper report that my raincoat was found wrapped round the body of Ansell. Now, I went out in that coat that night, but I hadn't got it when I woke up in the morning."

"H'm!" Blake grunted. "That isn't the sort of evidence that's likely to help you a lot. Anything else?"

The young man shook his head.

"Did anyone see you that night?" Tinker said.

Again Jim shook his head.

"Has anything unusual happened since?" Blake asked. "At your home, for instance?"

"Well—" Jim hesitated. "Yes. Jane has been acting very queerly towards me, but then I think it's my fault. You see, I was worried to death when I began to hear that

Ansell had disappeared. I began to wonder what I might have done that night, and I kept myself pretty much to myself until I could find out.

"I did find out—the night before last."

"What made you look in the cellar?" Blake asked, narrowing his eyes.

"On the night of the storm I looked down there, just to satisfy the old lady," Jim answered. "The night before last, I looked down there because it was the only place I hadn't looked."

"What did you find there?" Blake asked quietly.

"The whole place was different," said Jim. "On the night of the thirteenth, before the storm, the floor was mud— or rather earth, littered with old rubbish and muck.

"But the second time I looked in—the night before last—the floor was smooth as sand—like a beach. You see the flood water of the storm must have flooded the place, and carried down lots of liquid mud from the garden, and it had set solid."

Drake broke off, and fumbled in his pocket for a cigarette.

"But there were tracks in the mud," he went on. "Leading over to the corner, and a big trampled patch there, like a grave. I got a spade and dug, and then I found—"

His voice became hoarse and broke off. He lit a cigarette and his hand trembled.

Blake went across and looked down at the newspaper report again. The bare details which were set down there tallied with Jim's story.

"He was wrapped in your raincoat, which, according to this paper, was bloodstained," said Blake. "But you don't remember losing that coat?"

"I don't remember anything about the night of the thirteenth from the time I went out, to the time I found myself on my bed the next morning," said Jim, between his teeth.

"How did you feel when you came to that morning?" demanded Blake. "Did you have a headache? A taste in the mouth? Anything like that?"

"I hadn't been drinking, if that's what you mean," said Jim.

"I don't mean that," said Blake.

Jim scratched his jaw, now unshaven and rough.

"Yes, I did feel queer," he said at last. "I felt rough all that day."

"That is, on the Friday?" said Tinker.

"Yes, on the Friday."

Blake began to refill his pipe, and frowned towards the window.

"Ansell's father died very recently, didn't he?" the detective said, without looking round.

"Three weeks ago, I think," said Jim. "About that."

"Tinker," said Blake, "you might look through the papers. I think I saw his will published somewhere—a few days ago."

The assistant turned to the cupboard where the recent papers were kept for reference. It did not take him many minutes to find the item Blake wanted.

"Here we are, guv'nor!" said Tinker. "Ansell, George,

of Westhall Grange, Cheshire. He left £450,000!"

Blake did not show any surprise at the size of the fortune, but went on filling his pipe in a preoccupied way.

"That wouldn't be all in cash, of course," he said, still staring out of the window. "The value of the mills, the Grange and his property are all included. But it's a fair fortune, I must say."

He lit his pipe and sat down in a deep chair by the fireplace. For some minutes he said nothing. Tinker went on making a few notes in his book, and Jim watched the detective as a child might watch a conjuror.

"The situation is sticky," said Blake, after a while. "The evidence, as far as it goes, seems to point to you, and the police have made up their minds that it is you they want. Now it seems to me that if you're caught now, we shall have almost impossible difficulties in finding out what happened to you on the night of the thirteenth.

"I think," he went on slowly, "that we shall have to enter into a small conspiracy to deceive the police. It seems the only way, and if we can prove your innocence, it will have been the right thing to do.

"If, however, it turns out the other way—"

"I'll give myself up,' said Jim at once. "If I did do this terrible thing, I'll confess it."

Blake seemed to be watching the smoke clouds-rising to the ceiling, but now he looked round suddenly.

"This is the point the police won't understand," he said, an edge to his voice. "Why didn't you tell them as soon as you found Ansell's body in the cellar?"

"Because I didn't know whether it was my doing or

not," said Jim at once. "Instead I went into the wood and searched for traces of what I might have been doing on that Thursday night. I went as far as the Grange. I searched the wood in the dark, and after daylight—I spent hours on it.

"Then at last I decided to come back to the cottage, and I saw the police were already there. I knew the evidence would be too strong against me, and I decided the best thing I could do was to come to you for help."

"The evidence would be too strong against you?" echoed Blake, half to himself. "You know, Drake, that's the very thing that struck me from the beginning. The evidence against you is very strong.

"And the most curious feature of the case is that, but for Ansell's visit to Jane that night, you would have had no motive at all. I can't help thinking that's one of the most curious tricks of Fate that ever happened."

"How do you mean, guv'nor?" Tinker asked, puzzled.

"Just think of it, Tinker," said Blake. "A wealthy young man comes to a poor girl and tries to blackmail her into marrying him. Why? Heaven only knows! It's mad!

"But look at it from another angle, and then it seems that he went to the cottage that night and said: 'I want to be murdered. Here is the motive.'"

Tinker stared.

"I never heard of a man asking to be murdered!" he snapped.

"I have," said Blake. "Clive Ansell asked to be murdered. It's a hunch, Tinker. But at the moment it won't do us any good. We'll just bear it in mind while we get on with the hard work."

He got up, went across to the window and stared down into the street for some minutes. Tinker could see that Drake's case had fascinated the detective more than the ordinary case would. Sexton Blake could already see something strange and fantastic in a case that looked straightforward on the surface.

"We are in a jam," said the detective, turning back. "To find out anything about this case, I shall have to go to Westhall. And the mere fact of doing so is an admission that you have called on me, and that I am aiding and abetting you to escape the clutches of the law."

Jim started, and his jaw dropped.

"Hell! I hadn't realised that, Blake!" he gasped.

The detective chuckled and turned back from the window.

"It's a risk we shall have to take, if we're to do anything," he said. "Now I suggest, Mr. Drake, that you go with Tinker and have a shave and clean yourself up. I wish to think this over."

The detective went across to his chair and sat down again. The two young men went out of the room, leaving Blake alone with his pipe.

THE TWELFTH CHAPTER

Tinker Inquires.

TINKER WENT TO Somerset House, and there, with the usual formalities, saw the will left by the late George Ansell. It was a very simple will, in which everything of which that wealthy man had died possessed went direct to his son, if still living at the time of his father's death.

Mr. Clive Ansell, now also "the late," had been too busy in the pursuit of a good time to have made a will, and the estate therefore would be inherited by his next-of-kin.

Tinker left Somerset House, and went to the solicitors who had acted for George Ansell. It was a firm which knew Sexton Blake and Tinker very well, and the assistant had therefore no difficulty in getting an immediate interview with Mr. Hale, a junior partner in the firm.

Mr. Hale was a keen amateur criminologist, and never missed the opportunity to discuss crime with Sexton Blake whenever that gentleman was free to chat. The young man was therefore glad to see Tinker that morning.

"Another gory case?" said Hale, with a laugh.

"Pretty gory," said Tinker. "The Ansell case."

"Ah," said Hale, becoming more reserved. "Our clients."

"Exactly," said Tinker. "And I'd like a little information about the Ansell family—strictly confidential, of course."

"The family," said Hale, his brow clearing, "Well, there's no harm in that. I shan't be violating any confidences talking about them."

"Good," said Tinker. "Well, I've just looked up the wills, and I see that the estate is left to Clive Ansell's next-of-kin—if there is one."

"That's right," said Hale, nodding.

"And is there one?" queried Tinker.

"Well," said Hale, slowly swinging himself to and fro in his swivel chair, "there was, and maybe still is, though he hasn't been heard of for ten years. A cousin of George's who went to South America fifteen years ago."

"And he hasn't been heard of for ten years?" said Tinker.

"I'm afraid I've given you the wrong impression," said Hale. "I mean we haven't actually heard how he's getting on. We know he's still there, and we know he's alive, but that's all we do know."

"Come on," said Tinker encouragingly. "Open up."

"Arnold Grant is his name," said Hale, making a steeple of his fingers. "He is the black sheep of the family. A first cousin of George Ansell's.

"George Ansell got him a job in London, but after two years, found Grant was embezzling money. Grant's career was mostly embezzling money one way and the other, and finally George Ansell got fed up with him and packed him off to South America."

"And did Grant agree to go?"

"It was that or prison for embezzlement," Hale explained. "The old man took a firm line about it and Grant had to go. George Ansell then gave instructions that we were to pay Grant twenty pounds a month, through the Brazilian Trust Bank, which we have done until the old man's death three weeks ago.

"The money was drawn and signed for regularly every month, and as far as we know, Grant is still alive and kicking—unless he died in the last three weeks—no, two weeks. The last payment was drawn from the bank on the tenth of September last."

"And now he comes into half a million pounds?" said Tinker.

Hale shrugged.

"It won't be anything like that when death duties have been paid, but it'll be a good smack of worldly goods," he said. "What you might call worth while waiting for."

"And he's the only living relative?"

"The only one that's known," said Hale, nodding again.

"No one, for instance, in this country?"

"Certainly not. We should know if there was."

"I mean, Clive Ansell hadn't got a secret wife tucked away anywhere?"

"Clive—married?" Hale laughed ironically. "You didn't know Clive, did you? If you did, you wouldn't ask that question. Not wild horses would have dragged him to the altar."

"Oh," said Tinker. "And what sort of man was Clive?"

"A wastrel," said Hale, without hesitation. "Had he been left to his own devices, I think he would have made ends meet by the quickness of his wits, but with the expectation of his father's dough behind him—well, he never did anything at all, so far as I know."

"He was a fairly intelligent fellow, then?"

"Oh, yes. Sharp enough," said Hale. "He wasn't a nitwit, if that's what you mean."

"Just a lazy devil?"

"Yes. Just that."

"And was he strong willed?" asked Tinker casually.

"Always trying to get his own way," said Hale. "Got damn bad-tempered when he couldn't get it, too. He came here once and wanted us to give him some money. We wouldn't, and he threatened he'd have his father change his solicitors."

"Oh, I see," said Tinker slowly. "Mild blackmail. And what is your own personal opinion of him?"

Hale laughed bitterly.

"A damned dirty double-crossing little swine, and whoever did him in must have had plenty of reason for it."

"That's frank enough," grinned Tinker.

"Well, you asked for it," countered Hale cheerfully.

"And it's the sort of opinion I wanted," said Tinker. "Thanks very much."

Tinker hurried back to Baker Street, where Blake was in his room preparing for his journey north. The assistant quickly told the detective what he had found from Hale.

"Sounds like a dead end," grunted the detective. "I

was hoping there might be some near relative handy who would have had a good reason to kill Clive for the sake of that fortune."

"That's what I hoped, too," Tinker admitted. "As it stands now, it seems that the police case against Drake is as sound as a rock."

He sat down on the bed and watched the detective applying a very slight make-up to his face. It was only very slight—small enough to be unnoticeable—and yet enough to change his whole appearance.

"Do you think Drake did it?" Tinker said, after a while.

"I don't know," said the detective, peering into the mirror over the dressing table. "That's what I'm going to Westhall to find out. The whole case smells queer from the very start, although it seems straightforward."

"Do you believe his story about not remembering anything that night?"

"That, too, I'm going to find out about," said Blake, slipping on a jacket. "I have in mind a drug, but according to his story, he could only have had it at supper, in which case, the girl and her mother must have had some of it, too. That's the snag."

"Do you think he had a drug of some sort?"

"There's one small proof that he did," said Blake, glancing into the mirror for the last time. "How does this make-up go, Tinker? Joseph Blake, building surveyor."

"Good enough, guv'nor."

"Now I want you to keep Drake here until I send you word," said Blake, picking up his suitcase. "It may be to-morrow, but you must be ready at any time."

Tinker nodded and listened carefully while Blake gave him rest of the details necessary for their trip, and then went.

"I think you're up against a corker this time, guv'nor," murmured Tinker, when Blake had gone.

THE THIRTEENTH CHAPTER

The Surveyor Surveys.

THE MORNING WAS fine, and the detective enjoyed his walk from the town and through the spacious grounds of the Grange. The old house stood on the hilltop, almost hidden by a thick belt of trees, and there was no sign of life about it as he approached.

He settled his bowler hat more comfortably on his head, and mounted the broad steps of the terrace. The main doors were wide open, and the tall, black-clothed figure of Vernon was there, hands under his coat tails behind him, enjoying the morning air.

Vernon regarded the visitor with his heavy head cocked on one side, as if he did not altogether trust the detective.

"Good-morning," said Blake, raising his hat.

"Good-morning, sir," said Vernon.

"I am from Galway and Blake, surveyors," said the detective pleasantly.

"Indeed, sir?" Vernon replied, raising his eyebrows.

"I have been instructed by Mr. Ansell's solicitors to make a complete survey of the house and outbuildings," said Blake.

Vernon showed some slight sign of surprise, but it was very well mannered surprise.

"You know, of course, sir, that Mr. Clive Ansell is dead?" he said, with but the faintest raising of a heavy eyelid.

"Yes, I heard about that," said Blake. "A very tragic affair."

"Very tragic indeed, sir," agreed Vernon. "We were all very upset, as you can imagine."

Vernon was thawing a little. Now that he found that Blake was a surveyor, and not a gentleman, he seemed to become more friendly.

"I think, sir, you had better see Mrs. Marion, the housekeeper," he said. "She will give you all the facilities you require."

The butler turned and led the way in through the spacious hall, and through a green baize door which concealed his own quarters.

"I suppose you knew the young man very well?" said Blake in a confidential tone.

"Not very well, sir," said Vernon. "He was hardly ever here, you see. Not in his father's time."

"You, of course, must have been here for a long time," said Blake.

"No, sir. Not so very long," said Vernon. "I served Mr. George Ansell for just over five years."

"He was a good man to work for, I believe?" said Blake,

looking round him, as if already looking over the work he was supposed to do.

"Very 'good indeed, sir. It was a sad day when he died, I may say. We felt as if we had lost a friend."

Vernon sounded almost sepulchral, but there was in the heavy lidded eyes a look that made it seem he was putting it on for the visitor's benefit.

Blake had the idea that Vernon was genuinely sorry about the deaths—but only because he was likely to lose his job on that account.

Vernon came to a door and knocked discreetly. A sharp female voice answered from inside, and the butler opened the door.

"Mrs. Marion, sir—Mr. Blake, from the surveyors," he said, standing aside to let Blake through.

The black-clad woman was sitting stiffly at her table by the window, writing down her household accounts in an exercise book. She stared almost suspiciously at the newcomer, and nodded very curtly.

Blake explained what he had come for.

"Will it take you long?" she asked, her low metallic voice sounding clearly in the room.

"A few days, I expect," said Blake. "These rambling old places usually take some time."

"I am not sure that it would be right for us to offer you accommodation in the circumstances," she answered crisply. "We have instructions for the moment to carry on until we hear from the solicitors or Mr. Grant, and it would not be right to have guests—"

"I have a room in the town," said Blake. "I am putting

371

up at the Dragon, so that I shan't bother you very much."

She inclined her head as if in acknowledgment.

"Would you like to start work right away, Mr. Blake?" she said.

"Yes. There is no point in wasting time," said the detective. "But, first, I would like somebody to show me round the house. That will take some time, I think."

"I will show you round, sir," said Vernon, with a slight cough. "I have not a great deal to do, just at present."

There was a tinge of irony in his voice which rather amused the detective. It was clear that the wily butler had little time for the stark Mrs. Marion, and that the two did not see eye to eye about anything.

"Thank you," said Blake. "I think we might start straight away."

"Certainly, sir," said Vernon. "Where?"

"At the top," said Blake.

"Ah," said Vernon, and once more stood aside to let Blake precede him through the door.

The butler closed the door very carefully behind him, and then bent closer to Blake.

"A tough old cat," he confided in a whisper.

Blake chuckled. He had decided to make a friend of the butler. He had an idea that this genial and sly fellow would be a mine of useful information.

Vernon led him slowly upstairs through the main part of the house. Nothing hurried the butler, he went in his own slow time, pointing out various matters of interest as he went.

"And this was old Mr. Ansell's room," he said, pointing

through an open doorway. "That's where he died."

"What did he die of?" asked Blake curiously.

Vernon's eyes flicked round to him under the heavy lids, and the butler grinned faintly.

"Heart failure," he said. "'The old chap had a lot of trouble with his heart. Been kept in bed several weeks this year. Wouldn't take any proper advice and behave himself, so he died."

Vernon shrugged, as if to indicate that he had done as much as he could to advise the old fool, but his advice had not been taken.

"It would be a pretty draughty room with all those windows open," said Blake, staring round the room.

"Like the top deck of an iceberg," said Vernon. "I wouldn't have this room as a gift, but the old gentleman liked it. No accounting for tastes."

He looked round the place again.

"We were taking it in turns to look after him, that morning," said Vernon. "Early morning, it was, and suddenly the old chap tried to get out of bed. Think of it—with a bad heart! Of course he died practically on the spot."

"And then Mr. Clive came up to take over, I suppose," said Blake casually.

"Mr. Clive? No, he was here already," said the butler, closing the bedroom door. "Came up when he heard his father was ill."

"Did he always do that?"

"'Sometimes," said Vernon, and then gave a slow grin. "My word! You're a one for a bit of gossip, aren't you?"

"You needn't worry," said Blake with a short laugh. "I'm not a newspaper man in disguise."

They went on up another flight of stairs to the attics. Slowly the butler led Blake through the upper rooms, explaining everything and everybody who had ever lived there. There seemed to be no small item of gossip he didn't know.

The house was a rambling old one, and the whole tour took over an hour, during which time the butler supplied enough gossip to fill several books.

At the end of the tour he took Blake down into his private room and produced a bottle of wine, which he had clearly filched from the cellar.

"You don't seem to bear Clive's murderer any ill will," said Blake, raising his glass.

Vernon shrugged.

"I didn't care for Mr. Clive," he said quite frankly. "I don't think that young man will be greatly missed. Never did a good turn for anyone in his life. No"—he stared through his glass at the window—"I don't think anyone is sorry."

Blake finished his drink.

"I shall be back this afternoon," he said. "I believe there are a few cottages on the edge of the estate? I thought of going to look them over now."

"There is only one on the estate, sir," said Vernon, becoming formal again. "That is down through the wood—Laburn Cottage."

"I'll go down there now," said the detective.

"It was, of course, in the cellar there that the—er—corpse was found, you know," said the butler. "I hope that won't upset you."

Blake left the Grange and walked down through the wood to Laburn cottage. The distance was about a mile by a winding path through the wood.

When he came to the cottage the only sign of life was a thin wisp of smoke rising vertically into the still morning air from a chimney. The place looked so peaceful it seemed impossible that a foul murder had been discovered there only forty-eight hours before.

He knocked at the door, and Jane Wray answered it. Her face was pale and drawn, and her eyes very wide and bright. The tragedy she suffered was clearly marked in her expression.

"May I come in?" Blake said gently.

The girl agreed almost listlessly.

"Are you alone here?" went on the detective, when they were in the parlour.

"We are staying with mother's sister," she answered. "I have just come this morning to tidy the place up. We can't"—she broke off with a shudder—"can't stay here any longer. Not after that."

"Of course," said the detective softly. "I have an important message for you, but you must keep it a close secret."

The listlessness went out of her eyes and the fierce bright light of hope suddenly rose in them.

"A message?" she whispered, hardly trusting her voice.

"Drake is safe," said the detective. "He is at the moment in my rooms in London. I have come up here to help you—and him, if it's humanly possible. But in order to do that I must have your confidence. I want you to tell me absolutely everything you can remember about this affair."

The girl hesitated, her wide eyes searching his face.

"Who—who are you?" she said huskily.

"My name is Blake—Sexton Blake."

"The detective!" She stared for a moment then nodded. "I might have guessed he would go to you. He told me about your—er—dramatic meeting."

Her voice trailed away, and she sat down in a chair, her hands clasped tightly in her lap.

"Do you—do you think there is any hope for him?" she asked nervously.

"Of course there is hope," said Blake. "I can't tell you how much until I know as much as you do."

"I see," she said, wrinkling up her forehead. "I'll try and remember everything."

Blake brought out his pipe, filled and lit it while she told her story. He paced slowly up and down the little room, puffing slowly, and frowning at the floor.

When she finished, he halted by the open window and made a slight gesture of impatience.

"There seems to be no doubt then that a drug was somehow introduced into the salad that night," he said. "And there's no doubt that you had the smallest dose of the three. Now was there any part of the meal that you had only part of?"

She frowned for moment, then looked up.

"The salad dressing?" she said, as if asking a question. "I made some dressing, you see. Mother is fond of it, but I don't care for it very much."

"How did you serve it? In a cup or something?" asked Blake.

"No, I poured it on the salad."

"When?"

"When I made it," she said.

"Do you mean before Ansell came?"

She nodded.

"And where was the meal standing before you served it in here?"

She got up and opened the kitchen door. She pointed to a small table by the sink, and directly under the window.

"On that table," she said.

"Do you remember—was the window open or shut?" he persisted.

"Open," she said. "It was very close that night, because of the storm, and I was trying to get some air in. The window in this room was open, and the kitchen window."

"Did you shut it before the storm began?" Blake asked.

"Mother made us shut all the windows," said Jane. "She's terrified of storms."

"And the salad was standing under the open window," said Blake. "So that it would have been easy for anyone to reach in and pour the drug over the dressing?"

"Not easy, no," she protested. "The salad was in a glass bowl, and there was a plate over the top of it, to keep it fresh. And there were other plates and things with it, and I had some muslin over the top of them all, to keep the flies off."

Blake frowned.

"Was this muslin just laid over the whole lot?" he said.

"No. I always tuck it under the plates as well, so as to make sure no flies get under the edges," Jane said simply. "We get a lot of flies here."

"I see," said Blake slowly. "Then to put the drug in the salad someone would have had to lift off the muslin, which was tucked under plates, then lift the plate off the salad bowl?"

She nodded.

"And no one could have done that in the dark without making a noise—like one plate chinking against the bowl?" he said.

"That's right," she said. "It would be bound to make a noise, and I was in here all that evening."

"Was this door open?" said Blake, pointing to the door joining the parlour to the kitchen.

"Yes. To let the air circulate," she said, nodding again.

"Hm," Blake grunted in a disappointed way.

It seemed that all the information in this case was deliberately unhelpful. The more details he uncovered, the more difficult the case became.

No one could have got at that salad bowl in the dark kitchen without making a sound, unless it was a conjurer, and even he would have to be pretty slick.

Blake sat down on the window-sill and looked into the bowl of his pipe.

"Now you say Jim came back in that night at about three?" he said. "Wearing the raincoat which was in the devil of a mess, with mud and blood?"

She shuddered slightly.

"Yes."

"But you didn't mention that to him afterwards?"

"No. You see, it never occurred to me till just now that he did not know what he was doing," she said. "I thought he never mentioned it to me because it was something horrible to talk about."

"He seemed normal when he came in?" queried Blake.

"Well—no. Not normal," she said, biting her lip in an effort to remember. "He had a queer look—sort of not like his usual self at all. I didn't think, though, that he didn't know what he was doing. Poor darling!"

Her lip trembled and she looked for a moment as if she would cry, but she controlled herself with a magnificent effort.

"You see, Miss Wray," said Blake gently, "he did not speak to you about that night because for a whole week he was trying to find out what had happened to him during the storm.

"When at last he thought of looking in the cellar, his terrible suspicions were confirmed.

"He came to me not so much to escape the police, but to find out what he did do that night."

"I knew something dreadful had happened," she said in a low voice. "It was a sort of instinct, and you see, it seemed that Jim was the only one who could have—done it."

"It has been a terrible time for you both," said Blake warmly. "I believe that you have been callously thrown into the middle of a terrible murder that has nothing to do with you. But I have no proof yet of it, and that's why I'm here now."

He crossed the room and went into the kitchen. He stood there for some time, staring out into the garden, where the rubbish pile lay.

He returned to the parlour.

"Can I go up to your bedroom?" he said.

She led the way upstairs, and Blake stood at her window for some minutes, looking at the rubbish heap from several different angles.

He turned away at last, and they went downstairs again.

"Now I'm going into the cellar," he said. "I'll go alone."

He went out into the garden and through the bush into the cellar. The police had finished with it, and they had left things almost as they had found them.

But it was unlikely that any clues that might have been there were still remaining. It was going to be difficult for him to find anything of use there.

The floor which had been described to him as "smooth as a beach" had been trampled and churned up. Only in certain corners could he see the smooth, set surface that had covered the whole floor after the storm.

With the help of a flashlight he went over the whole place inch by inch, making a careful note of the state of the floor in every part of the cellar.

"When Jim Drake found the body, the tracks and grave marks were made on top of the smooth mud," he muttered. "Now let's see what this may mean.

"First, it may mean that the body was buried here after the storm, and after the mud had set, which would not be sooner than twenty-four, or forty-eight hours after the storm had finished.

380

"Second, it's obvious that if the body was buried on the night of the murder it would have been buried in liquid mud, which would have sealed over the grave and covered any trace the murderer may have left.

"The police think the tracks to the grave were made by Drake the night before last, but Drake swears they were there before, which is the reason he found the body.

"Which leaves two possibilities.

"One, that the body was hidden somewhere else first, and buried here a day or more after the murder: or

"Two, the murderer buried the body here on the night of the storm, and afterwards found the traces of it washed out. In which case he deliberately made tracks to the grave over the smooth floor, to make sure that it would be found.

"Which is it?"

He lit a cigarette and sat down on an old broken chest of drawers. Daylight streamed through the bush-covered entrance, sending long slanting sunrays down through the darkness of the cellar.

He realised that he was working under a severe handicap now. How could he go further unless he knew something of the state of the body when it had been found?

The real traces of the crime had been taken away by the police, and unless he found out from them exactly what the body had been like, he was working completely in the dark.

And how could he get in touch with the police without giving Drake away?

THE FOURTEENTH CHAPTER

The Sergeant Succumbs.

BUT AS SEXTON Blake sat there in moody thought, the answer to his prayers suddenly burst into the cellar, almost dragging the bush with him through the opening.

Once inside, the great figure of Sergeant Sale unfolded itself like a jack-knife opening, and regarded Blake with a look of cheerful suspicion.

"And what, may I ask, are you doing here?" he said, sticking his thumbs his belt.

"If you must know," said Blake, "I'm supposed to be surveying the place, and a more dank, dismal, damp and desolate cellar I've never come across."

"Ah," said Sale, nodding and looking round. "It's that. Like the Black Hole of Calcutta, it is. The young leddy said you were down here, so I thought I'd just see what you were up to."

"Nothing much to do down here," said Blake, getting up from his rickety seat. "I was having a quiet smoke, to tell you the truth."

"Haw!" laughed the sergeant suddenly. "Good place to pick for a quiet smoke. This is where that there body was found. You've heard about that, eh?"

Blake nodded.

"Yes. The people round here seem to talk about nothing else," he said, and then feigned a violent start. "Good heavens! You don't mean it was actually found in here?"

"I do," said Sale. "Right over there by where you're standing. Ha, ha! Gave you a shock, eh? Nothing to worry about, though. Everything's been cleared up, don't you worry."

"Well, I must confess it gave me a bit of a shock," said Blake, with a nervous laugh, and looked round. "Where was it? Over there?"

"That was the hole," said Sale, still cheerful. "Right there by the wall."

Blake stared down at the indicated spot, and from the corner of his eye watched the sergeant grinning at him.

The cheery sergeant was enjoying the surveyor's apparent uneasiness over this Chamber of Horrors.

"Buried him pretty deep, I suppose," said Blake, after a while.

"Not deep enough," said Sale knowingly. "Just under the surface. No more than nine inches on top of him. Careless, that was. Might have been here now but for that."

"Have a cigarette," said Blake, offering his case. "Phew! It's kind of warm down here."

The sergeant laughed and took a cigarette. He was in

384

a talkative mood that morning, and this was as good a place as any for a rest and smoke.

"What was he—shot?" asked Blake, lighting up again.

"Head bashed in," said Sale, puffing out a long streamer of smoke. "With a stone, or something like that. We haven't found the instrument yet. Fairly battered, though."

"Horrible!" said Blake. "Such a young fellow, too."

"No need to be sorry about that," said Sale, shaking his head. "Judging from all accounts, he was a first-class rotter. Took dope, too."

"Took dope?" echoed Blake, looking surprised in order to cover the sudden gleam in his eyes. "How on earth can you tell that?"

"The doctors find things like that at the post-mortems," said Sale contentedly. "There isn't much that gets past them, I can tell you. They find out all sorts of things."

"Rotten sort of job, though," said Blake, making a face.

"Messy," agreed the sergeant.

"The police suspect some young local chap, I hear," said the detective.

"Fellow that used to live here, up top," said Sale, jerking his thumb at the ceiling. "He did a bunk the day we found it, but we'll have him all right, don't you worry. We're watching the girl like a hawk. That's how I saw you come."

"I see," said Blake, nodding slowly. "You think he'll come back here, do you?"

"Oh, he'll try to get in touch, with her, you bet," said Sale, closing one eye. "She was his sweetie. They always try to keep in touch."

He yawned noisily.

"So you're watching the house," said Blake. "That's a pretty boring job, I should think."

"Darn boring," said Sale pointedly. "It's quite nice to have a chat, I can tell you—a relief."

"According to the papers," said Blake, "this chap wrapped the body up in his coat."

"That's right, he did," said Sale, nodding ponderously. "A damnfool thing to do, I might say. Why did he want to wrap it up for, anyway? The body had clothes on. I reckon he did it to get rid of the coat. Had blood on it, you see—blood and pine needles. Wouldn't have been any good as a coat, but still, he could have burnt it, or something."

"All murderers make mistakes," said Blake. "That's what they always say in the newspaper articles, anyway."

"Too true," said Sale. "And that weren't all. He left the dead man's handkerchief hanging on the bush by the entrance. That's what gave us the clue to where the body was. Like a ruddy signpost."

"Good lord!" said Blake. "And what sort of chap is he?"

"Oh, quite a nice sort of fellow, really," said Sale. "Pretty popular at his works and so on. I reckon he did this in a fit of rage—sort of saw red, if you see what I mean, and then didn't know how to get rid of the evidence."

"Extraordinary what people will do when they get into a panic," said Blake. "But it's very interesting."

"Well, if you're interested in it and got nothing to do this afternoon, you ought to go to the inquest," said the sergeant. "You'll get all the dope there, straight from the horse's mouth, as you might say."

The sergeant was savouring the last of his cigarette before he threw it down. In the distance sounded a church clock, striking twelve.

"Ah, well," said Sale, rising with a sigh. "I must get along, I suppose. Good-morning, sir. Don't forget the inquest. You'll enjoy that."

He forced his way out through the bush and disappeared. Blake waited a minute or two, then followed him out.

The girl was obviously waiting for him for she opened the kitchen door as soon as Blake came into the sunshine.

"Have you finished?" she asked loudly. This question was clearly intended for any distant watcher, and Blake acted up to it.

He looked quickly through his big surveyor's notebook, and then looked up.

"I'd like to see the parlour again, if I may," he said.

She stood aside, and when he was inside she shut the door.

"I didn't know that sergeant was here," she said quickly. "I only saw him just after you went down the cellar."

"Don't worry," Blake answered. "He turned out to be very useful indeed. He told me a lot of details that we didn't know. But please be warned by it, Miss Wray. Take care what you do, because it's obvious that the police are watching you in the hope that you will give them an idea where Jim Drake is."

She set her chin determinedly.

"They'll get nothing from me," she said with a trace of defiance.

"Good! Well, I must get back to the town—" He broke off and looked up at her again. "Oh, by the way, I suppose you'll be at the inquest this afternoon?"

She nodded and the shadow of fear passed across her face again.

"I am a witness," she said.

"Don't worry," he said. "It's nothing to be frightened about—quite a formal affair. Inquests always are." He looked at his watch, "Where is this one being held?"

"At the Grange," she said. "It's being held in the old ball-room there, because that's the only hall big enough near here."

"The ball-room?" Blake frowned. "Oh, yes. That's the room cut off from the house—just joined to the main building by a corridor?"

"That's it," she said.

"I shall be there," he said, and laid a hand lightly on hers. "Try not to worry more than you can help. We shall be seeing daylight soon."

THE FIFTEENTH CHAPTER

The Inquest.

THE BALL-ROOM WAS a huge place with a line of windows ranged along one wall, and through these could be seen the park and the trees of the wood.

Vernon had directed the laying out of the chairs in the room for the inquest, and everything was in position by two o'clock, when the first subdued members of the public arrived.

Several policemen were quietly on duty in the ball-room and guarding the doors on the outside. There was an expectant hush of whispering in the room as the public took their places.

Vernon himself stood unobtrusively at the back of the room, as if seeing that all was well. He nodded with a drooping eyelid at Blake when the detective came in through the door.

The atmosphere in the room was already getting warmer with the heat of many people, and it would have been unbearably stuffy but for Vernon's foresight in ordering three of the great windows to be wide open.

He had chosen the three which would give the most ventilation with the least draught, Blake noticed.

For all his lazy and insolent manners, he seemed to have the perfect manservant's eye for small details.

Dr. Rank, the coroner, came bustling short-sightedly into the room five minutes late. Several members of the public grinned, for no matter what appointment Dr. Rank made, he always arrived in a breathless hurry and five minutes late.

Here was the coroner, true to tradition, hurrying to his table at the end of the room, nodding to one or two acquaintances, looking at his watch, muttering and snorting breathlessly.

He sat himself down, sorted out his papers in a quick, nervous, confused sort of way, and at last indicated that he was ready to take the evidence.

The opening evidence was formal, telling how the body was found, where and when. This information was followed by the evidence as to the cause of death, and the condition of the body.

Dr. Rank coughed and regarded the police surgeon, as that witness stood behind the table which had been set to form a sort of witness-box.

"And how long would you say the body had been dead, doctor?" said Rank, peering over the top of his spectacles. "Could you give us some idea?"

"I estimate about a week," answered the surgeon. "I cannot say to the exact day, of course, but I should estimate that length of time to be about right."

The surgeon then proceeded to give the cause of death in highly technical language, but which in common parlance meant Ansell's skull had been cracked open with a heavy, blunt instrument, probably a stone.

"Now, sir, just as moment," said Rank, leaning forward. "Is it your opinion that this injury may have been caused by a fall?"

"The injury itself could easily have been so caused," agreed the surgeon. "But there are marks which clearly show that the dead man was being held by the throat at the same time that the blow was administered."

"I see," said Rank, and for some time he scratched away with a steel pen, writing down the surgeon's evidence. "Yes, we have that pretty clearly," he went on. 'Were there any other marks which might be of use to us?"

"There is very clear evidence that he was addicted to drug-taking," answered the surgeon.

"Really?" said Rank, stiffening.

The whole court seemed to lean forward in excitement at this revelation.

"What types of drugs?" continued the coroner.

"Cocaine and opium," said the surgeon. "Neither, as you know, dangerous in themselves, but in the long run having very serious weakening effects on the nervous system."

"Yes, yes," said Rank, nodding. "You mean that they eventually cause a man to act in a hysterical or irrational manner?"

"Exactly," said the surgeon, inclining his head.

"I think," said the coroner to nobody in particular,

"that we should bear that piece of evidence in mind as it may help us later on."

He scratched away with his pen again, and the surgeon left the witness table. There was some whispering amongst the public until the next witness was called—Jane Wray.

She told the story of Ansell's mysterious visit on the thirteenth, and the audience listened without a sound. But at the end of her evidence, quite a loud burst of chatter broke out, and Rank had to bang on his table for order.

The other witnesses came and went, and then Vernon, with majestic correctness, took up his stance at the table.

"You are the butler to Mr. Ansell?" said Rank.

"I was—to both Mr. Ansells," Vernon corrected him, with only the faintest glint of impudence in his eye.

"Do you remember the night of the thirteenth of September?" snapped Rank irritably.

"I do."

"Tell us what happened that evening—before Mr. Ansell went out?" said Rank.

"Mr. Ansell had been fidgety—on edge, you might say— during the whole of that day, sir," said Vernon smoothly. "His temper was never good, but it seemed worse than ever that day.

"I served dinner to him in the library—"

"Yes, yes! You are going too fast," said Rank. "What was Ansell doing during the day?"

"He seemed to be carrying out a search of the house, sir," Vernon replied.

"A search of the house?" demanded Rank. "What do you mean by that?"

"He seemed to be looking for something, opening drawers, looking through the books, searching the cupboards, and so forth."

"Had he done anything like that before?"

"No, sir. But then he had not been in the house very much, you see, sir."

"Did it seem to you that he had found what he was looking for?"

"No, sir. He seemed very bad tempered at dinner," said Vernon.

"He ate his dinner, did he?"

"No, sir, he didn't. But he drank half a decanterful of brandy before he went out."

"In short, you mean to imply that Ansell was in a highly nervous state on that day?"

"He was, sir. Highly upset, I thought."

"Would you say frightened, perhaps?"

The court seemed to lean forward again, as if to hear the butler's answer more clearly.

"No, sir," Vernon replied. "I would say irritated, short-tempered, and upset, rather like a boy who cannot get what he wants—that sort of tantrum, sir. But frightened, no."

The court sat back again.

"Right," said Rank. 'Now what happened after he had had—or rather, had not had his dinner?"

"He got up suddenly, sir," said Vernon. "He was in a foul temper, then—furious."

"This was after he had drunk the brandy?"

"Yes, sir," was the smooth reply. "And then he went out of the house, and we never saw him again."

"Did he say anything to you before he went?" queried Rank, cocking his head on one side.

"Yes, sir, he did," said the butler hesitantly. "He said, 'She'll have to do as she's told. I'm not going to be messed about like this.'"

Again the court sat forward. Clearly Dr. Rank also attached great importance to this remark.

"You are certain about that?" he persisted.

"Absolutely, sir," said the butler, and repeated it again.

From where he sat, Blake suddenly noticed the stiff, ramrod figure of Mrs. Marion shift with a quick movement of nervous impatience. It seemed to catch Vernon's eye, and he glanced towards her with faint, amused curiosity.

"And Ansell said nothing else?" said Rank, when he had written down the remark.

"He stopped at the library door, sir, and told me to leave out some whisky for him, and not to wait up," said Vernon.

"He told you not to wait up?" said Rank, writing again.

"Yes, sir."

"Meaning that he expected he would be late," said Rank, "And what time was this?"

"About eight-thirty, sir," said Vernon. "I cannot remember exactly, of course, but somewhere round about that."

"So that Ansell expected his visit to take some hours," said Rank, and his eyes roamed curiously across to where Inspector Grimes was sitting.

The inspector was making a jotting in his notebook, and seemed faintly puzzled. Immediately behind him sat Blake, his face bland and blank, like that of a courteous gentleman passing a quiet, but slightly improper afternoon.

Vernon returned to his seat at the back of the room, and upon her name being called, the stiff, black-swathed housekeeper marched quickly and rigidly to the witness table.

Her face was set and white, and Blake was surprised to notice that a sharp, fierce passion seemed to burn behind the black coals of her eyes.

She answered Rank's opening questions with a sharp intonation in which faint trembling could be noticed. Blake also saw that her black-gloved hands were tightly clenched in front of her.

"Did Ansell say anything to you before he went out that night?" said Rank.

She shook her head, but otherwise remained still and stiff as a statue.

"Did you hear him say anything before he went?"

"I heard the remark about the girl," she said, speaking quickly as if the last remnants of her iron control were falling away. "It wasn't what Vernon said. He's wrong. He knows he's wrong. What he said was: 'She'll have to do as she's told. I won't be black—'"

She stopped speaking, her mouth open, and her eyes staring as if in complete amazement. The dead silence of shock hung in the court at the suddenness of her stopping, and in that hush there came the sound of two rifle shots from the park outside. Then the stiff figure crumpled and fell forward over the polished top of the table. She slid slowly off the surface, and fell to the ground in a heap, with blood trickling from the side of her head.

Someone screamed, and then the startled voice of Inspector Grimes rang out:

"Stand right where you are—everybody! It's all right! Don't move!"

THE SIXTEENTH CHAPTER

The Man With the Gun.

SERGEANT SALE RUSHED to the doors, opened one and shouted an order through to his man outside.

Then he slammed the door again, and ran down to where Grimes was kneeling by the dead woman.

Everyone in the room was on his feet, all eyes turned on the crumpled heap by the table.

Only the eyes of Blake turned elsewhere, staring out through the open window behind the witness table to where the small figure of a ragged man was walking slowly towards the woods, the shape of a rifle under his arm.

Dr. Rank, the police surgeon, and Sergeant Sale were bending over the dead housekeeper.

"Good heavens!" gasped Rank. "Shot through the head! How did it happen?"

Blake appeared behind the coroner.

"There is a man out in the park there," he said, "It looks as if a stray shot came in through the window."

Grimes, the surgeon and Rank all turned and stared out of the window at the small figure. Even as they watched, the man put the gun to his shoulder and fired somewhere into the trees. The thin cracks of the shots came in a second or two after the shots had gone.

"After him, Sale!" snapped Grimes sourly.

The sergeant vaulted out of the big window and ran away down the slope towards the gunman.

Dr. Rank mopped his brow nervously.

"It seems almost as if there's a curse on this house," he said hoarsely. "Murder and accidents happening one on top of another. Dreadful! Dreadful!"

Blake looked back at the startled audience. Several women were sobbing; one had passed out in her seat and was being fanned by two others. In the far corner of the room Blake saw the white-faced, frightened Vernon, slipping something back into his hip pocket and wiping his mouth.

"I could do with a nip of brandy myself," thought the detective. "This has given me the jumps."

"Yes, there's no question about it," said the police surgeon in a low voice. "The bullet came in through the window, to one side and behind her. It's rook rifle size— .22."

"Perhaps a shot ricocheted off the trees and came in through the window?" suggested Grimes. "Anyhow, it's certain the shot could not have come from inside this room."

As he spoke, he nodded to Rank, who mopped his brow and turned to the public.

"The court is adjourned," he said. "Please make your way out quietly. This accident seems to have been caused by a stray shot from the park, so I ask you not to spread any alarmists' stories in the town."

Gradually the crowd began to disperse, stumbling out through the doors. Some were anxious to go; others seemed to want to stay and stare, but two constables quickly persuaded them to get out.

Blake went across to where Vernon was still waiting in the corner. The butler smelt of brandy, which confirmed Blake's suspicions that Vernon had been having a quick swig to help his nerves over this new crisis.

"Shook me to the core," he confessed hoarsely. "I know what it is, too. That damn fool of a stable-boy. I told him he could do some shooting provided he went right away from the house. Then he goes and shoots right through the blasted window!"

Vernon shuddered, then turned his heavy eyes from the group by the window to Blake.

"She's dead, is she?" he whispered.

"Quite," said Blake, nodding.

"Oh hell, oh hell, oh hell!" muttered Vernon. "I'll get the blame for this. Damn it! Why did I let the fool have a gun? I must have been crazy!"

"Is this the first time he's borrowed one?" asked Blake, keeping his voice low so that the party by the window would not hear.

Vernon shook his head and reached for his hip flask again, but decided it would be too risky, and dropped his hand again.

"No. He often goes shooting in the woods," he whispered. "He can hit a rabbit at two yards if the rabbit sits still."

Grimes looked across to Blake and Vernon in the corner. He frowned at the detective.

"What are you hanging about for?" he asked quickly. "Newspaperman?"

"Surveyor," Blake answered. "I'm working here for the next few days."

"I see," said Grimes. "Well, we shan't want you in here now." He waved his hand. "Ring the station, will you, Vernon? Tell the sergeant on duty someone has been accidentally shot. He'll know what to do."

"Yes, sir," said Vernon. "And will that be all?"

"I'll let you know if we want anything," said Grimes.

Blake and Vernon went out and down to the butler's pantry. Once there, Vernon produced a brandy bottle and two glasses.

"Hell! These things turn my inside right over," he said, sloshing out brandy. "Here, drink this. It'll do you good."

He drank off his own in one gulp, then nodded appreciatively and went out to telephone. The butler was very upset, and was doing his best to laugh it off. But he was not succeeding very well.

This was one thing he found he could not joke about. It had, as he confessed, "shaken him to the core."

Blake took a sip of the brandy and sat down to think.

He had been watching the woman during the giving of her evidence, and if she had been deliberately shot at she would have been an easy target because she had stood perfectly still the whole time.

But he had also been able to see out through the window into the park, and the only man in sight had been the stable-boy with the gun—and he had been too far away even for an expert shot to have hit her.

And he had seen for himself that the shot could not possibly have come from inside the ball-room—unless bullets can go round corners; and even the cleverest murderer would be hard put to find a way of doing that.

What was more, there had been no report—no sound of a bullet until the sound of the distant rifle's double crack had drifted in through the windows.

No. It looked as if Grimes was right this time.

Except that there was just one detail which stuck in Blake's mind.

The accidental bullet had struck at such a curious moment.

At the very second when Mrs. Marion had been giving the most important piece of evidence presented at the inquest she had been struck down.

Blake remembered the words—the corrected words—which she had been repeating.

"She'll have to do as she's told. I won't be black—"

Black—what? There were only two words Blake could think of that would fit this case.

Blackballed, meaning to be thrown out of decent society; or, blackmailed.

And everyone knew what blackmailed meant.

Blake took another sip of the brandy. If Ansell thought he was being blackmailed, then an entirely new facet of the case presented itself.

It was an angle which had occurred to no one so far, but one which fitted perfectly into the apparently crazy demand for marriage to Drake's girl.

Blake's train of thought was interrupted by the return of Vernon.

"I'll resign this job as soon as I can," he confessed, with a slight shudder. "I don't like the way people don't last in this house. There's a hoodoo on it."

"It certainly seems like it,' said Blake, with a wry grin.

"They've got Stiggins in there now," said Vernon, pouring out another helping of brandy for himself. "He says he shot at a rook somewhere over the house here. Silly young fool! What the devil did he want to do that for when he's got ten square miles to shoot in?"

"You mean he goes about taking pot shots?" asked Blake.

"That's what it seems like," said Vernon, "though he always tells me he goes for rabbits."

"Then if he didn't hit anything, there's no telling where the bullets might have gone," said Blake, with a shrug.

"We know where one of them went," said Vernon, and tossed down his drink. "Ah, that's better. I suppose," he went on, becoming gloomy again, "I shall have to take over all her accounts now. More work!" He sat down in an easy-chair and stretched out his legs.

"Do you ever feel as if all the people round you are going a bit barmy?" he asked, staring into nothing. "I've been feeling that this last few weeks. Everything falling to pieces, like. Ever since the old man died everything's gone wrong."

"Had Mrs. Marion been here a long time?" said Blake, sitting on the edge of the table.

"Since the Ice Age," said Vernon, then gave a sudden sly grin. "About thirty years, I believe. Started off as a girl, I understand."

Blake was thinking of the gun-room at the other end of the house. There were two dozen guns there, as far as he remembered.

"Are you supposed to lend guns to the boys here?" said Blake.

"Not supposed to," said Vernon. "But then, if I let them have one now and again it stops them pinching them, you see? Old Mr. Ansell was in favour of that."

He stared out of the window, and for a moment he looked a very tired old man, as if this succession of tragedies was wearing him down.

The detective slid off the table.

"I must get on with some work," he said.

He went out and up the stairs to the attics, leaving the forlorn butler with only the company of the brandy bottle.

Once in the attics, Blake lit his pipe and stared out of the grimy window at the park from which the foolish stable-boy had fired the fatal shot.

In his mind there was a fantastic theory slowly taking shape, like a grotesque phantom of smoke. It seemed to fit in with some of the facts that he had discovered, but it just would not fall into place with this last death.

That seemed part of another story altogether.

THE SEVENTEENTH CHAPTER

The Detective Wonders.

BLAKE WAITED IN the attic, staring thoughtfully out of the window, until the last police car had driven away, taking with it Inspector Grimes and all of his men but one, who had been left on duty below.

The detective waited, staring down from his little window to the stables which were set beside the house. From his viewpoint he could see down into the stable yard, and it was there that he saw the forlorn Stiggins, tramping slowly across the yard with his head down and his hands in his pockets.

Blake watched the boy halt by a horse-box and lean against it, his whole body the picture of misery and dejection.

No onlooker could possibly have doubted that this was the man who had unluckily fired the fatal shot.

Blake collected his big notebook and rule, and went downstairs. He hoped he would not meet the inquisitive Vernon on his way down.

Once the detective saw the silent butler passing the end of the corridor along which Blake was going. Blake went into a doorway and stayed there till the butler had gone.

The detective did not meet any of the other servants, and he was grateful when he found himself in the stable yard, which was empty but for the miserable figure of Stiggins.

The stable-boy looked up sullenly as the detective came across to him, and looked as if he would turn away, but Blake caught his arm.

"Don't let it get you down," said Blake quickly. "You weren't to blame."

"I weren't?" said Stiggins gruffly. "Then who was? I fired the bullet, didn't I?"

The growling, unhappy voice trailed away, and Stiggins became silent, scowling. Blake saw the horse-box empty, and he gripped Stiggins' arm more tightly.

"We can talk in there," said Blake softly.

"Talk?" Stiggins growled. "What about?"

"About guns and stray bullets," said Blake steadily. "What did the police ask you?"

Stiggins peered closer into the detective's face. It was pretty dark in the horse-box.

"What do you want to know for?" he demanded. "Who are you, anyway?"

"I'm just a man who might be able to help you," said Blake quietly. "I saw something this afternoon which might prove that it wasn't your shot which killed Mrs. Marion."

Stiggins became stiff, and his eyes opened wide.

"You couldn't prove that?" he said in a breathy whisper.

"Perhaps I could, if you told me what the police said to you," countered Blake. "But before you start, you've got to keep this meeting secret. Understand that?"

Stiggins licked his lips, and then nodded slowly.

"I'll mind that," he said, frowning. "Though I don't know as it's right to tell you anything, that I don't."

"You'll have to trust me," said Blake. "You'll have to take my word that I'm here to help you."

"Well, I dunno," said Stiggins doubtfully. "I never met nobody who wanted to help me before. Still, you look like a gentleman. What do you want to know?"

"I want to know what the police said to you."

"They said about the gun," said Stiggins vaguely. "It was the same size bullet what killed Mrs. Marion as what was in the rifle, see? A rook rifle, it were, twenty-two. Mr. Vernon often lets me borrow un from the gun-room."

"Do you get a lot of shooting practice?" queried Blake.

Stiggins shook his head. "I gets practice all right, but I don't seem to get no better," he said. "It's me eyes, you see. I can't see anything less it's right close. That's the trouble, sir—short-sighted."

"I see," said Blake. "You told the police that?"

"Yes, sir. I told um all that," said Stiggins, nodding.

"And did you fire towards the house at any time?" Blake pursued.

"Towards the house, sir?" said Stiggins, scratching his head. "I couldn't say for sure. The police was asking that, too, sir, but I couldn't be sure. I was firing towards the trees, you see, sir. Right up into the trees."

"You might have been firing over the top of the house, then?" said Blake, narrowing his eyes.

"Well, over the top of the ballroom, which is only one floor high—yes, sir. That might be. I might have been looking over the top of that, you see, sir, and not actually notice it. Because of it was a snap shot, you see, sir. I caught sight of a bird out of the corner of me eye, and swung round and shot at it—two shots, sir."

"I see," said Blake curiously. "Then you weren't sure in which direction you were firing?"

"There was some trees behind the bird, sir, like I told you," said Stiggins.

"Yes, but there are trees practically all round the perimeter of the park," said Blake short-temperedly. "Let's see—" He brought out a cigarette packet. "Now listen, Stiggins. You say you didn't see whether you were firing over the house or not because you looked straight up to where the bird was. But what about after you had shot? Surely you dropped your eyes then?"

"But I couldn't see nothing then, sir,' said Stiggins. "You see, the sun was in me eyes when I shot, and when I looked down all I could see was great red flashes in me eyes, like fireworks, you know, sir."

"The sun was in your eyes when you shot!" cried Blake.

"Yes, sir. Fair blinding it were," said Stiggins, nodding.

"I saw you in the park immediately after you fired the shot," said Blake slowly. "You were standing due south of the house, half a mile away."

"Were I, then?" said Stiggins.

"You were," said Blake, staring out of the open box

door to the gathering shades of evening. "And that's all the proof we want of your innocence!"

Stiggins' mouth dropped open and his eyes goggled.

"But I still want you to tell me what the police had to say to you," Blake went on.

"The police?" Stiggins echoed stupidly. "Why, old Sale came running out across the park and grabs me by the arm and says, 'Oy, you bin and shot somebody, you clumsy goat, Stiggins,' he says."

"He knew your name?" said Blake.

"What—Sale?" said Stiggins, with a twisted grin. "Bless you, mister, Sergeant Sale fairly haunted this here place till the old man went and died. Always about, Sale was, though mostly in mufti."

"What was he doing about the house?" said Blake, surprised.

"That I couldn't say," said Stiggins, shaking his head. "I thought as perhaps he was doing some job for the old man, as he was always about. And then, when the old man died, see, Sale didn't come so often.'

Blake was silent for a moment.

"Did Mrs. Marion know that?" he asked.

"The old girl?" said Stiggins, and scratched his head again. "She knew, but he kepp out of her way most times. She didn't like him there, and he knew it. Din't get on, they two din't."

"Did Mr. Vernon know?" Blake went on.

Stiggins gave a short chuckle.

"Mr. Vernon knows eyerythink," said Stiggins. "But he ain't the sort to make a fuss about what he knows. A good sort is Mr. Vernon. Easy going, like, and if you get into trouble Mr. Vernon's the one to get you out. You ask any of the servants, mister. They'll tell you the same thing."

"And Mr. Vernon didn't mind Sale being about the house?" said Blake.

"Mind? I reckon they was having a few drinks together when they could slip into the pantry, mister," said Stiggins, with surprising sharpness. "Mr. Vernon's a lonely man, Mr. Vernon is, and likes a bit of company over a pipe and bottle."

Stiggins had cheered up quite a lot since Blake had begun to talk to him. He was a simple young fellow, and quite ready to believe anything he was told.

He believed what Blake had told him.

Outside the evening was growing darker. Blake glanced out at the gathering shadows, and the few yellow lights shining in the windows of the great old house.

"I must be going," said Blake. "But in the meantime, Stiggins, don't worry, and keep your mouth shut. You'll be all right."

He went out, leaving the stable-boy to ruminate in the darkness of the box.

Blake quickly made his way back to the inn where he was staying, on the outskirts of the town nearest the Grange and the mill.

There was a telephone in the passage upstairs, and Blake went to this and put through a call to Tinker in London.

"That you, Tinker?"

"Sure enough," replied the assistant. "Everything's quiet here so far. No one has called to inquire about visitors."

"Good," said the detective. "Now listen. You're to come up here right away. It looks as if Drake is in the clear, but I'm not sure yet. If my guess is right, there is not one murder but three."

"Three!" gasped Tinker. "Gosh! Wholesale slaughter, eh?"

"On the contrary," said Blake. "A very quiet and clever exercise in killing."

"Sounds first-class," said Tinker.

"Anyhow, be up here by the morning," said Blake. "I'll fix up rooms for you here. Don't forget the instructions."

He replaced the receiver, then turned suddenly as he caught sight of something moving at the end of the passage. It was almost in shadow there, and difficult to make out.

Then a black cat strolled into the light of the corridor.

Blake sighed with relief.

"For a moment it looked like something else," he muttered. "But it's a sign of good luck, I hope!"

It was to be lucky in one way, because Blake lived to see the cat again the next day.

But it was unlucky in another, for the theory which Blake had built upon the mass of evidence which he had collected that day was entirely wrong, and it was that mistake which left Blake's flank uncovered.

His shield was up against the wrong man.

THE EIGHTEENTH CHAPTER

Probing for Facts.

SEXTON BLAKE THANKED his lucky stars that he remembered the address which Jane Wray had given him that morning during his visit to the cottage, for he never would have found the house otherwise.

Mrs. Wray's sister's house turned out to be a thatched cottage behind the mill. It was so small that it was possible to walk past it without seeing it hiding behind a six-foot bramble hedge which covered it.

When he arrived, Jane herself answered the door.

"I wanted to see you, Miss Wray," said the detective, "alone, if possible."

She looked quickly over her shoulder into the house.

"Mother is upstairs with her sister," she said in a low voice. "We can talk in the garden."

She closed the door softly behind her and went with the detective along the overgrown garden. The light of the new moon shone down through a solitary tree in a corner

413

of the wilderness, and on the other side the mighty blank wall of the mill rose like a cliff into the sky.

"Miss Wray," said Blake softly, "I have come into possession of certain information which I believe may solve this case of Clive Ansell's death. I think I can promise you that Drake had nothing to do with it."

"Oh, Mr. Blake!" she began, but he silenced her with a motion of his hand.

"I want you to try and remember the day that George Ansell died," he said.

He saw her frown in the moonlight.

"The old man?" she said. "But—"

"Yes, the old man," he interrupted. "Believe me, it's most important. What happened that day?"

"I went to work at the mill as usual," she said. "And at about ten there was a message for me to go up to the Grange and take some letters for Mr. Ansell."

She hesitated, staring up at the blank wall of the mill as if trying to remember more of what had happened.

"I went there, but when I arrived I found him too ill to be seen," she said.

"You actually saw him?"

"No. Mrs. Marion stopped me in the corridor outside his room," she said.

"What did she say?" Blake's voice was very quiet and firm.

"She said—" The girl frowned again and put a hand to the side of her head. "It's difficult to remember exactly. I think she said that Mr. Ansell had taken a turn for the worse and that they had sent for Dr. Angel."

"How long was this after you had had the message to go up to the Grange?"

"How long? Oh, perhaps half an hour. I went straight up there, you see."

"Who sent the message to the mill?"

"The old man himself," she said.

"But he was in bed, surely?" Blake looked surprised now.

"He had a telephone by the bedside," she explained. "He spoke to me himself."

"What did he sound like?"

"Pretty bad," she said, after a slight pause. "But no worse than he had been before, when he had sent for me."

"And after Mrs. Marion stopped you, what did you do?" said Blake, bringing out his pipe.

"I went downstairs and waited in the hall," she answered. "The doctor came soon after, and went upstairs. A few minutes after that I heard the old man was dead."

"That was all that happened, Miss Wray?" said Blake urgently. "Think now! Haven't you forgotten something?"

She bent her head in an effort to remember.

"No. That's all that happened," she said.

Blake slapped his pipe in the palm of his hand.

"Something's wrong here," he said, shaking his head. "If that's all that happened to you on that morning, Miss Wray, my theory of the murder of Clive Ansell is entirely wrong!"

"You mean that Jim is still in danger?" she asked breathlessly.

Blake stared up at the solitary shape of the tree against the melon slice of the moon.

"Miss Wray!" he said very sharply. "Think—think hard! Are you sure you haven't forgotten anything?"

"Perfectly sure," she answered helplessly. "I—I'm sorry, but there was nothing else to remember!"

Blake swore under his breath. He thrust the pipe back into his pocket.

"I want the key of Laburn Cottage, please," he said tersely.

"Of course," the girl said, staring with wide eyes. "I'll get it."

She turned to go and he caught her arm lightly.

"Don't let your mother know I've been here," he said warningly.

"I won't," she said softly, but she gave him a curious look before she turned again and went silently away through the overgrown garden.

She returned in another moment, and gave him the key. He took it and slipped it into his pocket.

"Miss Wray," he said, "it's always possible for someone to forget a detail of what happened a few weeks ago. Try and remember—try and recall every tiny detail of what happened that morning. The life of your fiancé may depend on it."

"I'm sure, Mr. Blake," she said, her voice trembling with emotion. "I haven't forgotten anything! Please believe me! I'd do anything to help Jim, you know that! But I've told you all that happened that morning."

The detective sighed, then uttered a soft, bitter laugh.

"Then I'm wrong," he said. "My reconstruction of the case is useless. I shall have to go to work again, and start from another angle. Never mind." He grinned in the moonlight. "We shall have it straightened out soon."

He squeezed her hand gently and reassuringly, and went silently out of the garden. He walked quickly past the mill and along the street until he came to a telephone box.

He went into the box and looked up Dr. Angel's address. Ten minutes after that he was at the doctor's house, and found that white-haired gentleman taking his ease before the fire after a busy day.

Dr. Angel had a red, cheerful face, but as he looked up there came into his eyes a puzzled light of half recognition as Blake entered the room and closed the door behind him.

"Sit down," said the old doctor, still frowning. "The maid said your name was Joseph Blake, but I could have sworn—" He stuck a finger into his ear and half turned it, as if this helped him to think.

Blake sat down in the seat opposite the doctor while the old man searched his face keenly.

"Yes, I could have sworn the first name was Sexton—" said Angel.

"You are right, Dr. Angel," said the detective. "But I want to keep it quiet, if possible. I am here on behalf of a client, but I don't want the fact generally known."

"I see," said the doctor, nodding slowly.

"I particularly wanted to see you about the death of George Ansell," said Blake. "I believe that you were attending him for many years before his death."

"I was," said the doctor, reaching out for a decanter on a table beside him. "Here, have a glass of port."

Blake declined, and the doctor poured himself a glass.

"What did you want to know about the old man, then?" he said.

"He died very suddenly, didn't he?" said Blake.

Dr. Angel shrugged.

"Suddenly for a normal man, yes," he said. "But with a heart like George Ansell's—no. Any shock would have been enough to put him away. As it was, he tried to get up out of his bed, and that was enough to finish things off."

"The strain of trying to get up?"

"Yes. Any shock like that," said Angel, and sipped his port. "He'd had a lot of trouble before, you know. He wasn't a healthy man at all. His eyesight was bad, his lungs were bad, and his heart was worst of all."

"His eyesight was bad, was it?" Blake asked.

"Very bad," said Angel, nodding. "Though you could never get him to admit it. Always tried to pretend everything was all right, but actually he couldn't see a thing unless it was put under his nose. No one ever saw him reading for that reason. It gave the game away. He had to hold the print less than a foot in front of his nose."

"I see," said Blake, sitting back in his chair. "Now I'm going to annoy you, Dr. Angel; and I want you to forgive me in advance."

The doctor laughed.

"My dear Mr. Blake, I know enough about you to forgive you almost anything," he said jovially.

"Thank you," said Blake. "But I'm going to suggest to

you that George Ansell was murdered."

There was a silence. The doctor became quite still with his eyes fixed on the detective. Then he lifted his glass and took a sip, still keeping his eyes on the detective.

"Nothing in this world is impossible," he said at last, and set his glass down. "In fact, to murder George Ansell would be the easiest thing in the world. Any sudden shock could have done it. Any sudden excitement. Yes, it would have been easy."

"You weren't surprised to find him dead when you got there?" Blake queried.

"Surprised?" said Angel, raising his eyebrows. "My dear boy! I was told he was dead before I went to him!"

"You were told!" said Blake, sitting forward in his seat. "By whom?"

"By the son, Clive. He telephoned me," replied the doctor. "He'd just gone in to see the old man and found him on the floor by the bed, so he rang me straight away."

"And told you that his father was dead?"

Angel nodded.

"He said he thought he was dead," said the doctor. "No breathing and no heart beats. It was a right conclusion. That's the only way a layman could tell."

Blake sat back again and drummed on the arm of his chair with his fingers.

"What makes you think that George Ansell may have been murdered?" the doctor asked shrewdly.

"A half million pounds," said Blake slowly. "It's too much money to be floating around at a loose end, just passing from one dead man to another. There must be a reason behind those deaths, Dr, Angel. I'm convinced that there is, and the only reason I can think of is that fortune. It's enough to make any man think about murder."

The doctor poured another glass of wine, and this time his hand shook a little.

"Yes, there is reason enough," he said, nodding. "But who benefits? The father is dead, so is the son. Who comes after that?"

"A cousin in South America," said Blake dreamily.

"Surely you would mean a cousin who has come back from South America?" suggested the doctor keenly.

"No. Unfortunately, I mean a cousin who must still be in South America," Blake said, frowning.

The doctor spread out his hands in a helpless gesture.

"But, my dear boy, how—"

"Exactly. How?" said Blake, nodding slowly. "That's the very thing that's bothering me. You see, this fellow must be in South America, because he signs at the bank there for his remittance every month!"

"Conclusive proof that he is still there," said Angel smoothly. "In short, the motive for your murders is five thousand miles away and couldn't have done anything about murder—unless he did it by cable!"

The doctor laughed, and Blake smiled wearily.

"I agree, that's what it looks like," he said. "But I cannot see how Cousin Grant could bash his kinsman's brains out with a rock from that distance. He couldn't cable a rock, could he?"

The doctor's eyes twinkled and his hand went out for the port decanter again.

"Here. I'm sure you could do with a glass of this, my boy," he said, pouring one out. "It'll do you good. You're tired. At least, you look it."

"I'm not so much tired as bad tempered," grinned Blake, taking the proffered glass. "I had a perfect theory of this crime all worked out and fitted together like a jigsaw, and then one little detail didn't fit and the whole darned lot has fallen to pieces."

He drank and then sat back to look into the fire again.

"You found nothing unusual in George Ansell's bedroom on the day you found him dead?" he said, looking up at the doctor again.

Angel shook his head firmly.

"Except that the patient was out of bed—nothing," he said. "But then, even supposing he was murdered, there would not have been much evidence. You see, a person pretending to smother him with a pillow would have been sufficient to send him off, perhaps. Any cruel practical joke such as that might have done it."

"I see," said Blake. "His heart was really as bad as that, was it?"

"Quite as bad as that," said the doctor, sipping his port again. "It was in as bad a shape as it could be."

"What state of health was Clive Ansell in?" Blake asked.

"Well—" The doctor scratched his head noisily and cocked his head at the fire. "I couldn't say with any certainty. I hardly ever saw the man. But he was nervous and jumpy at times, and gave every sign of being in the habit of taking drugs. I gather subsequently that that guess was true."

"Was he a powerful man?"

"No. Probably a little weaker than most. His stamina would have been badly impaired by drug-taking, of course."

"He wouldn't be able to put up much of a fight against a powerful man?" said Blake sharply.

"None at all, unless he got a lucky blow in first. He'd have been practically all in after the first second or two of strain."

The doctor chatted for a while longer, and then Blake rose to go.

"Pleased to have met you, my boy," said the old doctor, shaking the detective's hand. "If there's any way I can help you, let me know. Always glad to assist where possible."

THE NINETEENTH CHAPTER

Interlude for Death.

BLAKE WALKED SLOWLY along the country road thinking hard. The trees of the Grange wood stood against the silver sky, and the white walls of Laburn cottage shone in the moonlight like sugar icing.

The detective turned in at the gate and walked slowly into the garden. His eyes darted quickly about him, as if searching for something which might be hiding there, and then he opened the cottage door with the key.

He went into the parlour and closed and locked the door behind him. Moonlight streamed in through the uncurtained windows, throwing weird colourless patterns on the floor and jumbled furniture.

Blake brought out his pocket torch and held it ready in his hand, although the moon gave enough light for him to see by.

He went into the kitchen and once more looked out through the window into the garden. After a moment he bent and made a close examination of the sill and the table with the help of the torch, but too long had passed since the night of the storm.

Any mark which the murderer may have made while doping that salad had long since been removed by careful cleaning.

"Sometimes a sloppy housekeeper is better than a careful one," thought Blake. "Good clues can stay preserved under layers of dust, but this is hopeless."

He went over the kitchen carefully, then went upstairs to Jane's bed-room. In the moonlight the rubbish heap below did look queer.

He could see now that in the sudden distorting flash of a lightning flare, that heap might look like the huddled figure of a man lying on the ground.

He watched it from various angles, half-closing his eyes to get a more vivid effect, and then suddenly he snapped his fingers.

"It does look like a man," he said half aloud. "But if there had been two figures there already, that heap would have made it look like three, and not two! What she saw was one man bending over the heap and beating the heap itself!

"But why beat the heap?"

A sudden grin came to his face. He turned and hurried downstairs. The back door was locked, but the key was in it. He turned it, let himself out into the garden and locked the door behind him, slipping the key into his pocket.

Both front and back doors were then locked, and both keys were in Blake's pocket.

He crossed to the heap and under the moonlight examined it. It was a pile of dead rotting leaves and vegetation, mixed with soft earth and ash from fires. The mass was soft, and crumbled easily between the fingers.

Blake got a short stick and began to probe about in the pile of rubbish. For a long time he found nothing but small pieces of ash and clinker, but then suddenly the stick dug into something tough.

The detective scraped the stuff away from the object, then pushed his hand down in the soft earth and pulled the thing out.

The damp, wet mould fell away from the object as Blake held it up, and he brushed the rest off with his fingers.

The thing was a small key wallet, and inside were three small keys and a name tag made of celluloid upon which was written the name

CLIVE ANSELL

Blake put the wallet in his pocket and continued his search. After a while he found two or three coins. A half-crown, three pennies, a two-shilling piece—just as coins might have fallen out of a man's pocket.

Blake bent and shone his torchlight carefully into the holes he had made in the damp mould. For some time he searched without result, and then faintly he could see patches of a darker stain than ordinary damp.

He scooped a little up and put it into an envelope.

"And if that's not bloodstain I'll eat my hat," he muttered.

He looked around again, then returned to the cottage, let himself in at the back door and closed and relocked it.

"It seems to me," he murmured, "that the police jumped at the obvious conclusion and didn't bother to look too closely at the rest."

He went back to the kitchen window again and made another minute examination of the sill. A silence as heavy as a muffling curtain hung in the air. Even the old clock in the other room had stopped for want of winding, and nothing moved at all.

Then suddenly, from somewhere behind him there came a faint, high-pitched whispering, like a string being whirled round in the air.

Instinctively, the detective moved to one side and half-turned.

Into the bright beam of the moon through the window there shot a silver streak, flashing like a huge, sparkling star and whizzing towards him.

He stepped sideways, and his foot caught in the leg of the table. He staggered and went over backwards with a crash as the table clattered across the floor.

He did not care that he had lost his balance so long as he got out of the way of that murderous sliver of steel that sped in the silent air.

He crashed to the floor, striking his head against the skirting.

The blow almost knocked him out. Stars shot in his sight and a blackness descended over his brain, but with the strength of supreme will power he fought the numbing effects of the blow, grasped the table leg, and dragged himself up.

Through the ringing in his ears he heard the front door

slam, and the sound of quick footsteps drawing away along the path.

He swayed dizzily, pressing his forehead between his fingers to try to drive off the giddiness. He could see the bright beam of the moonlight streaming through the window and the brighter, gleaming steel of a dagger stuck deep into the woodwork of the window frame where he had been standing.

He regained proper control over himself and went into the parlour. He turned the handle of the front door and pulled the door open.

Yet he himself had locked that door, and the key was still in his pocket.

Through the doorway the countryside lay still. Nothing moved in the silver light and deep shade of the night.

"Someone is a good deal cleverer than I am," he said to the empty night. "He knows who I am, but I don't know who he is!"

He closed the door again and leant against the wall. His head was aching abominably from the effects of the blow against the skirting, and yet that was better than the feel of that murderous knife in his back.

He had avoided it by a split second. If he had not heard the faint sinister hiss of its coming, he would have been a dead man now.

But the gloves were off. The purpose of his disguise was gone.

So far it had been successful. It had deceived the police, but it had not deceived the murderer.

Somehow the unknown had recognised him, and had

guessed what he had come there for. That fact should have been a clue in itself.

Blake had never met anyone in this part of the country before. Dr. Angel alone had recognised him almost, but then the doctor had many years before held a practice in London. A fact which Blake well knew, and because of that had not hesitated to reveal his identity to the doctor.

Who else could have recognised him? Who else was there who might have met him somewhere?

He knew of no one. He had kept his own name for the masquerade as a surveyor, but then it was a custom of his, for Blake was by itself a very common name, and there was hardly any danger of it being recognised.

Blake had learnt that lesson from criminals, who had refused to use their own names of Smith or Jones, and had assumed one like Devereux, which is instantly noticeable. Those men had attracted attention at the very time when they were trying to attract none.

Blake had not made that mistake. His curiosity at the Grange had been little more than any normal man's who found himself in what had begun to look like a charnel house.

But there was someone who knew what Blake was up to, and there were facts about this mysterious person that Blake now knew.

He could throw a knife, which was not a very common accomplishment.

He had a key to the cottage, since he had unlocked the front door to let himself in.

He was someone who knew what Blake had been doing

that day, either by seeing for himself or by indirect means.

Blake thought of the people who might fit the last requirement, but after a minute or two he gave it up.

He could think of people who knew what he had done that day (but without knowing his real purpose). There were Jane Wray, Sergeant Sale, Vernon, Dr. Angel, Stiggins, and a half dozen servants at the Grange, who had seen him there.

But then the murderer might be someone he had not seen that day, someone who had been told about him by one of the people he had met. For instance, Jane Wray might have told her mother about Blake; Stiggins might have told an unknown friend; Sale might have mentioned his meeting to a colleague—

The more he thought of it that way, the clearer it became that to try to find the murderer by this means was hopeless. Any one of the people he had met might have told any one of forty thousand people in the town.

But there was one thing which struck him now as a matter of urgency. Whoever the murderer was, that man had been watching him.

It was more than likely that he had seen Blake visit Jane Wray at the cottage by the mill, and if so, the girl herself now stood in danger.

Blake locked the cottage and set out along the road heading back towards the town. He kept his eyes wide open, used every trick he knew to surprise anyone who might be following him along the moonlit road.

After a few minutes he was certain that no one was following.

The murderer had gone, believing Blake to be dead. The murderer had not stayed to make sure of what the knife had done, but had gone at once.

"Most unusual," Blake thought. "Either he did that because he fully believed the knife would do its work, or because he was keen to leave the very fewest clues in the cottage.

"To have come into the kitchen would have left more signs to be detected."

He frowned at the road. Once more the quiet and unusual touch of the murderer fascinated him. By comparison to the usual run of murderers, this man seemed almost delicate in his silent plans.

These things gave a characteristic which baffled detection at the start, but in time Blake knew that that characteristic would help more than anything else to identify the criminal.

He reached the little cottage behind the hedge. It stood silent and still in the moonlight. The inmates were asleep, and there was no sign of any disturbance.

Blake settled himself in the shadow of a hedge to watch.

THE TWENTIETH CHAPTER

Safe Arrival.

AT FIVE, WHEN the dawn rose, Blake left the cottage. No lurking shadow had appeared there all that night, and the detective had not dozed for a second.

He was cold and tired, but when he arrived back at the inn and let himself in with the key they had given him, the smell of frying eggs and bacon came to him.

He sniffed appreciatively, and then, as he was about to mount the stairs, the door opened by the bottom of the stairs and the smell came out strongly, followed by the inn maid.

"Coo!" she said. "You bin out all night? Your friends is here. In the breakfast-room."

She watched him with a curious dark stare, and Blake knew that to leave her to wonder where he had been would have been to invite a lot of stupid guesswork and wild stories.

"No, I haven't been out all night," he said cheerfully.

"Had to go out early, that's all. Any breakfast for me?"

"Corse," said the girl, nodding, and disappeared, banging the door to.

Blake went into the breakfast-room, where two men were sitting. Tinker was smoking a pipe, and Drake was nervously smoking a cigarette.

Drake's appearance had altered considerably, for his hair was black now, and a few deft touches here and there by the expert Tinker was enough to change him. His smartly-cut clothes, too, had altered him a lot from the loosely covered, happy-go-lucky Drake of a week or so ago.

Blake closed the door.

"Pity we had to alter your appearance, Jim," he said. "I hate any sort of disguise. Too dangerous, but in this case I didn't see what else we could do."

"I'm getting used to it," said Jim, with a brief grin. He looked expectantly at the detective.

"Well, guv'nor?" asked Tinker, watching Blake.

"Unwell, Tinker," said Blake and dropped into a pew by the freshly lit fire. "My theories are falling to pieces like rotten wood. You see, if we're going to prove this murder at all, Miss Wray must be in possession of evidence which incriminates the murderer. Understand that?

"Yet she says she isn't. She swears she knows nothing which incriminates anybody.

"I believed then that she knew something important, but did not realise it. But if this were the case, then she would have been in some danger from the murderer last night. I watched, and no one came. And that piece of evidence, which apparently doesn't exist at all, is the pivot of my whole case!"

Drake's face fell. Tinker watched the detective with his head cocked on one side.

"Suppose you tell us what you mean, guv'nor?" he said.

"I mean this, Tinker," said Blake, bringing out his pipe. "I believe old George Ansell was murdered, and in order that the rest of this case should follow on that, Miss Wray must have seen that murder taking place!"

Both listeners became rigid.

"What?" said Drake incredulously.

"I mean, of course, that she must have seen something which was in actual fact the murderer at work, but, course, she did not recognise it as such."

"Who murdered the old man, then?" demanded Tinker. "Can't we get at the problem from that angle? If we know who did it, then we can find out what it was the girl should have seen."

"I don't know who killed him," said Blake. "But I do know that Clive Ansell believed that he did!"

"But surely a man would know whether he'd done a murder or not?" said Tinker slowly.

"Normally," said Blake, "But with a man who took opium, no. The effects of that drug are pretty constant, and while under its influence a man may be told to do something which he will do—as if he were hypnotised—without question. And afterwards he will have no knowledge of what he has done.

"That is what happened to Clive Ansell. At the time of his father's death, Clive Ansell was under the influence of a drug, such as opium. He did not know what happened, but he was told that he had murdered his father— Good Lord!"

The detective broke off with a sudden start, and a gleam came into his eye. Drake did not seem to have noticed the detective's sudden excitement. He was staring into the fire.

"That's practically what happened to me," he said. "I was drugged that night. There's no doubt about that. I left the house feeling dizzy, and after that goodness knows what might have happened."

"I know what happened," said Blake quietly.

"You do?" said Drake eagerly.

"I do. Now, listen to me first, so that you understand what I have to explain," said the detective. "Dope has a curious effect on people who take it for the first time. You feel it coming on, trying to rob you of consciousness, and what's your natural reaction to that?"

"You try to fight it off?" said Drake.

"Exactly. And in the course of that your mind reaches out for something which will help you defeat the drug. An order which you were given before you took the drug, perhaps, will come into your mind, and you will obey it again, just as if you had not done it at all the first time."

"That is a form of hypnotism," said Tinker. "Making you do something which you don't really intend to do."

"That is exactly what the opium type of drug does," said Blake. "Now, then, Jim Drake. Think back to the night of the thirteenth. Did anyone give you an order that night?"

"An order?" Drake scratched his head and frowned terribly. "Not as far as I remember— Oh! Unless you'd call Mrs. Wray's storm precautions an order!" A faint grin came to his face.

"What did Mrs. Wray tell you to do?" said Blake.

"To go into the cellar and see if there were any old mirrors," said Drake. "She believes they might be struck by lightning."

Blake nodded.

"Did you do that when she asked you?" he said.

"Not exactly," said Jim. "I just looked down the cellar. That's all."

"Right," said Blake. "When the drug took effect, later on, you became dizzy on the edge of the wood, and then into your mind came that order again. You remembered that you had to go into the cellar—and that's where you did go!"

"What!"

Jim Drake was on his feet.

"That is where you went, Drake," said the detective. "Down into the cellar and sat there, huddled in a corner, not knowing what you were doing, while the storm water was pouring in, soaking your shoes and socks, your coat and trousers. You didn't step into any ditch, my friend. You were huddled in a sort of drugged stupor in the cellar.

"And because of that, the murderer could not bury the body of Ansell down there until the next day! That is the proof of where you were that night, a proof supplied by the murderer himself!"

A dead silence fell in the room, then along the passage came the sound of slippered feet and the chink of china on a breakfast tray.

The maid came in with the breakfast and kept up a cheerful chatter while she laid it. The three waited with impatience until she had gone, and then they began to talk and eat.

"You obeyed an order to go into the cellar," said Blake. "Clive Ansell believed it when he was told that he had murdered his father. Jane Wray believed she saw two men in a mortal fight in the garden, because she knew of your jealousy and had been afraid of violence, which was enough of an order to her to see a scene in the garden which was not actually there.

"In all three cases, blind obedience, varying with the amount of the drug taken. The exact symptoms of drugs of the opium type."

"But in the case of Mrs. Wray the dose she had was too strong, and she just slept," said Tinker.

"But just a minute," said Drake keenly. "If Jane didn't see two men fighting in the garden, what did she see?"

"She saw the murderer temporarily burying his victim in the rubbish pile," said Blake.

"I see," said Drake, very slowly. "But then why did the murderer take him out of the pile and bury him in the cellar next day?"

"He was afraid that the body would be found too soon, if left in the loose earth of the pile," said Blake. "According to his plan, he wanted time to pass before the body was found."

"Why?" said Tinker.

"Because after a week a witness will remember only half of what happened, and after a fortnight even less. What's more, the greater the period between, the less memory is to be trusted. The murderer wanted your evidence to be as confused as possible, so that in the confusion any evidence against him would become lost."

There was a thoughtful silence while they ate, and then Tinker said:

"This murderer seems to be a cut above the average."

"He is the most fascinating criminal I remember," said Blake slowly. "He is making all the actors in this drama do exactly as he wants, as if they were puppets dancing at the ends of the strings on his fingers.

"He is a psychologist. He knows exactly what each person is going to do when confronted by the set of circumstances which he creates. He studies them first, then forces them to act in such a way as to cover himself and lay the blame on someone else.

"He is an artist, but, like all artists, his brushwork will be recognised perhaps sooner than he thinks."

They finished breakfast, then went upstairs to their rooms.

Drake went to his own room, and Tinker went with Blake into his.

"Drake must stay in his room all to-day," said the detective, going across to the wash-basin. "As he's been travelling all night it won't make the landlord curious. But he's got to stay there."

"O.K., guv'nor," said Tinker, sitting on the edge of the bed. "Now tell me what's been going on."

The detective did so. As he talked, he washed, shaved and changed his clothes, but he never seemed to interrupt his story for a second.

"I see," said Tinker slowly. "So our friend has taken a pot at you now, has he?"

"He has," Blake admitted. "And that is his first real mistake."

"How did he get on to you?" Tinker asked.

"I've been thinking that over," said Blake quietly, "and I've come to the conclusion that he heard my phone call to you yesterday evening."

"Where did you ring up from?"

"From just outside this room."

"I see, somebody in the pub," said Tinker, lighting a cigarette.

"Yes. But don't forget a pub has lots of customers. I heard a lot of talk and laughter in the bars below when I came up. It might have been any one of fifty customers."

"Or just somebody who followed you in at the hotel door?"

"Perhaps," said Blake. "In fact, I believe that's more likely the answer to it. You see, that was the only time yesterday when I was careless. I admit it, and I believe that carelessness nearly put a dagger in my back."

"You'll have to look after yourself," said the assistant sharply. "You take too many risks. One of these days—"

Blake cut him off with a laugh.

"Yes. It may happen one of these days," he said. "But I'll be waiting for it, and it's all in the luck of the game."

"Well," said Tinker sourly, "even if you are a fool, I'd like to see you enjoy a restful old age."

"That's kind of you, Tinker," said Blake. "But I think a

restful old age would drive me to drink—or worse."

Tinker grunted.

"We have a pretty stiff day's work ahead, Tinker, but by the end of it I think we shall have the murderer," said the detective, and knotted his tie.

"I hope so," said Tinker. "'Otherwise the murderer might have you!"

He got up and began to walk up and down the room. "But I don't see this point about the girl. Why did Ansell try to force her to marry him?"

"Surely that's obvious now, Tinker," said Blake quietly. "He believed that she had seen him kill his father, but failed to realise it. Therefore, he went to her, because once she became his wife she would be unable to testify against him."

"Oh, Lord, yes!" said Tinker, stopping. "Then what did the girl see that day?"

"She saw nothing," said Blake. "And I can see now that that is the key to the whole business. She saw nothing at all which could have implicated Clive Ansell."

Tinker's forehead began to clear. He threw his cigarette into the empty fireplace and grinned.

"I see. So the murderer didn't change his style of game at all! He stuck to it all the way through."

"And until he attacked me he never changed his tactics at all. As I say, that knife-throwing act was a blunder. It's a mistake. It isn't cricket." Blake broke into a grin. "Hang it! It isn't even English!"

"And nor," said Tinker, "was the knife."

"Exactly," agreed the detective.

THE TWENTY-FIRST CHAPTER

Shadow at the Grange.

THAT MORNING BLAKE walked up the to the old mansion with Tinker. The assistant was carrying all the necessary books and rules and looked about him with interest as they approached the house.

On the front terrace Vernon was taking the air, but he welcomed the detective with his usual affability, and but for the early hour he would clearly have invited the gentlemen in to share a small bottle with him.

"We are starting the measuring-up this morning," said Blake. "That is why I brought my assistant."

"Of course, sir," said Vernon, with a faint smile at Tinker. "One should never do too much oneself. Fatiguing."

When they had gone into the house and left the butler Tinker jerked his head back.

"I reckon he's a gay old bird when he's on holiday," he said.

"A droll fellow," said Blake. "A philosopher, too. You

want to beware of his brandy bottle, though. He pours it out like water."

They turned to the right along a wide corridor.

"We'll start off in the ball-room and work our way through the ground floor," said Blake loudly. "We should have it done by midday."

The detective led the way into the ball-room, where the fatal inquest had been held on the previous afternoon. The chairs and tables still stood about where they had been left yesterday afternoon, and only the windows were shut.

There was a dead, heavy silence in the huge old room, and the bright sunshine streaming through the windows seemed cold, and curiously out of place in that death house.

"Now look at it, Tinker," said Blake in a low voice. "She was standing there, straight as a ramrod, quite still, and the shot came through one of those three windows behind her."

They crossed to the table where the witness had stood.

"And it's dead certain Stiggins didn't fire the shot that killed her?" said Tinker.

"Definite," said Blake. "The shot came from somewhere outside—somewhere quite near."

"But you didn't see anybody outside, did you?" queried Tinker.

"I saw no one," said Blake. "But then I didn't hear the killing shot, either. I heard Stiggins' shots, but not the one that killed Mrs. Marion."

He crossed to one of the three windows and opened it.

For some seconds he stared out. Then he turned back and looked around the room again.

There were three big ventilators in the ceiling, formed by copper grilles, made up like the wicker seat of a chair. The holes in between the network of copper strips were half an inch in diameter.

Blake stared at these for a while, and Tinker followed his glance.

"Is there anything above here, guv'nor?" he queried.

"Just the roof space, that's all," said Blake. "This is just a single storey annexe built on to the house. There's no way up there except by unscrewing one of the grilles and going up through the ventilating holes."

"But couldn't our man have got up there that way and hidden there during the inquest?"

"He could have got up there, Tinker, but who screwed the grille back in place after he had got up there? He couldn't do that himself, you see. The screws point downwards into the room."

"And the grilles were all in place yesterday afternoon?"

Blake nodded, and looked at the three big chandeliers which hung down from the ceiling. He stared at them for a moment, then back to the three grilles again.

"The shot could have come from one of those vents," he said. "The end one there would have given about the same angle to the bullet as one coming through the window."

"I see there's a big ladder lying down just outside these windows," said Tinker. "We might as well get up and have a look at those vents."

They got the ladder in—it was actually a high pair of folding steps—and stood it beneath the end grille nearest the witness table. Blake clambered up to the top and closely examined the grille.

The copper screws fixing the grille to its wooden frame in the ceiling were bright with scratches. They had been unscrewed very recently, for the scratches were new.

Blake peered between the network of the copper, but the roof space above was dark. He brought out his torch and shone it through the lattice work.

A giant network of criss-cross shadows was thrown on to the sloping boards of the roof above the grille, and in the light of the torch Blake could see some carelessly laid electric cables running along from one chandelier to the next.

These wires seemed to be bunched together any old how, but they were coloured red, black, blue and yellow, so that an electrician could easily distinguish which was which.

And these colours were bright. There was no dust on the wires at all near the grille.

"Here's the rule, sir," said Tinker suddenly.

Blake looked down as Tinker handed up a long ruler, and prepared to make notes in his book. The detective took the hint and the rule, and as he did the door came open at the far end of the room.

The big, broad form of Sergeant Sale came in and looked curiously at the two surveyors.

"Three feet by two foot six," sang out Blake, measuring the grille. "One copper open mesh ventilating grille," he added, and climbed down the steps. "And the other two are the same size, I judge."

Tinker wrote industriously in his book, and the detective looked towards the sergeant.

"Good-morning, sergeant," he said. "We seem to be constantly meeting."

"It's a small world," Sale replied, his eyes on Tinker. "Still hard at it, eh? What's the idea of measuring this place up?"

Blake shrugged.

"Possibly they're going to alter it, and turn it into something else," he said.

"Ah!" grunted Sale, looking round. "Have to measure the electric light fittings and all, do you?" His eyes drifted up to the ceiling.

"Everything," said Blake evenly.

Quite suddenly Blake realised something very queer. Yesterday morning the sergeant had said they were keeping Laburn Cottage under observation in case Drake came back.

But had there been anyone watching the cottage last night? If so, either the murderer and himself had been seen entering, or else the murderer was the man watching the cottage!

Or was the story of the cottage watching a lie?

"I should think," said Sale, "that you have to be careful, poking around in these old places. Never know what you might find, eh?"

"You're right," said Blake. "You never know. This is my assistant, by the way," he added, nodding at Tinker.

"How do?" said Sale blandly. "I thought you were working on your own," he went on, turning back to Blake.

"Oh, no!" said the detective. "Too much hard work in a place this size."

"Yes," said the sergeant, ignoring Blake's remark. "This is the sort of house I should be careful in, what with stray shots coming in at the windows now and again."

"And old men dying suddenly in their beds," said Blake.

The sergeant started visibly, and the pinkness of his face faded. He grinned again to cover the momentary lapse, but he could not hide the hard, suspicious pinpoints of his eyes.

"What do you mean by that, exactly?" Sale asked.

"Well, old Ansell did die in his bed, didn't he?" said Blake innocently. "Or have I got the story wrong?"

"Oh, I see what you mean," said Sale, bland again. "I thought you meant you thought he was shot, too."

"Good lord, no!" said Blake, with a short laugh. "You wouldn't have to use a bullet on an old chap like that, would you? A blank cartridge would be enough, I should think. That would frighten him to death."

Sale did not answer for a moment.

"It seems curious to me," he said at last, "that your surveying takes you into all the places where things have been happening. I suppose that's coincidence?"

Blake laughed again.

"Coincidence? Why? These things all happened in practically the same place, as far as I know."

There was a silence, and then the door opened and Vernon appeared.

"You're wanted on the telephone, sergeant," he said quietly.

"Thanks," said Sale, and marched out.

The butler closed the door behind him and yawned.

"Always buzzing around like a giant bluebottle," he said insolently. "Can usually be found here, there, and everywhere, but mostly here."

He eyed the surveyors with his heavy lidded, humorous glance.

"Would either of you gentlemen care for a little refreshment?" he said. "This must be dryish work, one way and another, and since I understand the new heir is a teetotaller he surely won't notice a few bottles gone from the cellar."

"Oh, he's a T.T., is he?" grinned Blake.

"So I understand, sir," said Vernon, putting his hand up to another yawn. "Pardon me! What tiring weather this is."

"Have you ever seen this Mr. Grant?" said Blake.

"Oh, no, sir," said Vernon. "He was a good deal before my time. He was what I believe is known as the black sheep, sir, or Remittance Man."

He put a hand into his pocket and rattled something there.

"I'm afraid we've too much to get through this morning to accept your invitation," said Blake. "Sorry."

"As you wish, sir," said Vernon. "Shall I send in some coffee?"

"That would be an idea," said Blake.

The butler nodded and went silently out.

"He's a card all right," grinned Tinker. "I shouldn't think anybody else's property is very sacred to him."

Blake did not reply but went quickly up the steps again. Once more he shone his torch through the grille.

He saw the coloured wires and the bright, gleaming strips where the covering had been rubbed or cut away from two of them.

That was all there was to see, and he came down the steps again.

"Somebody was up there," he said in low tones. "Looks as if the gun got caught in the wire and tore the insulation off. But I don't know how we're going to get up there and have a closer look."

He glanced round.

"We've got to get to the gun-room. It's half-way along the corridor leading to this one, but we'll have to measure our way along, so as not to arouse suspicion."

Tinker nodded.

"I've got a feeling," he said, "that we're on tricky ground."

"Very tricky," said Blake tersely. "And the murderer's somewhere about, watching us."

Startled, Tinker looked round him. They were alone in the room, but as he looked out through the window he could see Inspector Grimes talking with Stiggins at the entrance to the stable yard.

They went out of the ball-room and went slowly along the passage, taking down measurements as they went. The corridor was empty, and they got into the gun-room without being seen.

There were two dozen sporting guns there, standing in racks, and Blake went quickly through them. He found only two which could have fired the fatal shot, and these stood alongside an empty stand.

In this stand had been the gun which Stiggins had borrowed, but that weapon was now in the hands of the police.

Blake examined the other two, but could find no unusual mark on either. All the guns were spotlessly clean.

"No good," said Blake. "The guns have been cleaned this morning."

Blake opened the door of the room and went out into the corridor, leaving Tinker to pretend he was measuring the door. Vernon was approaching silently along the passage with the promised coffee on a tray.

"Where shall I put it, sir?" he asked.

"Oh, might as well put it in here," said Blake, pointing into the gun-room.

Vernon carried the tray in and set it down, then eyed the range of shining guns with almost an affectionate eye.

"Lovely things, aren't they, sir?" he said. "I enjoy cleaning them more than all the other things in the house. And while I'm cleaning 'em, I like to think of all the people I'd like to bump off with them. That's the real pleasure of cleaning guns, sir."

Blake chuckled again.

"I confess I hadn't thought of it like that," he said. "You cleaned them all this morning, I suppose?"

"Every morning, sir," said Vernon. "The old man was very particular about them, sir, though what for I don't know, as he couldn't see further than the end of his nose. Sadly short-sighted, sir, he was."

"Collected guns, did he?" said Tinker, drinking coffee.

"Yes, sir. Though heaven knows why, because he was scared to death of the things. Always bellowing to guests to be careful not to point the muzzle at him, sir. He was once accidentally shot at point blank range, sir, while out shooting, and that frightened him for the rest of his life."

"How dreadful!" said Blake, with a look of sudden interest. "Ah, well, we must get on with the work. I have to get down to my hotel before twelve." He looked at his watch. "Which means I ought to get going now. Will you carry on till I get back?" he added to Tinker.

The assistant nodded, drank some coffee, and went to work. Blake went away, walking quickly down the drive.

He had got to get hold of Jane Wray.

He reached the little cottage behind the hedge and knocked at the door. Old Mrs. Wray answered it, looking as bright and chirpy as a sparrow.

"My name is Blake," said the detective. "I want to see your daughter, if she's in."

"No, no. I'm afraid she isn't in yet," said the old lady quickly. "But she won't be more than five minutes. Do come in and wait, Mr. Blake, do, please."

Blake went into the tiny place.

"Mrs. Wray," he said, "you have lived here all your life, I believe?"

"Why, yes of course, Mr. Blake," she said.

"Then you must have known George Ansell's cousin— Grant?"

450

She shook her head so violently that it looked as if she would shake it off.

"Oh dear, no! He was a wastrel, you understand, and old Mr. Ansell used to keep him as far away as possible."

"I know Ansell sent him to South America ten years ago," said Blake. "But surely he came here before that time?"

"No, Mr. Blake, not even before that," she said, her mind switching rapidly from one subject to another. "And oh! Isn't it dreadful about poor Mrs. Marion? Why, it seems almost as bad as Mr. Ansell going—the old one, of course. She was at the Grange for years and years. She was young Mr. Ansell's nurse, you know—and oh, how she loved that boy!

"Couldn't do anything wrong, young Master Clive. She was like a mother to him—really, she was. It must have broke her heart when he died, too, in that terrible way."

"Clive's mother died a long time ago, I suppose?" said Blake.

"Oh, gracious me, yes! She died a year after Mr. Clive was born, so that the poor boy never had a mother, which may be why he was so funny in many ways."

The door opened, and Jane came in. She halted in the doorway as she saw Blake, and her cheeks flushed.

"Miss Wray!" said the detective, without wasting time. "One more question about the day George Ansell died. Did you at any time before you reached the house hear a shot?"

"A shot?" said the girl, startled. "Yes, I did. But that's not an uncommon thing to hear in the park."

"Of course it isn't, Miss Wray," said Blake, with a sudden grin. "And did you happen to know that old Mr. Ansell was frightened of guns?"

"Oh, yes," she said. "I remember once the butler came into the room with a long roll of paper with the accounts on. Old Mr. Ansell thought it was a gun, and was terribly frightened. I thought he was going to pass out. He couldn't see very well, you know, and couldn't tell the paper roll from the barrel of a gun."

"Thank you, Miss Wray."

The detective wished them both good-bye, and went out with a new liveliness in his step. He returned to the inn where he was staying and went up to Drake's room.

The prisoner was pacing his room, and whirled round violently as Blake came in.

"Jim Drake, you're as near a free man as makes no difference," said Blake, with a short laugh.

"You've found the murderer?" gasped Drake, his eyes wide.

"Not yet," said Blake. "But I know now how the murders were done, why they were done, and when they were done. I don't yet know who the murderer is, but unless I do find out in the next few hours there will be another corpse, and it will be me this time!"

Drake looked disappointed.

"But—"

"Listen, Drake," Blake interrupted. "We've got to rig a trap for this man, and the chances are that he's too wily to fall for it. Never mind. We've got to try it. And you'll have to play a big part."

Drake squared his shoulders.

"You can count on me for that," he said, between his teeth.

"Good!" said the detective, and went out of the room to the telephone in the passage. He put through a call to London, and after some conversation, he hung up again with a frown.

"They can't get confirmation before seven this evening," he muttered, going into his own room. "That's a curse. Still, it can't be helped."

He went to the mirror and stared into it. The slight disguise which he had worn for the past two days was a matter of seconds to remove. He removed it, left the room again, and once more went to the phone.

He got through to the Grange in no time, and the quiet, half-humorous tones of the butler answered.

"Is my assistant there?" said Blake.

"Oh, it's you, sir!" exclaimed Vernon, obviously glad to hear from an old friend. "Yes, I'll just get him if, you'll hang on."

There was an interval, and then Tinker answered.

"Tinker, I want you to hang on there until this evening," said Blake quickly. "Keep your eyes open for anyone hanging about. I've got a lot to do this afternoon, and we can't act until after seven to-night."

"O.K., guv'nor!" Tinker replied in low tones. "That fat sergeant is still hanging around as if he suspects something, but the inspector's gone."

"Right! Just keep ready to spot anything unusual and— look out for yourself."

"You bet!" Tinker breathed into the telephone.

Blake hung up and left the inn. He went quickly to the police station, where he asked to see Grimes. He was shown into the inspector's office almost at once.

The inspector was busy, but he got to his feet as the detective came in and held out his hand. There was no glint of recognition in his eyes for the "surveyor" whom he had seen in the ball-room the day before.

"I'm glad to meet you, Mr. Sexton Blake," he said. "I take it you have come to see me on business?"

"Yes, on your business, I'm afraid," said Blake. "I am interested in the Ansell case."

"Oh?" Grimes became a little colder, and frowned. "But that is practically over. We haven't actually got Drake yet, but it's only a matter of days."

"No; you haven't got Drake, because I've got him," said the detective tersely. "I have definite proof now that Drake is innocent, and I want you to listen to what I have to tell you. I have been on this case for two days."

"You have!" said Grimes, starting, watching the detective's face, and then he snapped his fingers. "You were at the inquest!"

"Right again, inspector," said Blake. "But you didn't know who I was."

"I certainly did not," said Grimes, astonished. "No, I did not, ha!"

"I will tell you briefly what happened," said Blake, and quickly went over the rough details of his work, since the previous morning.

"And you were attacked in Laburn Cottage last night

by the murderer!" gasped Grimes.

"I was. And there is proof enough that my attacker was the murderer of Ansell," said Blake. "You see, I had by then proved beyond doubt that Ansell's body was first hidden in a rubbish heap, and here is a sample of the bloodstained earth from there."

He put the envelope of earth on the inspector's desk.

"If you have that analysed you will find that it is not only blood—but Ansell's blood. The murderer must have seen me get this sample. He obviously knew that I had rumbled his game, and that was why the attack was made on me in that cottage."

"Yes, yes, ha!" said Grimes impatiently. "That is self-evident. But how does this prove Drake innocent?"

"Drake was in the company of my assistant on board a train from London at the time the attack was made," said Blake clearly.

"Good lord! He was?" The inspector's eyes bulged. "Well, it seems that you have a stronger case than we have, Mr. Blake. Hell! But it puts us back to where we started!"

"Not quite," said Blake. "I believe that I can trap the murderer this evening, but it depends on you keeping Drake's innocence secret for the time being."

"It does?" said Grimes. "But can't you tell me roughly why?"

Blake spread out his hands.

"I can't tell you anything until I have a confirmation of my theory from London," he replied. "That confirmation cannot reach me before seven this evening. I'm sorry, but there it is."

"Ha!" grunted Grimes, making a face.

"But I can promise you this," said Blake slowly. "If you will come to the Grange to-night with Sergeant Sale, I promise to prove how and why all three murders were committed."

"All three what?" roared Grimes. "There's only one murder that I know of!"

"One death from shock, one murder, and one accidental shooting," said Blake evenly. "Well, all those three deaths are murders, inspector. All are part of one of the cleverest and most diabolical plots I've ever had the misfortune to come across. I'm hoping to-night to force the murderer to reveal himself, but if he boxes as cleverly as he has done till now he may get away with it yet."

"Not while I breathe!" snorted Grimes.

"And this man is clever enough to see that you don't—if it suits his fancy," said Blake, grimly humorous. "He nearly had me last night."

Grimes stuck a finger down his collar to ease his neck.

"I'll be there, Mr. Blake," he said. "With a pistol. I'm thinking we might need something of the sort to catch this customer,"

"Please yourself," said Blake, "but it's certainly a good idea."

THE TWENTY-SECOND CHAPTER

Blake's Visitors.

WHEN BLAKE HAD gone, Tinker returned to the ball-room, climbed the ladder and looked through the grille in the ceiling. It was difficult to see exactly what had been done to the wires there, for the grating threw weird, distorting shadows into the musty darkness of the roof space.

He came down again and stared out through the window. He could see the big, softly moving figure of Sergeant Sale coming towards the house, his hands behind him, and staring at the house itself.

The door of the ball-room opened and Vernon appeared.

"Have you finished with your coffee, sir?" he queried. "I see your cup in the gun-room is still half full."

"Yes, I've finished with it, thanks," said Tinker, looking down at his notebook. "By the way, Vernon, is there any way of getting up into the roof space above here?"

The assistant pointed with his pencil, and the butler stroked his jaw.

"Well—there is, sir," he said doubtfully. "Though I must confess it's a messy sort of procedure, and I've never cared to go up there myself."

"I don't want to go up unless I can help it,' Tinker confessed. "But the place has got to be measured, and I don't see how I can do it from down here."

"Quite, sir. Quite," agreed Vernon, gazing up at the ceiling. "Well, the only way is up the roof slope from outside, sir, and then in through a sort of dummy dormer window, if you see what I mean."

He dropped his eyes to Tinker's grey suit.

"You're hardly wearing the right thing to go scrambling about on roofs, sir, if I may say so," he added, shaking his head. "Filthy things, roofs, sir, once you get to know them."

He chuckled, and Tinker grinned at him. There was something about the fellow's cheerful insolence that attracted the young man.

"Ah, well," Tinker sighed, "it'll have to be done, I'm afraid."

"Very well, sir," said Vernon. "I'll get Stiggins to put a ladder up outside. Though, if I were you, I should take it as measured."

Again he chuckled as he went softly out of the room again.

Tinker turned suddenly towards the window again. A passing shadow there had caught his eye.

He was just in time to see Sergeant Sale pass out of sight behind the edge of the nearest window.

"That sergeant again," Tinker muttered. "What the

devil is he doing up here? He seems to be watching the damned place like a cat watching a mouse-hole."

Tinker wandered slowly round the room, looking at small details, as if there he might find the answer to the riddle of Mrs. Marion's death.

Blake was sure it was murder. Tinker knew that, but he could not see how in the devil's name murder could have been committed in the middle of the room full of people including policemen, doctors, and keen-eyed newspaper men.

"Perhaps the murderer actually bribed Stiggins to fire the shot," Tinker thought. "Stiggins is a dull sort of fellow, and might agree to take a pot-shot, providing the price was high enough.

"Or—more likely!—he might have been bullied into doing it!"

Tinker's sudden gleam of hope faded again as he grunted.

"But the range was too great. He couldn't have done it from that distance. Even with good eyesight it would be doubtful."

And that left only one possibility.

Mrs. Marion must have been shot by somebody inside the room!

Tinker sat down on a table and lit a cigarette.

It sounded impossible, of course, yet it was the only possible explanation which fitted in with all the facts!

"The only possible explanation," snorted Tinker, getting off the table. "But in of all these people—how? Gosh! Through the gun-room wall!"

He almost ran across to the back wall of the hall-room, and examined every inch of it. He knew that at the back of that wall lay the gun-room, but after a few minutes he also knew that there was no opening—not even the size of a pinprick, through the wall.

Therefore no shot could have been fired through that.

He lit another cigarette and turned to stare up at the ceiling grilles again. They offered the only hiding-place that a murderer could have used.

They were the only openings through which the gunman could have fired the shot at the angle which had struck Mrs. Marion.

But, as Blake had said, the screws which fixed the grilles were underneath, pointing down into the ball-room.

The murderer could have unscrewed them and got into the roof space, but he could not possibly have refixed the grille again.

There was no possible shadow of doubt about that.

Tinker turned as Vernon came in again.

"I've got Stiggins to put the ladder up against the roof, sir," he said. "Though I think you'll find it a dirty journey."

"Never mind," said Tinker, grinning to hide the gleam in his eyes.

The murderer, of course, could have got into and out of the roof space through the dummy dormer window in the roof!

He followed Vernon out of the room and round to the other side of the ball-room building, where the silent Stiggins was standing by the ladder which he had erected against the eaves of the roof.

"Ye'll need to watch 'er, sir," said the stable-boy. "She be a bit on the shaky side."

Tinker looked up to where the dormer window poked out of the tiled slope of the roof, and then he frowned.

There was no window there. It looked as if the dummy frame had long since been taken out, and the opening was nailed up with old weather-beaten boards.

"You'll need a hammer, sir, to get the boards down, sir," said Vernon.

"I'd forgotten the place was nailed up. Stiggins! Run and fetch a claw-hammer."

"Yessir," said Stiggins, and began to move off.

"No, don't worry," said Tinker, halting the boy. "It's hardly worth it. The darned thing's been boarded up for years."

There was no doubt about it. From where he stood Tinker could see the weathered boards and the rusty heads of the nails which had not been disturbed since they had been driven in there years before.

Vernon stroked his jaw.

"If only I'd remembered it was boarded, I could have saved you the trouble, sir," he said. "But the best way up there—and the cleanest—is through the grilles in the ceiling, sir. That's the way the electricians always get up when they have anything to do up there."

Tinker hesitated.

"I think I'd better wait until Mr. Blake comes back before I start pulling anything to pieces," he said at last.

The assistant did not want to make it seem as if he thought the roof space was of too much importance.

And, indeed, now that he had found the only entrance to the roof space was the ceiling grilles, he did not see how they could be of any importance at all.

Certainly, a murderer could have hidden up there, but such a murderer would have had an accomplice to screw the grille back in position.

And Tinker was sure that this murderer was too clever to share his terrible secrets with another man.

"Practising to be a steeplejack, sir?" said a voice behind Tinker.

The assistant looked round at the wide, bland features of Sergeant Sale who had somehow arrived without being heard by any of the three men around the base of the ladder.

"I was thinking of it," said Tinker. "But have since given the idea up."

"Dirty work, that sort of thing," said Sale, with a nod. "Don't care for it myself. I'm not the right shape for a ladder."

Tinker eyed him for a moment as the bland-faced man stared up to the ladder top.

"This is a difficult house to get about," sighed Tinker. "All bits and pieces and no proper entrances. Just one bit stuck on another, higgledy-piggledy."

"Yes, it is an odd place," agreed the sergeant. "One of the oddest I can remember."

"Certainly some of the oddest things happen inside it," said Tinker, turning away. "Stiggins, you may as well take this ladder away. I shan't be going up there to-day."

"Yessir," said the stable-boy, and seemed only too anxious to take down the ladder and move away with it.

"Ah well," said the sergeant, pulling out of his pocket a great chain with a watch attached to the end. "I'd better be getting back to the station, I suppose. Time's getting on."

"Time," said the butler softly, "usually does."

The sergeant gave a quick look back at the smiling Vernon, then turned and strode off on his way.

"A parasite," murmured Vernon.

"Sergeant Sale?" said Tinker, with interest.

Vernon shook his head sadly.

"Yes, I fear so, sir," he said. "That man does nothing but hang about this place. Has done for months before the old man died. What he's up to I don't know, but judging from that great bladder of lard which in normal people is called a face, I should say no good."

"Hard words, Mr. Vernon," said Tinker, with a faint grin.

"Alas, sir, yes," agreed the butler. "But there is always the type you could not trust with a blind man's collecting can, and I'm afraid the sergeant always seems to me to be just that type."

Tinker laughed outright at this.

"You would probably care for some lunch yourself, sir," said the butler, changing the subject. "Will you allow me to arrange something for you?"

"That's very kind," said Tinker. "It would help a lot as I haven't time to get away from here."

"No sooner said, sir, than done," said Vernon, and stole away with his usual, half-humorous silence.

Tinker returned to the ball-room, and then wandered into the gun-room. The guns were all there in their places, yet somehow there seemed to be something thing wrong about their arrangement.

He stood in the middle of the room staring at them, but he could not see what was wrong about them.

"Fond of guns, sir?" said Vernon, coming in silently behind him. "I should look these over if I were you, sir. Judging by the way things are going, you should have a good chance of buying what you want at a reasonable price!"

The butler stood aside from the door.

"If you'll follow me, sir, you'll find everything ready for you," he said.

Tinker followed him along to the old dining-room—a huge place that had not been used for a long time. Blake's assistant felt very small and lonely sitting at one end of the great dining table while Vernon served him with smoothness and silence.

"You know," said Tinker, after a few minutes, "I'd feel better if you sat down with me. It's so lonely here."

"Too true, sir," agreed the butler, taking a seat. "I often thought that myself when serving the old man, sir. He nearly always dined alone, as you know, sir. His son would never come home unless it was to ask for money. Even then, sir, if wasn't often that he came."

"Curious bird, wasn't he?" said Tinker curiously.

"Very curious indeed, sir," said Vernon. "Were I not the family servant, I should say a pretty poor character altogether," he added, with charming insolence.

"Did he drug himself very much?" Tinker asked.

"Quite enough," said Vernon, with a tinge of sharpness. "There were some days when he had no idea of what he was doing at all. Very violent, too, he was, sir—very violent indeed."

"He sounds pretty unpleasant," said Tinker.

"He sounded like that to me, sir," said Vernon piously.

After the meal Vernon left him, and Tinker went back to the ball-room.

The problem of the shooting of Mrs. Marion was still on his mind, and it was one which fascinated him so much that he sat there quite silently on one of the chairs, thinking hard.

And while he was sitting there, there was a sudden noise.

At first it seemed like the scuttling of a rat behind the wainscot, but then, as it came again, he noticed that it was coming from above him.

He started to his feet, staring upwards towards the grilles in the ceiling. He made no sound at all.

Once more the sound came, and this time there was the faint soft thud of a footstep with it.

"Somebody dragging wires along the rafters overhead," Tinker thought, stealing forward, his eyes still turned upwards.

On the metal edges of the mesh of the grille the light of a torch reflected from the gloomy space above, and then was gone. Silence came again.

Whoever had been in the roof space had disappeared again into the shadow from which he had come.

Tinker raced across the big room without making any sound. It was a movement that he was used to, and he did it well.

He raised the sash of one of the windows and climbed

through. He turned to where the ladder had been standing that morning, but it was no longer there.

He looked up at the boarded dormer window, but that too was sealed just as it had been before.

"Then there is another way into that damned roof space!" Tinker muttered. "And I'm going to find it!"

He climbed back into the room, took his notebook and rule from a chair where he had left it, and went out into the main hall.

The day was becoming overcast, and the great hall was gloomy and empty, like the entrance to a museum nobody ever visits. The shadows grew like black ghosts in the panelled corners of the place, and the black oak staircase sprawled with great stretched paws like a monstrous panther from another world.

The silence was deadly, hanging like a stifling curtain in that grim place. Now at last the evil of the place seemed to be materialising—the devilry which was slowly killing everyone in it was coming to the surface at last.

Tinker stopped at the foot of the stairs and looked round him.

There was no one to be seen.

He went upstairs and walked through the darkened corridors in the direction of the ball-room.

As he went he stopped several times and looked back. There was a crawling sensation at the back of his neck which made him feel that someone was following.

Yet each time he looked back he saw nothing, but the faint, dull gleam of armoured figures standing silent and forgotten against the walls.

He listened, but there was no sound from anywhere in this part of the house.

"Must be me noives!" he thought, with a twisted grin, and went on again.

The corridor came to an end with a wall and a big window in it. That window looked out over the roof of the ball-room below.

Tinker looked down through the window and saw the tiled slopes of the ball-room roof meet the brickwork of the house wall just below the sill.

"So that the entrance to this roof space must be somewhere close to me now," he muttered, and bent down, flashing his small torch at the panelling of the wall below the window.

There was no sign of any opening there, but as he bent nearer to the floor he saw that there was a gap of nearly a quarter of an inch between the skirting of the floor board, and this gap extended for about three feet.

Tinker's hands explored the mouldings of the panelling. It was a search he was used to. With Sexton Blake he had found almost every ingenious type of hidden opening, and this one was not one of the best.

He found the key panel and pushed. Three feet of the panelling swung open inwards like a small cupboard door.

"Vernon didn't know anything about this way into the roof!" grinned Tinker. "Though that's not surprising. That man's too damn lazy to be alive."

He crawled through the opening into the gloomy cavern of the roof space. The beam of his torch showed the cobwebs and silver dust on the arched rafters overhead.

Along the joists of the hall-room ceiling ran the snaky lines of the electricians' wiring, in which Blake had been so interested, but Tinker was not interested in them any more.

The light of his torch showed the joists and the wiring cables to be clean and dusted. There were no cobwebs there. All traces of a recent visit had been removed.

Tinker stepped over the joists and came to the nearest grille. He bent until he was almost squatting on the beams, and peered down through the grille at an angle.

He found himself looking directly down at the witness table, at which Mrs. Marion had met her death so suddenly.

"No doubt about it now!" Tinker muttered, and turned to examine the boards and beams around that grille.

There were one or two small fresh cuts in the wood, made with a penknife. Tinker frowned over them, but he could not make anything of them at all.

The bared wires shone brightly in the torch-light, but Tinker saw that other wires had been joined to the bared copper—a pair of wires which led away out of the roof space in the direction of the house.

"I suppose the guv'nor couldn't see those from below," he muttered.

He was right. Sexton Blake had not seen those wires, for they had not been joined to the bared cables then. They had been joined up since, and Tinker was examining the trap which had been set for his own death.

"Good gracious, sir!" came the voice of Vernon from several yards away. "How did you find this?"

Tinker shone his light towards the secret opening, where the butler was crouching down and looking through the hole with quite a lively interest.

"Found it by accident," replied Tinker, stepping back towards the opening. He crawled out through the opening and stood upright beside the butler.

"Well, do you know, sir, I've been in this house all these years and never knew that opening was there," he confessed. "Good lord! It means the whole house might be covered with secret passages!"

"That's one of the items we surveyors have to find out," said Tinker.

"Exactly, sir,' said Vernon, stroking his chin, with a curious frown on his face. "Do you know, sir—something has just struck me, sir. Something rather terrible!"

"What do you mean?" said Tinker, eyeing him narrowly.

"Why—terrible in one way," said Vernon, "and yet good for me. You see, sir, I felt rather responsible for Stiggins having that gun when Mrs. Marion was shot, though I never could understand how he could have fired at such a distance. But now—"

"Now what?" said Tinker.

He knew that the butler had thought of the same explanation of the murder as he, but he wasn't going to admit it first.

"Why, sir," said Vernon slowly. "A murderer could have got in here without being seen, and could have shot Mrs. Marion by pointing the rifle down through the grille there!"

"He could, that's true," Tinker agreed. "But what

about the sound of the shot, man? Surely you would all have heard it in the room below?"

Vernon took him gently by the arm and bent his head to whisper.

"Pardon me, sir, but there is a silencer in the gun-room! A thing for fitting on to the end of the nozzle of a rook rifle!" His voice was a tense whisper. "If I may suggest it, sir, we ought to go and see that it's still there!"

"Too true!" said Tinker. "I say! Fancy us turning out to be a couple of detectives!"

They went downstairs together to the gun-room, and Vernon opened a cupboard on the wall. From this he took out the small silver cylinder of a silencer, and as he did so his eyes flicked up to the window of the room, and he slipped the silencer under his coat.

"Can't be too careful, sir!" he said. "There's that damned man again!"

Tinker looked through the window and saw the figure of Sergeant Sale approaching the house.

"Come to my pantry, sir," said Vernon. "We can examine this silencer at our leisure and sample a little drink at the same time. I must confess that this sort of excitement makes me very dry in the throat."

He led the way out of the room, and Tinker followed.

THE TWENTY-THIRD CHAPTER

The Visitors.

THE EVENING WAS growing dark when the young man walked confidently in at the main door of the Grange. The butler was strolling through the hall when he saw the visitor, and turned towards him.

"Are you looking for someone, sir?" said Vernon smoothly.

"No; but I think someone must be looking for me," said the young man. "My name is Drake."

"Good gracious!" said the butler, raising his eyebrows. "Not the Drake?"

"That's the one, yes," said the young man, grinning.

"Well, well!" said the butler, staring. "It's a strange world, is it not? I suppose I am safe?" He chuckled.

It seemed that nothing upset Vernon's sly sense of humour, not even the sudden appearance of a wanted murderer.

"Well now, what can I do for you, sir?" he said.

"I am looking for Mr. Blake's assistant, actually," said Drake.

"Really, sir?" said Vernon, his eyebrows popping up again. "But he's been gone an hour or so."

Drake looked surprised.

"Gone, has he? Oh!"

"He said he would be back, sir, but he didn't say when," said Vernon. "Would you like to wait until he does come?"

"Yes, I'll wait," said Drake. "Mr. Blake will be here, anyway."

"Mr. Blake is coming back here to-night?" said Vernon, glancing at the gathering darkness through the doorway. "What odd times these surveying gentlemen do work!"

Drake laughed cheerfully.

"Surveyor!" he said. "That man's no surveyor! His name is Sexton Blake."

"What—the detective?" said Vernon, raising his eyebrows again. "Good gracious! And I never guessed it! Why, he behaved exactly like anybody else."

"He doesn't think the same, though," said Drake, and glanced at his wrist-watch.

The time was half-past seven.

The overhead lights shone brightly in the vast hall, and the beams suddenly reflected off the polished panels of the main door as it swung open again and a tall, slim man walked in carrying a brief-case.

The butler went towards him.

"My name is Hale," said the stranger. "I'm a solicitor from London. I wish to see Mr. Blake."

"Mr. Blake is not here yet, sir," Vernon apologised. "Would you care to wait with this gentleman?"

He pointed across to Drake, and then turned with a frown as the untidy figure of Stiggins came into the hall.

Vernon strode majestically across to him.

"What are you doing here, Stiggins?" he whispered. "We have visitors. Go away!"

"Mr. Blake told me to come and wait here," said Stiggins, with marked obstinacy.

"He told you to wait here?" said Vernon, astonished. "Good gracious! Has the man no idea of proper manners?"

The butler turned away, disgusted.

Before he could return to the two men waiting by the stairs, the main door opened again and little Mrs. Wray walked in, darting her head quickly about, as if trying to see as much as possible in the first few seconds.

"Madam?" said the butler, approaching her curiously.

"I've come to see Mr. Blake," said the old lady, gripping her umbrella with great firmness.

"What is this—a game?" breathed Vernon, and added aloud: "Right, madam! If you'll sit down over there—" He indicated a seat, across the hall.

The little old lady took the seat indicated, and the butler took the liberty of scratching his head delicately, as if wondering what on earth this was all about.

He swung round once more as the door opened for the fourth time and Inspector Grimes strode in, followed by Sergeant Sale.

"Blake here yet?" said the inspector.

473

"No, sir, not yet," said Vernon, and then with smooth insolence he added: "Do you happen to know if Mr. Blake is giving a party?"

"I believe he is—of a sort," said Grimes with a short, twisted grin.

Sergeant Sale's bright eyes were fixed on Drake, who had gone across to talk with little Mrs. Wray. The sergeant nudged the inspector and blankly indicated the wanted man.

"Drake!" hissed the sergeant.

"I know," said the inspector, quite pleasantly.

Sale stopped with his mouth open. He did not understand this at all. He had not been told of Blake's visit to the inspector and still believed Drake to be the wanted man.

Once more the door opened, and the big, cheery, untidy figure of Dr. Angel came in. He nodded cheerfully to all present.

"Mr. Blake here yet?" he said loudly.

"No, sir," said Vernon. "Mr. Blake is perhaps the only person in the town who has not yet arrived."

The doctor chuckled.

"Sly dog!" he chortled, and brought out a snuff-box from which he took a hearty pinch.

Drake had stopped talking to Mrs. Wray, and now a deep silence fell on that strange, assorted company. People looked uneasily at one another, but did not speak again.

The door came open for the last time, and Sexton Blake came in. The detective's eyes swept the company, as if calling a silent roll.

He seemed satisfied that everyone was there and crossed directly to Mrs. Wray. He spoke to her in low tones, and she nodded like a little bird, with bright eyes.

Then suddenly she shook her head instead of nodding it. A moment later the detective straightened up and stood back.

Mrs. Wray got up and trotted quickly out of the house again. Everybody watched the spring door swinging and flashing in the light.

"Right, gentlemen," said Blake, looking round again with a slight frown. "I should be glad if you will come with me into the ball-room. Vernon, will you please lead the way there?"

"Certainly, sir," said Vernon, rather more pleased now that Blake had arrived to take charge of the situation.

He led the way, and the party of men followed. Stiggins tried to hang back, but Blake tapped him on the shoulder, and with a reluctant grunt the stable-boy followed the others.

Vernon switched on the ball-room lights, and stood aside for the guests to pass him into the room. Blake came in last and closed the door.

The detective's face was white and there was a sign of strain in his eyes.

The chairs and tables were still set out as for the inquest, and Blake asked the company to sit down. They all did, with the exception of Vernon, who kept his proper place standing by the door in case he should be wanted.

"My assistant appears to be missing," said Blake, suddenly bringing out a cigarette-case. The movement was jerky and betrayed a certain nervous tension. "Has anyone seen him?"

"He went, sir, over an hour ago," said Vernon quietly. "But he said he would be back."

Blake lit his cigarette and nodded his acknowledgement.

"Well, Blake," said the inspector impatiently. "What happens now?"

The detective gave a short laugh.

"Perhaps the murderer knows," he said. "But I must confess that I don't."

He looked round the puzzled, frowning faces.

"Gentlemen," he said, "we all know there is a murderer loose, but who he is, only the murderer knows. He may be in this room now, and he may not. The evidence I was waiting for is not here.

"My assistant, Tinker, knows now who the murderer is—but Tinker is missing. That is the difficulty."

The inspector fidgeted in his seat.

"Supposing you tell us what you know, Blake? Your assistant may be back before you've finished."

"I hope so," said Blake softly. "You see, the problem is a very difficult one. The murderer is a man who has used drugs and his own will to pull the strings that worked his victims.

"The evidence all tends to incriminate innocent people, and those people themselves have wiped out any clue that might have pointed to the real culprit. I have found out a lot—perhaps I have found the whole story—but there is not one shred of proof to support it, and the murderer knows that."

"There is, as the inspector will tell you, a constable posted at the main gates. He was hiding in the bushes by the gates, and found a piece of folded paper on the gravel there, addressed to me. He gave it to me as I came in through the gates just now, and here is the message."

He pulled a folded sheet of paper from his pocket, and read it out.

"'My dear Blake—Your trap has been turned against you. Forget this case. Let sleeping dogs lie, or you will be the loser.'"

"That message is written on a sheet torn from my assistant's notebook, and is written in pencil—in Tinker's handwriting."

There was a gasp which seemed to come from two of three men. Sergeant Sale's face was pasty white, and he licked his lips. Dr. Angel was frankly goggling, and looked nervously round him. Vernon clicked his teeth, and looked as if he had at last come upon something which had surprised him.

"Hell!" said the inspector.

The solicitor brought out a very white handkerchief and mopped his brow, although the room was cold.

"I don't much care for this," he muttered to the man next to him.

But that man was Stiggins, who sat like a lump of clay, watching Blake as he might have watched a fox, dully suspicious.

"But I'm not going to change my mind," said Blake

suddenly. "I have to take a risk. It must be done or there will be more deaths in this accursed house."

He looked determined, but his face was very white now. He had made up his mind, but was depending on his own theory to save Tinker's life.

If his guess was right Tinker would be safe. If it wasn't Tinker would be dead.

Never in all his career had such a price been put upon the correctness of his work.

"I am going to tell you the story of these murders," he said, in a hoarse voice. "I shall tell you the story which I know is true, but I cannot tell you the name of the murderer, because as yet I do not know it. But I must use some name, so that you will understand the story as it goes along, and I shall use the name of a man five thousand miles away—Arnold Grant."

In the silence that followed the scrape of the inspector moving his feet was the only thing to be heard.

THE TWENTY-FORTH CHAPTER

How, Why and When.

"I AM CONVINCED," said Blake, "that the motive for these murders is the gain of the Ansell fortune. Half a million pounds is more than enough to tempt a killer, and I am certain that it was—and still is—the bait.

"First, we must understand who stood to gain that fortune. George Ansell had it, his son would have it after, and if the son died—Cousin Grant came into it.

"But there it ended. If Grant was dead then no one stood to gain it. There is no other descendant. The whole fortune would go over to the State.

"Therefore, it is reasonable to assume that Cousin Grant is the murderer of the Ansells, and of the housekeeper, Mrs. Marion, since no one else in the world stood to gain by their deaths."

Hale, the solicitor, interrupted.

"That's true, Mr. Blake," he said; "but don't forget that we have proof that Grant was in South America until two weeks ago—and actually signed a document there and drew money from the bank there more than a week after George Ansell died."

"Five thousand miles is the devil of a long way to shuttle to and fro between murders," commented the inspector sceptically.

"We'll examine that in a minute," said Blake. "Let us get on with the story.

"George Ansell was the easiest victim that any murderer could pick. A bad heart, likely to go at the slightest shock, and a ghastly fear of guns. What easier set of conditions could you wish for? And, what was more, should anyone suspect that George had been murdered, suspicion would immediately fall on the weak, wastrel, drug-taking son. But there was no reason why murder should be suspected.

"On that morning, when the old man was ill in bed, Grant was at this house—"

"From South America?" jeered Sale.

"We are not considering South America, if you remember," said Blake dryly. "We are merely using the name, because we don't know the murderer's real one."

Sale grunted.

"As I say, on that morning there was the old man in bed. The son was in a haze of a drug of the opium type, and had then no idea of what he was doing. Vernon, what was Mr. Clive doing that morning?" Blake asked suddenly.

The butler pulled his nose and frowned at the floor.

"That morning, sir," he said slowly, "I believe he was lying on his bed. Yes, I'm sure of it. He would not have any breakfast."

"Right," went on the detective. "So that all Grant has to do is to get a gun from the gun-room, put into it a blank cartridge, go upstairs and point the gun at the old man. There was no danger of being recognised. George Ansell couldn't see anything distinctly if it was some distance away, but he could see the gleam of a gun barrel.

"Miss Wray has given evidence of a previous example of this.

"By this means Grant terrified the old man, who tried to struggle out of the bed to save himself from the murderer, who then shot the blank cartridge and killed the old fellow as surely as if he had shot with a real bullet.

"The sound of that shot was heard by Miss Wray, who will testify to these things at the proper time.

"Grant then went into the drugged man's bed-room, put the gun in his hands, pulled him together as best as he could and told him that he, Clive, had just killed his own father.

"You see, gentlemen, what a perfect game it was. Clive knew from experience that under the influence of drugs he could do things that he knew nothing about. Naturally, then, he had no difficulty at all in believing that in a drugged dream he had committed this frightful deed."

"Good Lord! What a devilish idea!" breathed the butler.

"Clever, though!" said Drake, between his teeth.

"The first part of the plan is complete, and passes off as intended, without the police being suspicious. But the first part was only the cradle for the second part and carried the scheme for the death of Clive himself.

"How brilliantly contrived this was can be seen from the way that the police were completely deceived and were led to do exactly what the murderer had intended they should do. Listen carefully to the way it was planned.

"The old man was dead, but Clive was half-mad—haunted by the fear of what he had done. But at that time only Grant shared the secret with him, and he could buy off Grant. And that wasn't good enough for Grant; he wanted the lot, or none at all.

"Jane Wray had come to the Grange that morning—a fact which Clive knew, because he had seen her there, when the shock of the supposed murder had cleared his head of the drug.

"Grant then pretended that the girl had been to him and had told Grant what she knew of the murder. Grant then told Clive Ansell this, and roused the young man's fear that she would give the game away.

"There was only one thing to do, Grant said. Clive must marry the girl and keep her mouth legally shut forever. It was the only solution.

"It was an easy thing to suggest to a young man, whose mind and will were weakened by continual drug-taking.

"Therefore, on the night of the thirteenth, he decided to go and force her to marry him. It was that night, in the library, when he suddenly said, 'She'll have to do as she's told. I won't be messed around like this.' Isn't that so, Vernon?"

The butler scratched his head.

"Well, as you know, sir, memory is a tricky thing. I thought that was what he said, but Mrs. Marion seemed to think different. Anyhow, it was something like that. He didn't say it to me, you see, sir. He was sort of talking to himself, over by the library door."

"But you believe that's what he did say?"

"I believe so, sir," he said. "But if Mrs. Marion was behind the door she would have heard more clearly than I did. The library is a long room, sir."

"We'll take your version as correct," said Blake. "The young man decided to go to Laburn Cottage.

"See now how brilliantly the plot is conceived, because the girl whom he must marry is already engaged to a powerful and intelligent young man, known by his friends to be violently jealous of his fiancée.

"In other words, Clive Ansell himself goes off and provides the alibi for his own murderer!"

"Heavens above!" grunted Dr. Angel. "The man's a genius."

"An evil genius," murmured Vernon.

"Clive is at the cottage, the windows are open back and front, and under the kitchen window is a salad ready for the Wrays' supper. Grant puts some of Clive's drug in the salad and goes away.

"He therefore makes as sure as he can that not one of the three people in Laburn Cottage will remember clearly what happened that night. In fact, when the evidence piled up against Drake, neither Mrs. Wray nor her daughter would be able to defend him."

Hale mopped his brow again and gave a low whistle. He looked rapidly over his shoulder, as if suddenly fearful that someone might be lurking behind him.

"And only one thing went wrong in the whole of that plan," said Blake. "Drake obeyed his instinct to obey an order which he had not carried out, and went into the cellar, which the murderer had meant for the disposal of the body.

"You see, Grant did not want the body to be found for some weeks, when evidence would be blurred over and forgotten—except that which pointed to Drake.

"He had to bury the body in a rubbish heap, where he knew it would be quickly found. And so later—after the rain-washed mud of the cellar had set—he reburied the body in the cellar and left clear traces which Drake found too soon.

"Even then it seemed the plan was still working all right. Nobody suspected Grant. The dice were too heavily loaded against Drake, motive, evidence and all!

"And Drake, not knowing whether he was guilty or not, disappeared and made his guilt seem clear. At that time, it seemed, Grant had nothing more to do but sit back and wait for the inheritance to come his way."

Hale shifted uncomfortably in his seat.

"All this is brilliantly clever," he said irritably. "But you must realise that Grant cannot be in this country. I thought I had made that clear."

"I think Grant has made it fairly clear, too," Blake answered dryly. "But we cannot consider that for the time being. We must get on with the rest of the story."

He looked at his watch again. It was a quarter to nine.

There was no doubt now what had happened to Tinker. Had all been well he would have been back long before now, so that Blake's fears were well founded.

"You have the most difficult fence to clear yet, Blake," said the inspector. "You say that the death of Mrs. Marion was murder, but you'll have the devil's own job to prove that."

"We were all in this room when it happened," said Sale, with a jerky sneer. "Are you trying to tell us we're all deaf, dumb, and blind?"

Stiggins gave a nervous titter, then shut up immediately and looked around him guiltily.

"You yourself took the evidence of Stiggins," said Blake slowly. "He told you that he fired at a bird, but couldn't see the house because the sun was in his eyes.

"You know where he was standing—south of the house.

"You know—or you should know—where the sun is at three o'clock in the afternoon. It is west-south-west, which means that the shots Stiggins fired travelled directly away from the house. In fact, they went off in almost exactly the opposite direction from that of the window the bullet was supposed to have come through.

"No bullet can come back in the opposite direction from a ricochet. It can go off at an angle, but it can't come back on its own tracks."

The inspector looked suspiciously at Stiggins, then stroked his moustache and frowned.

"No, the game wasn't that at all," said Blake. "Stiggins in the park was just another stool pigeon. The fatal shot was fired from inside this room."

"Rubbish!" snorted Sergeant Sale. "We should have heard it."

"You would have heard it normally," said Blake, "but this gun happened to be fitted with a silencer."

"Oh," said the sergeant. "And what about the smoke and smell of cordite? I suppose the murderer put that in his pocket and walked out?"

"Don't be a fool, Sale!" the inspector snapped.

"The shot," said Blake, pointing upwards, "was fired through the grille up there."

Every head turned upwards to the ceiling, where the copper mesh mouth of the ventilating grille shone in the reflection of the lights.

"That is a ventilator," said Blake. "Hot air from the room rises through that and goes out through slots in the roof. It was hot in here yesterday afternoon, with all the people here, and the smell and smoke of the shot merely went upwards and out through the roof. That is why nobody detected it."

"You mean there was somebody up there all the time?" demanded Dr. Angel, glaring.

"No, no one was up there," said Blake. "There was a gun fixed there, and trained on the witness table. And that gun was fired by electric contact. The bare wires, where the insulation was scraped off to make the circuit can be seen up there now, if anyone would care to get up and look."

There was a silence, but nobody seemed keen to get up and look for himself.

Vernon coughed.

"You'll pardon me, sir," he said, "but I appear to have let myself in for something, haven't I? I mean, I lent the gun to Stiggins that afternoon, and that therefore it makes it look as if I—"

"You're just another stool pigeon," snapped Grimes impatiently. "It seems that everybody in the district has been implicated by these devil's tricks. I've never came across anything like it! Carry on, Blake."

"Yes, carry on," said Hale, leaning forward. "Why was Mrs. Marion murdered by this ingenious device? Why was she murdered at all? She wasn't in the way of the fortune."

"No, that's true," said Blake. "But Mrs. Marion was passionately fond of Clive Ansell. She had been like a mother to him while he had been a child, and that love for him never died.

"When he was killed she was heartbroken. But she was a tough type of woman. She did not show what she felt. Instead, she set patiently about the business of getting her revenge. She was a cold and deliberate woman.

"She knew that if she accused the man she suspected, he would kill her without a second thought. But if she gave him away in public, then she would be safeguarded by the presence of the police, and also she would make sure that the murderer got his due.

"But she was being watched. Grant was on the spot, in and out of the house at odd times, and he was closely enough in touch to know what she had in mind.

"Therefore he rigged up the trap in the grille. When the inquest began everything was ready. The gun could be fired by the light switch that controlled the centre chandelier."

All heads turned to the door where Vernon was standing by the six light switches, and where he had been standing during the inquest.

"But it should be noted," Blake went on, "that there are three separate switches which control the central chandelier, as is usual in rooms of this huge size.

"One is by the door, where Vernon was. Another is between the two windows over there, where Sergeant Sale was standing, and a third was opposite the windows, on the far wall, where the main body of the police were sitting."

"Ah!" grunted Grimes. It was a long, noisy, disappointed sigh. "So that anybody might have fired the shot?"

"Anyone might have done," Blake agreed. "But only one man did."

Vernon suddenly whirled round to the door and dragged it open.

Everyone started. Grimes stood up, knocking over his chair.

"No one there," said Vernon, and closed the door again.

He bent down, and was about to pick up something from the floor, when he stopped and looked up at Blake.

"I saw this come under the door, sir," he said, in a shaky voice. "It's a note. Shall I pick it up, sir?"

The detective strode to the door and picked up the small square of folded paper from the floor. He dragged the door open and looked into the dim passage beyond.

The faint lights from the distant hall shone yellowly at the end of the corridor, and deep shadows lay everywhere along the corridor, but nothing moved.

Blake closed the door, turned back towards the light and unfolded the message.

It was written on another sheet from Tinker's notebook,

and in a copy of his handwriting.

"Give it up, Blake. You probably know by now how Mrs. Marion died. Your assistant is hidden in this house now, with a gun at his head, connected up just as the other one was. Blow the gaff, Mr. Blake, and you blow your man's brains out.

"That's all. The choice is up to you."

Grimes stepped up to the detective.

"What's it say?" he demanded gruffly.

Blake handed him the note, and looked at his watch. One minute to nine.

"I'll just finish off my story," Blake said. "Grant has not been in South America for many years. He has never appeared at the bank there. He sent someone to collect the money, and that someone brought back the signed receipt to the bank.

"Those receipts were forgeries arranged by Grant before he left. An accomplice of his received that money every month and signed for it.

"I asked your senior partner, Mr. Hale, to cable for confirmation of my suspicion. I got the answer this evening. The bank has not seen Grant in person for eight years.

"As I told you before, Grant had bigger fish to fry. He wanted half a million. It was worth working for years to get such a fortune legally into his hands. And that was what he did.

"He came back. He came to this town, where nobody knew him. He knew that his cousin George Ansell would

489

not recognise him because George Ansell could hardly see. Clive Ansell had never seen him at all.

"And so, Sergeant Sale—"

At that second the lights went out. There was a loud shout from Vernon, mixed with cries from the others. Chairs bumped over in the darkness, and then someone dragged the door open and flung it back with a crash.

Blake rushed in the direction of the door, and grabbed in his pocket for his little torch as he went. He shone the beam ahead, but it was too faint to reach the shadow of the fleeing man ahead of him.

The murderer was no more than a distorted black shape running fast towards the hall.

In the ballroom behind them, the shouts and cries and crashes of the falling chairs made an unholy din. Blake ignored it, but kept on running fast.

He had to keep his light on to retain the figure ahead, but light unfortunately also showed the fugitive the way.

Grant reached the hall and made one tremendous bound for the stairs. He fled up them like a black wraith, with the detective some distance behind him.

The light shone on the black polished stairs as Blake ran up behind Grant. At the top, the figure of a suit of armour stood rigidly by the stairhead, passively watching the mad race for life through the ancient building.

Grant reached the top, flung out a powerful arm, caught the armour round the neck and sent it toppling down the stairs towards the detective.

Blake swerved to one side to avoid the mass of metal that thundered down towards him. He pressed himself against the banisters and the body of the thing crashed past him. One flailing metal arm struck him a terrific blow on the shin as it went, almost crippling him.

He went on, limping heavily up the stairs, still keeping the figure of Grant in sight, though the murderer gained a lot by his ruse.

Blake ran on as hard as he could, his teeth clenched to help him force his injured leg from collapsing under him.

Grant turned and raced into George Ansell's bed-room. Blake followed as well as he could.

He knew now that it was a trap, but it was himself or Tinker, and he knew that his assistant would be in no position to defend himself now.

He ran through the door, holding the torch out to one side, and as he came into the room he switched it off altogether.

Moonlight was streaming in through the many windows, and Blake kept out of the range of the silver beams.

But in the bright searchlight of the moon he saw Tinker bound to a big carved chair. The assistant was tied and gagged so rigidly that he could not move at all.

Beside him, lashed to another chair was a rook rifle, with two wires trailing from the trigger to a plug in the wall skirting. Blake stopped in the shadow close to the door, held his breath and listened.

There was a sudden laugh from somewhere across the room.

"I must say I thought your reasoning very clever," said Grant. "But you mustn't mind if I feel a little bitter about it. You prevented me bumping off your man here, but you only delayed it for a while."

Blake only half-listened. He was looking quickly round him for a way to cross the room without going across the tell-tale moonbeams.

But there was no way. The moonlight cut the room in two, with himself in the shadow of one side, and the murderer in the blackness of the other.

"You know that the inspector brought a pistol, don't you?" Grant went on. "Well, the inspector is a careless man. I got it out of his pocket just now, and a very good pistol it is, too."

"Maybe," said Blake. "But, of course, you won't get away with this now."

"Oh, I know that," said Grant softly. "I'm not a fool. But you must admit I have a score to pay off. But for you, I should have had half a million smackers in my fist to-night. I should have had a fortune, Mr. Blake, but for your cursed interference!"

The man hissed now. There was no mistaking his tone. He was cornered, and he was going to die for what he had done, but he would not die alone.

He meant to have the final satisfaction of shooting down the man who had wrecked his scheme.

"You missed me last night," said Blake. "You'll miss me again."

"You, yes! But surely I can't miss this one here, can I?" said the voice from the darkness. "I'm not such a bad shot as all that!"

Behind him Blake heard a movement in the doorway. He glanced quickly round and saw a faint shadow slide into the room close beside him, and the dull gleam of a long barrel showed at his side.

"I shall show you, before the others come," said the voice across the room. "I was a crack pistol shot in South America."

Into the beam of the moonlight across the room there slowly appeared the brilliant, glinting shape of a nickel pistol.

Crack!

Flame spat from Blake's side, and the pistol jerked violently into the air and fell to the polished boards with a clatter.

Like lightning the detective sprang across the room. He leapt on to the great bed and off the other side with a bound that brought him down close to the pistol.

He kicked the weapon aside as he ran, switching on the torch again and directing it into the shadows beyond the moonbeams.

The circle of light on the wall looked yellow by comparison with the moon, but it showed the figure of the murderer leaning back against the wall, holding a broken, useless arm with his left hand.

Behind them, Drake came across the room with the smoking rook rifle still held ready before him.

"Er, put that blasted thing down," said Vernon, with a wry grin. "One bullet is enough for me."

From below came the running shouts of Grimes and the others, calling wildly for Blake. Then suddenly the house lights came on again.

Blake stepped back and tore the wires from the gun on the chair.

Vernon gave a groan of pain, then grinned again.

"There is one thing I would very much appreciate," he said. "I have a flask in my hip pocket with brandy in it. Be so good as to give me a sip. The pain is ghastly."

"Shall I?" said Drake, half-turning his head to Blake.

"Yes," said the detective, with a brief glance. "He'll faint otherwise."

Vernon was in too much pain to struggle. Drake got the flask from his hip pocket, and the butler dropped into a chair by the wall, still holding his broken arm.

"Here," said Drake holding out the flask.

"Thank God," said Vernon, in a queer voice.

"Stop!" cried Blake and turned from unfastening the hapless Tinker. "Don't let him—"

But he was too late. With his one good hand, Vernon snatched the flask from the startled Drake and poured the contents down his throat.

Blake snatched the flask away, but he knew that it was too late now. Vernon laughed into his face.

"Why, Mr. Blake," he said. "You should have thought of it before. You know there is quite a store of drugs in this house—"

His smile became suddenly fixed, and when the inspector and the others came rushing in at the door, Vernon had followed his three victims out of this world.

"I was a fool," said Blake. "But perhaps it has saved a lot of trouble."

"Saved us a lot of trouble, anyway," said the inspector, turning away.

THE TWENTY-FIFTH CHAPTER

Mr. Blake Goes Home.

"THERE IS ONE thing I wish to know," said the inspector, with a grim look at the unhappy Sergeant Sale who stood beside him. "Why did you accuse Sale?"

"Vernon had rumbled I was after him just too soon," said Blake. "I had to stave it off until the lights went out, otherwise he would have pressed the switch behind him and killed Tinker. Accusing Sale was just enough to make him believe there was a hope yet."

"I see. And why did the lights go out?" demanded Grimes.

"Because I suspected that Tinker was in this position, and I knew I'd never get the chance to find him alive if I openly started searching for him," said Blake. "I arranged with Miss Wray to be in the servants' quarters by the main house switches. I synchronised my watch with hers before I came to-night. Then when I found Tinker was not here, I told old Mrs. Wray to give the message to her daughter to switch off the power at nine exactly.

"That rendered the electric gun useless, but only by a split second!"

"Gosh!" broke in Drake excitedly. "I wondered why Jane wasn't here to-night when everybody else was!"

"Well, she is here," said Blake. "You'll find her still waiting downstairs."

"Will I?" gasped Drake, his eyes bright. "Gosh! I— Crumbs! Here, hold this, inspector!" He jammed the rook rifle into the inspector's startled hands. "Good lord!"

Drake rushed to the door, and hesitated there, holding on to the doorpost.

"See you later, boys!" he shouted, and tore off along the passage and down the stairs like a war-horse.

Blake laughed, and so did the aching Tinker, who was sitting on the bed massaging his cramped limbs.

"And just how did he get you in this position, Tinker?" asked the inspector.

"Very simply, I'm afraid," said Tinker, with a grimace. "He asked me into his pantry, and went in first. I followed him, and suddenly he slammed me in the wind with his elbow and kicked me on the shins. At the same moment, he spun round and swiped me over the head with a bottle. I must confess, I wasn't expecting it."

"I shouldn't have been expecting it myself," admitted Grimes. "Even that little trick was a clever one. The man had brains."

"Pity he used them for such work," said Blake, and lit a cigarette.

"Ah," said Grimes. "We'd better get the last body removed, I suppose. I hope it will be the last!"

"It certainly will," said Blake with a grin. "You've seen the last of Mr. Grant's tricks."

Blake and Tinker left the room and the police to get on with their work. The detectives had done their work, and it was up to the police to find such evidence as Vernon had accidentally left about the house.

In the hall below, they found Jim Drake, Jane and Mrs. Wray. All three were looking up towards him as Sexton Blake came down the stairs.

Judging from the faces of these three, there seemed no doubt that their happiness had been restored with the removal of the shadow from their lives.

"Mr. Blake, I can't thank you enough," began Drake, approaching the detective.

"Then don't start at all," said the detective, grinning. "I hate it."

"But really, Mr. Blake—" said Jane.

"Please!" said the detective plaintively.

"Oh, well!" The girl laughed and turned to her fiancé with a helpless shrug.

At that moment, the solicitor, Hale came down the stairs behind them and saved the detective from any further attempts at thanking him.

"Well that was a nice little performance you gave, Blake," he said with a chuckle. "I've never been so frightened in my life. The sweat poured off my brow. And the brazen insolence of the man! Actually throwing down forged notes inside the room where we were, pretending they'd been shoved under the door!"

"He was never lacking in impudence," said Blake. "He

seemed sure of himself right to the end."

"Did you really know that it was Vernon?" Hale asked curiously.

"That was my guess, but I could not be absolutely sure until I made him give himself away," said Blake. "There was only one thing that gave me the idea at first, and I worked on that."

"And what was the one thing, Mr. Blake?" said Jane, frowning.

"The doping of the salad," said Blake. "The way you'd covered it, only a conjurer, or a man well used to handling crockery silently could have done it. No one is more used to handling things silently than a butler."

Drake whistled. "Heavens! I might have thought of that myself!" he said.

"Then there was the mistake of the attack on me at Laburn Cottage," said Blake. "That man had a key of the cottage. Now, apart from the tenant's keys, the only place another would be found would be at the landlord's, and only Vernon was likely to have had control over the estate keys."

Tinker offered Blake a cigarette which the detective took and lit.

"I still can't understand," said Hale, "how that Brazilian bank didn't rumble that the monthly receipts were forgeries done by a friend of Grant's."

"Because it was done by agreement with Grant," said Blake. "My dear fellow, if somebody perfectly forged your signature, and you did not tell anyone, do you think any outside person would rumble it? Of course not. No complaint, no suspicion. It was obvious—and, what an alibi!"

"True enough," said Hale slowly. "And simple enough, too, when you think of it. Well"—he looked at his watch—"I must fix up at a hotel before they all shut up. Oh! And by the way," he added, "did you know there was a codicil to old Ansell's will?"

"I didn't," said Blake, surprised. "What is it?"

"That if both his son and cousin should die intestate, the whole of the Ansell fortune should be used for the establishment of a hospital in this park, and whatever remains to be used for the development of the mill," Hale said.

"Is that so?" said Blake. "So the old man had a strain of generosity in him after all. Pity he didn't leave it like that to start with. He would have saved four lives."

Hale shrugged.

"Perhaps your measuring up will be useful after all, if they're going to alter this place into a hospital," he said ironically.

"Ah," said Blake, sadly shaking his head. "But I'm afraid no one can read my figures."

Hale laughed and went out. Soon after, Blake and Tinker left the Grange.

As they walked away down the drive, glinting like sugar icing in the moonlight, Tinker threw down his cigarette end and said:

"What was the mystery of Sergeant Sale? He never seemed at ease the whole time!"

"It was nothing much," said Blake. "You see, old Ansell

was frightened someone was going to murder him. That was obvious from his behaviour. So he employed Sale in his spare time to act as a sort of bodyguard and general snoop.

"Sale, of course, would get into one hell of a row if that was known."

"So that was why he lied about watching the cottage, when he found you that morning?" said Tinker.

"Of course. He was watching the cottage all right, but unofficially, trying to find out if he was going to get mixed up in it, because of his spare time job," said Blake with a short laugh. "Ah, well, it's all over, Tinker, and thank goodness you've still got a head on. Not," he added slowly, "that it's much use—"

"If you really want a slanging match—" grinned Tinker.

"No, I think we'd be better without it," said Blake, showing crossed fingers.

They walked on down the drive until the black shadows under the trees by the gates swallowed them and left the moonlight empty.

THE END

BAKER STREET, LONDON

SEXTON BLAKE CLOSED the periodical and put it back into the binder.

He frowned and said, "Those days, they were the last for what you might term the traditional detective. By the 1950s, changes in the law made it more difficult for us to operate independently. Also, advances in official police procedures were fast making us redundant. I was faced with a stark choice: I could either resign myself to photographing cheating spouses and exposing insurance frauds or—"

A soft trilling interrupted him.

He pulled a mobile from his pocket and put it to his ear. The phone was unlike any I'd seen before. An unfamiliar brand, slightly curved and transparent.

He murmured something into it, listened, and exclaimed, "Already? ... Yes ... All right, straight away. Whatever you do, don't let him out of your sight for even an instant, young 'un!"

He stood, pocketed the device, and handed me the binder.

"I must go, but we've finished for today anyway, I think?"

"Yes," I replied, as I got to my feet. "Young 'un? Was that Tinker?"

"It was."

We crossed the room. He opened the door. I hesitated on the threshold.

"The choice, Mr Blake?"

"Choice?"

"Spouses and frauds or—"

He ushered me out onto the landing. "Or shake things up."

"Time to establish a new order in your affairs."

"And that," he said, as I descended the stairs, "will be the topic of our meeting tomorrow."

It was.

However, on the following morning, it was not Sexton Blake that I met in the Baker Street house.

Next:
The Sexton Blake Library

ANTHOLOGY V: SEXTON BLAKE'S NEW ORDER